Mona Lisa Smiles

KATE LLOYD

UNION BAY PUBLISHING

CHAPTER ONE
Mona Lisa

I wrestled myself to consciousness, up through the heavy sheath of sleep, and heard a doorknob turning and grinding, then it released, producing a click.

Was I dreaming? I opened my eyes, but none of the inky silhouettes made sense. *Dove mi trovo?* I lapsed into the Italian of my youth—what my parents spoke when they didn't want me and my little brother to understand.

I turned on the bedside lamp and saw my childhood bedroom, with its window seat, faded wallpaper—strands of pink roses—and tall bookcase, still displaying my high school annuals, my novels, and my Canon AE-1 camera, once my favorite possession. With Mama in a retirement community and my dearest Papa dead for over ten years, the family home gaped like a tomb.

From downstairs, Mama's Doberman pinscher, Figaro, let out a throaty bark. Another noise rustled my eardrums, and the house's air pressure dropped as a door shut. Most of the doors in Mama's old house complained, thanks to Papa's invention, The Squeaky Door, a composition that made hinges whine like a soundtrack from an Alfred Hitchcock movie. "A poor man's burglar alarm system," Papa had maintained when he came up with the idea.

Leaving the warmth of my covers, I bolted to my feet. The

springs that supported me through my tumultuous teen years creaked; my toes dug into the worn shag carpet. I rifled through my purse for my cell phone and opened it with a shaking hand. Or should I use Mama's telephone to call 911 so her address would show up on the Seattle Police Department's caller ID? No, Mama had contacted them with so many trivial concerns that the operator would roll his or her eyes and say, "It's that nutty Buttaro woman again."

I stood, waiting for another sound. A jet cruised overhead, then receded southward into the blackened sky toward Sea-Tac Airport. Off in the distance, a siren moaned, moving away, lessening.

Holding my breath, I wondered if the house was haunted. Since I moved in three months ago, Papa often visited me in the depths of my sleep, shadowing me and whispering in my periphery, always out of reach when I tried to embrace him.

I reasoned that if someone had broken in, Figaro would have barked furiously, or I would have heard glass shattering and footsteps as intruders rushed around stuffing pillowcases with loot. Mama's TV wasn't worth carrying away, and her stereo system was thirty years old. But meth addicts might target an old woman's house. They'd poison the dog, then if they found nothing of value on the first floor, they'd swarm upstairs searching for jewelry and find me. I was tempted to cloister myself in the bathroom and lock the door, but I could imagine my deceased father seeing that act as cowardice. Too many times, I'd let my parents down. I'd soiled the Buttaro reputation by living with Kevin, who'd refused to marry me when I announced I was pregnant. As far as I knew, he never found out I'd miscarried. Today, Kevin might think he had a one-year-old son who looked just like him, but he hadn't cared because I was part of the package.

Dressed in pajamas, a hoodie, and my fuzzy leopard-skin slippers, I crept into the hallway, still clutching the phone, and padded down the darkened staircase.

Another vibrating rumble rattled a windowpane. Was the neighbor kid's car stereo cranked up? Had rats infested the walls? Was someone snoring?

"Figaro, come on, boy." I wanted the dog to accompany me down to the basement. But he glared at me with glassy black eyes. My mother, born in Naples and brought up south of Seattle—once dubbed Garlic Gulch—spoke to Figaro in Italian. So I tried, "Figaro, *andiamo!*" But he ignored my command and closed his eyes. Stupid dog.

I tiptoed down the stairs into the basement, stopping at each step to listen. The vibrating sound ceased, leaving in its absence a hollow silence. The overhead light stretched my shadow, and the narrow, curved stairwell closed in on me. The hairs on the back of my neck prickled when I reached the bottom, nearing the stand-up vacuum cleaner, menacing in the darkness. A box filled with Papa's old clothes headed for the Goodwill looked ominous, as if it could spring to life.

I rounded the corner and saw Joey's bedroom door—closed, like it always had been when he had lived at home. The image of my brother—*mio fratello*—snoozing in his old bedroom made me cringe. In his best interest, I'd placed my only sibling in a group home several months ago. I'd begged Mama to move Joey into a group home so he'd learn independence, but she worried he'd run away, end up living under the freeway or, worse, commit suicide. After Papa's death, Mama might have sold this house and moved into a spiffy new condo near their restaurant if it weren't for fears about her son's future.

My hand trembling, I took hold of the doorknob and cracked the door enough to see Joey's bed bunched up against the wall under the window well and his profile illuminated by the dim light entering through striped curtains. Fear spiked into me. Reeling, I stepped backward into the hallway and bumped into Figaro, who'd snuck up on me, his massive shoulder blocking my retreat.

Joey snorted, gasping for air. Then he rolled onto his side and muttered an expletive in Italian.

3

Both incredulous and outraged, I stepped toward the bed. As a little boy, he was a tousled-haired lad, *un bel ragazzo*, but in his teens, he grew into an odd duck. In his second year at community college, he began withdrawing, closing in on himself, dropping his buddies, missing classes, and finally admitting to Mama that voices had infested his brain, warning him not to leave the house or speak to anyone who would twist his mind into a pretzel. Once out of school, he slept during the day; I assumed to avoid people. What did he do all night? He had no friends that I knew of. He hadn't dated since high school.

"Joey, it's Moni, wake up." Scorn shrilled my voice. Although I loved him, I was furious and had every right to be.

Figaro moved to my side, his ears pricked. He sniffed my hand, his moist nose making me flinch, then ambled over to the bed and sat facing me like a soldier waiting for orders. Did he consider Joey the dominant member of our pack, lowering me in the pecking order? I adored fuzzy little fluff-ball dogs and was always worried Figaro would turn on me. We knew nothing of his history.

Joey's eyes blinked open, and he yawned. He looked sweet—the way he shaved his face at least twice a day, scissored his own curly brown hair to the scruffy length that's popular these days, and laundered his clothes heavy on the bleach so his white T-shirts glowed blue like overly lightened teeth. "What are you doing here?" He yawned again.

"I could ask you the same question. You scared me to death. How dare you break in?"

"I didn't. I used a key."

"But I took your key away from you." And brought in the spare that used to reside behind the hose at the side of the house. "Where did you get it? Did Mama give it to you?"

"No, I had another—"

"Joey, you promised not to come back. What if we'd already sold the house and a child was sleeping in this room? What if the new owner kept a gun under his pillow for protection? You might be dead!"

4

"Your car was out front. I figured you were here."

"And that gave you the right to come in?" My ire ratcheted up another notch. "Get out of bed this minute."

"No, let me sleep." He jerked the covers over his face, shutting me out like a spoiled brat refusing to go to school.

"For heaven's sake, act your age. You're thirty-five years old." Two years my junior.

My annoyance expanded like a fractured dam. "Look, I need to drive you back to the group home, then in three hours get to the restaurant." I noticed my reflection in the mirror over Joey's bureau and saw my scowling face, flushed red, and my slitted eyes. At one time, I was considered pretty in a classical sense. Not like the popular girls in school, what with my olive complexion, dark hair, and Buttaro nose that verged on beakiness. My face was beginning to show the signs of too many early mornings waking at five o'clock to go into Booty's Café, ignite the flame under the soup of the day, order fresh produce, and refill the salt and pepper shakers.

I tapped Joey's shoulder through the covers. "You can't ignore me." But he was a mole, burrowing deeper under the covers.

"Why didn't Mrs. Landis at the Caring Home call me?" I wondered aloud. She maintained a ten o'clock nightly curfew and was supposed to contact me if he didn't check in.

I wanted to unload a lifetime of resentment toward Joey, the heir to the Buttaro family name. He was our parents' favorite, his every achievement magnified and celebrated, while I never enjoyed the spotlight, even when I'd aced most of my classes.

I grabbed hold of the covers and whipped them back to expose Joey's wiry frame. He was wearing only an undershirt and boxers. Lying on his side, his head was bent forward, his hands tucked under his chin, and his long, skinny legs curled into a fetal position. Nothing in life had prepared me for this moment. I searched for a comedic element the way Papa would have—he always kept us in stitches. My brother's got chicken legs, I thought, trying to find humor. And Mama had always told me to look on the bright side, even when it was raining at a picnic—not unusual in Seattle. I was glad she wasn't here; she'd welcome Joey home. "Blood is thicker than water," she'd say. "Be nice to your little brother." Joey this. Joey that. When I signed up for this life on Earth, where in the small print did it say I'd have to be my brother's keeper?

He pulled the covers up to shield his lower half and flipped over on his back, his lips pressed together, his sunken face warped. I was torn between pity for him and frustration for his wasted, joyless life—he was my brother, after all. We shared DNA. But tonight, he might as well have been a stranger. I didn't know what to expect.

I had no one to count on but myself—no one to bail me out of this jam. I steeled my gut, reaching into myself for courage and finding none. What were my options? If I were a burly man like Papa had been, I might pick him up and haul him out to the car, but I stood five foot three and weighed one hundred and twenty pounds. Gangly Joey was almost six feet tall. And Figaro might defend him.

"Do you realize Mama doesn't live here anymore?" I asked, but Joey made no response, like he was stoned or drunk. He lived on an allowance from Mama. I doubted he could afford booze or drugs. I sniffed the air for alcohol or the damp, woodsy odor of marijuana but smelled none.

"Joey, have you been to visit Mama?"

"No, too many old people. Sick. Germs everywhere."

"Mama's selling this house." What I'd told him repeatedly. "I could put it on the market any day." But he gazed at me blankly, like he was made of wax, his skin smooth and pale from lack of sunshine. No laugh lines either.

Was he passive-aggressive? A nutcase? *Pazzo*?

"I'm too tired to deal with this drama tonight," I said. "But tomorrow you're out of here." Leaving Figaro by the bed, I backed out of the room. My little brother and that wretched dog had won this round, but tomorrow I'd find a way to rid myself of both of them.

CHAPTER TWO
Joey

Joey's heart pounded like it might explode. He yanked the covers up around his Adam's apple as he listened to Moni mount the stairs to the first floor. Sensing Joey's distress, Figaro rotated his body and laid his head on the edge of the mattress. The dog had more empathy for him than his own sister did.

"Leave me alone!" Joey called out, in case Moni had tiptoed back downstairs and was skulking outside his door. No, the kitchen floorboards overhead creaked, and then he heard footsteps climbing to the second floor. She was out of earshot—or had she bugged his room?

He'd never get back to sleep now. His thoughts were doing cartwheels, and his legs had that itchy, jerky feeling that kept him awake many nights. He got the urge to throw on his jeans and bolt out the kitchen door, disappearing into the slippery, cool night, never to be seen again.

"That's exactly what she wants you to do, Jo-Jo," said Saint Signore, the voice in Joey's head. "Hold your ground. Don't let her win this hand." The middle-aged man spoke with a gravelly Italian Brooklyn accent. "You shouldn't have allowed her to move you out of here in the first place. But what else is new?"

Joey sank into the mattress like it was quicksand. "She claimed Mama was dying and the house was going on the market."

"Admit it, Jo-Jo, you've always been gullible."

"Stupid is more like it."

"No, you're kindhearted and expect people to treat you with honesty. But they never do. Not to worry, we can handle your sister." Over the years, other voices, both male and female, had nattered in Joey's head—as loudly as real people—but Joey trusted only Saint Signore, his mentor and secret friend since age sixteen. Joey didn't think he was mentally or physically strong enough to stand up to Moni.

"Now, calm down, Jo-Jo." Saint Signore could grasp Joey's thoughts before they even crystallized. "*Ho un'idea*," Saint Signore said—I've got an idea. When the Saint spoke in Italian, Joey could understand him, but he never let Moni or anyone else know Italian was his second language. They'd use it to control him.

Saint Signore said, "We'll find out your sister's dirty little secret—everyone has one. Then you'll have ammunition."

"Are we talking about blackmail?"

Saint Signore guffawed. "I like to think of it as friendly persuasion."

Joey tried to remember the dirt he knew about his sister. *Niente.* Nothing. It was no secret that she had huddled in the nerdy crowd in high school or that she studied photography in college but wasn't apparently good enough at her craft to make the cut. And even Mama guessed that Moni only attended church a couple times to snag a husband from the singles group, but so far, she had been sadly unsuccessful.

"We'll keep a sharp eye on her," Saint Signore said. "She'll get overconfident and tip her hand."

Joey imagined himself hacking into her laptop computer, reading her emails, or checking under her bed for evidence. But then what? "If I find something incriminating, what should I do? Papa was the only person Moni obeyed, and he's dead. At least I think he is. We had a funeral, and I saw the obituary in the paper. But I've wondered, did he actually move to a tropical island like the painter Paul Gauguin and start a new family?"

8

"No, Jo-Jo, your father is in heaven. No subterfuge there. For the most part, he was a fine man."

Moni had worshipped Papa; she would have done anything to get his attention. "She was such a goody-two-shoes as a little girl. Sickening."

"Pathetic," echoed Saint Signore. "But don't worry. I have a plan. And Mama's on your side. So is Figaro. He'll protect you until his real owner shows up. Then we're all in trouble."

CHAPTER THREE
Mona Lisa

As I neared Booty's Café the next morning, I glanced up at the sign and noticed a bird had left a white splat across its painted surface. An ill omen? "Bad for business," Papa would say.

My folks had opened Booty's fourteen years ago, named after Papa's lizard cowboy boots and a play on their last name, Buttaro. They'd hung a boot-shaped sign out front that looked like Italy to anyone with half a brain, according to Papa. My parents claimed the café would entertain them into retirement. I figured they'd hoped to give Joey a place to work. But he'd balked at the mention of clearing germy dishes and assembling sandwiches and panini made of cheeses and sliced meats, a potential home for hazards like E. coli or salmonella. Or handling money, which had passed through—who knew how many filthy fingers?

I was exhausted from lack of sleep but would have to haul the ladder out of the back room, climb up, and scrub off the bird droppings. I hadn't learned to delegate responsibilities, not that my cook, Ramon Lopez, had time for such menial work. When he arrived at 10:05, always running late, he'd have plenty to juggle. And by noon, when one of our dishwashers and our waitress showed up, the sinks were chock-full of dirty pans and dishes.

I opened the restaurant's front door and inhaled the familiar smells of garlic and of the Clorox used by the cleaning service, which would dissipate as soon as I cranked up the heat and got the daily soups warming. Since quitting my job at an optometrist's office, I was now prepping, waitressing, and counting the till six days a week. Thankfully, we were closed on Sundays.

I walked across the doormat and disarmed the alarm system, punching in 1028, my parents' anniversary date, then stepped past the register to the waist-high, L-shaped counter with its eight vinyl-topped stools. I never saw the twelve-foot-long hardwood plank without thinking of my father, who'd collapsed and died of a heart attack behind it several months after Booty's grand opening. He'd passed away after closing time, luckily, since death is also bad for business. After the service, Mama swore to keep the café open. As sole proprietor, she'd pared down the operation, ordering bread instead of baking it herself and modifying the menu to include a few plain old American sandwiches that were easy to prepare. She'd hired a cook, Ramon, and a waitress. My determined mother had done a fine job running it until last fall, when she tripped and tore the cartilage in her knee. Then a month later, she caught a virus, which turned into pneumonia, followed by another fall in her backyard.

I headed to the coffee maker and started the urn. Listening to the first spatters of java, I rubber-banded my shoulder-length hair into a ponytail and tied on a white apron, then checked in the vegetable cooler, a six-foot-high wooden-framed structure that had to be eighty years old. I lugged out onions, carrots, and garlic—I threw a couple of cloves of garlic in every vat of soup, in memory of my father. I had enough leftover minestrone soup to see us through the day but needed to get the vat of split peas I'd soaked overnight on the burner and start sautéing the chopped vegetables.

I dumped the diced onion into the fry pan, the morsels letting out a hiss as they hit the warming olive oil. A college-aged young man peered through the front window, but I ignored him. Booty's was opened only for lunch. My parents had spoken of offering dinner but didn't get around to it. They'd never lacked for customers. With Mama manning the cash register, the lunch crowd queued up twenty people deep some days, an endless stream of hungry stomachs and grouchy quips about waiting so long. But business had recently slacked off without Mama's engaging personality entertaining her guests, as she called her customers. As soon as I built profits up again, I'd locate a realtor specializing in businesses and sell the place.

An hour later, with my soups slowly warming—I'd once made the mistake of burning a vat of split pea soup and had to chuck the whole batch—I wandered around the restaurant, tidying and filling paper napkin dispensers. Long gone were the red-and-white-checked tablecloths and votive candles my parents once used. With Mama in assisted living, I'd changed the background music from festive accordion or the Three Tenors to soothing jazz. Were there any traces of my folks left? Yes, framed watercolors of the Amalfi Coast still hung from the rough-hewn cedar walls, representing a sliver of Buttaro heritage. And I continued to reproduce Mama's recipes as best I could. So far, none of the customers had complained that her minestrone soup had lost its zest.

I heard a key working the front door lock, then Ramon strolled into the kitchen at 10:10. His raven-black hair was still damp from showering, and his shirt collar was open to the third button, exposing bronze skin. He stood five foot seven but possessed the confidence of a giant, dwarfing men a foot taller.

"Good morning, beautiful." His gaze traveled the length of my torso, then took in my face.

I didn't smile because I'd asked him repeatedly to call me Mona. All my life, I'd begged friends to save me from the embarrassment of being named after da Vinci's painting of a woman with a Gioconda half-smile.

He sighed. "I mean, good morning, Mona." Then he broke into Nat King Cole's hit, "Mona Lisa, Mona Lisa..." and started waltzing me around the kitchen.

"Stop it." I struggled out of his embrace while containing a bubble of laughter. "Mama may think your playful antics are amusing, but I don't." Although I admit I found him attractive; most women would.

I re-gathered my poise. "Ramon, I'm not wearing my

dancing shoes. And—and we open in thirty minutes, and you haven't sliced the meat."

"There should be plenty left over from yesterday. I stayed late."

"Well, what about slicing tomatoes?"

He grinned. "I'll get right on it."

But I understood his underlying message—that he'd like to get right on me. And some days I was tempted, but always reined myself in. I needed Ramon as an ally, not a boyfriend. I depended on the thirty-three-year-old cook and intended to hang onto him. Last month, when he'd been sick, I'd nearly drowned in the kitchen, overwhelmed by the demands for special orders. My opposite, Ramon functioned like a Cuisine Art, his body swaying to the background music while he flirted with female customers, who could chat with him through a shoulder-high open window as they stood in line waiting to order.

Cinching his apron strings low on his hips, he glanced my way and lifted his brows. "You look tired. Busy night?"

"I was in bed at nine thirty."

His full lips widened into a smile.

"Alone," I said.

"But something disturbed your sleep?"

"Yes, a troll moved into Mama's basement." I could see confusion in his brown eyes and realized he'd never heard of the story. "I'm referring to *The Three Billy Goats Gruff*, one of my favorite childhood books. It was my brother, Joey, who sneaked into Mama's house at two in the morning." I gave the minestrone soup a stir with a long-handled ladle that once belonged to my grandmother in the old country. "With any luck he'll be gone by the time I get off work." I sounded mean-spirited, which is how I felt. Mama would not be pleased.

"If you have a problem with your brother, perhaps I can help. I could spend the night."

"Thank you, but I couldn't inconvenience you." I kept my face from revealing my annoyance. Or did I enjoy attention from this sexy man?

He winked. "It would be no imposition, I promise."

"No, thanks." To change the subject, I said, "I'm thinking about adding a couple of new items to the menu."

"I make a fresh cilantro, avocado, roasted red peppers, and Monterey Jack cheese panini that will knock your socks off."

"Sounds great. I'll order cilantro, and we'll give it a try." While he rinsed a dozen tomatoes and set them on a cutting board, I mounted the step stool and erased the blackboard above the cash register with a damp cloth. I wrote the soup of the day, split pea, on its gray surface in the neat, slanted handwriting I'd acquired in fifth grade.

Minutes later, Annie, our petite busboy/waitress, strode in, shouldering a bulging backpack as big as a twenty-pound bag of potatoes. She stowed it under the counter next to the keg of beer, but instead of her usual routine of putting on an apron, she came over to me.

"Good morning." I was always glad to see the hardworking young lady. Her raisin-black hair was lopped short and spiky.

"Can we talk?" Her gaze set itself on my feet.

"Could it wait until after the lunch rush?"

"This will take only a second," she blurted out. "I need to give you two weeks' notice."

"Is there a problem? I was planning to give you a raise." I wasn't, but I should have. Annie's tips were meager. Our customers had to stand at the register when placing their orders. "Have I done something wrong?" I asked.

"No. You and your mother have been very kind to me. I'm returning to LA, at least through the summer."

"Nothing I can do to change your mind?"

"My boyfriend lives down there. But I might come back for fall quarter."

I didn't plan to be in the restaurant business in six months but wouldn't divulge that information. "I can't wait that long. I'll need your replacement the moment you leave. I guess I'd better put an ad in the newspaper." I had no idea how to hire personnel.

14

"Post the job on Craigslist," she said. "Or put a Help Wanted sign in the window. That's how your mother hired me."

If only Mama were here to handle this. "What if one of our regular customers applies for the job? Like the scraggly man who sometimes sits at the counter nursing his coffee cup for hours."

"I don't mind being the bad guy." Ramon left the kitchen area, drying his hands with a bar cloth. "Let me handle it."

"In other words, we're hiring a young beauty?" I asked.

He sent Annie a smile. "That would be a bad thing? It's what your mother did."

"True, Annie is lovely." I wondered if the two had ever been an item. I told him, "If I can't find the right person by the end of the week, you're on."

For the next two and a half hours, Ramon, Annie, Kavi (our nineteen-year-old Thai dishwasher, who barely spoke English), and I muscled our way through lunch madness, customers filling all twelve of the tables and the stools hemming one side of the counter twice—meaning two sittings. As Ramon cranked out the meals, while also filling his weekend social calendar, I welcomed customers, trying to emulate Mama, and took their orders. Whenever a free moment presented itself, Annie and I flitted around delivering meals, topping off coffee cups, and clearing away dirty dishes.

To add to the melee, Ramon ran out of provolone at one o'clock and had to substitute with Swiss cheese, then we ran low on homemade Italian dressing, and I hurriedly concocted another batch. And disgruntled Frank DiAngelo, one of our regulars and an old friend of my parents, returned his split pea soup because it was too salty. "Kiddo, are you trying to give me a heart attack?"

It was exhausting but rewarding work once the onslaught subsided, and I counted the till to find we'd covered expenses: food costs, wages, rent, insurance, utilities, and taxes. Great, another few weeks of profitable days like this and I'd find a commercial realtor eager for the listing. Then I'd go back to my old job at the optometrist's? No, Dr. Kamahuri had filled my position. And I was ready for something radically new. But what? As a teen, my passion was to imitate Ansel Adams, the master of black-and-white photography. But Papa talked me into studying art history in college, focusing on the Italian Renaissance. He'd assured me a dynamic museum career awaited me, but there weren't any job openings in Seattle.

Leaving Booty's, I stopped by the bank to make the deposit, then swung by Mama's assisted living home. As I entered the four-story brick structure with its substantial lobby, it occurred to me that Mama might have given Joey her key to the house. When I got home, I would call a locksmith and have the locks changed. Wouldn't Joey be surprised when he couldn't get in?

I took the elevator to the third floor and found Mama's room several doors down. I knocked, but she didn't answer. I was about to check the dining room, but then Mama came strolling my way with Frank DiAngelo. Had he come to complain to her about his lunch?

Those two looked chummy, their heads tipped together, unaware of my presence until we were only feet apart. Mama wasn't using her cane, and she looked different. Younger. Her grizzled hair was newly cropped and hennaed, and she'd applied too much rouge and lipstick to match her fire engine-red sweater. Since when did she start wearing bright colors? Black and beige used to dominate her wardrobe. And she was cradling a dozen yellow roses enclosed in green tissue.

"Mama?" I wanted to get her attention before she bumped into me. Her face showed more surprise than pleasure at my unscheduled visit.

"Mona Lisa, hello *cara*. I wasn't expecting company." She glanced at Mr. DiAngelo. Had he also stopped by unannounced, or was this a planned rendezvous? If I didn't know better, I'd have said the silver-haired, mustached, seventy-five-year-old gent, in his worn pinstripe three-piece suit, was blushing.

"Nice to see you, Miss Buttaro." He spoke formally, as if I hadn't just served him lunch two hours ago, when he'd called me "kiddo." Was he losing his memory? Good, then he wouldn't complain to Mama about his salty soup.

"A pleasure to see you too." I smiled. "I trust you found something to meet your satisfaction at lunch."

"Yes, the French dip sandwich was good, considering its country of origin. But after I finished my meal, upon exiting the front door, I noticed a bird had - how you say in English? — defecated? - all over the sign. *Che schifo!* Enough to make a man lose his appetite."

"I think you mean *defecated*." I turned to Mama and described the bird's unpleasant signature. "I forgot. I meant to clean it off."

"You should have called your brother and asked him to do it."

Was Mama joking? "He's the last person I'd think to call," I said. "Joey never lifts a finger to help anyone. When was the last time he even answered the telephone?"

A door further down the hallway cracked open, and a gray-haired woman peeked out. Mama said, "Mona Lisa, you're bothering my neighbors with your arguing."

"I'm not arguing, just stating the facts."

"Would you please keep your voice down?"

"Mama, are you going to let me in?"

She shrugged in Frank DiAngelo's direction, like there was no way she could rid herself of her pesky daughter.

"I was just leaving." He brought his feet together and made a small, courtly bow in her direction. "*Ciao*, Barbara." His voice lingered on her name like he was singing a line from *West Side Story*. Then he added briskly, "You, too, Miss Buttaro."

"Come back any time." Mama's voice fluttered. She was batting her eyelashes! "Don't forget about dance class on Thursday night."

"I'll be there, Barbara." He departed, a jaunty swing in his step, and Mama finally opened her door. I followed her into her one-bedroom unit. On the walls hung three framed watercolors of Positano, the village Mama called the pearl of the Amalfi Coast.

17

Every inch of horizontal surface was adorned with colorful Italian souvenirs and ornaments.

Mama moved to the kitchenette, more of an alcove with a pint-sized refrigerator and a microwave oven and reached under the sink for a vase.

"Are the flowers a gift from Mr. DiAngelo?" A creepy uneasiness tightened my stomach. I assumed Mama would remain a single woman. I didn't want a stepfather. No one could fill Papa's shoes, and I felt like a traitor even contemplating the idea.

"Yes, they are." She splashed water into the clear vase, then set about clipping an inch off the roses' stems, as if admirers presented flowers to her every day of the week. "How was the lunch crowd today?"

"Steady."

"And Ramon?"

"He was whistling when he left." He'd had a woman's telephone number scrolled on a paper napkin in his back pocket.

"And the ice machine is still working?"

"Yes, Mama, but I'm afraid that dinosaur is on its last leg." It was secondhand when my parents bought it.

I noticed Joey's high school portrait positioned next to Papa's photo on the mantle and remembered my unpleasant mission. "I had a visitor last night. Joey came back."

She left the roses on the counter next to a bottle of sherry. "Isn't that nice? Did you two have a pleasant chat?"

"No, we didn't." I folded my arms across my chest. "He sneaked in like a thief. In the middle of the night. If I'd summoned the police, he could have been hauled off to jail."

"Now, *cara*, why would you call the police?"

"Because I thought he was an intruder. In fact, he was. Unless you gave him your key."

Kicking off her one-inch heels, she glided over to the couch and cleared a space for me to sit, moving aside a shocking-pink shawl I'd never seen before and draping the slinky fabric on a chair. Again, I was taken aback by the brash color. Papa wouldn't

18

have cared for it. Had she bought the shawl for herself on a whim, or was it a gift?

I didn't want to sit; I stood my ground. "Did you or didn't you give Joey your key?"

"I don't think so, but I might have." She scooped up her purse and turned it upside down on the couch. Out tumbled a small tin of mints, a comb, and a laced hanky. "Maybe he took it off my key ring when he was here last week."

"Joey visited you? How did he get here?" He'd never learned to drive.

"He took the bus. He's memorized the Metro schedule for every single run in the whole city. Remember, Joey was always good at math and algebra."

"But his teachers complained he didn't follow their rules."

"That's because his brain takes shortcuts." She finally located the key ring under a sofa cushion and lifted it up with pride. "It looks like my house key is missing. And now that I think of it, I might have given it to Joey. He wanted to pick up some of his things."

"You mean the boxes of trash I threw away?"

"Why must you take that tone, Mona Lisa? I'm sure your brother had reasons for his 'collection.'" She quoted the word with her fingers. "He's not happy living at The Caring Home. Joey says his roommate, Adam, bothers him. The man sounds mentally ill."

"Mama, Joey isn't your average ordinary guy either."

Her hands flew up to partially cover her ears. "I will not listen to you bad-mouth your brother."

"Okay, I'm sorry. But he can't stay with me. I sublet my apartment to a visiting professor from Wales, and it will be vacant again in a few weeks. I'm planning to move back. And Joey isn't capable of living in your house alone."

"Why? I thought it was a mistake moving him out in the first place, but you strong-armed me into it when I was flat on my back and thought I might be dying." She was right, but I'd done the Herculean deed for everyone's good.

19

"When are you moving back home, Mama?"

"Never. I can't. I'm on a pinochle team here with Loretta from church, Marsha Schwartz, and Lois Valentino from the old neighborhood, who lives two doors down. We girls get together for tea every afternoon." She inclined her head toward the kitchenette at the bottle of sherry. No teapot in sight.

"All the more reason to sell your house." I noticed a ticket stub to the Fifth Avenue Theatre. "How long can you afford to continue living here?" I eyed the balcony, with its two wicker chairs. "It must cost $5,000 a month to stay here."

"That's nothing for you to worry about, *cara*. Consider the lilies of the field, how they grow."

"Yes, yes, I get your point. God will provide. But in the meantime, how can you afford to live here unless you sell the house?"

"I can't sell. What would happen to Figaro?"

"The same thing that happened before when someone picked him up foraging through garbage cans. I'll call the canine rescue lady and find another person to adopt him. I don't trust that dog. He reminds me of a detonated hand grenade."

Standing almost my height, she took hold of my shoulders. "Mona Lisa, listen to yourself. What happened to my fearless daughter, the tenderhearted girl who loves animals?"

Her words sank into me like darts. Sure, I was a brave tyke when a *ragazzina* of eight. What changed me? Then I remembered the fiasco that sent my world spinning on a new trajectory.

CHAPTER FOUR
Mona Lisa

The next morning, Booty's lunch rush loomed like a tidal wave, Friday being our busiest day of the week - if all went well.

Ramon brought out mayonnaise, scooping blobs into a stainless-steel bowl. I stifled a yawn, because if I covered my mouth, I'd have to wash my hands again. One of Mama's rules for hygiene. "Hot date last night?" he asked.

I leaned into the cooler and hauled out the tub of leftover chopped lettuce. "You know me. Party till closing time."

"I could have been your designated driver and escorted you home."

I sent him a crooked smile. "That's a kind offer. I'll keep it in mind for next time. Not that I drink anymore. In my twenties, I assumed Italians could hold their liquor, that sipping red wine ran in their genes, but I learned the hard way I turn into mush when I overindulge."

"Have you tried margaritas? I know a place - " He capped the mayonnaise jar.

"Ramon, are you trying to be a bad influence on me?"

I noticed yesterday's lettuce had wilted - my fault, I'd prepared too much. So, I dumped the greens into the bin provided by a pig farmer who came by to pick it up at closing time. More of Mama's rules: serve only fresh lettuce and let nothing go to waste.

"So last night?" Ramon returned the mayonnaise to the cooler and pulled out jars of roasted red peppers and pitted olives. "Nothing exciting. I started going through Papa's desk." Drawers stuffed with papers and receipts - some fifty years old. And cancelled checks. He kept everything, including several boxes of sketches and notes. His inventions never took flight. But there was one idea I kept on the back burner of my mind: a possible way to produce income for my mother and me, if I could find it.

"I didn't get very far. It put me in a funk, made me miss Papa, and then I slept badly, every little sound jarring me awake."

"Any trolls in the basement?" His tone was playful, but his dark eyes, framed by black brows and longish sideburns, revealed concern. Or was I reading sentiment into them because I needed someone to care about me?

"Thankfully, no. To make sure I didn't have uninvited visitors, I put the chain across the front door and dragged the kitchen table in front of the back door."

"Where did your brother sleep?"

"I have no idea. I decided when he gets tired and hungry enough, he'll return to The Home." I felt the weight of guilt heavy on my shoulders. "Maybe, in spite of myself, worrying about him kept me awake last night."

"That's no way for a young lady to spend time." Ramon said, moving to my side. "Let me take you out to dinner tonight."

Much as I would have enjoyed an evening of flirtatious chitchat, I said, "Don't you already have a date?" Chances were he did.

He shrugged. "Give me the word, beautiful, and I'll cancel." He snapped his fingers. "Like that, and I'm all yours."

"I'm too old for you, Ramon."

"No, you're not. And since when does age matter in affairs of the heart?" He helped me remove a carton of iceberg lettuce from the cooler, then set it on the counter next to the sink. "Your mother told me your age. We're only four years apart."

"She did? Mama made me promise never to tell anyone how

old she is. That's a double standard. I'm tempted to write her age on the menu board." As we extracted half a dozen heads of lettuce, his elbow brushed against mine. I stepped back to gain distance from him. "What else did she tell you?"

"Only good things."

An hour later, I was working busily, making extra efforts to greet the customers I recognized by name, the way Mama did. "Good morning, Mr. DiAngelo," I said when the mustached gentleman schlepped up to the register, his wingtip shoes sliding across the floor. Same three-piece suit. "What can I get you? I made a point of not putting too much salt in the lentil and vegetable soup today, just for you."

"I don't like lentil soup - give me a bowl of minestrone." His domed, balding forehead shined under the overhead light. "And…" He tugged on his earlobe. "Call me Frank. We've known each other so long we're like family. No?"

Was that his excuse for acting surly most of the time?

I reached into the till for a dime and three pennies. "Don't forget your change, Mr. DiAngelo - I mean, Frank."

"Keep it, as a tip."

"Thank you so much." I dropped the change into the tip jar. When he moved away to sit at his usual table, a tall man stepped in front of the register. He was what you'd call a hunk with his wide shoulders, wavy brown hair, and blue eyes. And he seemed vaguely familiar.

"Mona Lisa, how are you?" His laugh lines framed his smile. A smile that came too easily.

Gawking at his face, I scrutinized his rugged features and finally recognized him. Mr. Popular from our large public high school. He'd aged with creases on his tanned forehead and a few graying hairs at the temple, but he was still handsome and probably knew it.

"Is that you, Cliff?" I asked, all blasé, when in fact a battle of emotions made me punch in a panini sandwich when he hadn't ordered anything yet.

"Yep, it's me." His large hands rested on the counter. "A few years older, but many times wiser. I didn't know you were working here." His gaze pierced right into mine. Did he still think of me as a *wop* or *dego*? Not that I ever heard him use those derogatory terms, but one of his buddies had.

"I started a few months ago - long story." I recalled with horror the crush I'd had on Cliff from afar. And, darn it all, I still found him gorgeous. "What would you like today?" I asked, as if he were any old customer. I'd learned a lot in the last decade about hiding my true feelings.

"The soup-and-sandwich special - roast beef on white, heavy on the mayo - and a chance to catch up. Would you have time to stop by my table?"

Catch up on what? Cliff and I had never spoken to each other before this moment.

I looked down the line of customers, six deep, and shrugged. "Not for thirty or forty minutes. You'll probably be gone by then." I felt a vague sadness in my chest, like a missed opportunity was sailing me by. What was I thinking? We were opposites. Case closed.

He said, "I'll find a newspaper and eat slowly." But I figured he wouldn't.

When the bulk of the lunch rush subsided, I asked Annie to take over the till, and went out to refill coffee cups. I was surprised to see Cliff hunkered in the back corner at the table under a map of Sicily. He noticed me and set his newspaper aside. I refilled his cup to the rim - how would he manage to drink it without spilling? Mama would not approve. I wished she were here.

"I'm on the twenty-year high school reunion committee," he said, as if this would interest me. He probably wanted me to contact the unpopular kids to invite them. "Hard to believe that much time has gone by," he said.

"Can't argue with you there." I checked his left hand. No ring. "You married Janette Wilkinson, didn't you?"

He gave me a thoughtful look. Was he reliving the good old days with the queen bee of Roosevelt High School?

"We took the plunge straight out of college," he said. "She and I stuck it out together for eight years. We had a daughter, Patricia Ann, now fourteen years old. Nicknamed Panda. A beautiful girl, but the rest of the marriage got ugly." He glanced around, maybe checking to see if anyone was eavesdropping. But the two women sitting near him were busy in conversation. "And how about you," he asked.

"Never married. No kids." The words tasted like week-old fish. Why had I revealed my pitiful condition? I busied myself, taking his plate with the other hand.

"Would you like to join the reunion committee?" He dabbed the corners of his mouth with his napkin. "We meet two evenings a month at Duke's on Union Bay."

I envisioned the kids in high school who never acknowledged me: Vicki, Deidre, Chick, and TR. I was too old to be invisible again. "No thanks, I don't have much spare time." I stepped a few yards away to replenish a coffee cup on a nearby table, then returned and lowered myself onto the chair across from Cliff because Mama expected me to be polite to customers. "I'm swamped with work and helping my mother sell her house." No way would I mention Joey.

"I remember your parents orchestrating the spaghetti feed. They were great."

"Thanks." My parents had turned the high school fundraiser into a symphony but had embarrassed me with their jokes and stories about the good old days in Italy. I couldn't tell if the kids were laughing with them or at me. "My father died over ten years ago."

"Yes, I read his obituary in the newspaper. I hadn't known he was an inventor."

"A slight exaggeration. Although he did come up with a few ideas, I'm surprised you remember." I glanced at Cliff's worn jeans and collared shirt. Northwest casual. "What kind of work do you do?"

"I own a small construction business. Some new, but mostly

remodeling. These days, half my clients are adding another story or expanding their kitchen."

"I could use a handyman," I said. "According to Mama's realtor, two dozen repairs need fixing before I can list her house. And her back fence is about to topple."

"I have a young man, Thomas, who could get those done for you. Why don't I come by and give you an estimate?"

I envisioned Figaro grabbing hold of Thomas's hand, what Mama labeled a playful gesture but what I took to be an act of dominance, then Joey flashing by in his skivvies. But I needed help. "Sure, that would be great. Send Thomas over." I wrote Mama's address on a paper napkin and handed it to Cliff.

He folded it in half and slid it into his pocket. "I'll need to look at the job to make sure he can handle it on his own. How about five thirty tonight, on my way home? And while I'm here, you want me to clean off your sign out front? I've got a ladder in the back of my pickup."

"Uh, sure, thank you. I'll pay you for your time."

"No need."

Ramon delivered a salad to a nearby table, meaning I was needed back at the register. Or had Ramon come into the seating area to scope out Cliff? I dashed back into the kitchen before the two men could meet.

* * *

Hours later, Figaro stared into the void behind me as I entered the front door. No doubt he was anticipating my mother's arrival; I hoped he didn't hold me responsible for her absence. He stalked over to sniff my pant legs for traces of food. He must have weighed eighty pounds, maybe ninety, but he padded silently across the carpet.

"Hi, Fang," I said. "Didn't I leave you out in the backyard this morning? Joey must have let you in." I gave the dog's hip-high withers a pat, feeling his rigid outer coat. He raised his head and stared up at me, like he was waiting for attention. When Mama took the dog in, he bonded to her like a private to his drill sergeant in a mere twenty-four hours. Mama called him her little pup. *Il mio cagnolino.* That's how she treated everyone - with open arms. I wondered who Figaro's former owner was. What kind of idiot would let their purebred dog run off leash and then not come looking for him?

I'd heard dogs could intuitively read body language, so I forced myself to relax my arms and shoulders. Who knew? Maybe I'd be glad to have his company when Cliff got here.

Entering the kitchen, I noticed the clock above the stove proclaiming it was already quarter past five. Why had I agreed to let Cliff come over in the first place? Because the house needed all sorts of repairs, and the fellow Mama hired last month, a retired carpenter, never showed up. So why was I rattled? I didn't like strange men in the house, that's why. Was Cliff a serial killer who looked ordinary on the outside? Yikes, my mind was turning paranoid like Joey's. I needed to get a grip. Cliff would come to the house once. After the work was completed, I'd send him a check in the mail and never see him again.

I looked in the sink for dirty dishes, evidence that Joey had eaten breakfast or lunch - empty. Then I checked the dishwasher, also empty, save for my coffee cup from this morning. I opened the refrigerator door and found its contents - milk, eggs, the remains of Thai takeout I planned to have for dinner - as I'd left them. I didn't bother to lift the Styrofoam lid and check on my Rama Rong Song; no way would Joey sample my unsanitary leftovers. That would be like offering him a lick of my popsicle or a swig of my Coke. The corners of his mouth would draw back in disgust. I remembered a party when he was in high school, one of our parents' guests double dipped a potato chip and he shouted that the whole bowl of Mama's artichoke dip was contaminated. After that incident, Mama indulged him by scooping a small portion and serving him separately. Then he refused to attend my parents' parties at all. If only Mama had treated him as a normal kid, maybe he would have developed differently.

27

The door to the basement stood open. If Joey was napping downstairs, I wanted to wake him before Cliff showed up because I needed to show him Joey's dungeon of a bedroom. I'd never known anyone who slept more than my brother, like he'd just finished a marathon when, in fact, he moved very little. I made my way down the stairs, Figaro tailing me, his muzzle inches from my calves. I hated confrontations and resented Mama for designating me Joey's overseer. Yesterday, she'd given me his monthly allowance, which she just happened to have in cash, because Joey wouldn't enter a bank with a check and had no personal identification anyway.

I found Joey's bed as neatly made as a five-star hotel room, like it had never been slept in. Thank goodness. Had he skedaddled out the back door when he heard my five-year-old Toyota cruising up to the curb minutes ago? Or did he take off shortly after I left for work?

I checked the window wells to see if Joey was prowling around the side yard and spying on me. I wished our parents had installed a burglar alarm system. *Quit fretting.* Joey was back at The Home by now.

"Are you hungry?" I asked Figaro, and he dipped his chin like he could understand me. Good grief, I was talking to the dog like Mama did.

Back in the kitchen, I filled Figaro's bowl with kibble and positioned it on the wooden crate Mama brought home from Booty's to save the dog from getting a crick in his neck. While he crunched into the food with powerful mandibles, I called The Home. When I asked to speak to Joey, Mrs. Landis said, "We went all over this, Barbara," and I realized she thought she was talking to my mother. Had I begun to sound like her? The next thing I knew, I'd be staring at her face in the mirror.

"This is Joey's sister, Mona Lisa Buttaro." I stressed my last name to add credibility because legally I had no control over his actions. I wasn't his guardian and didn't have power of attorney. "May I please speak to him?"

"He isn't here." She sounded defensive. "Your mother said he was with you."

"He was last night. Why didn't you contact me when he didn't come in? You have my cell phone number. After my mother, I'm next of kin."

"I called your mother, and she told me not to disturb you."

Imagining the trials of running a house for mentally disabled men, I couldn't blame Mrs. Landis for being frazzled. I said, "Would you please check his room to see if he's shown up, so I can let my mother know?"

"I talked to his roommate, Adam, ten minutes ago. He hasn't seen Joey in twenty-four hours."

"When my brother returns, would you call me?" I said. Mrs. Landis agreed, then called me Barbara again.

Cliff was supposed to be here right now. To keep myself from pacing by the front door like a teenager waiting for a date, I headed upstairs to check my email. In my bedroom, I opened my laptop and found an email from Uncle Vito, Mama's brother, a widower living in Naples, whom I hadn't seen face-to-face since Papa's funeral. At his invitation, we'd exchanged emails ever since.

Mona Lisa, Carissima, your mama called yesterday begging me to come to Seattle to help her family, but I am an old man, and my lumbago is bothering me. Be a good girl now and do what your mama asks. Take care of Joey. Is he shy? Then introduce him to a nice young woman, maybe with money of her own. And how about you? Isn't it time you are marrying? Your mother needs grandchildren, then she won't worry so much. I have an idea. You and Joey, come visit me. I'm living in Rome now. If you can't afford the tickets, I'll pay for them.

Another idea: I know a bachelor who's looking for a wife. He is twenty years older than you, but this makes him wiser, no? And he owns a winery (very excellent Chianti) and five apartment houses in Rome, all high rent.

I could picture Uncle Vito's jaunty goatee and his small, merry eyes. He'd taken on the role of family patriarch and was indeed the oldest male in the extended family, with apparently too much time on his hands to meddle in my affairs. If he thought I was going to marry an old coot I'd never met, he was crazier than Joey.

Searching for a polite way to stave off my uncle's snooping, I pressed the reply button on my computer screen. Then, out front in the street, I heard two car doors open and close.

CHAPTER FIVE
Cliff

"This is my daughter, Panda." Standing on Mrs. Buttaro's craftsman-style front porch, Cliff glanced down into the fourteen-year-old girl's scowling face. He felt awkward bringing Panda along while bidding a job. She'd dyed half her bangs, a swatch of her brick-red hair, bright green, and she looked, well, freaky wearing miniature combat boots with thick soles, and skin-tight black clothing. "At the last minute, her mother - you remember Janette - couldn't pick her up." He was doing his best to act professsionally.

"That's okay," Mona Lisa said. "Hello, Panda." She extended her hand to shake Panda's, but his girl folded her arms, covering her small breasts. "What grade are you in?" Mona Lisa asked.

"I'm a senior," Panda lied. Fair enough, Cliff told himself; Panda didn't want to be here. Janette had dumped her into his lap again without warning. But if he refused to fetch Panda after school, Janette might play hardball with him for months.

"Glad to meet you," Mona Lisa said. "Please, come in." As she stepped back into the front hall, a black-and-tan Doberman marched onto the front porch and poked his nose against Panda's flat abdomen. "Sorry." Mona Lisa grabbed hold of his collar. "I meant to put him outside before you arrived."

"I love dogs," Panda declared.

"She's always been an animal lover." Cliff laid his hand on her shoulder, but she shrugged it off.

"His name's Figaro, and he's looking for a new home." Mona Lisa lifted her brows as she glanced at Cliff. He sent her his sternest frown. The last thing he needed was a pushy woman offering his daughter a dog and making him into the bad guy.

"Daddy, you promised to get me a puppy when I was old enough to take care of it."

"That was when your mother and I lived together. We went all through this. I can't keep a dog in my apartment. Especially a Doberman pinscher the size of a pony."

She stomped her foot like a demanding three-year-old. "He's the perfect size." Her voice rose in pitch and volume. "You should buy a real house, Daddy, with a big yard."

No way would he expose his financial problems in front of Mona Lisa. "Sweetheart, can we talk about this later, in private?"

Panda stroked the dog's arched neck, then under his chin. "He likes me."

"Of course he does," Cliff said. "Everyone likes you."

"I'm sure I will, once I get to know you," Mona Lisa said, with what seemed to Cliff to be pseudo-enthusiasm. She gave the dog's collar a tug and backed him into the front hall. On a round table stood a silk flower arrangement atop a doily. A wooden banister curved up to the second floor. Out of habit, Cliff reached out to wiggle the banister and found it wobbly.

"My little brother and I used to slide down that," Mona Lisa said, a smile emerging.

"Cool, I want to." Panda shed her quilted parka and trotted up several steps.

"Whoa there, partner, no one's riding down it today," Cliff said. "It needs tightening, big time." He extracted a pad of paper and a mechanical pencil from his pocket and wrote *repair banister*.

"We should have taken care of that years ago," Mona Lisa said, color rising in her cheeks.

"It's typical of these fine old houses." Cliff thought of his mother's rattrap, the empty gin bottles under the kitchen sink. Her name was Grace - a ludicrous name, if he'd ever heard one; there was nothing gracious about her. Deep in his chest, a familiar ache resurfaced. "What else do you have for me?"

"Since we're headed in that direction, we could go upstairs first." She glanced at Panda, who glared back, her thin lips pressed together.

As Mona Lisa and Cliff initiated their assent, Panda slipped past them down the steps to pet Figaro.

"Will you be all right by yourself?" Cliff asked her.

"I don't know the dog's temperament very well," Mona Lisa said. "Mama hasn't had him long."

Cliff felt himself bristle inside. How dare she put his daughter at risk? "Better put Figaro outside," he said.

"He's fine! I'm fine!" Panda shouted over her shoulder, then she strutted into the living room, out of sight, Figaro tailing her.

"I guess it's okay. This won't take long." He'd work faster without Panda's obstinate presence. She didn't make loving her easy. But of course he did. "Shall we?" he said. He watched her swaying hips mount the staircase. He should be attracted to her narrow waist and her thick waterfall of coffee-brown hair streaming across her shoulders. A man could run his fingers through the waves and caress the nape of her neck. But he was off women, for now. Unlikely he'd ever marry again, unless it was to a knockout leggy blonde who'd make redheaded Janette seethe with jealousy.

Forcing his gaze away, he noted the carpet underfoot needed replacing. "How much money does your mother want to sink into the house?"

Reaching the second floor, she paused. "I don't really know. Mama's realtor said anything she invests in the house will come back to her when it sells. But I'm not sure how much she can afford."

"I look forward to seeing Mrs. Buttaro again." A real, live mother, the opposite of his own. He'd come into Booty's over the years and gotten to know her a little. "Is she around?"

"No. She lives in a retirement home." Mona Lisa led him to her mother's room, a wallpapered area with two window seats and billowy lace curtains. The top of the bureau had been swept clean- of family photos, knickknacks, or perfume bottles. Only a framed photo of Mr. Buttaro adorned one wall.

Mona Lisa tipped her chin up and eyed a hair-thin crack dissecting the ceiling.

"From the earthquake about eight years ago?" he asked.

"I think the crack's always been there, but the earthquake deepened it. Is that something your young man, Thomas, could fix, or do I need to bring in a painter?"

"I could smooth that plaster for you myself and then have Thomas paint the ceiling. I'm working on a job a few blocks away. A kitchen remodel. Then I've got nothing set up." He had three bids out, but the homeowners kept waffling. He needed to keep Thomas busy or lose him.

She gave Cliff a worried look, her full lips pursed. Was it pity, or did she fear that he and Thomas were incompetent? He regretted exposing his meager work calendar, but hadn't he recently promised himself and God, he'd be honest with every person he met? No more lies. He needed the money. During their marriage, Janette had spent faster than he could earn - had she been siphoning off their savings and squirreling it into a hidden account? Her attorney had saddled Cliff with inflated spousal and child support. Recently, Panda had been accepted at pricy Puget Sound Prep, and she was getting braces next month; both demanded hefty down payments.

Mona Lisa said, "That would be fine. There's a crack in every ceiling on this floor. And Mama's bathroom has a few problems." They squeezed into the peach-colored tiled room, dominated by a bathtub large enough to accommodate a Sumo wrestler. She yanked the plastic shower curtain back to expose the dripping shower fixture jutting from the wall at eye level and, below it, the tub's rust-stained enamel.

"At least I don't see any mold." He turned on the tub's hot

water, then twisted it off with all his might, but the dripping persisted. "I need to know how much your mother wants to spend. We could change the washer and hope that stops the leak and clean up the tub or take the tub out and replace it with a new shower stall. The tile in the back needs to be re-grouted. And we could paint the vanity and put in a new light fixture."

"Let's go the cheapest, quickest, easiest route."

Stingy with her mother's money, he thought. "As my father once said, don't trip over the dollars to pick up the pennies." But he never did find those dollars. "A little investment will go a long way. It's a beautiful old home." Cliff would probably never own his own again. Janette would see to that.

Stepping back into her mother's bedroom, Mona Lisa glanced around, her gaze landing on the ceiling light fixture, missing one of two bulbs. "I'm feeling overwhelmed. If I were taller…" She was a slim little gal, only an inch taller than Panda. He imagined her standing on a chair, the light fixture still out of her reach. He couldn't help feeling sorry for her.

"We'll take care of that," he said. "If it would help, I could let Thomas come over by the hour. We'll set up a list by priority and see how much he accomplishes in three or four days."

"Okay, whenever he's available." She led Cliff into the hall and then to another smaller room, a bedroom with blue walls and flowered curtains. The single bed, covered with a paisley bedspread straight out of the sixties, was pushed up against the wall and heaped with old magazines: *Scientific American*, *Popular Science*, and *Discover*. The wooden desk, sturdy in character, was buried with loose-leaf binders and papers. A pencil holder perched on the corner was jammed so tightly that it looked ready to explode. A swivel chair supported a book entitled *Million Dollar Ideas*. A ceiling-height bookcase displayed a hodgepodge of balsa wood, scrap metal, and Lego models, some wheeled and some winged, of exactly what he wasn't sure. One six-inch-high structure resembling a crane stretched out into the room, dangling a magnet from a string. Doodads - assorted flashlights, can

35

openers, cigarette lighters, tie clips, and sunglasses - huddled in groupings on the lower shelves.

"My father liked to tinker." Mona Lisa's hand wrapped the back of her neck. "There's more of Papa's stuff in the basement and garage. I've got to go through everything. Either that or throw it away."

On the floor lay a half-dozen cardboard boxes, their tops folded shut and marked with words in a foreign language. "Is that Italian," he asked, and she nodded.

"Mostly our parents insisted we speak only English." She busied herself pushing the chair, with its carved armrests and brocade back and seat cushion, against the desk, like no one would ever sit there again. "But they lapsed back into Italian when they argued." A smile gathered on her face, raising the corners of her mouth. "And in times of celebration, which usually included wine and too much food, if you didn't speak Italian, you didn't understand what was being said about you." She released a sigh as if she were deflating. "Those times are gone."

"I know that feeling," he said and she narrowed her eyes at him as if he couldn't possibly understand her loss. He got the urge to reveal the details of his dismal childhood; he bet hers was a fairy tale compared to his. But why bother?

"I'd better check on Panda and then get her to her piano lesson. Are we done?"

"Not quite." Mona Lisa guided him through the rest of the second floor - another small bedroom, which he gathered was hers, and a bathroom with a leaky toilet he could easily repair. Finally descending to the first floor, he stepped into the living room to find Panda and the dog gone, leaving a dent in the couch and a silver cigarette case sitting at an odd angle, like it had just been examined.

"Nice crown molding." He glanced around. "And I like the fireplace." But where was Panda? As he moved back into the front hall, he heard a door at the back of the house open and close.

"The kitchen is this way." Mona Lisa strode across the front hall to the kitchen, the same vintage as his mother's, gold-colored appliances and all. But this yellow-walled room was neat, with crisp white curtains on the windows above the eating nook and the sink. No dirty plates or mildewing empty soup cans strewn across the counter.

He scanned the room while his thoughts remained on Panda. "Do these appliances all work?"

She let out a chuckle, her head held at a tilt, as though she'd finally decided he was okay. "Actually, one of the stovetop burners is broken. And the broiler hasn't worked for years."

He pulled a chain - the kind made of tiny metal balls - to switch on the fan above the stove. The blades commenced rotating with an angry hum - "That racket would drive me nuts. Do you do much cooking?"

"I used to enjoy it when I lived in my apartment. But living alone, why bother? And I have food coming out of my ears at Booty's." She moved to the sink, and Cliff followed.

"By the way, the disposal doesn't work either." She shrugged. "And there's a leak under this sink." She looked out the window to the backyard, where Panda was trying to coax Figaro into chasing a stick, without success. When his girl bent to pick up the stick, her fleshy midriff exposed itself provocatively. Her tight slacks encompassed her derriere and slender legs like a hooker. How could Janette allow their daughter to go to school dressed like that?

The dog turned its chiseled head to stare into the kitchen window, and Mona stepped away from it.

"Are you sure you don't want a dog? I'll throw him in free when your job's finished." Her dubious humor quirked into him, making him grin.

"Sounds tempting, but my landlord doesn't allow pets." He looked past her out the window and spotted movement in the garage. "Hey, there's a man out there."

CHAPTER SIX
Mona Lisa

I spun around and spotted Joey's lanky silhouette in the darkened garage. Light slanting in through its small side window highlighted his gaunt cheekbones, his flyaway hair, and his plaid Pendleton shirt Mama gave him decades ago.

"I saw that guy begging for money at the freeway entrance." Outrage flared through Cliff's voice. "He had a cardboard sign saying Vietnam vet, as if he's old enough to have been in Nam."

Before I could assure him it was only my brother who would never do such a thing, Cliff rushed to the back door. His hand tore at the knob; he yanked it with such force that the door shuddered on its hinges. He dashed down the back steps onto the grassy yard and wrapped a protective arm across Panda's shoulder. Figaro's head swung around looking for a common enemy; the hairs on his withers prickled, and his legs straightened.

My mouth gaped open. Would Joey bolt for the alley and run away, as Mama feared? I wished she were here to coax him into the house.

I hustled to the back door and got to the porch in time to see Cliff escort Panda to the bottom of the steps. Then he turned to the garage with fists clenched and his jaw squared, like he was ready for a high school brawl. Hadn't he grown up? Was his mind stagnating in that punch-them-up-after-the-game mindset? At least Figaro was calmly snuffling some bushes.

"Cliff, that's my brother." I snagged his attention. "He must have stopped by to look for something. A gardening tool." An absurd statement; I was covering up the way Mama did. But I couldn't expose our family skeleton to Cliff, who probably came from a sophisticated, perfect family that dined with cloth napkins and candlelight.

Cliff's posture remained rigid. "I never forget a face. I saw him panhandling."

"Joey wouldn't. He's too shy. And he wouldn't hurt a flea." But I didn't know that for a fact. My thoughts twirling back to childhood, I recalled how Violetta, our family cat, disappeared when I was fifteen. Papa had said our beloved kitty had probably been hit by a car, and Mama surmised an elderly neighbor lady serving saucers of cream had lured her away. But it occurred to me now that Joey could have killed the Persian and buried her in the garden behind Mama's hydrangeas. No, Joey would have been thirteen at the time; he didn't start behaving strangely until several years later. That I knew.

As if reading my thoughts, Joey receded into the shadows of the garage.

"Joey!" I called, and Figaro turned to me, his elegant ears pivoting to catch suspicious sounds. It seemed like the whole world fell silent.

"Maybe your brother went out the other door," Cliff said.

"No, the electric garage door opener has been broken for ages."

Cliff's gaze remained fixed on the garage until Joey finally cracked the side door, the one Mama used last year when bringing groceries into the house. His Rip van Winkle eyes - he looked like he'd been asleep for one hundred years - squinted under the overcast sky, and a fuzz of whiskers shadowed his pale face. He hadn't shaved? I thought his sanity hinged on tidiness. I could see why Cliff had mistaken Joey for a vagrant. My brother's rumpled shirt and jeans sagged several sizes too big.

He shuffled closer, his gait stilted like an old man.

"This is my brother, Joey." I tried to fabricate pride the way Mama would, but I wasn't a good enough actress to pull it off. I recalled when I first laid eyes on Panda, with her shock of kelly-green hair, which had to draw stares, and her tight pants. She had an angry aura to her, her brown eyes defiant. Joey couldn't appear any odder than she did. But I knew she was trying to make a statement, as I had in my teenage years. Joey was just weird.

His mouth severe, Cliff put out his large hand to shake Joey's, but Joey slouched into a military-at-ease stance, his hands grasped behind his back. Cliff's arm hung midair, until finally Joey extended his slender white fingers and shook Cliff's hand. In his trade, Cliff was probably used to blue-collar workers - men dressed like Joey. Men doing odd jobs didn't wear Armani suits. But Joey's smooth hands were a giveaway that he spent his days indoors.

"You remember Cliff from high school?" I said to Joey. "He was in my class."

"I think I might." Joey rubbed his hands together; he'd probably scrub them with disinfectant soap later. "A football player? Homecoming king?"

"My claim to fame," Cliff said. "But I've seen you recently." He gave Joey a good looking over. "Earlier today, in fact."

"No, I've been here all day."

"In the garage?" I wondered if he was pulling my leg.

"Yup, I took a nap in the back of Mama's Cadi."

"You're setting up house in her car?" I pictured him cocooned in Papa's musty sleeping bag, exhumed from the basement closet.

"She wouldn't mind."

"Mama's car is an oldie but goodie," I explained, so Cliff wouldn't think we were loaded and raise his hourly rate. "A 1972 Cadillac. Quite the gas-guzzler."

"I love vintage cars." Cliff walked over to the garage and glanced through the window. "It's a beauty. And is that an Alfa Romeo in there?"

40

"Yes. It was Papa's. I need to sell both cars, but first I have to get the garage door open." That wasn't my only hindrance; I'd toyed with selling my lackluster Toyota and driving Papa's cherry-red roadster, but I couldn't use a stick shift. And all reason suggested it rained too much in Seattle to drive a convertible.

"The garage door opener may need a new motor or be off its track," Cliff said. "I'll add it to my list."

"It may not be that easy. Before his death, Papa monkeyed with it. One of his inventions. His idea was that an electric eye would recognize Mama's car and, presto, the garage door would open, then close again a few minutes later. But the door opened and shut every time a full-size sedan motored down the street. When Papa passed away, Mama disconnected his contraption and went back to using her handheld clicker, but it never worked right again, and then finally quit."

"Maybe it just needs a new battery or isn't wired correctly," Cliff said. "One way or another, we'll get it fixed so your mother can get her car out."

"Thanks, that would be great. But I may not tell Mama. The world's a safer place without her behind the wheel."

Cliff chuckled. "I can relate. My mother drives like a maniac, but she won't give up her license." I imagined a meticulously coifed woman in a luxurious Mercedes-Benz.

At that moment, Panda sidled up to us. Cliff turned to Joey and said, "This is my pride and joy, my daughter, Panda." His solemn words sounded more like a warning than an introduction.

Both Panda and Joey's mouths formed an O. In recognition? They couldn't know each other. Then they said, "Hey," in unison. My brother stood a head taller than she did, but they stared into each other's eyes, holding the connection for several seconds longer than appropriate.

Apparently, I wasn't the only one to think so because Cliff slipped a hand under Panda's elbow and said to me, "We need to be on our way. I'll bring Thomas over tomorrow afternoon. Can you give me a key?"

Joey shifted his weight to one foot. "She'll be at work, but I could let you in."

CHAPTER SEVEN
Joey

"See you tomorrow, three o'clock," Joey said to Cliff.

"Thanks for coming," Moni said, her voice taut. "You, too, Panda. Nice to meet you."

Panda made no response. She gave Figaro's shoulder a pat, and the dog leaned into her skinny leg. Then Joey watched Cliff steer her around the side of the house and shut the gate so Figaro couldn't follow them.

"Come, Figaro," Joey said, although Saint Signore had let slip that the dog's real name was Max and that his owner was hunting for him, planning retaliation against the person who'd stolen him.

As Figaro trotted to Joey's side, Moni turned to the house, her hands gathering at her chest. "She's scared of that dog, and he knows it," said Saint Signore.

Joey had noticed the dog taking a shine to Panda and hoped Cliff would bring her with him tomorrow.

"I remember that pretty girl - *una bella ragazza*," Saint Signore said. "Two weeks ago. On the Ave. One block away from the University of Washington campus We were walking behind her and her girlfriend, their hips wiggling, trying to capture the attention of frat rats. Then a guy selling dope stopped them, and we saw Panda give him a couple of twenty-dollar bills, then stash

43

a packet into her purse." Joey admired how Saint Signore never missed the tiniest detail.

"How old were you when you started popping LSD?" Saint Signore asked, prodding into Joey's memory. "Fifteen? What a trip." Joey recalled with clarity the neon snowflake patterns expanding onto the pavement ahead of him as he walked home after partying with a friend who'd amassed a medley of psychedelic drugs. Trees had swayed like hula dancers, and lampposts evolved into eels, their scales flashing like sequins. But as Joey's trip ended, his mind dove into the dark recesses where demons lived. That's when Saint Signore first spoke words of assurance in his ear. "Your mama wants me to watch over you," he'd said.

"Who are you?" Joey had peered into the mirror above his bureau and saw his distorted image: his nose hooking more than usual, his eyes black holes, sucking him in.

"Call me Saint Signore. If I gave you my real name, the magic would be lost. And for heaven's sake, don't look in the mirror when you're stoned. You want to turn suicidal?" Joey had heard other voices in his head before but was amazed to find a saint lurking in his brain because his family was no longer Catholic. According to Uncle Vito, Mama's brother, Papa was practically excommunicated from the church, one reason he moved his family out of south Seattle and why he and Moni hadn't attended parochial school.

"I'll have to leave work early tomorrow," Moni said with a snap, bringing Joey back to the present. "You won't be here."

"She's trying to intimidate you," Saint Signore said. "Stand up to her."

Joey returned her glower. "I'm not going back to The Home. You lied before. You tricked me. You said Mama was dying."

"That-a-boy," Saint Signore said. "Make your papa in heaven proud."

"I thought she was." Her eyes glistened, forming a veneer of tears. Saint Signore whispered it was a ploy to garner Joey's sympathy. "But it doesn't matter," she said. "Mama is happily settled at the retirement home."

Joey scanned the neighbor's house and saw a curtain moving. The old bitty next door was an informant, spying on him since he was a child. "Moni, I'm not going to argue with you out here where the whole world can hear us."

"The neighbor lady's a bigmouth, *una boccalone*," Saint Signore said. "Remember how she used to tell Mama when you were skipping school? Now, hurry up and get your sister in the house, *subito*, before she looks in the garage."

Joey moved toward the back porch; he didn't want Moni anywhere near the garage where he was hiding his newfound treasures, which were still unclean. Later, Saint Signore would help him with the purification ritual.

Fortunately, Moni spun around in a huff and stomped up the back steps.

"She's a piece of work," Saint Signore said, with an edge of sarcasm. "A class act."

In the kitchen, Moni opened her purse and extracted a white envelope that Joey recognized as coming from Mama's bank. "Here's your allowance." She unsealed the sticky flap, taking out the twenty-dollar bills to count the $300 in front of him. Mama went to great lengths to find brand-new twenties straight from the mint - no creases, markings, or smudges - but Moni was further contaminating them with her germ-ridden fingers.

"Don't complain," Saint Signore warned Joey. "She'll keep the money for herself."

If Joey could only make his own income, he would be free from his sister's domination. Cliff had been right when he said Joey had been standing on the corner at the freeway exit. This morning, while ambling along Forty-Fifth Street, a panhandler latched onto his arm. The man's sunken eyes floated in the caves of his sockets like a dead goldfish, and his hair was matted and stringy like dried seaweed. "Hey, buddy," he'd said, his breath stale, "stand here until I get back." Then he handed Joey an empty cottage cheese container and a cardboard sign that said he was temporarily homeless and a Vietnam vet. Saint Signore had told Joey, "You'd better do what this guy asks." So Joey stood there for two hours, staring into the cars that stopped at the red light, then slithered onto the cross street when the light changed green. Several cars lowered their windows and beckoned him to step closer, then dropped money in the container. Finally, the panhandler returned carrying a brown bag twisted around what appeared to be a bottle of booze and said, "Buddy, get off my corner. Hand over what you collected and give me my sign. If I ever catch you here again, you're dead meat."

Still grasping the white envelope, Moni put out her other hand, palm up. "Let's make a trade. I give you this money, and you give me the house key."

"No, I'm keeping it." Joey slipped a hand into his jeans pocket and fingered the cool metal.

"Later today, go to the hardware store and make nine more copies," Saint Signore said. "Hide them all over the yard."

Joey nodded in silent agreement. "I'm never going back to The Home," he told Moni. "My roommate Adam's dirt-ridden fingernails and greasy hair are detestable. And five other grubby residents live there, not counting the one who disappeared last week. No one knows what happened to him." Joey wondered if Mrs. Landis had poisoned the young man, then disposed of him in the dumpster.

"That's got to be hard." Moni's voice softened. "Could you divide the room in half and stay on your side?"

"As if bugs can't crawl over to your bed?" Saint Signore quipped.

Adam, if that really was his name, claimed he got saved at the Gospel Mission two years ago and mumbled scripture, hoping his words would infiltrate Joey's mind. That's why Joey never allowed himself to fall asleep with Adam in the room.

"We share a common bathroom," Joey said.

"Keep at it," Saint Signore said in his ear. "You're getting to her."

Joey asked, "How would you like to share a shower stall with five men? Hair and grime everywhere. No privacy."

Her shoulders gave a shudder. "That's different. I'm a woman."

"Playing the defenseless female card again?" Saint Signore said. "She's trying to lead you into a no-win subject. Never mind. Fix yourself lunch. If I didn't remind you to eat, you'd starve."

Joey's stomach gave a lurch at the thought of sustenance. "Moni, do you mind if I eat something?" Not waiting for her answer, he opened the refrigerator door and glanced in long enough to ascertain there was nothing he'd dare ingest. The smell of aging milk and cheddar cheese almost suffocated him; he turned away, trying to exhale and empty his lungs. He moved to the cupboard where Mama stocked her canned goods and brought down a tin of Progresso vegetable soup. Squinting, he scanned the ingredients to make sure the company hadn't added animal by-products to their recipe. He ate strictly vegetarian. Fewer chances of contracting diseases.

Leaving the can on the counter, he lathered his hands with liquid soap and scrubbed them, singing "Row, Row, Row Your Boat" to himself, giving time for an adequate rinse. He scrubbed the soup can lid and the can opener, then dabbed his chapped hands with paper towels. The man who invented paper towels deserved a Nobel Prize. How did people manage before them? "They died of the bubonic plague," Saint Signore said. "I warned you about leaving the house without wearing disposable latex gloves. And look at you, you haven't even bathed or changed your clothing."

But Joey was so hungry he ignored Saint Signore. He reached under the counter and brought out a saucepan, which he inspected for debris, then flushed it with water, again humming about rowing a boat. Then he dumped the soup into the pan and turned the burner up. Food should always be brought to a thorough boil. Even so, some bacteria survived. He should have asked Papa to invent a bacteria zapper before he died. "Come up with your own invention," Saint Signore suggested, and Joey thought he just might do that.

"Where are you going?" Moni challenged Joey as he headed for the basement stairs to take a shower with the hottest water he could tolerate.

"To get changed," he said.

47

"You'll never change," Saint Signore joked.

"Joey, come back, you left the stove on high!" Moni said as he scuttled down the steps into the tranquility of the basement.

CHAPTER EIGHT
Mona Lisa

I heard Joey's bathroom door shut, then water running full force in the basement - another one of his marathon showers. I resented Joey's wasteful habits. Had our parents never taught him about energy conservation?

I lowered the heat on the stovetop to medium and gave Joey's soup a stir. If I weren't here, the mass of diced vegetables would burn, smoke billowing through the house, but Joey wouldn't smell it. Down in the basement - his den - he was oblivious. Or was it an act? A ploy to scare me away and gain possession of the house? I'd heard about adult children refusing to leave their parents' nest out of laziness or feelings of entitlement. Neurotic or not, Joey was a mooch, but what could I do? I was powerless to ask the police to place a restraining order on him. The house wasn't in my name, and I couldn't strong-arm Mama into making him stay at The Home.

Dragging the spoon along the curve at the bottom of the pot, I gave the soup another stir. If only Papa were alive to help me. What advice would he give? "Chin up," he might say. "You're not a helpless little lamb. *Un'agnellina*." Imagining his gravelly voice gave me a shot of courage. Would Papa approve of my hiring Cliff and Thomas to refurbish the house, like on The Home Improvement Channel? Soon, the realtor would list it at a reasonable price. I hoped Papa would agree that now was not the time to hold out for top dollar. Some nice couple would buy it. Marking the end of an era. The end of the Buttaro family in the Pacific Northwest. It didn't appear Joey or I would have children. "Sorry, Papa," I whispered. "No grandkids for you and Mama."

The luxury of embracing a child had at one time, been my all-consuming desire and part of my motivation for my relationship with Kevin, for whom I'd bent every rule. My throat tightened as I imagined myself a spinster at ninety. No, I must not let my mind return to roost on my losses. Who knew? I might meet a widower or a divorced man with children already. I thought of Panda, the jagged, secretive cut of her bangs, partially concealing steely navy-blue eyes, her small mouth set in a scowl. Her whole attitude showed cheekiness and defiance. And the little schemer seemed to be flirting with Joey, who was old enough to be her father. Should Cliff remarry, I pitied his future wife, the woman forced to attempt to warm up to Panda. I felt a prick of guilt for my hostility and vowed to find something to like about her if I ever saw her again - as long as she kept her distance from Joey.

Someone rapped on the back door, alerting Figaro, who scrambled to it, his toenails clicking on the linoleum floor and his stubby tail wagging, signifying a friend. I opened the door to find my mother dressed in clingy black slacks and a knit sweater with a plunging neckline. I stared at the tiny gold cross hiding in her cleavage. "Va-va-voom," Papa would say.

"Knock, knock!" she sang out in an uncharacteristic manner, then stroked the dog's broad skull. She must have given Joey her only house key; she never knocked on the door. "Surprise! We've got dinner. Chinese food." Another first. I couldn't remember Mama ever bringing home takeout, not when there was pasta and marinara sauce in the pantry. I glanced past her and saw Frank DiAngelo bending into an aging white Lincoln Town Car sitting a foot from the curb. He extracted a large brown paper bag, then ambled toward the house, his feet barely clearing the concrete brick walkway as if his shoes were filled with water.

"When did you start eating Chinese food?" I asked Mama, instead of voicing my real question - what's he doing here?

"Frank and I have a favorite restaurant that offers an early evening special for oldsters like us." Oldsters? Again, an expression I'd never heard her use.

"You're not old," Frank said, closing in behind her and admiring her curvaceous hips. "*Bellissima*," he uttered with a sigh. Mama's cheeks heightened with color, her lips forming a grin, like she'd just eaten a chocolate-covered cherry, her favorite candy.

"Mona Lisa, may we come in?" She was asking admittance into her own house. For a moment, I was tempted to politely say no, not tonight, because she would interfere with my plans to escort Joey back to The Home to beg Mrs. Landis to give him a private room - a solution I should have thought of earlier. Who knew? Mrs. Landis might have a private bathroom tucked away in her three-story group home.

"Of course, Mama, come in. It's nice to see you." I'd be lying if I said I was happy to entertain Frank DiAngelo. Why did Mama spend time with him? She had many lifelong friends.

Clutching a red patent-leather handbag, she moved forward into the house, her arm grazing mine. As I stepped back to make way for her, Frank shuffled in, bringing with him the aroma of sweet-and-sour sauce mingled with the aftershave and cigar odors clinging to his suit jacket. Papa had smoked a cigar, and I'd always enjoyed its fruity scent, but Frank's odor made me recoil. He struck me as being ancient - a balding, dried-up apple. But of course, Papa would be almost his age if he were still alive.

Figaro sniffed Frank's cuffed pant legs with suspicion, but Frank paid no attention; apparently, he wasn't afraid of big dogs.

Mama's gaze landed on the steaming soup and then the empty Progresso can. "Mona Lisa, is this your supper? Don't you cook from scratch anymore?"

"Not after working all day at Booty's. And our refrigerator's empty."

"You should have gone to the grocery store."

"No time. After working around food all day, the last thing I want to do is shop for it. That's Joey's soup. He's in the basement."

"*Perfetto.*" Her amber-brown eyes sparkled as if they held the punch line to a tantalizing joke. "The whole family will be together for my special... announcement."

"Tell me now, Mama."

"No, first we eat." Mama escorted Frank into the dining room to Papa's old chair, the only one with a high, carved back and arms, and feet like lion paws.

I yelled out, "No, not there." Figaro ducked his head and retreated into the front hall.

Mama's full lips formed a half-smile, the unreadable one I was often accused of wearing. "Where else should we seat our honored guest?" she asked. "In the kitchen by himself?"

I felt chastised but still wanted Frank to park himself somewhere else. No one had ever sat on Papa's chair, what we called his throne, while he was alive.

Pulling Papa's chair away from the table, Frank stood in front of it and ripped open the brown paper bag. He extracted a half dozen white cartons; the aromas of sesame seeds and soy sauce wafted out. He moved the boxes to the center of the table, then he lowered himself onto Papa's chair. His hands fingered the armrests, like he was claiming the wood for himself, then he walked the chair in against the table. "Very comfortable, Barbara."

"I'm glad." Mama gathered place mats and her silverware kept for fancy occasions from the sideboard, while I brought ten plates into the dining room, the extras to put under the boxes so the heat wouldn't mar the table's surface.

I returned to the kitchen and called down into the basement. "Joey, Mama's here." I wouldn't tell him we had company. Joey had known Frank DiAngelo since we were kids, but he might hide until Frank was gone. Because, given the choice, Joey lived like a hermit. As if to prove me wrong, his slippered feet pattered up the stairs, then Joey appeared with damp hair, parted and combed like they did in the 1940s but - already a curl was lifting as it dried. I thought he might bolt when he heard Frank's voice, but Joey reached into the cabinet for his favorite pasta bowl, served himself soup, then set it in the microwave oven for a minute until the ingredients started spitting and crawling over the sides of the bowl. Then, donning hot mitts, he removed the bowl and inched into the dining room, careful not to spill.

"Good evening, Mr. DiAngelo. Hi, Mama." My brother could act like an ordinary guy when he made the effort. Annoying as all get-out.

Mama glided over to Joey and kissed the air near his ear. "*Mio tesoro*," she said. "My treasure." She pulled his chair out, and he placed his soup bowl on a dinner plate and sank into his usual spot, farthest from the kitchen, so he wouldn't have to get up and fetch things or clear later.

"Just like old times," she said.

"With a stranger at the head of the table?" My words tumbled out of my mouth, and Frank frowned. Not that I blamed him. I was acting like a brat but couldn't control my snarled words. It felt like an ill omen was churning through the room. Was Papa sending us a warning from the grave? I was tempted to bring his photo down from upstairs to set on the sideboard. Or better yet, place it on the dining room table where Frank was sitting.

"Mona Lisa Buttaro, where are your manners?" Mama asked. "Frank's no stranger. And even if he were, that's no way to treat a guest."

"Sorry, Mr. DiAngelo." But the sight of him dominating Papa's chair made me feel like I was captured in a surreal painting where reality was warped out of shape.

I reached for the box of ginger beef, but then Mama cleared her throat and bowed her head, her fingertips meeting under her chin. "Shall we thank the Lord for our blessings before we eat?"

My stomach growled with hunger. It must have been obvious I didn't pray before meals when on my own, or ever, really, unless I was with Mama or at the church I attended occasionally because

53

they had a singles group. I was still mad at God for letting Papa die. I'd begged God to spare his life, but my entreaties hadn't made a whit of difference. Over the years, I'd even prayed Joey would miraculously turn normal and go back to school or get a job. Fat chance. Then, when I got pregnant and Kevin dumped me, I fell on my knees and begged God to change his heart. One day, after praying out loud, I felt so pumped up that I'd tried contacting Kevin, but he didn't answer his cell phone, no doubt because he saw my number on his caller ID.

"Frank, would you say grace?" Mama asked.

He crossed himself. "We give thanks to thee, Almighty." He closed his eyes. "Bless us, O Lord…"

My mouth gaped open in outrage. She'd asked a man other than Papa to be the family's spiritual leader. I stared at him, his forehead shining under the lights in the brass chandelier. His mouth hardly moved when he spoke, like he was a hand puppet.

"Amen," Mama and Frank finally said, and I echoed a weak "Amen," realizing I hadn't heard most of the prayer.

"Mama," Joey said between tidy mouthfuls, "You look different somehow."

"You could always read me like a book, *mio tesoro.* As a matter of fact, I'm happy. Can you guess why?" But Joey shrugged and swallowed another spoonful of soup. Mama turned to me. "Notice anything different about me, *cara mia?*"

I scanned her attractive face. Her eyebrows had that just-sculpted look, her lids were overly shadowed with a shimmery mocha color, and her mascara was applied with a heavy hand. She was prettied up, that was for sure. She'd gone to the extra trouble for an old codger like Frank?

"Well, you two?" She put out her left hand to show off a ring - what must be a two-carat ruby surrounded by small diamonds, residing where her wedding band had. Since yesterday? When had she removed it?

I leaned closer to get a better look. The ruby's setting looked antique; the stone brilliant enough to reside in the window of

Tiffany's. Frank was a widower with four children. Had it once belonged to his former spouse?

"Stunning, isn't it?" Mama asked.

"Yes." I squirmed in my seat. "An early birthday present?" Her birthday was in July, making ruby her birthstone.

"It's an engagement ring, silly." She wiggled her ring finger. "Frank and I are engaged!"

Joey dropped his spoon; it clanked against the side of his bowl. He must have been as surprised as I was—appalled is a better word for my reaction.

"Mama," Joey said, "at Papa's funeral, you swore you'd never marry again."

"Yes, I know, *mio tesoro*. I was devastated. But that was over ten years ago. It's time for me to move on."

"To forget about Papa?"

"I'll never forget him. He was my first love."

"But you've found a replacement?" I asked.

"*Basta!* There's no reason to get worked up." Frank forked into the sweet-and-sour shrimp and served himself a generous portion, taking the largest pieces. "Your father and I were best friends - like two brothers. *Due fratelli.* In the old days, it would have been considered my duty to marry your mother when she became a widow." His face broke into a grin, chiseling a network of fine lines across his cheeks. "An excellent practice, don't you think?"

"No, I don't." The angry words spilled out of my mouth. "It sounds archaic."

"Like from the Stone Age," Joey said. For once I agreed with him.

"Then think of us as a couple of Neanderthals," Mama said with her usual good humor. Frank chuckled, then brought out a cloth handkerchief and wiped the corners of his eyes.

"Have you set a date?" I hoped they'd opt for a five-year engagement.

"We haven't sorted out the details yet." Mama portioned rice onto her plate - a neat mound of white granules. "For instance, where the ceremony will take place."

"At Saint Patrick's, of course." Frank stuffed a shrimp in his mouth.

"Now, Frank, I haven't attended Mass or gone to confession for over twenty years. And I like my little nondenominational church."

Frank chewed quickly and swallowed his mouthful. "With a female minister? You wish to have a woman perform the ceremony? Impossible." He held his fork like a gavel. "My ancestors would roll over in their graves if I got married in anything other than a Catholic church."

"Then why don't you just live together?" Joey asked.

"And be a bad influence on you two?" Mama tilted her head toward Frank. "If we can't agree on a church, we could use a justice of the peace."

"No, no." He flattened his hands on the table. "Let's not be hasty. We'll discuss this later, my dearest Barbara. In private. I'm sure we'll come to an agreement."

"One question, Mama." I plunged my fork into a slice of ginger beef but had lost my appetite. "Are you moving back here?"

Mama's gaze scanned the framed print of the Trevi Fountain dominating one wall and the built-in china cabinet in the corner, laden with Venetian glassware. "I love this old house, but there are too many memories."

"Barbara and I need our own marital bed," Frank said matter-of-factly.

I shrank back from the table. The image of our mother snuggling between the sheets with Frank DiAngelo soured my stomach. I laid my fork aside and wadded my napkin into a ball.

Across the table, Joey chuckled. But I found nothing to laugh about. What happened to our mother?

CHAPTER NINE
Joey

Joey couldn't help chortling at Frank's ridiculous allusion to a roll in the hay with Mama. He was too old and might suffer a heart attack if he saw Mama in a lacy negligee. Gross! A disgusting thought. Joey was having a hard enough time sitting at the table with Mama in her cleavage-baring sweater, an item of clothing meant for someone Panda's age.

As thoughts spun through Joey's brain, Saint Signore spoke in his ear. "Think about it, Jo-Jo. After they get married, Frank will make you call him Father. Legally, he'll stand next in line to inherit the house and all its possessions. Your possessions. Your father's inventions. He could move his own children and his obnoxious grandchildren in here and turn the place into a menagerie."

Joey polished off the last of his soup.

"Are you getting enough to eat?" Mama asked him. She nudged a white carton in his direction; the top was open, but no one had eaten any of it. "Try this vegetarian special I bought specifically for you. With tofu. High in protein."

Joey was still hungry but said, "No, thanks." He appreciated Mama's generosity and was sorely tempted to dig in, but takeout food was a health risk.

"Good move," Saint Signore said in his ear. "There's no way

of knowing if the cook bothered washing his hands. He or she could have splashed in chicken stock crawling with salmonella and used vegetables from Chile, alive with parasites, and then not brought the concoction to a boil. It's never safe to eat restaurant food. Take-out, which can sit at room temperature for hours, is a regular little laboratory for breeding bacteria."

"I just came up with a brilliant idea," Moni announced from across the table. "Joey, if you spend the night here, you're coming to work with me at Booty's tomorrow morning."

"That's wonderful," Mama said. "It's been my dream that he work there."

It sounded like a nightmare to Joey. He made a face, curling his upper lip.

"Better go along with them," Saint Signore said. "Don't worry, I've got a plan."

Joey nodded. "Okay. Fine, I'll do it."

Moni jumped to her feet and started clearing the table. She sent him a phony smile. "Better get to bed early, little brother. I'll wake you at five o'clock in the morning."

"She expects you to be long gone," Saint Signore said. "She thinks she has you licked, but tomorrow we'll give her a day she'll never forget."

CHAPTER TEN
Mona Lisa

When I descended into the basement the next morning to fetch Joey, I was surprised to see light bulbs beaming and his bedroom door open. I heard water running, then snapping off in his bathroom around the corner through the laundry area housing Mama's washer and dryer.

Worried he'd emerge from the bathroom naked, I announced myself. "Joey, I'm downstairs." But he moseyed out of the bathroom fully clothed, clad in one of Papa's old bowling shirts - yellow with a black collar, the fabric too broad in the girth and hanging on Joey's skinny frame like a kid playing dress-up. The garment looked recently laundered and ironed and smelled of Tide detergent. "Where'd you get the shirt?" I asked, wondering the same thing about the baggy slacks, which were turned up at the cuffs and belted tightly at his waist.

"From the giveaway box. I washed them last night. Twice." He ran a hand across his smoothly shaved chin and neck. Had he stayed up all night?

"You look nice," I said. Goofy was more like it, but what did I care? For the bulk of the day, I'd keep him in Booty's kitchen under Ramon's, Annie's, and my watchful eyes. The customers would never see him.

"No time for coffee." I stifled a yawn. "I'll make it at the restaurant." After Mama and Frank had departed last night, I couldn't fall asleep, then I woke up in a tangle of sheets and blankets. Were lovey-dovey Mama and Frank serious about getting married, or were they pulling a prank at my expense? It occurred to me that Uncle Vito might have told Mama he'd invited me to visit him in Rome. Could her engagement be a ploy to send me traipsing off to Italy instead of emptying her house? Which reminded me: I hadn't returned my uncle's email.

With Figaro fed and left in the fenced backyard, Joey and I headed to my car parked in the driveway. The same driveway where my childhood friends and I played our version of hopscotch while Joey rode his big wheel. Back then, he'd seemed average - except he never matured into riding a bicycle like the other kids in the neighborhood or learned to drive a car when he turned sixteen. Once he was old enough to use the city bus and had money in his pocket, he was off to who knows where.

Ordinarily, I'd have appreciated the chirping of the nesting birds in the flowering plum trees lining the street and the morning sun's rays spilling over the neighbor's shingled roof, but I was too distracted with worry about the dubious day unfolding ahead of me.

Last night, when I told Joey he had to go to work with me, my goal was to send him scurrying back home. I was sure I'd wake up to an empty house, but my plan had backfired. My little brother was out-faking me. Should I admit defeat now and let him return to bed?

As I unlocked the car door, I was considering his motives for obeying me, but as I withdrew the key, his face grew fearful, his mouth twisting, and I thought he might bolt for the garage or down the street. But he mumbled, or rather, seemingly argued with himself. "Okay, okay, I'm going," he muttered.

Glancing into the car's window, I could see the front passenger seat was littered with receipts and a newspaper. I leaned in and tossed the debris into the back seat, and he got in on the other side for the first time, ever. Honestly, the two of us had not been in a vehicle together since I was in college, making this outing a monumental occasion I wished Papa could see. When our father passed away, I don't think he realized the depth of Joey's "limitations." Mama had shielded her son and made-up excuses for his antisocial timidity. But this was over ten years later; Joey had shrunk further from society into lethargy.

He tucked his hand into his long jacket sleeve to shield his fingers when he closed the door. Was he trying to keep his elbows from touching the velvet seatback? I wasn't a neat freak, but my car seemed plenty clean to me. But now was not the time to antagonize Joey. Or was it? Once again, I questioned my reasoning for bringing him with me. He didn't know how to cook and had never waited tables or worked the cash register. I bet he'd set foot in the restaurant only once - the day it opened.

I started the engine and backed out of the driveway. Twenty minutes later, inside Booty's kitchen, I stood before the stainless-steel sink, rinsing vegetables - carrots, cauliflower, broccoli, potatoes - then setting them in the colander. Joey lingered nearby. Wearing latex gloves he'd brought from home, he unfolded the white apron I'd given him, wrapped it across his chest instead of his waist, and cinched the strings under his armpits. But I wouldn't make a wise crack. He was here. For him, this was a huge achievement.

Using a brush, I scrubbed a black smudge off a potato. "Joey, I've decided to make vegetarian soup today, in your honor, but I don't have a recipe to follow." Without using chicken or beef stock, I wasn't sure how to make it palatable to our customers. I'd hate to have to dump the vat of uneaten soup out at the end of the day. "I should have Googled recipes and downloaded them from the internet before leaving home."

Joey swayed back and forth. "Can't you find a recipe in one of Mama's old cookbooks? Or did someone steal them?" This wasn't the first time he'd expressed fears of thievery, when in fact the missing article—a glove, pen, or book of matches—had been misplaced. In the past, I'd told Mama that Joey suffered from paranoia and needed to be examined by a psychiatrist, but she'd dismissed my concerns.

"No one stole anything," I assured him. "Look for yourself next to the spice rack. But I doubt those books have vegetarian soup recipes in them."

He double knotted the apron strings. "Shouldn't you wash those vegetables with soap?"

"You mean dish soap? What for?"

"To kill the bacteria."

"Is that what you do at home?"

"Yes, then I rinse them in bleach."

"Yuck-olla. I don't think our customers would appreciate the taste. Frank DiAngelo would demand his money back."

"Spices mask it," Joey said. "Cleanliness is next to godliness."

That was the reason he washed his hands repeatedly? "Did Mama teach you that?"

"No, a friend". His lips clamped together, cutting off his words.

I'd always wondered if he had friends, but secretive Joey never spoke of his social life; this was his first mention. "A man or a woman?" I prodded.

"Neither."

I wasn't amused by his evasiveness, but curiosity got the best of me. "Is this a riddle?"

He angled his face away and got busy covering his head with a clear plastic shower cap he must have brought from home too. He looked like he was going into surgery.

"Would you please help chop vegetables?" I brought out a knife and passed it to him, using care to put the handle in his hands. He stared at the blade's metal surface, where my fingerprint resided, then hurried the knife to the other sink and lavished it with soap and hot water.

"Mama would approve of your thoroughness," I said. "You'll need a cutting board." I brought him one. He inspected the plastic rectangle board on both sides, then brought it to the sink and scrubbed its surface. He started dicing the potatoes into proficient, neat cubes. I thought I was going to have to give him a lesson, but apparently, he'd done this before. Mama must have taught him.

"You want a cup of coffee?" I asked as I moved to where a fresh pot sat.

"No. Caffeine makes me jumpy. Do you have bottled water?"

"Behind the bar, with the soft drinks."

He stiffened. "I can't go out there. That's where Papa died."

I hadn't been in Booty's the day Papa collapsed but had envisioned the incident a thousand times: Papa grasping his chest in agony, sinking to the floor. I wasn't sure of my facts because I'd found it too painful to ask Mama for details.

I wouldn't let Joey know how much my own mind dwelled on the tragedy. "Joey, if you want to get technical, Papa passed away in the ambulance, not in this building."

Joey's brown eyes enlarged. "Still, Papa's ghost might live here."

"His soul is in heaven, with Grandma Maria's and Grandpa Antonio's. Papa is surrounded by loved ones."

"I don't think so, Moni. Papa sinned, then refused to ask God for forgiveness."

"You're way off base, little brother. Papa never did anything wrong. He was a humble man. If he'd made a bad decision, he'd have been the first to admit it."

Joey's head jerked slightly, like he'd heard a noise behind him, then his gaze came back to meet mine. "I know something about Papa…"

"A secret?" I felt outrage tightening my throat. "Then spit it out. I will not tolerate anyone badmouthing our father."

He shook his head; a curl of hair slipped out of the cap and down onto his forehead. "Never mind, it's nothing."

"I thought so. If anything, Papa spoiled you, and this is how you repay him?" I felt like expelling Joey from the restaurant, but that would be indulging him further. I said, "What kind of job shall I give you? Slicing the meat?"

"No. I'll finish making the soup. We could add canned, crushed tomatoes. Too bad you didn't soak pinto beans last night."

"How would I possibly know you'd need them? But you're in luck, I have canned beans in the pantry."

While Joey chopped and sautéed the rest of the vegetables, I went to the pantry and brought out tins of pinto beans and crushed tomatoes. So Joey wouldn't have a cow, I rinsed off the can opener before handing it to him. "Nice and clean," I said, but he took it from me and washed it again.

"Moni, you should buy organic vegetarian soup broth." He was chatting more than he had in years. Was it the early hour? He reached up to the rack and started splashing in Italian seasoning, like he'd thrown together hundreds of batches of soup in this kitchen.

"So now you're a chef?" I quipped. "Where did you learn to cook?"

"Watching the Cooking Channel. I know a lot more than you think I do."

I couldn't let his mysterious statement slip by. "For instance?" I had no clue how he spent his days.

Ignoring me, he flicked pepper into the soup. I tried another tactic. "Read any good books lately?"

He spun around. "Who informed you I went to the library?"

"A lucky guess. Which surprises me. I can't picture you there. Aren't library books dusty and handled by hundreds of people?"

His head gave an involuntary shudder. "Yes, they're filthy, but I wear these." He held up his latex-gloved hands.

"What kinds of books do you read? Or are you on the internet? Do you know how to use a computer?"

"What I do with my days is none of your business."

"Whatever. No offense meant." I chided myself for trying to carry on a conversation with him.

With the lunch rush approaching, I didn't have time to quarrel. I brought roast beef out of the refrigerator, turned on the meat cutter, and started slicing. The whirring of the round metal blade sent Joey shivering against the counter for support.

Later, when Ramon came in, I introduced Joey as my little brother.

"I've heard of you, Joey." Was Ramon envisioning a troll under a bridge? He put out a hand and said, "Welcome aboard."

Joey raised his gloved hands as if to signal he was keeping them sterile.

"I see a family resemblance." Ramon turned to me. "Your brother takes after your mother." Ramon had never met Papa. Still, he was right. Mama and Joey's dark brows and brown eyes slanted slightly, when Joey wasn't squinting. It occurred to me that he might need glasses, but how would I talk him into seeing an optometrist when he wouldn't even have his blood pressure checked?

"Annie's replacement?" Ramon asked.

"Yes," I said, not meaning it. "Joey, as long as you're living at home, you can earn your room and board by bussing tables and emptying the dishwasher. You can pocket your tips."

"Dirty dishes?" Joey balled his hands to his chest.

"I'm not asking you to clean the bathrooms. We have a service that comes in at night."

The house telephone shrilled, but I decided to ignore it until opening time. Then my cell phone chirped, and I dug into my purse to find Annie on the line, calling in sick. "I woke up with a stuffed-up nose and a cough," she said, so I told her to stay home.

I said to Ramon, "Annie's sick. I hope it isn't the flu bug that's going around. She could be out for a week."

"Or longer." Ramon's hands stayed in motion. "I know a young woman who might come in—"

"A new girlfriend?"

"Say the word, and I'll give up all other women."

"For how long?"

"As long as you wish." The conversation had taken a U-turn

into forbidden territory. But I let my mind venture into the future, envisioning an evening spent with Ramon at his condominium. In the past, he'd offered to fix me dinner. He'd described his deck with its two chaise lounges and view of the Olympic Mountains, his lush carpet surrounding his fireplace, and his cushy sofa. Would I ever sink into the luxury of a man's arms again?

I reined in my runaway thoughts. "Ramon, we need to concentrate on the impending disaster known as the lunch rush. I should have put a Help Wanted sign in the window two days ago."

"We'll be fine. Your brother's here."

"Dressed like that, he'll scare people away."

Obviously listening to us, Joey glanced over his shoulder. He looked like a sorcerer with a caldron in the way he kept stirring the vat of soup. Couldn't he see there were a dozen other chores that needed to be accomplished before opening time? No, of course he didn't. I barely did myself. Until recently, I'd been only a customer here.

"When Joey takes off the plastic hat and gloves, he'll be fine." Ramon's sentence went up at the end, like a question.

Joey pulled the long-handled spoon out of the vat, a spatter of soup falling to the floor. "Doing what?" He grabbed a paper towel and dabbed up the mess.

"Delivering orders and clearing away dishes," I said.

His shoulders hunched forward, and his face took on a look of disgust. "Moni, you never said I'd have to touch dirty dishes. You should have warned me."

My ire ratcheted up another notch. "This is a family business. That means all of us pitch in."

"Why not call your mother?" Ramon suggested. "She might help."

"Great idea. Why didn't I think of that?" I went to the phone, dialed her number, and found her in.

"Sure, if you wish, I'll come in for lunch," Mama said. "Then I'm getting my hair done."

"Perfect, we open in twenty minutes." For the first time all morning, my stomach relaxed. "Can you get here by then? You'll work the cash register, and I'll take out orders."

"You expect me to work? You can't be serious. I could fall again, and then where would I be?"

I pressed the receiver against my ear. "Mama, you'll stand safely behind the register. You can sit on a bar stool if you like. Our customers have missed you." As soon as Mama got going, she'd slide into her former routine and love every minute of it.

"*Cara mia*, I can't. It's too much for me. I've slowed down over the last few months. My knee…"

I was feeling as desperate as I sounded. "I'll do all the leg work, take the orders out, and clear the tables. With Joey here—"

"He's here with you? *Grazie, mio Dio.* Thank you, God in heaven. How did you manage, *cara*? Never mind, it doesn't matter. So you don't really need me. You were planning a surprise. I'm so happy."

"Mama, I do need you. It was a miracle prying Joey out of the house and into my car, but now he refuses to do more than stir his soup."

"He made soup? All by himself? I'm sure it's excellent."

"I don't know if our customers will think so. You'd better come in and sample it." I glanced through the front window and saw a woman with three squirrelly little boys waiting to gain entrance. We had only two highchairs. "Please, Mama, I'm begging you. Come in."

"All right. Frank and I will stop by for lunch in an hour or so—as customers. I can't wait to see how my Joey is doing."

CHAPTER ELEVEN
Cliff

Cliff nosed his recently washed and polished anthracite-gray metallic Porsche 911 into the driveway in front of his ex-wife Janette's home, what used to be their love nest - where he thought he'd spend the rest of his days, a happily married family man.

Thirty minutes earlier, Panda's school had called his cell phone to report Patricia Ann - her legal name - had missed her first two classes. The attendance office had tried without success to get in touch with Janette, and Cliff was listed as an alternate contact, like he carried no more significance than an uncle or neighbor.

He shoved his foot down on the - brake pedal and eyed Janette's double-car garage door, shut - way to tell if her car was inside - and the manicured grass framing the thirty-year-old Northwest contemporary two-story house. She must hire a yard maintenance company, he thought. In the old days, Cliff did the mowing, pruning, and raking of the three maple trees he'd planted for fall color.

Where was Janette? Inside watching soaps or out showing a client property? Twenty minutes ago, Cliff had tried calling her but didn't get an answer. When he phoned her office, a coworker said Janette was out of town and couldn't be reached. Which had to be a mistake. No one had informed Cliff.

This had better not be a joke, Cliff thought, getting out and straightening his long legs. The past several times he'd shown up at Janette's house to pick up Panda only to find she was spending the weekend with a girlfriend. On each occasion, Janette claimed she'd mentioned switching weekends earlier and let slip Panda hated going to Cliff's cramped apartment where she didn't have her stuff. Six months ago, Janette informed him he must look after Panda for a long weekend while Janette bounced off to Mexico with her new beau, an announcement that stabbed Cliff like a screwdriver to the heart. He hated that he'd ever loved Janette at all. He assumed she would marry the stud she'd played around with during the last year of their rocky marriage, but now she adored some dude named Dennis.

Cliff strode to the front door, passing a newspaper still in its plastic bag. He rang the bell and listened to the chime vaulting through the four-thousand-square-foot home. No one answered. To make sure, he knocked on the door and stabbed the bell again. Finally, the speaker, which he'd installed, clicked on, and Panda said in a froggy voice, "Who is it?"

"Your father. Are you sick, honey?"

"Uh, no. I was sleeping. I have the day off. A vacation."

"I know that's not true because the attendance office called me. Come down and let me in immediately."

"I'm not dressed."

"Then put something on."

Minutes later, Panda unbolted the front door to let Cliff in. Her eyes were swollen from recent sleep, but other than her mussed hair, she seemed fine. Although her knit PJ's allowed Cliff to see too much of her breasts; she'd filled out into womanly proportions these last six months. And when she turned, he noticed a tattoo on her back at the waist, peeking out above her low-riding pajama bottoms. Panda was only fourteen years old. Why had Janette allowed it? He imagined their daughter through the eyes of the boys at school and felt protective.

"Where is your mother?"

"On a trip."

"She left you here alone to fend for yourself?"

"Not exactly. I was supposed to go to Jillian's, but her mom's a drag. She makes us do homework right after school and no TV after ten o'clock."

"So you decided to stay by yourself? For how long?"

"A week. Ten days? I can't remember."

"Janette said nothing to me. What if there'd been an emergency?" As far as Cliff was concerned, this was an emergency. "Where did she go?"

"Hawaii. With Dennis."

"To Maui? To the Grand Wailea?" The family's favorite hotel. She wouldn't be that vindictive, would she? Sure she would; she'd taken the diamond - the sparkly stone Cliff had worked overtime to afford - out of her wedding band and reset it into a charm in the shape of a rat for her bracelet.

"I don't know. She didn't tell me." Panda yawned, not covering her gaping mouth. "Dad, I think they're getting married."

His jaw tightened, and the lump in his throat threatened to block off his air supply. Feeling faint, he leaned against the door jam. The enormity of his reaction struck him as ludicrous. He didn't love Janette anymore. He despised her narcissism and the way her world orbited around herself. And here she was, deserting her own child.

"Why didn't she take you with her?" Cliff asked.

"Like, on her honeymoon? Anyway, I hate Dennis."

He chuckled in spite of himself. He agreed with her assessment of Dennis. Cliff had despised the man immediately when they'd met. His straw-yellow curls, the fact he wore a neatly pressed and collared shirt on a Sunday afternoon, and his smug expression that said, *your former wife and daughter are now my property.* Cliff had heard frightening stories of predatory boyfriends taking advantage of children. But how could Cliff prevent it? He'd been denied parental custody because Janette's lawyer successfully portrayed him as unstable. At that time, he was.

"Get ready for school." Cliff averted his eyes so he wouldn't see her swaying breasts or the lines of her thong underwear. "Pack a bag and bring a bathrobe. After school, you're coming home with me." Having her would carve into his busy work schedule, but he reminded himself this would be a time to prove himself, to forge a father-daughter bond, an opportunity he'd long awaited. He loved Panda more than anyone.

While she dressed, Cliff wandered into the kitchen he'd remodeled five years ago. He experienced a momentary wave of pride as he surveyed his handiwork, but seeing the beauty of the seating area in the added bay window and the granite counters filled him with resentment. He wondered if Janette had planned to leave him long before he'd finished his remodel, if she'd kept him around like a mutt on a leash to finish the job.

He noticed her laptop sitting on the built-in desk against the sidewall - also his design and handiwork - and was tempted to open her computer to survey her emails, the way he had when she'd first told him she'd wanted a divorce. He'd been out-of-control crazed, a compulsive detective searching for clues as to why she didn't love him.

No, he wouldn't let himself stumble into the jealousy pit again.

Panda wandered into the kitchen dressed in skinny jeans and a scoop-necked T-shirt and fired up the espresso machine. Her hair was still a tangled mess, but she'd applied dark eyeliner and mascara. Cliff thought she was too young for so much makeup, and for coffee, for that matter, but what could he do? Janette caved to all of Panda's demands. Maybe she liked Panda's provocative wardrobe. He'd heard of mothers pretending to be their daughter's sister to make themselves seem younger.

Pick your battles, he told himself. The fact that Panda was skipping school and had lied to her parents was the bigger issue. As he watched her slurp her cappuccino, he thought he wouldn't mind one himself but didn't want to be a bad influence. And it would get back to Janette that Daddy had made himself at home, and she might reinstate the restraining order.

He headed for the house phone. "I'll try your mother again.

If she sees this number on caller ID, she'll be more likely to answer."

"She can't. Their plane's somewhere over the Pacific Ocean."

"Well, if she tries calling home, she'll find you at my place. You can't stay here by yourself."

"Why not? I'm old enough and perfectly safe."

"Not on your own, you're not. What if you came home from school and found an intruder in the house?"

"No one can get in. We have a burglar alarm."

"You might forget to set it. Or someone could disarm it."

"Then you should get me a dog like Figaro. He'd protect me." When Cliff answered with a steely silence, she said, "Or you stay here. This used to be your house. Mom bought a new king-sized mattress and just had the bedroom repainted."

Even though Cliff knew pain awaited him at the top of the stairs, he was tempted to jog up them and allow the floodwaters of rage to engulf him once more. At least he'd feel alive. Then an amusing thought hit him: if Cliff slept here, Dennis would come home with his new bride to find Cliff lounging on the bed, his scent permeating the room. Janette said she could always detect his aftershave, even in a crowd.

"I'd better not. Your mother wouldn't like it."

"Why don't we fly to Hawaii and stop the wedding?" she said, her chin raised.

"We don't know the island or hotel. Even if we located her, how would I explain our bizarre appearance?" She'd laugh and say this was an echo of Cliff's immature thinking that had gotten him in trouble before.

"Honey," Cliff said, "we need to let go and let God," quoting something his AA sponsor might say. Cliff's thoughts were buzzing around like hornets, too frantically to land anywhere. So he recited the Serenity Prayer in his head: God grant me the serenity to accept the things I cannot change…

He reminded himself that he looked forward to a time of closeness with his beloved daughter - moments they hadn't shared since she was in elementary school. He remembered pushing her swing at the park as she begged to go higher.

"What your mother does is out of my hands." Noticing Panda's surly expression, he said, "We'll have fun tonight. Order pizza for dinner."

"Nah, I eat gluten-free now. My doctor said my skin would clear up if I stopped eating foods with gluten, like bread and pasta. And my stomachaches would go away."

Cliff had never heard of gluten. He'd noticed her skin was broken out much of the time - like other teens - but didn't know she suffered from stomachaches. This made him feel like a stranger. A stranger in a familiar kitchen; he who could reach into any drawer and know what to expect, but he didn't know his own daughter.

Minutes later, after finding her backpack, they headed out the front door.

"Good, you're not driving the dump truck today," Panda said, referring to his pickup.

"I stopped by my apartment and swapped cars, especially for you."

Panda had complained that riding in his Ford pickup embarrassed her; when in it, she ducked her head, hiding for fear someone she knew might see her. And it wouldn't have hurt Janette to notice him driving his sporty coupe - a chick magnet, Bernie, his buddy since high school, called it.

Cliff backed down the drive and slid the transmission into first. He rarely drove his Porsche - nicknamed "Cliff's midlife-crisis revenge car" by Bernie. Cliff had purchased the vehicle right off the showroom floor the day after Janette said she was suing for divorce. The steel-gray metallic Porsche had a tough-guy sounding muffler, and its back tires sent gravel flying, but driving it rarely brought Cliff the joy he'd anticipated, rather it reminded him of all he'd lost. Just like coming here did, as if he'd shrunk in stature, an outsider looking in on someone else's paradise.

"I'm hungry," Panda said. "Stop somewhere for breakfast on the way to school, please, Daddy."

He checked the clock on the dashboard and saw it was 11:30. "Why didn't you have cereal?"

"The milk's gone bad."

"Well, then eggs and toast."

"Toast has gluten in it. And you didn't give me time to cook eggs. You were in such a hurry to leave. Let's go to Starbucks."

"No more coffee, young lady."

"You think it's going to stunt my growth? You wish I were taller like Mom, don't you?"

He'd wondered why she stood several inches shorter than Janette's five-foot-six. Had the divorce stopped their daughter's growth? "Honey, I like you exactly the way you are."

"Yeah, right."

He slowed as they approached Booty's Café. "Booty's might serve globulin-free food."

"It's called gluten."

"I know the owner—you met her. Mona Lisa Buttaro. She might be willing to fix you something special. A tuna sandwich without the bread?" He had no idea if that was true but took a left onto the main arterial and saw the boot-shaped sign hanging above the sidewalk where a swarthy man was putting out a sandwich board. He strode back inside with an air of confidence that made Cliff hesitant to go in. Cliff had noticed the man in the restaurant several days earlier and had wondered if he was Mona Lisa's lover.

As they reached Booty's - the restaurant stood shoulder to shoulder in a row of other two-story buildings - Panda craned her neck to see into the wide front window that opened into the kitchen. "There's Joey!"

Cliff tapped on the brakes. "That guy's an oddball. He's too old for you."

Her head spun around. "What do you think we're going to do - have sex right there on the restaurant floor?"

Cliff gripped the steering wheel with arms that felt like two-by-fours. He hadn't lost his temper - stormed and hollered - in a couple of years. Was Panda purposely provoking him, or was she acting like a typical teenager? He reminded himself that whatever he said would be forwarded to Janette verbatim. "Do you speak that way to your mother?"

"Don't go ballistic, Daddy-o."

He needed to keep calm. "Honey, I should be at work right now, finishing up a kitchen remodel. The homeowners are cooking out of their basement, using a microwave oven and the tiny refrigerator their son once used in his dorm room. Maybe you can eat at school. It's almost noon - lunchtime."

"My friends wouldn't be caught dead in the cafeteria. I'd have to sit by myself with the losers. And there's nothing good to eat that doesn't have gluten in it."

"A salad?" he said. "Carrot sticks?"

"Do I look like a rabbit?"

Again, he felt the gush of anger, his stomach knotting. He took a calming breath. But then he thought about how miffed Janette would be if she knew he was taking Panda out to lunch on a school day, and he reconsidered. "I do need to speak to Mona Lisa about this afternoon. If Joey's here, how are Thomas and I supposed to get inside Mrs. Buttaro's residence to start work?" He pulled into the parking spot near the front of Booty's. He was hungry, too, now that he thought about it, and playing hooky together might be a memorable time for him and Panda, something for them to laugh and talk about later.

CHAPTER TWELVE
Joey

Joey stood at Booty's waist-high kitchen counter, slicing tomatoes, each flat circle an echo of its predecessor, either growing or diminishing in size. He was tired and wished he could lean against the counter for support but didn't want to dirty his apron. He'd stayed up all night. Nothing new - he often did, ordinarily collapsing into bed at daybreak. But this morning before sunup, Saint Signore had bugled into his ear, alerting him to be dressed and ready to leave when Moni descended the stairs. "Don't turn your back on her," Saint Signore had warned him.

The day had slid downhill ever since. Joey felt like a miniature poodle at obedience school, with Moni emulating Cesar Millan, the Dog Whisperer. If Saint Signore hadn't coaxed him through the hours, giving him cooking tips and soothing his anxieties with words of assurance, Joey would have unclipped his leash, bolted for the door, and kept running, back to Mama's, his refuge - for now.

"This reminds me of my time in North Africa in the trenches," Saint Signore said as Joey cut into a new tomato, one with a worrisome blemish. "World War Two," Saint Signore said with pride.

Joey carefully removed the tomato's brown spot and discarded it into the compost can. "You were in the war with Grandpa?"

"Yes and no. I was a hero, although I let others take the credit, while your grandfather spent most of the war in an internment camp with other Italians in this country because he hadn't become a citizen. The treatment of Italians during the war was disgraceful. I'll fill you in when the time's right. You already know too much about him and your father, enough to break your mother's heart."

"Yes. Poor Mama." Joey noticed Moni speaking quietly to Ramon, like they were talking about him. Had Joey been moving his lips inadvertently? Or were they laughing at Papa's outdated bowling shirt? It was the Saint's idea to wear it, since Joey was spending the day in what was once Papa's restaurant. And because most of Joey's clothes were still at The Home. Where they'd stay, as far as he was concerned After bleaching and washing Papa's shirt in hot water a half-dozen times, it still carried the trace aroma of cigar smoke and the briny essence of their father. Joey couldn't wait to go home and change his clothes.

"Make yourself busy, your sister's looking for an excuse to get on your case," Saint Signore said. Joey transferred tomato slices into the aluminum bowl provided by Ramon, who stood with Moni on the other side of the counter, in the stove and cooking zone.

"You're not going back to The Home." Saint Signore harrumphed. "But you don't want to end up living under the freeway or behind an office building after hours. No bathroom. No running water."

The thought sent a dizzying shiver through Joey; he'd rather be committed to a mental institution.

"No, you wouldn't," Saint Signore said. "Picture some battle-axe nurse forcing mind-altering pills down your throat. She'd plug your nose until you swallowed them. And you'd be surrounded by imposters. Play-actors as sane as sardines, planted by the government."

Joey wondered why spies tailed him.

"They're after your father's secrets," Saint Signore whispered.

Joey scrolled through his memory to find the list he kept in the dark crevices in the back of his mind. He'd promised Papa never to divulge the truth - or did Mama already know? Joey didn't dare ask her, and his father was gone, so he couldn't release Joey from the burden of secrecy. At least he thought Papa was dead. Joey had attended his memorial service but never actually saw Papa's body. Anyone could have been entombed in that varnished box. Maybe Papa was living the grand life in Italy with a new wife who looked like a movie star. Is that what the priest at the memorial service meant when he spoke of the afterlife, or was he referring to living in the presence of an all-merciful God? Joey looked forward to heaven so he could exhale all the way and finally relax for once. In the meantime, he was trapped in his earthly body, his mind spinning like a lopsided top. Death loomed like a gaping uncertainty.

Saint Signore had repeated, "You must wait for God's perfect timing," when Joey was tempted to check into Paradise early.

Joey carved into another tomato, the plump orb's rind surprisingly tough and its innards like his own: red and squishy. He wondered what would happen if he sliced into his wrist, if the tomato's contents would match his blood, or if the liquid would spurt out blue, the color of his veins.

"Jo-Jo, keep on task," Saint Signore reminded him. "You want to end up in the ER? The waiting room is chock-full of sick people, a breeding ground for streptococcus, which first consumes your flesh, then gnaws into your organs."

"But life - especially today - is too hard."

"Sorry, Jo-Jo. Like I said, you don't get to decide when to check out. That's a cardinal sin."

Joey's thoughts turned to another guarded secret, Papa's so-called inventions.

"That's a laugh," Saint Signore said with a throaty chuckle. "As a kid, you gave your illustrious father all his good ideas. He gathered them greedily and filed them away. Your mission is to find those plans and destroy the evidence before your sister gets her hands on them."

Joey remembered that, as a kid, he'd been flattered that his father made use of his ideas. Joey couldn't have put them into life without Papa's tools, expertise, and money for parts. But then it became evident his father was amassing his inventions, pretending they were his own, basking in Joey's limelight. By his early twenties, Joey informed his father his reservoir of ideas had dried up, which wasn't true in the slightest. After that, Papa distanced himself; Joey had lost his usefulness.

"Your sketches and diagrams must be upstairs in one of the cardboard boxes," Saint Signore said. "Tonight's your best bet. Make sure Mona Lisa's out of the house."

"But Papa's study is teeming with dust mites."

"Tell me something I don't already know. They're everywhere in your mama's house, even in your pillow, dangerously close to your brain cells." Five years ago, Joey had talked Mama into buying a vacuum cleaner with a HEPA filter, supposedly able to weed out 99.9 percent of dust particles, but still the air billowing out of the vacuum was laden with germs.

"What if there are spiders and mice?" Joey shivered.

"Bring Figaro upstairs with you for protection," the Saint said. "Dog's noses are four hundred times more discerning than your own."

"He'll have a field day sniffing around the floor in here."

After several minutes of flirtatious chitchat, Moni left Ramon's side and moved about the kitchen. Without washing up before or after, she swiped the back of her hand across her forehead, taming several strands of long bangs, then picked up a used towel. Her apron was covered with smudges and oily splats.

"Ugh, Moni," Joey said. "Wash your hands."

"I washed them five minutes ago." She seemed proud of the restaurant's cleanliness, but Joey saw layers of grime like veneers of varnish on hundred-year-old furniture. He held his lips together to stifle a yawn rather than sucking in extra air. Even taking baby breaths, germ-ridden sludge was gathering in his lungs - he could feel the weight of it. Is that what caused unexplained lung cancer?

Mama's friend Patsy, who loved cooking, had died of it, and she never smoked a cigarette in her life.

"You should have brought a face mask." Saint Signore's voice sounded as loud as Moni's and Ramon's - but they didn't react. Joey nodded. Often, he wore a paper face mask when on the bus or in the library doing research. People gave him double looks, but Saint Signore said, "Who cares what those morons think?"

"Hey, man," Ramon said from across the counter. "That's enough sliced tomatoes. That'll last us for days."

"Uh, okay." Joey mounded the rest of the slices into the container and passed it to Ramon. Then Joey carted the knife and cutting board to the sink and scrubbed them vigorously in water so hot that his latex gloves felt like they were laminating onto his fingers. He laid the board and knife in the drying rack, peeled off the gloves, and discarded them, replacing them with a pair from his pocket, leaving only two pairs left. "You should have brought the whole box," Saint Signore scolded. "Too late now. Go check your soup to make sure a fly isn't using it for a jacuzzi."

Cringing, Joey crossed the short space to the burners, where his vat of soup sat next to the warming minestrone - left over from yesterday - a hotbed for bacteria as far as Joey was concerned. He dipped a clean ladle into his soup and stirred it for the fifty-seventh time - first clockwise and then counterclockwise. He'd always counted in his head: how many footsteps it took to walk home from school, how many times his toothbrush swept against his upper teeth so his lower teeth would receive the same attention. His fingers automatically tapped out and counted the beats of every song that rapped, waltzed, or tangoed through his mind. Sometimes the same tune would circulate through his brain for hours and hours.

"You're going to turn that soup into mush if you fuss with it too much." Moni immersed a tablespoon into it and supped a taste. "It needs salt." She reached around him and added a dash and a clove of garlic.

"Hey, you're ruining it!"

"Our customers will complain if it's too blah. Except for Mr. DiAngelo. But I doubt he'd try vegetarian soup in the first place." She hovered next to Joey, scrutinizing him. He could feel her energy coiling around his torso in a tangle of electricity. Why was she intent on controlling his every move? He'd heard of viruses showing up on computers, infiltrating people's minds. That's why he wouldn't use the one at home. Maybe his sister was taking commands from some unknown entity.

Moni discarded her spoon in the sink. "Joey, how many times have you been in here anyway?" A stupid question. Or was it a trap?

"Once," he said. "The day before opening. Remember, I designed the sign out front."

"No, you didn't, little brother. Papa made it."

Joey felt like a swimmer trapped at the bottom of a pond.

"Stand up for yourself," Saint Signore said, giving Joey the courage to dive to the surface to gasp for air.

"Moni, I'm the one who came up with the restaurant's name. Booty was my nickname in elementary school. And I designed the sign in the shape of a cowboy boot, making it look like Italy. Papa took my blueprint…"

She shook her head in disbelief, as if he were speaking gibberish.

"I did," Joey said, with Saint Signore's approval. "Papa traced the design onto a piece of plywood and cut it out. Then I painted the wood and scribed on the letters."

The corners of her mouth curved up. "I don't have time to argue. We'll ask Mama about it when she comes in."

CHAPTER THIRTEEN
Mona Lisa

I prepared the drink orders - an iced tea (Booty's unique blend with sliced oranges, lemons, and crushed mint) and three cups of apple juice - for our first customers of the day, a late-twenties woman with her three preschool sons. Hearing the boy's squabble over who would sit where, I pitied the frazzled mom for her life of servitude: playing referee, swabbing runny noses, and enduring sleepless nights.

No, not true. I envied her. I was childless and my biological clock was melting down toward menopause, like Salvador Dali's distorted clock draping across a tree branch.

I delivered the drinks and strode back to the kitchen. Joey was stirring his soup methodically and evenly, first in one direction and then in the other. "Double, double, toil and trouble," he muttered to himself.

"The order's ready." Ramon set three grilled cheese panini sandwiches on plates and relayed them across the counter, dissecting the kitchen. Using a tray, I hustled them out to the waiting children, along with a bowl of minestrone soup for their mother.

As I reentered the kitchen, I was happy to see Joey had stepped away from the soup to speak with Ramon, who was explaining how to read the orders I'd printed from the cash register so he could set them up for delivery. "I add side orders like pasta salad and tossed green." Ramon pointed to the stainless-steel containers housing Italian, blue cheese, and raspberry vinaigrette dressings. "Then the server - Mona Lisa or you - dollops on the salad dressing."

I stood beside Joey, who'd managed to keep his apron as pristine as newly fallen snow. I told him, "We check to see if the customer wants the dressing served on the side in one of these little dishes. Once you get the hang of it, you can deliver the orders too."

Joey's brows lowered, the corners of his mouth drawing back. "You want me to wait on people? You said Mama was coming in to help. Why isn't she here yet?"

"I'm not sure. Once she arrives, our regular customers will swarm around her with hugs and good wishes. She won't be able to resist stepping back into her former position as Queen of Booty's." My shoulders relaxed as I imagined her abundant energy. "She'll be delighted to find you here, Joey." Trying to view him through her eyes, I felt a ripple of pride. He was doing better than I'd expected, following Ramon's and my instructions, proving he could work under supervision. My worst fears hadn't come to life. Joey hadn't tipped over the vat of soup with his constant stirring, dropped a knife, or sneaked out the back door. On the other hand, it seemed he would have continued slicing tomatoes until closing time if Ramon hadn't stopped him. And Joey mumbled to himself, bringing a smile to Ramon's lips. I reasoned that we all talked to ourselves. Ramon often hummed or sang, his sultry voice filling the space with a bossa nova or Latin song, making my limbs sway with the rhythm. And I admit, I heard Papa's words in my mind and occasionally answered him. But he never answered back.

"I'm tired, you said I'd have to stay for only a couple hours," Joey said to himself, his lips barely moving. He released a lengthy sigh and stared past Ramon, out the window, onto the street. I followed his gaze to see Cliff exiting a spiffy Porsche coupe that must have cost a bundle. I remembered back in high school he drove a Corvette Stingray, the envy of every young man. I assumed he'd had to work long hours after school to afford it, or his wealthy parents spoiled him. I had to admit that after all these years, the man still retained his rugged good looks, muscled shoulders, and trim waist. Sure, he had a snazzy, showy car. But it's not as if Papa hadn't torn up the roads in his red Alfa Romeo coupe. He'd even lowered the top in midwinter on a sunny day.

A far-fetched idea unfurled itself in the back of my mind. "Joey, we should sign you up for driving lessons." But he gave me a one-shoulder shrug, like I'd told him it wasn't too late to become an astronaut. "We could get you a learner's permit, and I could teach you," I said. "My car is an automatic. You just point it where you want to go, and the transmission makes the decision when to change gears."

"Nah." In spite of Joey's negative response, his interest seemed heightened, his posture straightening. I noticed his attention was fixed on Panda climbing out of Cliff's car. As she slinked to the sidewalk, she tugged her T-shirt down to cover most of her belly, leaving a small slice of pink flesh. To me, there was nothing appealing about the girl. Her jeans were too tight, the hems frayed, and her face, pretty as it was, wore a sullen expression.

She moved to the window and knocked on it, trying to snag Joey's attention. No need. He was already watching her but didn't wave back. Cliff placed a hand on her petite shoulder and spoke in her ear. She whirled around, wriggling out of his grasp, and launched a spray of words into his chest. I couldn't hear their conversation through the window, but it looked as if he were trying to coax her back into his car. Arms folded, she marched to the restaurant's front door and shouldered it open. Cliff followed her.

I wished Mama would waltz in to take their orders. I'd spent all my surplus energy coaxing Joey along. I doubted I had a smile left in me.

I turned to Joey, who stood transfixed, watching Panda and Cliff move toward us.

In a minute, Panda and Cliff were standing at the counter, so I was forced to say, "Good morning. Welcome to Booty's."

"Hello." Cliff's voice sounded strained. "You remember my daughter, Panda?"

"Yes, of course. Nice to see you."

"Hey." Panda's gaze cut into me as if I were her least favorite teacher, the one who sent her to detention. Which I bet happened often. She scanned the board hanging above me. "Vegetarian soup. I'll take a cup."

"Okay," I said.

Joey moved in behind me as I rang up her order. He ignored Cliff, but when Panda asked for a complicated vegetarian chef's salad, Joey said, "I'll make that for you right away."

Her whole demeanor softened, and she giggled. "Can you sprinkle it with sunflower seeds?"

"Sure, anything you like."

Was Joey flirting with a girl half his age? From Cliff's pinched expression and severe mouth, I guessed he was picking up on the same vibes.

"And may I have a Diet Coke?" She lengthened her words into a teasing drawl.

"Did you get all that?" Joey asked me as I punched the drink order into the cash register.

"Yes, I did, thank you." I addressed Panda, "Don't you have school today?"

Her spiky green bangs flopped forward to partially obscure her eyes. "None of your business."

"Panda, honey, don't be rude," Cliff said, without much enthusiasm, like she mouthed off on a regular basis. If she were my child, I would have given her pert little rump a smack, but I was too stunned to do anything more than stare.

"Sorry, Daddy." She finally aimed a sickly smile at me. "Ma'am, I'm cutting school today." *Brat* was too generous a word to describe her. I'd rarely been treated so rudely. I felt like retaliating, sending her a left jab over the counter.

Cliff scanned the menu. "I'll have a roast beef sandwich on white bread, heavy on the mayonnaise, no onion, a bag of chips, and a glass of milk." Again, he'd ordered the most boring items on the menu, as far as I was concerned. Which told me a lot about him. He handed me a twenty-dollar bill, and I counted out his change. He slipped a dollar in the glass tip jar, then ambled away to find a table. Panda lingered, her hand snaking into the jar to retrieve the dollar like a pro. She palmed it, stashing her loot in her jeans pocket. My mouth opened in silent surprise. Should I tell Cliff, or did he even want to know?

In a flash, she was gone, shadowing her father to a table against the wall.

"Can you believe that?" I asked Joey, but he'd stepped to the tub of chopped lettuce and was fashioning Panda an elaborate salad.

CHAPTER FOURTEEN
Cliff

From across the table, Cliff watched Panda pick the sunflower seeds off the top of her salad with her fork, one by one, dawdling.

He reined in his escalating temper. "Hurry up, honey." The severe brightness of the room warned him of an impending headache. "I need to take you to school and get back to work. I'll write you an excuse explaining you overslept, and I took you out to lunch."

"That won't cut it. They'll give me an unexcused absence. You'll have to make something up. Tell them I was sick."

His chest tightened. "No, I won't lie." He'd promised himself no more lies. "I'll tell them the truth. Your negligent mother skipped out of town."

"Don't blame everything on her. If you lived at home…" She forked into her salad and crammed a tomato wedge into her mouth.

His thoughts turned to Janette, as if she still held the string to his kite. How could she abandon their daughter? The answer was as blatant as a billboard - Dennis was more important to her than Panda. But Cliff couldn't voice his opinions; Panda might repeat them to her mother or, worse, be crushed, in spite of her tough facade.

Maybe Cliff should call Bill, his AA sponsor, the only person he confided in. The man knew more about Cliff than anyone.

"Daddy, what are you doing?" Panda said with an air of disgust.

Cliff felt moisture in the palm of his hand and realized he was crushing his roast beef sandwich, the mayonnaise oozing out the sides and dripping onto his plate. When he was a kid, he used to ball bread into wads and throw them against the kitchen wall - what he'd like to do to Dennis's head.

He loosened his grasp and wiped his fingers on his paper napkin. "Panda, you've got ten minutes to finish your salad, then I'm taking you to school."

"What's the hurry?" She located another sunflower seed and crunched it between her molars. Still gnawing, she said, "My health teacher says you're supposed to chew every mouthful twenty times for proper digestion."

"I hardly call one sunflower seed a mouthful." As he bit into his flattened sandwich, he wondered if Panda even took health class. Had his daughter inherited his propensity for falsehoods? His mind spun back to when he was a kid; he'd lied to his folks all the time, and they never caught on. What was he talking about? His father took off when Cliff was in third grade. He never admitted to his friends that Dad lived on the other side of town and showed up at the house only once a year on Christmas Eve to deliver an excuse for a present. In hindsight, Cliff figured his father came by to see how Mom was spending the child support money, if he sent any. Cliff had no idea how his mother, working as a secretary, made ends meet. When in her twenties and thirties, she was quite a looker, wearing sleazy clothing, gobs of makeup, and too much perfume. She invited creepy male friends to spend the night; they brought gifts - boxes of See's chocolate and wilting carnations that never made it to a vase - and left twenty-dollar bills on the coffee table. She still had male friends, but no more flowers. Couldn't Cliff's father have seen she was a lousy drunk who had no business raising a child?

As he gnawed into another bite of his sandwich, Cliff had to wonder about himself and if he was just as inadequate, shirking his parental duties. Maybe he could change all that starting today. But how?

Mona Lisa strode past their table carrying a tray with two savory-smelling panini sandwiches and delivered them to a college-aged couple at a nearby table. Cliff was still hungry enough to eat dessert, but that meant giving Panda more time to skip school. Yet why sit there with nothing to do while she picked at her lunch?

"Mona Lisa," he said, as she turned back toward the kitchen, "would you please bring me a slice of pie? Apple, if you have it. I'll pay you on the way out."

She spoke over her shoulder. "Want to try one of our house specialties? Tiramisu or zabaglione?"

"No, I'd prefer plain old apple pie. À la mode." Like his mother never made.

"Yeah, we have it." She glanced to the register where two customers waited, then sent Cliff a stern look.

He said, "About this afternoon, I need a key…" but she'd hightailed it back to the register and wasn't listening.

"You shouldn't eat pie," Panda said. "You're getting porky."

His hand moved to his waist. This morning, while dressing, he'd noticed a ripple of flab. He didn't have time to make it to the gym - but he didn't appreciate being razzed.

"If anything, Panda, you're underweight. You could use a few pounds."

She dropped her fork in the middle of the salad. "I'd rather be a beanpole than a blubber gut."

"An extra five pounds doesn't make me fat, young lady." He felt like ordering a tall glass of beer and really shocking her. But Panda would tell Janette. And he was off booze. He hadn't touched the seductive liquid in two years.

The front door opened, and Mrs. Buttaro entered the restaurant, her hand resting in the crook of an aged gentleman's arm who looked like he'd stepped out of *The Godfather*. Good, Cliff could get a key from her.

"Mama, it's about time." Mona Lisa spoke with a twist of impatience. "Where have you been?"

"I've had a busy morning."

"But we need you. Look, Joey's here. Come into the kitchen and help him."

"Joey? That's wonderful." Ignoring Mona Lisa's suggestion, Mrs. Buttaro moved regally past her and the customers waiting to order. She slipped behind the bar to the sound system and spent a moment changing the background music from soothing jazz to peppy accordion, which Cliff guessed must remind her of the old country.

Mrs. Buttaro came around the bar, sidled up to it, and sat on one of the stools. Her escort climbed up on the stool next to her—not an easy feat. He must have stood around five six and was dressed in a fitted three-piece suit and wingtips.

"Joey." Mrs. Buttaro yoo-hooed into the kitchen. "Come out and say hello to Mr. DiAngelo."

Mona Lisa turned her face away from her customer at the register to snap her words at Mrs. Buttaro. "Joey refuses to leave the kitchen. Annie's home sick. We're shorthanded."

"Yes, yes, you told me."

"Well, don't just sit there, Mama!"

Cliff could see Mona Lisa was understaffed and overwhelmed, but her curt attitude offended him; she should be grateful she had a healthy and vivacious mother. His own was probably still sacked out in her bed between sheets that hadn't been laundered for months. Cliff would never let Panda spend the night there, for fear some slimy pervert was skulking around.

Rather than responding to Mona Lisa's entreaties, Mrs. Buttaro focused her attention on trying to coax Joey out of the kitchen. "*Mio tesoro*, come say hello to me and Mr. DiAngelo. Bring us some coffee, please, won't you, darling son of mine?"

Joey finally poked his head out. He was wearing a hair net. Or was it a plastic shower cap like Cliff's mother wore? Joey's gaze canvassed the room until it landed on Panda, who stopped eating her salad and smiled at him. His grim expression brightened somewhat, and he stepped back into the kitchen. He returned without his hairnet, placed two cups and saucers on the bar, and then fetched a coffee pot.

"Don't fill Mr. DiAngelo's cup too full," Mrs. Buttaro said.

"My hand shakes." Mr. DiAngelo held his gnarled fingers out to demonstrate.

His face serious, Joey dribbled coffee into Mr. DiAngelo's cup.

"That's perfect." Mrs. Buttaro's voice rang with enthusiasm. "Fill mine to the brim. *Grazie*. Now, Joey, please take this coffee around and fill empty cups."

Cliff could sense Mona Lisa was listening to her mother's conversation as she rang up more customers. Ramon, the cook he'd seen the other day, dashed out of the kitchen to deliver an order, then jogged back again.

Mrs. Buttaro noticed Cliff and waved. She lowered herself off her stool, leaving her elderly friend. "Cliff, how nice of you to visit Booty's again. And who is this lovely young lady?"

Panda held in a smile, but her face finally relaxed into a grin when Cliff introduced her. Mrs. Buttaro insisted both call her by her first name, Barbara. "Mrs. Buttaro makes me feel old."

Mona Lisa rushed out of the kitchen with a triangle of apple pie and a ball of vanilla ice cream and skidded the plate onto Cliff's table.

"That pie looks stone-cold," Barbara scolded. "You didn't heat it?"

Mona Lisa looked frantic. "No time."

Barbara picked up the plate. "We'll put the pie in the oven—not the ice cream," she told Cliff, who chuckled at her levity, but Mona Lisa scowled, bringing sharp lines to her forehead. Her snarly temperament reminded him of his own daughter.

Barbara raised a hand. "Joey, come here to your mama." Carrying a coffee pot, he was meandering aimlessly among the tables with his shower cap sticking out of his back pocket. Barbara handed him the pie plate. "Give this to Ramon to heat."

91

Joey eyed the pie with suspicion before transporting it into the kitchen. Cliff couldn't put his finger on it, but Joey was what his grandmother - his mother's mother - would have called "touched in the head." Part of Cliff's impression was Joey's yellow bowling shirt. Was he going for a retro look? In any case, Cliff was certain he'd seen Joey panhandling. A friend on the police force once told Cliff that panhandlers easily raked in one hundred dollars a day.

"About the key," Cliff said while he had Mona Lisa's and Barbara's attention. "Thomas and I need to get into the house this afternoon."

"Mama, can you get a copy made for Cliff?"

"If I could find mine…"

"Mama, I can't believe you gave Joey your last copy. What were you thinking? Please take his back and get it copied. You see how busy I am."

"Yes, *cara*, business looks good. Papa would be pleased." Most of the tables were filled. But only half of the customers were eating, the rest waited for their meals. Several people lingered at the register for their to-go orders.

Cliff glanced up at Barbara and Mona Lisa. Both classic beauties. Mona Lisa had maintained her curvaceous but trim figure. Her face had grown more attractive since high school: olive complexion, liquid brown eyes, full wavy hair pulled back to frame her sculpted neck, loose curls around her ears. But her mother radiated generosity and contentment, while Mona Lisa's glower and raised shoulders revealed pent-up anxiety. Not that he blamed her; he'd never be able to cope with her multitasking job.

"Never mind, I'll do it myself." She shot Cliff a fierce look, like the missing key situation was his fault. "I'll swing by the house at three o'clock on my way to the bank. Okay?"

"Sure, that'll work."

Twenty minutes later, Cliff pulled his car up in front of Panda's private school, which he could not afford. But he'd agreed to pay the hefty tuition during the divorce settlement.

Janette's attorney had outmaneuvered Cliff's - a poker night buddy - and by then Cliff had used up his fighting stamina.

Listening to the engine idle, he wished he hadn't indulged in that apple pie à la mode. What was he thinking? His belt cut into his waist, but he couldn't loosen it in front of Panda. With his high school reunion coming up, he'd promised himself he'd work out at the gym every day to hone his body into prime condition, figuring Janette would show up with Dennis. And he wanted to look svelte in front of his old crowd. Several of the guys still entered triathlons and had grown financially successful. Cliff wished he had some beauty to bring as his trophy girlfriend. In the next month, he'd find someone. He might break down and try one of those online dating services.

Using his ruled pad of paper, Cliff scribbled a note for the attendance office. *Please excuse my daughter Patricia's late arrival. She was with me.* There. Not completely accurate, but not lying.

Panda snatched the paper from his hand. Her bulky backpack clinging to her shoulder, she hopped out of the car, took off on foot, and dodged around the side of the school.

CHAPTER FIFTEEN
Joey

Joey stood at the restaurant's front window examining the void Cliff's car left after whisking Panda away. Leaving the curb, the Porsche's engine had sounded like the low purring of a panther—soothing but dangerous.

Saint Signore said, "Jo-Jo, maybe you should take up your sister's offer to teach you how to drive."

His words flapped through Joey's brain like bats trapped in an attic. The idea of sitting behind a steering wheel terrified Joey. What if the car took on a mind of its own and crashed into another automobile? What if Joey himself, possessed by an uncontrollable urge, turned the steering wheel and intentionally drove into Lake Washington? When he was a boy, he'd heard his parents speak of a horrifying accident - someone they knew spinning off a bridge. The image had indelibly etched itself in Joey's mind. Drowning in a car was one of his greatest fears. In dreams, he'd experienced the helplessness of sinking and suffocating. Doors locked. Windows sealed.

Seattle had two floating bridges spanning the width of Lake Washington and several smaller bridges crossing the Ship Canal, not to mention the elevated Aurora Bridge and the towering freeway. Driving in Seattle without crossing a bridge was impossible.

"You do fine on the Metro bus," Saint Signore said.

"You know full well I close my eyes and pray when the driver takes us over a bridge."

"You're working here today, aren't you?" the Saint reminded Joey. "I'd call what you've accomplished at Booty's close to miraculous."

"Thanks." Joey had surprised himself. "But driving a four-thousand-pound vehicle is more complicated than filling coffee cups or making soup." He watched a white Mustang swish by. He'd always accepted the Saint's wisdom in the past, so he dared to imagine driving Panda somewhere. Just as friends, laughing.

"Panda's a cute little dish," Saint Signore said.

Joey spoke out of the side of his mouth so no one else would hear. "She's just a kid. Way too young."

"In Italy, men marry younger women. Your father was much older than your mother."

"The last thing I need is a wife."

"Why not? Someone to wash and fold your laundry. And keep you warm at night. Preferably a woman with an inheritance or who works at a job with enough income for both of you."

"It's out of the question. I haven't kissed a girl since high school." Joey remembered his first kiss, when he was ten, playing spin the bottle in Julie's basement while her parents entertained out on the patio. Then he recalled his girlfriend in junior high - they'd exchanged embraces in the dark during movies. In high school, he'd fallen hard for Debbie Webster, a real girlfriend, for a month, until she dumped him before the junior prom, leaving him feeling devastated and unlovable. Then, through newspaper articles, TV specials, and science class, Joey learned how sexual intimacy transmitted disease. Even kissing and holding hands spread viruses and bacterial infections.

"Joey, can you help?" Ramon aimed his words at him. "This order's getting cold."

Joey left his disturbing thoughts and moved to the counter, where two panini sandwiches sat on white plates. The aroma of warm goat cheese and bread filled his nostrils. His stomach twisted with hunger, but he'd have to wait until he got home before he ate. Or was it safe to sample his vegetarian soup?

"Put the plates on a tray and take them out," Ramon said, not looking up from his preparation of a caprese salad. "You know the routine. The number's on the ticket." Joey knew that the order number matched the location number the customer took to their table.

Saint Signore walked Joey through the task of finding a plastic tray, exiting the kitchen, and delivering the sandwiches to two women almost Mama's age, who practically grabbed their food off the tray.

"They waited fifteen minutes for their lunch," Saint Signore informed Joey. "The service has been too slow, like a snail. There's no way around it, you're going to have to pitch in."

Bringing the empty tray back to the kitchen, Joey noticed a businessman dressed in a narrow lapel suit and skinny tie. A government worker or member of the FBI? A restaurant critic from the *Seattle Times*? The man, waiting for his lunch, glared up from his paper and gave Joey's shirt a glance.

"We need to get him served and out of here," Saint Signore said. "The sooner the better." Joey returned to the kitchen to ask Ramon what needed to be delivered next.

"Great, man," Ramon said.

A moment later, Joey exited the kitchen, carrying a sandwich to the man in the suit, who set his newspaper aside to make room on the table. "Where's my coffee?" he demanded and glanced at his watch.

"I'll get it." Joey turned back to the kitchen. In his haste, he tripped on another man's foot. The empty tray flew out of Joey's hands and scudded across the floor. All heads turned. Someone chuckled - the FBI guy?

Feeling a bruised hip, Joey pulled himself upright, hoping his slacks hadn't gathered germs from the floor tracked in on the bottom of people's shoes.

"Pick up the tray and get the man his coffee," Saint Signore reminded him. He filled a coffee cup with shaky hands.

"Good boy," Mama said from her stool as he passed by, supporting the cup with both hands. Even Moni, still at the register, thanked him. The man didn't look up from his paper as Joey set the coffee cup on his table. Fine with Joey; he wanted to go unnoticed. He wished he were invisible.

On the way back to the kitchen, Saint Signore warned Joey to tread carefully and beware of pranksters trying to trip him.

Joey felt dizzy and woozy. He slid onto the stool next to Mama, who was supping on a large bowl of vegetarian soup. Frank sat on her other side, gobbling up minestrone by the tablespoon, but she didn't seem to notice his uncouth table manners. Joey leaned his head against her shoulder.

"Your soup is very good," she said.

"Thank you, Mama." But could he believe her? She was still wearing Frank's engagement ring, a blood-red ruby. Had its dazzling sparkle cast a spell over her, making her forget about Papa? Joey remembered Frank's dominating the dining room table like a king ruling over his newly conquered domain.

"You should have taken better care of Mama," Saint Signore said. "You and I, we'll find a way to get rid of Frank."

CHAPTER SIXTEEN
Mona Lisa

Papa had disapproved of tardiness, and here I was, running thirty minutes late. I needed to give Cliff a copy of Mama's key, show him several more items in her house that needed fixing, then race back to Booty's. I'd left Ramon and Joey in the kitchen, looking like a tornado with indigestion had whirled through it. I needed to balance the till - count the cash and checks and tally up credit card receipts - then make the deposit at the bank before it closed.

I steered my car onto Mama's tree-lined street and spotted Cliff parked out front of the house talking on his cell phone. My mind repeating the Italian word *tardi* – late - I pulled into Mama's short driveway, hopped out, and hurried across the grassy front strip. I stood by Cliff's sleek Porsche on the passenger side, but he didn't notice me. Engrossed in conversation, his voice muffled. He closed his eyes and pinched the bridge of his nose with his free hand.

"Cliff?" I rapped on his window, startling him.

He shut off his phone and lowered the window. "I just about gave up on you."

"Sorry. It took longer - there was a line at the hardware store. I found a couple more things that should be repaired. The back porch light …"

"Not now." Cliff stretched one hand out, palm up. "You have the key?"

"Yes." I extracted the newly copied house key from my purse and handed it to him. The moment he possessed it, his window slid up halfway, like a wall shutting me off. I was miffed that he didn't get out of his car, let alone thank me.

I bent forward to speak to him. "Could you come in for a moment?"

"No time. Panda's waiting for me to pick her up at school."

"Okay." Obviously, he was worried about her. But the headstrong girl who'd sassed me at Booty's earlier today looked like she could fend for herself. Who would dare kidnap her? No, that was wrong thinking. Panda might be standing like a waif out front of her school, waiting for her father.

"She's staying with me until her mother gets home." Cliff jiggled the keys in his pocket. "Where's Thomas? He was supposed to meet me here. You can let him in."

"No, I can't. I need to get back to the restaurant immediately." I didn't want to get pulled into Cliff's drama. When I'd left Booty's an hour ago, Mama and Frank DiAngelo were also leaving so Mama could get her hair done. I'd begged her to stay to keep an eye on Joey, but Mama told me he would manage fine. "Give him a chance to spread his wings, *cara*," she'd said, like she was blaming Joey's antisocial behavior on me.

Standing in the afternoon sunshine outside her house, I recalled the post-lunch cleanup chaos awaiting my return.

"I have to go." Cliff disengaged his parking brake. "I'll call Thomas and ask him not to show up until later."

"In that case, you could have come back to the restaurant to pick up the key," I told his departing car as it thundered around the corner.

Figaro woofed from the backyard. I should get him inside before Mama's neighbors complained. I saw mail sticking out of the slot by the front door and a small package sitting on the porch, signaling to the whole world that no one was home. I was already out of my car, so I opted to quickly take care of the mail, bring in the dog, and give him a snack to tide him over until dinner. Who knew when I'd get back?

I usually entered via the kitchen door but climbed the front porch steps to retrieve the package - addressed to me. I didn't recognize the return address. The print was too small to decipher without the reading glasses. Vanity kept me from wearing them all the time. But I could tell it wasn't from Lands' End, the only mail-order business I'd used in the last few months. The box was the size of a plump paperback but heavier. I suspected it was Mama's handiwork and probably had something to do with Joey. I'd open it later. Cliff wasn't the only one on a tight schedule.

In the front hall, I shuffled through the mail, finding an invitation to my high school class reunion, titled "Blast from the Past." Cliff's buddies had come up with the event's name, which made me think of a high school kegger. No doubt there would be heavy alcohol consumption that evening, and his crowd would revert to its juvenile behavior. I took a moment to scan the mailer, which asked me to sign up on a website and contact the committee with other students' missing email and home addresses. I didn't have the energy or interest to examine the long list of escapees, who were probably enjoying their anonymity.

Late as I was, I got distracted sorting through the rest of the mail, consisting of bills and recycling information. How had I gotten saddled with overseeing Mama's bills? I would ask the mailman for a forwarding postcard. After the house sold, Mama wouldn't need to concern herself with utility bills.

Carrying the package and the mail, I walked through the core of the house to find Figaro scratching at the back door, which needed repainting before I listed the house. But then Figaro would scrape the new enamel with his nails, which needed clipping, a job I didn't have the nerve to tackle. More impetus to find him a home. Anyway, what realtor would dare walk clients through a place with a Doberman pinscher guarding it? I needed to locate the dog rescue group, or maybe find one that specialized in Dobermans, if there were such a thing.

With the same reluctance I always felt upon seeing the dog, I opened the back door, and Figaro bounded inside, circling me and sniffing my hands and pant legs. He caught the scent of the package, stalked to the counter, and inhaled vigorously. Had Mama sent me homemade biscotti she'd baked in her tiny kitchen or a ricotta cheesecake needing to be refrigerated? I pulled the tape off the box and slid out the contents to find a Panasonic digital camera that I hadn't ordered. It came with an instruction book but no invoice.

"What am I supposed to do with this?" I asked Figaro. He pricked his ears and sniffed at it again. I hadn't used my old camera in ten years, maybe fifteen, not even to capture family birthday parties the way I used to. Photography had once been my passion. But I'd lost interest in recording full moons rising at sunset or rainbows over Lake Washington, and at family gatherings, I'd grown weary of the feeling of being on the outside, peering in, snapping photos while others blew out candles, and had fun. Then friends and relatives started arriving with digital cameras, producing instant viewing, making my old Canon obsolete.

I set the camera on the counter and turned to the dog. "You hungry, Fang?" I sprinkled kibble in his bowl. The dog gulped it with mammoth jaws, swallowing without bothering to chew.

While he was still eating, I left the house, jogged to my car, and sped back to Booty's. Entering the closed restaurant, I noticed a new Help Wanted sign in the front window. I found Ramon standing at the sink, washing a fry pan. The sight of him brought a tear to my eye. I knew he could easily find a job at an upscale restaurant like Benjamin's or Canlis, but he had remained loyal to me.

Noticing my teary eyes and solemn expression, he slid off his gloves. "Are you all right, beautiful one?" His arms reached out, his hands landing on my shoulders, then sliding around them to give me an extensive hug. I sank into his embrace, resting my head on his chest, feeling his breath rise and fall in unison with mine. His hand moved to the back of my neck, and he massaged away the tension, my muscles softening. It felt good, so comfortable, accepting his healing touch. How long had it been since I'd kissed a man? I thought of Kevin. It was pathetic, I knew, but I missed him. My body ached, deep inside, like I hadn't eaten a full meal in months. Maybe the only way to get over a man was to replace him with another. But I couldn't endure the agony of being dumped again. I needed to find Kevin's opposite, a man with my father's honesty and integrity. Was he standing in front of me?

I imagined Papa watching me and shaking his head with disapproval. In less-than-perfect English, he'd remind me that good business policy demanded I not fraternize with employees.

I stiffened and stepped away, wiped the corner of my eye. "Ramon, I'm sorry I left you with this mess."

"Don't worry about it. I didn't mind." He slipped his hands back into his gloves, rinsed the fry pan, and set it in the drying rack.

Still feeling a tingle of desire, I put on an apron and brought out a towel to dry the pan. "I'm afraid to ask where Joey is."

"He vamoosed right after your mother left. Is your brother on staff permanently?"

"I have no idea. Thanks for putting the Help Wanted sign out. Even if Joey returns, we'll need someone." Although it would bring payroll up higher and look bad on the books for a buyer.

Should I tell Ramon that I was selling the restaurant? He deserved the truth. He was obviously more than an employee.

CHAPTER SEVENTEEN
Cliff

A couple blocks from Panda's school, Cliff rehashed his recent conversation with his assistant, Thomas, who'd remained in the Wiltons' uncompleted kitchen, installing the cabinet hinges. "Tell them I'm sorry we're running behind," Cliff had instructed the twenty-year-old. "I'll be back in the morning to wire the new hood over the stove and the chandelier above the table." Then Cliff had fled the house, jogging down the back steps to his Porsche, to swing by Barbara Buttaro's to get the key from Mona Lisa on his way to pick up Panda. Not his usual modus operandi. Cliff liked to complete jobs ahead of schedule; running late made him feel out of control and in need of a crutch. Why, he even longed for a cigarette, and he hadn't smoked in ten years.

"God, help me." His voice filled the car's small interior. But as usual, except for the engine's purring, the air hung silently around his ears.

As he downshifted and hung a right off the main street onto school property, his thoughts landed on Mona Lisa. She was to blame for his tardiness; she should have called him on his cell phone to say she was going to be late. He could have fetched Panda first, then gotten the key. But Mona Lisa, who had no children of her own, didn't understand his bind. The words *spinster* and *old maid* came to mind. She wasn't even a favorite aunt, what with her weird brother? Who would marry either one of them?

Okay, maybe he wasn't being fair to Mona Lisa. He'd heard on the news that some women chose to remain single and childless and claimed to be perfectly content.

Up ahead, several students idled on the sidewalk, chatting, their backpacks heaped together on the pavement. At the curb, in the pickup area, his daughter was speaking with Mr. Patterson, head of the middle school, a black man who stood a foot taller than Panda. As Cliff stopped at the curb in front of the two-story brick building, Mr. Patterson strode around to the driver's side. Cliff lowered his window and heard him say, "We were sorry to miss Patricia at school today."

Huh? "There must be some mistake; I dropped her off after lunch." Cliff cut the engine. "I wrote a note for the attendance office."

Mr. Patterson's frown told Cliff he was perturbed. "Could you come in for a chat tomorrow?" he said.

"How about right now?" Cliff reached for the door handle.

"No. Too late today. Tomorrow at ten?"

"Sure, okay." Cliff would have to get up early the next morning and arrive at the Wiltons' before the young professional couple left for their downtown commute. But then how would Panda get to school?

Panda bopped into the passenger side and tossed her backpack behind Cliff's seat, atop the grocery bags housing her clothes. He had given her a matching set of luggage last year. Had Janette borrowed the suitcases for her honeymoon?

"What's the story, young lady?"

For once, Panda clipped on her seatbelt without being asked. She must have carried makeup in her backpack; her eyes were rimmed with additional black liner and globs of mascara, making her look cheap. "The bell rang the minute you dropped me off, so I went straight to my science class. The old bat probably counted me as absent. She needs glasses."

"And your class after that?" Cliff didn't want to admit he didn't know her schedule.

"French? *Oui. J'étais la.* I was there."

"I met Madame Dupont at an open house. She didn't strike me as the type to miss seeing a student. Did you hand in my note?" He turned in his seat to catch her mouthing her lower lip.

"Oops. I forgot?" She reached into her purse and brought out the folded and creased paper, opening Cliff's note on her lap. "Blame it on my ADHD."

"Since when?"

"Mom had me tested last month. Ask her yourself, if she ever comes home."

Cliff wasn't sure if he was more irked at hearing about Panda's psychological testing without his consent - Janette would no doubt send him the bill - or surprised at Panda's comment about her mother's return. "Why wouldn't your mom come home?" he asked.

"She deserted you, didn't she? Maybe she and Dennis will like Maui so much they'll never come back."

Cliff noticed a car in his rearview mirror. He started his engine and rolled forward. "Your mom will be back. She'd miss you too much."

"Not since she met Dennis. He's all she talks about. Makes me want to barf." She opened her mouth and pointed her finger toward the back of her throat.

"I thought you and your mother got along."

"That was last year." Her small shoulders slumped forward.

"You want to call her?"

"And interrupt her wedding? She'd have a cow."

He chuckled, more out of anxiety than lightheartedness. He found nothing amusing about Janette's elopement.

"Daddy, what time is it in Maui?"

"Two or three hours earlier. You can call her tonight after we get you settled at my place." He headed south across the University Bridge, then up Capitol Hill, traveling parallel to the freeway. He wondered if Janette and Dennis would tie the knot on a beach or in an intimate chapel. Had fat-cat Dennis presented her with a hulking two-carat diamond, dwarfing the ring Cliff had given her? Would she wear a white gown even though she'd been married before, or something sassy and sexy? She'd always enjoyed showing off her curves and long legs.

Halfway up the hill, Cliff turned east onto a residential street, nearing his apartment - really, part of the second floor of a 1920s home with five units, including his landlady, Mrs. McCloud's.

"Do I really have to stay here?" Panda said.

"Come on, now, honey, it won't be that bad. You haven't spent the night with me for three or four months."

"That's because I'm busy." On his designated weekends, she and Janette always had an excuse. Either Panda was dying to attend a party or Janette had planned a shopping expedition, overshadowing Cliff's parental rights. But now he and Panda had a whole week to bond, to get to know each other again, even if it was inconvenient as all get out. After work, Cliff usually vegged out in front of the TV to decompress or did household repairs for his landlady in lieu of paying rent. Tomorrow evening, he'd planned to attend his high school reunion committee meeting. How would he arrange to go to the meeting? He certainly couldn't rely on his mother to come over and watch Panda. There were always Janette's parents, the Do-Gooders. He'd nicknamed Harvey and Isabel Andersen because they wore perpetual phony smiles, even when testifying against him in divorce court. They'd been instrumental in getting Janette sole custody, with visits for Cliff every other weekend. They'd paid for her pit bull attorney and their accusations about Cliff's liquor consumption and unreliable behavior painted him as a loser. Bottom line: They never liked Cliff and thought Janette had married beneath her.

He pulled into an alley and parked behind his landlady's three-story Queen Anne-style Victorian between his pickup and the garbage cans.

"The Addams Family should live here." Panda eyed the twin turrets and the peeling paint.

"Is that show still on TV?" Cliff was determined to keep the mood light.

"Not anymore. It's like you, too old to even be a rerun." She snapped her fingers twice. "Remember, you gave Mom a Charles Addams cartoon book for Christmas."

"No, I didn't." Only child support and an alimony check. "Dennis must have given it to her."

"Yeah, I remember. You're right. He says she has a good sense of humor. Do you think she does, Daddy?"

"Sure, I guess." At one time, Cliff assumed Janette's laughter and joking meant she was happy. They'd had their share of arguments, but he'd been stunned when she demanded a divorce. "If she ever gives up real estate, your mom could be a stand-up comedian." He was unable to contain his sarcasm. He got out and reached behind the driver's seat for the two paper bags. With Panda trailing him, he carried them up the porch steps, then the back staircase to the second floor, to his door, marked 201 with brass numbers. Taking a pass through his living room, he lugged the bags into his spare bedroom—what he called Panda's room.

"Panda dumped her backpack on the floor between the two twin beds. "I want to check my emails on my laptop. And do research for a history paper."

"I'll put the computer in the living room. Where I can keep an eye on you."

"I have my own TV at home." She surveyed the room that Cliff had gone to great trouble to pretty up for her sake: pale pink walls and flowered bedspreads.

"Where am I supposed to put everything?" She stood facing the doorway.

"In the new bureau." He'd recently sanded and stained the four-drawer dresser, a garage sale find, to match the cherry-wood headboards. "And there are plenty of hangers in the closet." Earlier today, when picking her up at her mother's, he'd seen Panda's room, her dirty clothes strewn across the floor in layers, a regular pigsty. "Would you like me to help you put your things away?"

"Nah, I won't be here that long."

"Honey, if your mom's out of town for a week..."

"I don't want to stay here. I hate pink. It reminds me of babies."

"Then let's repaint the walls. What color do you like?" He realized he didn't know her favorite anything. "How about Tuscan Yellow?" He'd admired the golden hue at Barbara Buttaro's.

Panda scanned the room. "I want the walls and ceiling eggplant purple. *Aubergine*, as my French teacher calls it."

"I'm not sure my landlady would go for that. She's in her late eighties. Dark colors are hard to paint over."

"If you're not interested in my opinion, why ask? Let's forget the whole thing and stay at Mom's."

"No, I can't risk her coming home and accusing me of trespassing."

"Dad, you're acting like a wimp."

He and Panda wandered to his living room. It was a beautiful room, complete with a sectional couch and a flat-screen TV. The windows faced east with a view of the Cascade Mountains. With its breathtaking view and high ceilings, it must have originally been the master bedroom of this grand old mansion. But it didn't feel like home to Cliff, with its walls blank except for a landscape print of a Scottish loch surrounded by bleak hills that Mrs. McCloud had lent him. She'd insisted he take it.

Panda stepped into the kitchen, once a walk-in closet. She swung open the refrigerator door. "I'm starving, but there's nothing to eat."

"Sorry, I didn't know you'd be here until this morning." The refrigerator was empty except for the basics. "We'll go shopping, and you can choose anything you like. Or we can go out to a restaurant for dinner." He should be at the Buttaro residence meeting Thomas right now. He could bring Panda along, but that would mean seeing the Doberman and possibly Joey, both potential threats to his daughter. He wondered if Panda was old enough to stay here by herself. Fourteen was babysitting age, but he didn't want to leave her here on her first night.

Panda opened the cupboard and pulled out a bag of chips. "Any dip?"

"Just a jar of salsa. Come on, let's go to the grocery store and stock up."

An hour later, they returned from a store that had an eclectic assortment of patrons, to say the least. Panda seemed to fit right in there. No one - neither the other customers nor the checker - took notice of her stripe of green hair.

After eating macaroni and cheese, Panda emptied the contents of her backpack - several notepads and books - onto what Cliff called his dining room table, his only table, sitting in the corner of the living room. She brought out her iPhone, positioned AirPods in her ears, then fiddled with her homework. She insisted she could concentrate better while listening to music, which made no sense to Cliff. Any song could capture Cliff's attention, dominating his thoughts and dragging him back into the past he was trying to forget. That's why he never listened to music while working, especially when up on scaffolding or a ladder, where concentration was essential.

With Barbara Buttaro's key still in his pocket, he rinsed their dirty dishes and filed them in the dishwasher. "How will I manage to get you to school tomorrow?" he wondered aloud, figuring she couldn't hear him above her music.

Realistically, there was no use rushing to the Wiltons' then coming back for her. Should he take her to work with him before school? No, he'd witnessed her surly mood this morning. If she got up that late today, how would he get her to bed at a reasonable hour tonight? The whole process seemed insurmountable. She'd never been a normal sleeper. When she was a little girl, she'd wake up in the night hysterical, in a half-dream state, her eyes wide open and her vision blank. "Night terrors" is what her pediatrician labeled her screaming fits. Cliff had to give it to Janette, after twenty minutes or so, she was able to soothe Panda back into her bed.

Finally, around age seven, Panda's night terrors stopped and were replaced by something more peaceful but equally as frightening when Cliff considered the possibilities.

He turned to her. "Hey, Panda?" He had to know. "Do you still walk in your sleep?"

CHAPTER EIGHTEEN
Mona Lisa

By the time I left Booty's, the bank was closed. For safety's sake, I brought the deposit home with me and stashed the zippered money bag in my closet behind a stack of shoeboxes, where I hid my diary as a kid. Earlier, after Ramon and I tidied the kitchen and reset the tables, I'd spent several hours trying to balance the books. But no matter how many times I counted and recounted the cash, checks, and credit card receipts, we were missing eighty dollars. A lot of money for our small restaurant. When Mama couldn't work at Booty's anymore and begged me to take over, she explained our staggering overhead: daily expenses of rent, insurance, utilities, wages, and the high cost of food. And taxes. Small businesses paid more than their share.

Where were the eighty dollars? I kept asking myself. I remembered Panda's hand snaking into the tip jar to nab her father's dollar bill. But she couldn't have gotten her mitts into the cash register, could she? Which left Mama, Ramon, our dishwasher Kavi, and me. And Joey? I didn't want to believe Cliff's assertion that Joey had panhandled at the freeway exit. Or was it the entrance? No matter, Cliff claimed Joey was begging for money, and the truth was, I had no idea how my little brother spent his time when he wasn't with me. Or what he was capable of.

I sat down at my childhood desk. Checking my email, I

deleted some spam, then clicked on a note from Uncle Vito with the subject: "Buon Compleanno!" Which made me smile because my birthday had been two months ago.

Cara Mona Lisa,

Did my gift arrive? I bought the camera, a late birthday present, over the internet so you wouldn't have to pay duty. Please send me pictures of your mother and Joey. And, please, take several of yourself. Someone here is anxious to see what you are looking like. When will you come visit? Let me know, and I will purchase your plane ticket, an early Christmas present.

Love from your Uncle Vito

Mystery solved. My uncle in Rome was playing matchmaker. He wanted me to send photos of my smiling self to attract his ancient *amico,* who was looking for a spouse. Once I figured out how to use the camera - if I could - I'd contort my features into a clown's face and take a few hideous mug shots. That would scare the old geezer away.

I mulled over my uncle's invitation to travel to Italy. I would like to see the Trevi Fountain and Saint Peter's. But that wouldn't happen until I sold the restaurant and the house.

I scanned through the rest of my emails and was shocked to recognize Kevin's email address. He was the last person I expected to hear from. As I read the subject line "Miss you," I was transported to my internal courtroom, where two opposing lawyers, speaking with Italian accents, argued their cases in my mind.

"Don't open it," one asserted. "Kevin inflicted irreparable damage on you. He demonstrated egregious behavior. He showed no regret."

"Examine the evidence," the other insisted. "What could it hurt?"

"No, press delete."

I paused, my hand hovering above the keyboard. Was Kevin

searching for a missing tie or some other personal item? I'd found a razor, toothbrush, and pair of socks after he moved out, and I'd shoved them in the garbage under the kitchen sink, then dumped uneaten chili over them for good measure. Most likely, he was getting married and wanted to hammer home the good news.

I summoned up his image. A perfect Irish nose And mouth. Pearly white teeth. He carried himself like a late-thirties John F. Kennedy, with ease and confidence but some slight stiffness, which I thought indicated good Northeast breeding. He was originally from Cape Cod, but I'd never met his family. I'd been delighted when he'd first driven his Mercedes coupe to the optometry shop and asked for my opinion on frames. Everything looked good on him, but I'd checked my enthusiasm and pretended I wasn't wowed beyond belief, enough to capture his interest, because minutes later he asked me to dinner at Ray's Boathouse on Shilshole Bay, which later became our favorite restaurant.

"*Buona fortuna* - a dentist in the family," Mama had gushed later when I'd told her about Kevin, as if he'd already proposed. Which he never did.

We had great times together - at least I did. I even bought hiking boots to accompany him on mountain walks through the Olympic rainforest, exhumed my old bike from Mama's garage so we could ride on the Burke Gilman trail together, and played tennis with him, physical activities I hadn't attempted since my twenties that left my thighs and knees aching for days. But I'd relished the discomfort as proof that I was finally up to the challenge of dating a jock.

Until something happened that I still didn't understand. He didn't love me anymore. Maybe he never had; he hadn't actually said the words "I love you." I'd just assumed he felt the same way I did.

My curiosity was doing cartwheels. I was over Kevin. *Finito*, Papa would say. But I couldn't help myself from opening Kevin's email. I held my breath and read:

Hi, Mona, you've been on my mind. When I called your
cell phone last month, Joey told me you'd moved to
California. Then I went by your job at the optometrist's,
but the new girl said you didn't work there anymore.
Your former boss was busy with patients. Do you ever
get back to Seattle? I need to talk to you.
  Love, Kev

Talk about what? I'd spotted him tooling around with a
woman a week after we split. Through his car's tinted windows,
I'd seen them laughing. Had he sampled the fruits of other women
and decided I was the crab apple he should have settled down
with? Unlikely. Was there some unfinished financial matter, and
he thought I owed him money? Or had he heard from a mutual
friend that I'd miscarried, and he wanted to offer his condolences?

Hey, wait a minute. Joey had answered my cell phone and
didn't tell me. The creep. My outrage shifted from Kevin to my
little brother. How dare Joey not notify me?

I reached out to hit reply.

No, I'd acted hastily too many times in my life. I'd better let
my answer percolate for a few days. Because I didn't have one.

I heard the kitchen door opening, but Figaro didn't bark.
"Joey, is that you?"

"Yeah."

I considered going around Mama's house with a can of WD-
40 to silence the hinges. Although, maybe Papa had the right idea,
the whiny doors alerted me to intruders. I should sort through
Papa's papers in hopes of finding his formula for The Squeaky
Door or some other invention - something to carry Mama through
retirement. Once she was gone, who would support Joey? He'd
never attended college or collected a paycheck. A friend had
advised me I should contact the Social Security Administration to
see if Joey qualified for benefits, but she'd mentioned they'd
require testing to prove he was incapable of supporting himself.
So far, Joey had refused to see a psychiatrist. I made the decision

to locate a counselor or social worker this week. Certainly, Joey wasn't the only misfit oddball in the city of Seattle.

Down in the kitchen, he was carrying on a one-sided conversation with Figaro? At least I hoped he was talking to the dog. Lord, please tell me he hadn't been begging on the freeway and had brought back a homeless person. No, Figaro would be barking.

I supposed I should congratulate Joey for sticking it out at Booty's most of the day. "Good job," I could say, the way Mama would. I was reminding myself of her more and more. I'd coddled Joey through the workday instead of treating him like a regular employee.

I heard footsteps padding up the staircase and then a rustling noise in Papa's old office. I tiptoed around the corner and saw Joey sitting at Papa's desk, rummaging through the drawers. His head jerked when he noticed me.

"What are you doing?" My words came out as an accusation. "Leave everything the way it is. You don't have any more right to Papa's things than I do."

I knew Joey's propensity to collect papers and could envision him compulsively stacking Papa's notes and diagrams in the basement just when I'd cleared the area out.

"I intend to examine every scrap of paper." I closed in on him.

"In search of a million-dollar invention?"

I was surprised by his question, but I supposed his desire for money was a good sign. "After all the years of Papa's tinkering," I said, "there has to be a moneymaking idea somewhere."

"You'd better find it before our sister does."

"Huh?" Further proof that he lived in a make-believe world. We didn't have other siblings. "Joey, when we move out - you do realize we're selling the house, don't you? We'll have to make this place look like a showroom on The Home improvement channel. I'll box Papa's papers and take them with me if need be." Maybe Joey learned some of his bad habits from our father, who kept every scrap of paper. And Papa did have a hard time parting with outdated clothing. I figured Mama thinned out his wardrobe every once in a while, because sometimes he'd ask us if we'd seen his old plaid jacket or some item of clothing from the '60s. Wearing her half-smile, Mama would shrug and say, "*Non lo so.*"

Joey seemed itchy, like the label on the back of his shirt was bothering him. "I saw a strange camera in the kitchen."

"It's mine, a late birthday present from Uncle Vito."

"Mama's nosy brother? How do you know? I didn't see a card."

"He sent me an email explaining…"

"Are you sure he's the one who sent the email? A hacker could have sent it."

Paranoia à la mode, I thought. "It really doesn't matter, because I don't have a clue how to use digital cameras."

"I could read the directions and charge the battery, if you promise you won't take pictures of me." His chocolate-brown puppy-dog eyes stared into mine. "But you have to promise, no pictures, cross your heart and hope to die."

"What's wrong, little brother? Rob a bank?" I was joking, but he winced. Then I remembered the missing money. Was guilt needling into him?

CHAPTER NINETEEN
Joey

"You're doing fine, Jo-Jo," the Saint said. "Get her out of this room. You and I can meet back here later, when she's sleeping."

"Let's go downstairs." Joey got to his feet and stepped toward the doorway, but Moni blocked his retreat. She wore navy-blue sweats, and her dark hair hung limply at her shoulders.

"Wait a minute, little brother." She narrowed her eyes at him. "Did you answer my cell phone within the last few weeks?"

Joey remembered hearing its chirping ring while Moni was putting out the garbage. With Saint Signore's prompting, Joey had extracted the phone from her purse, recognized Kevin's name on the caller ID, and answered it so Kevin couldn't leave her a message. Should he fess up?

"Now's not the time," Saint Signore had advised him. "You want her groveling back to that scoundrel?"

No, but Joey felt sorry for his sister. She came across as cranky and was a regular pain, but she was still attractive. Saint Signore had mentioned more than once that she was as beautiful as the original Mona Lisa. And Joey wanted to see her happy - whatever that meant to her. She wanted a husband and kids, no doubt, but her childbearing window was shrinking. Maybe their uncle was right. According to Mama, Uncle Vito knew a wealthy widowed father of six looking for a wife. In one marital transaction, Moni could become a stepmother, gain financial solvency, and then perhaps have a child of her own.

"Your Uncle Vito's friend has enough moola to maintain this house for us, Jo-Jo," Saint Signore had told Joey. "With Mona Lisa living in Italy, every day would be *una festa*. Party Town, USA." Moni crossed her arms and waited for an answer.

Joey said, "Scientists believe cell phones cause brain cancer. If you have one, you should dispose of it immediately." He pretended to find interest in a small-scale windmill perched on Papa's bookcase. Their father had dabbled in wind power since Joey was a toddler. Papa even built a windmill in the backyard, but a storm toppled it over, providing wood to build an elaborate play structure.

"Did you or did you not speak to Kevin Shaughnessy?" Moni let out a huff.

"The name sounds familiar."

She wiped her damp forehead in a show of frustration and spat out the words, "My old boyfriend?"

"I'm glad you didn't marry him."

"I didn't have much choice in the matter." Her hands dropped to her sides. "Are you sure you didn't answer my phone?"

"Moni, have you ever seen me speaking on a cell phone?"

"No. But if Kevin called, you'd tell me, wouldn't you? He claimed you said I moved away."

"The man's a liar. You already know that." Joey couldn't tell her what Saint Signore had reported about Kevin's extracurricular activities without inflicting more pain on her. "As a rule, I avoid dentists."

"Kevin specializes in TMJ, so it's unlikely you'd need his services."

"Yeah." Joey's hand moved to his jaw. Recently, when he yawned, he'd felt a clicking. But he wouldn't tell her.

"While I'm here, I might as well get started." She bent down and hefted up one of Papa's cardboard boxes and set it on the desk. Like an archeologist rooting into a tomb, she opened the flaps to

118

reveal rows of envelopes, standing like a battalion of soldiers, filed in what appeared to be chronological order.

"Looks like our parents kept every cancelled check for thirty years," she said. "I think we can toss away everything older than seven years. I'll ask Mama's accountant." At random, she exhumed an envelope and read the return address aloud, "Washington Mutual." She opened the envelope, pulled out a couple dozen checks, and fanned them across Papa's desk. "These are dated 1995. Why would Mama keep them?"

"In case she got audited? Or maybe they gave her a sense of security." Joey could relate.

"They look like household expenses." She sorted through them, her hand coming to rest on a check in the middle of the stack. "Here's one for Teresa Moretti. Two hundred dollars. I wonder who she is."

"Red alert!" Saint Signore said in Joey's ear, and Joey's hands rose up to cover them. Then, more calmly, the Saint said to Joey, "Maybe it's just as well Mona Lisa finds out about your older sister. She will eventually." But Joey couldn't face the impending tidal wave of Moni's tangled emotions. She had no idea Papa had fathered an illegitimate child back in Italy, a girl - now a woman - whose mother, in essence, had blackmailed Papa. Then, when Papa died, she'd kept quiet all these years.

"Teresa? The name doesn't sound familiar." Joey swallowed and steadied his voice to mask the flagrant lie. "She could be a dressmaker. Remember Mama's favorite Chianti-colored taffeta evening gown?"

"Yes, it was gorgeous. Mama sewed it. She sewed most of her clothes."

"A babysitter?"

Moni frowned at the check. "Who would pay a babysitter that much back in 1995? Not our folks. I always got stuck looking after you."

"That's true. Papa was pretty tight with his money."

"An understatement." She restuffed and closed the envelope, filing it into the box.

"You're right about talking to the accountant before throwing these out," Joey said. Anything to delay destroying them. He tried not to inhale the dusty air stirred up from the box, but he felt a sneeze approaching. "There might be something in there concerning Booty's. The check for the ice machine."

"No, Papa used a separate checking account for the restaurant." Moni pulled another envelope out from the back of the box. She located the date stamped by the Post Office. "Here's the most recent, April 2013. The year Booty's opened. It's hard to believe Papa's been gone that long." She sighed, her chin lowering and her chest sinking, like she alone carried the weight of his death. Joey missed him too. But Saint Signore kept in contact with Papa, lessening Joey's sense of loss. If he ever had a question for Papa, he just asked the Saint.

Joey sneezed twice into the crook of his elbow - he never used his hands. "God bless you." Saint Signore had told Joey that a simple blessing would keep the devil from diving down his throat.

Moni opened the envelope. "Same kind of stuff. Bills. Water, garbage, electricity." She selected a check from the bottom of the stack and laid it atop the others. "Here's another check written to Teresa Moretti. I'll have to ask Mama who she is."

"I wouldn't do that," Joey predicted Mama's outrage upon hearing Teresa's name.

Moni turned to face him. "Why not?"

"Stones better left unturned?"

Not an Italian saying, but it was all Joey could think of.

"Meaning what?" She placed the check written to Teresa on the corner of the desk, then put the others away and folded the box's lid. "I'll buy a shredder and get rid of this junk."

A prickly feeling spread all over Joey. He could picture the shredder's jaws slashing the checks, making him shudder as though the blades were cutting into his own flesh. "I think we should save them."

"If it were up to you, we'd keep everything. This house would be wall-to-wall junk."

"It beats throwing away valuables by mistake."

Mama's cordless house phone rang, drawing Moni out of the room. Joey could hear her say, "Hi, Cliff." Then, in a nonplussed voice, "I wasn't planning to go to the reunion." Another pause. "Tomorrow night? I'm not sure…" She carried the phone with her down to the first floor.

"Find an empty container," Saint Signore advised Joey in a whisper. "A shoebox would be perfect. Transfer some of your papa's checks into it, a few at a time. She'll never know the difference." Joey sneaked into Moni's room. He wasn't the only one who didn't throw unworn clothes away. In the closet hung a frumpy prom dress and several other outfits. Below them stood a dozen shoeboxes.

While Joey eyed the shoeboxes, Saint Signore sang the first line of *"Meglio Stasera"* …"It Had Better Be Tonight"…from *The Pink Panther*, one of his favorite oldie-but-goodie movies.

"Domani chi lo sa, quel che sarà?" Joey echoed. It loosely meant, "Who knew what tomorrow would bring?" Joey enjoyed the song's melody and kicky percussion playing in his head. He thought about it. Really, did anyone know what the future held?

He would have kept mouthing the words, but Saint Signore reminded him to stay on task. "That top box is perfect for our mission."

Joey took a fresh pair of latex gloves out of his pocket and slid them on. *Like a doctor ready for surger*y, he thought. Then he lifted the box's lid, extracted a pair of Moni's black pumps, and tossed them into the shadows in the back of the closet. They didn't thud onto the wooden floor but instead landed on something soft, then slid off to the side.

"Better check it out," Saint Signore said.

Using two squares of Kleenex to protect his clothing, Joey kneeled down, peeked around the shoeboxes to stare into the darkness, and spotted a zippered deposit bag.

"It looks like Mona Lisa's stealing money from the restaurant," Saint Signore said.

Joey couldn't imagine another explanation. "Now what should I do?"

CHAPTER TWENTY
Cliff

Wearing an old Hardwick's Swap Shop T-shirt and boxers, Cliff sat in bed, wishing he had a good but soothing book to read. He couldn't watch TV without disturbing Panda.

Bill had suggested Cliff pray for those who'd hurt him, but Cliff couldn't bring himself to ask God to bless Janette. Why should she get everything she wanted when Cliff's world had been ripped apart? He'd lost his wife, his home, his relationship with his daughter, and half his friends, who'd sided with Janette - she'd poisoned their minds with lies about him. He had good reason to hate her. And Dennis was a regular jerk who sported a suntan year-round and clung to his University of Washington Huskies football fame. According to Janette, fans still stopped him on the street to reminisce about the good old days. Cliff knew this shouldn't bother him since he himself had played football in high school. But he hadn't made the cut at Washington State, Janette's and his alma mater.

Feeling a twinge of guilt for his snarly attitude, Cliff slipped under the covers. How could he pray when his heart was filled with antagonism and worry? Whole nations suffered from the ache of poverty, and here he was, full stomach, a roof over his head, and his daughter in the next room doing homework, her books and papers strewn across the table.

Cliff had offered to help her with her math, but she'd rolled her eyes, like he was too dumb. At one time, he'd been good at algebra and geometry, but he guessed he wouldn't know how to use her new-fangled calculator, with its rows of foreign buttons that made no sense. He hoped Panda wasn't lagging behind on her homework. Why did Mr. Patterson want to speak to Cliff? He dreaded the meeting. How would he get everything done tomorrow? He should write a priority list. First, make Panda breakfast. Waffles. No, he didn't own a waffle maker anymore. The one he'd bought years ago was at Janette's. Pancakes then. He'd fix Panda breakfast, take her to school, rush to the kitchen remodel, return to school to speak to Mr. Patterson at ten o'clock, then go back to the remodel.

His head sank into the warmth of his pillow, and he dozed off in spite of his well-lit room. The next thing he knew, it was midnight. He'd napped for two hours. He could hear the TV on in the living room. Panda wasn't supposed to watch anything until after her homework was done. And she'd promised to turn in by eleven.

He got out of bed, thrust his arms into his bathrobe, and cinched it at the waist. In the living room, he found Panda sleeping sprawled out on the couch. Asleep, her angular features had softened, her lips parted slightly, and her razor-cut bangs fell to the side like strands of silk thread.

He flicked off the TV and slid his hands under her sleeping body. She wasn't too heavy for him to carry. When she was in this serene dreamland state, he was strong enough for both of them. He recalled her as a little girl, before adolescence set in and before the divorce. His thoughts traveled back to her birth, the day he thought his heart would burst with joy. He'd never experienced such glorious elation. He'd brought a stuffed panda bear to the hospital and set it in their new daughter's temporary plastic bassinet. "We'll name her Patricia Ann, after my mother and aunt," Janette had declared from her hospital bed. "Cliff had disliked Pat, his mother-in-law, but was too content to protest their daughter's name. And he'd hoped this peace offering would gain his mother-in-law's approval. No such luck.

When Patricia Ann was three years old, Cliff had called her Panda while she and her other teddy bears (brown, black, polar - only one panda) were listening to "Teddy Bears' Picnic" on her cassette player. She'd been delighted with the nickname and after that refused to answer to her real name - by him anyway. He wondered where Mr. Panda was now. The stuffed animal had remained her favorite toy for the next ten years. She'd cuddled into bed with her furry friend at night and insisted on bringing him on family trips and overnights, much to Janette's consternation.

If only there was a way to turn time back onto itself. Would he want to be younger again? Sure, he'd make better choices. But if he'd married a woman other than Janette, he wouldn't have his beloved daughter. There was no way to win.

Cliff lifted and transported Panda into her room with care so her toes didn't bump the doorway. He wished he could relax half as well.

As he trudged back to his own bedroom and nestled under the covers, he mulled over the following day and questioned his inviting Mona Lisa to the high school reunion meeting had been a good idea. Well, if Cliff's scheme fell through, she could help entertain Panda. With Panda there, he'd be less likely to drink - still a temptation when hanging out with his old friends. He pictured Mona Lisa and Panda sitting at the table in the restaurant. Panda doing homework, and Mona Lisa being attentive to her needs while he caught up with his buddies. Should Janette's friend Cindy show up, it would look like Cliff had a date. Mona Lisa wasn't bad looking. In fact, over the years, she'd become quite beautiful—the way an immature peach might ripen into a mouth-watering piece of fruit. Not to mention, she could pass for a younger version of Barbara Buttaro, who was still a head-turner.

Mona Lisa had hesitated when he invited her to the meeting. "It'll give us time to talk about your mother's house," he'd told her.

The sound of footsteps padding through his apartment woke

him. He dragged himself to a sitting position, opened his eyes, and made out Panda's ghost-like shape, pausing at his doorway. He'd left his door ajar and a nightlight on in the hall.

"Panda. Are you okay?"

She made no notice of him. Gracefully, like a pirouetting dancer, she turned on her heel and floated toward the kitchen.

His heart racing, he sprang from his bed and followed her past the table, where her homework still lay in a chaotic heap. He rounded the corner in time to see her opening the door to the cupboard above the sink. He knew from experience that she was sound asleep and not responsible for her actions.

"Baby, wake up." He came to stand beside her, wrapping his arm around her bird-like shoulder. Her muscles tensed slightly, but she didn't look in his direction. Her eyes were hollow voids, staring straight ahead. She'd told him she'd outgrown sleepwalking, but obviously that wasn't true. Or maybe she honestly thought she had. Why didn't Janette mention she still walked in her sleep? He felt like calling her and giving her a piece of his mind, but when Panda had tried to contact her earlier no one answered. Panda had left a message, but so far Janette hadn't responded.

"Can you hear me, Panda?" He wished he could better understand her, that he could step into her dreamscape and become part of her dream.

Like a zombie, she moved to the refrigerator and opened the freezer drawer, where the two ice cream cartons they'd purchased several hours ago lay. The frigid air drifted out, surrounding them. Cliff was relieved. All she wanted was dessert. He was tempted to wake her and share a bowl of chocolate chip cookie dough ice cream, but they both needed sleep. He pushed the drawer closed and said, "We can have ice cream for breakfast, if you like. Right now, let's get you back in bed, okay?" He sensed she couldn't hear him, or was she faking?

Finally, her mouth moved. "Joey," she whispered in a slurred voice.

His head snapped around. "Did you say Joey?" His question

hung in the air between them. "Joey Buttaro?" Was she dreaming about Mona Lisa's oddball brother?

He took Panda's hand and led her back to her bedroom. He didn't dare leave her alone again.

CHAPTER TWENTY-ONE
Mona Lisa

As I neared the University Bridge heading south, I heard the clanging warning bell up ahead, then saw the crossing barriers lower. Drat. Several vehicles in front of me slowed to a stop. Only minutes ago, I'd rechecked the dashboard to make sure I had enough gas and then checked the oil pressure gauge. I had a premonition - something was going to go wrong.

I saw the mast of a tall sailboat coming into view. My thoughts spun ahead. Why was I going to this reunion meeting? As if I cared when, where, or how the gathering took place. What was Cliff's motive for inviting me, the girl who'd floated invisibly through the halls of our high school? Well, at least I didn't have to worry about running into an old flame the way Cliff did, because my one boyfriend - a three-month fling that never went beyond kissing and holding hands - had attended another high school. I rather hoped Cliff's ex-wife, Janette, would be there tonight. I knew I was being mean-spirited, wanting to see Cliff squirm with discomfort. He'd mentioned he was bringing Panda - oh joy, I'd get to see his obnoxious daughter again. I pictured the grumpy teenager with a swatch of green hair sitting smugly between her uncomfortable parents, once called the cutest couple in our high school yearbook.

I was tired after working at Booty's all day. I bet I'd walked five miles - distance of circling Green Lake twice on foot.

My day had started off wrong. My intention had been to make yesterday's deposit on my way to work, but I'd forgotten about the cash bag hidden in the back of my closet and would need to deal with it tomorrow. The rest of the day had gone smoothly. Annie was still out with the flu, and Joey filled in for her again. With my prodding, he'd improved somewhat. After arguing with himself - did he have a make-believe friend? - he sporadically cleared tables and took around coffee. Now if I could just get him to remove his latex gloves and shower cap and smile at customers, or at least make eye contact.

I glanced to my right, up to the towering freeway, and wished I'd taken it across to Capitol Hill so I could see if Joey were panhandling at the entrance on NE Forty-Fifth Street, the way Cliff had claimed. Joey wasn't home when I left. Where did he spend his time? I remembered the James Thurber book, later made into a Danny Kay movie, *The Secret Life of Walter Mitty*. I imagined the title *The Secret Life of Joey Buttaro* -a screenplay I'd write on a movie theater's marquee. Growing up, Joey's whereabouts and erratic behavior had been taboo topics in our household, with Mama always defending him or Papa discounting my concerns.

I tried to remember when Joey stopped appearing at the dinner table and felt a spike of exasperation at my parents for never discussing his decline, which was steady and forceful like the tide rushing in, bringing with it driftwood and trash.

Joey collected matchbooks as a kid - nothing unusual. But later on, when I was in college and he was in high school, I'd come home to use the washing machine. I glanced into his room and saw thousands of matchboxes heaped in one corner. I called Mama, who stood around the corner by the basement door sorting laundry, and asked if Joey had hoofed around to every restaurant in Seattle collecting them, but she wouldn't come look. I stepped into his room to see that his desk was buried under a mountain of papers - candy wrappers, receipts, used envelopes - many had fallen to the floor between the desk and wall. And under his bed lay dozens of crumpled plastic bags. Although Mama would never admit it, her prayers for Joey had never helped him crawl out of his quagmire; he'd only sunk deeper since then.

The bridge began to lower and the vehicles in front of me rolled ahead a few feet. Moments later, the crossing barriers lifted, and I was propelled forward by the long line of cars that had accumulated behind me. I crossed the bridge and saw Duke's ahead on the right-hand side. A cheeseburger and fries sounded good. Having worked all day at Booty's, I hadn't eaten a decent meal - only coffee and a cup of minestrone soup while standing at the counter. After speaking to our accountant on the phone this morning, I concluded we couldn't afford to hire a replacement for Annie when she left permanently, not if we were paying Joey minimum wage. Which was more important? Socializing and training my little brother so he could eventually find a job and support himself, or whipping the restaurant into shape to sell it?

I glanced into the parking lot. It looked full. That moment, a car pulled out, giving me a spot near the front door. I should be grateful. I spent too much energy griping and worrying.

I ventured through the restaurant's front door. The aroma of grilled meats, fish, and sautéing onions filled my nostrils. Peering past the hostess, I saw Cliff, his back to me, sitting with two women and three men at a table for six. The crowded room vibrated with conversation and the clanking plates; busy waiters carrying trays of drinks and food zigzagged between the tables. Out the windows I could see boats on Union Bay. It was a beautiful sight, but what was I doing here? Why would Cliff want my input? I had zero interest in the high school reunion.

The hostess stood by the podium. "How many, ma'am?"

"I'm meeting some people. Or do you make to-go orders? I could smuggle a burger and fries home and relax in front of the TV instead."

The hostess smirked. "I'd join you if I could. My feet are killing me." She handed me a menu, then greeted a couple coming in the door. "I can seat you in ten minutes," she told them.

I stepped to the side and scanned the extensive menu.

Because Cliff and Thomas had finally showed up to work at Mama's house this morning didn't mean I owed Cliff an appearance here, although he'd mentioned one of the men coming tonight worked at a business brokerage. I needed to find a pro to list Booty's and didn't want to take a chance with the realtor I'd chosen to handle Mama's house. She was a nice woman but she'd admitted she knew nothing about selling restaurants.

As I stood pondering my options, Cliff's head turned, and he waved at me. He got to his feet and wove his way across the room. The hostess smiled brightly as he approached, as if she were hoping to snag his attention, making me reappraise his appearance. Tall and wide shouldered with strong features, he was ruggedly handsome in a way most women find irresistible. And he was a capable workman. Papa would have liked him.

I closed the menu and held it in front of me like a shield. Why would I think Cliff or any other man would choose me over a cutie like this darling young hostess? A better question was, why was I wasting gray matter contemplating something I didn't want?

"You made it." Cliff took my elbow. Maybe he sensed I was ready to scram out the door.

"Sorry I'm late, I got stuck on the other side of the bridge."

"That's okay. I'm glad you're here."

Why? This was his turf, his friends, and his gig. Cliff placed his hand on the small of my back like he was guiding a child in the right direction toward his table. I got a dizzying sensation, like I was stepping into someone else's history. He'd mentioned he and his clique had hung out here, but I never did.

Slowing, I turned my head. "Where's Panda?"

"At my apartment. My landlady offered to look in on her. Panda has a history paper due tomorrow. She'll be fine. I hope." His mouth tightened and his lips pressed together.

As we closed in on the table, I heard laughter from my five former schoolmates, the nucleus of the popular crowd at our large high school. I recognized the bad boy, Bernie, had been a goof-off and sat next to me in science class my sophomore year. With him sat homecoming queen Cindy, once Janette's best girlfriend, and Deidre, also in their tight circle. Bernie, TR, and Chick. I imagined they were laughing at my arrival, trying to figure out what to say to me. But that was paranoid, immature thinking. We were all adults now, playing on a level field. Still, I felt heat rising up my neck and my cheeks reddening.

When we reached the table, Cliff announced in a loud voice that brought their conversation to a halt, "Everyone know Mona Lisa Buttaro?"

"The mysterious Mona Lisa?" Bernie Goldman said, half standing. Mysterious? Was that a politically correct way of saying I was shy in high school? In our senior year, Bernie and my lockers stood next to each other, but he rarely acknowledged me. "How've you been?" he asked.

"Fine." I figured he didn't want a blow-by-blow description of the last twenty years, or even the shortened version.

He looked me over and nodded his head in approval. "You're looking good."

"Thanks." I was wearing my favorite size eight petite black slacks. When pulling them on earlier, I'd noticed they hung looser. Working at Booty's had trimmed my thighs and waistline. I also wore a fitted jacket and a jewel-neck sweater that flattered my neck and shoulders. I hoped I didn't look like I'd spent too much time fussing with my appearance. In fact, I'd tried on half a dozen outfits, hoping to get a thrown-together-at-the-last-minute look and even fluffed my shoulder-length hair so it would seem casually tousled.

I noticed Bernie had gained some twenty pounds since high school, and his dark, curly hair was trimmed shorter, maybe to camouflage a receding hairline. He reached behind us to take hold of a vacant chair from a nearby table and squeezed it between his and Cliff's.

On the other side of Cliff sat TR Wincheimer, who stared at me blankly. "I can't quite remember you." No surprise there.

"Her folks put on the spaghetti feed," Cliff informed him. "The fundraiser."

"Oh, yeah," TR said. "I remember, sort of."

"Her parents saved the day," Cliff said. "Without their help, the dinner would have been a bust."

I lowered myself and walked my chair in. "They enjoyed themselves."

The menu on my lap, I shrugged off my jacket and draped it over the back of my chair. In truth, my folks had had the time of their lives, but there'd never been another reason for them to become involved with school activities. Neither Joey nor I played a sport. Our parents would have loved cheering from the sidelines and bringing snacks for halftime. My main interest in my teens - what my folks called a hobby - was photography, a solo pastime. It consisted of stealthily moving around snapping candid shots of others having fun or setting up my tripod to capture fleeting sunsets and then immersing myself for hours in the dark room.

A waitress swished over to take my drink order, a Diet Coke, and refill Cliff's 7UP at the same time. He must not drink alcohol anymore? That surprised me - he was a heavy consumer in high school. Not that I didn't take nips from my parents' open bottles of Chianti, and once my girlfriend Sally and I made ourselves sick on rum and lemonade, a combination that still made my stomach lurch when I thought about it. She'd provided the rum and I brought the pink lemonade. We'd snuck off to the park for an evening of drunken hilarity, followed by gut-wrenching vomiting. Maybe it was a blessing; I never overindulged again. Moderation in all things, Papa would say. But playing it safe was boring.

I scanned the rectangle table and saw the others were either nursing a beer or a mixed drink.

"Long time, no see." Cindy Fenning spoke to me from across the table, the first words she'd ever uttered in my direction. Over the years, I'd seen her beautiful self at the grocery store, but she'd always glided her cart right past me without a show of recognition. She wore her Ann-Margret red hair pretty much as she had in high school, and the same frosted-green shadow echoed her round eyes.

Next to her sat Deidre Elstrom, older but still looking like a Nordic princess, her creamy blonde hair swept back into a meticulous French roll. No wedding ring.

Next to Deidre sat Chick O'Day, former class president and all-around jock - what we called a stud back in school. His tie was loosened and his notched collar open. He must have come from his downtown office, clad in a navy-blue suit. An attorney? He was still alluring with a full head of sandy-colored hair, and a great physique judging from the way his shoulders filled his suit jacket. I recalled going to stupendous lengths to sit next to him and Cliff in assemblies and at lunch, but they'd ignored me.

One of the many things I'd learned while entertaining guests at Booty's was how to feel at home in restaurants talking to strangers, or at least how to fake it, so I fell into my workday routine: a fabricated show of warmth. "Nice to see you, Cindy. And Deidre. Hi, Chick. Good to see you."

"Hey, Mona Lisa," Chick said. "How's life been treating you?" His smile seemed genuine - or was he also in his at-work mode? He'd probably just learned my name from Cliff. I wondered what Chick saw when he looked at me. Did I still look like an insecure little nobody? I remembered an Eleanor Roosevelt quote, "No one can make you feel inferior without your consent." Well, I refused to give my consent, and yet I felt a tug-of-war going on inside of me.

"Couldn't be better." I forced enthusiasm into my voice. "Say, I hear one of you is in commercial real estate." I wanted to get the conversation rolling in a different direction so they wouldn't quiz me about my nonexistent husband, my nonexistent kids, and my nonexistent career.

At the words *commercial real estate*, TR's face came alive. "That would be me." He reached into his bulky wallet, produced a business card, and thrust it into my hand. He was a tall fellow whose face had softened over the years. But could I trust selling the restaurant through a man who still went by his initials? I surveyed his card and read Torrance Randall Wincheimer III.

Okay, I understood why his friends dubbed him TR; I didn't need to be judgmental. Didn't Theodore Roosevelt use his initials?

"I'll call you," I said, and his brows lifted. "To talk about a possible listing," I said.

"You bet, any time." He jimmied his wallet back into his jeans' pocket, then took a sip of beer.

"We're all here," Chick said, like he was still president of the senior class. "Let's get this meeting in order and discuss our problem."

"We'd better fill Mona Lisa in," Deidre said, her gaze not quite fixing on mine. Did I have lipstick on my front teeth? I ran my tongue across them to make sure they were clean.

"We're having the reunion, Blast from the Past, with spouses on a Saturday night in October," Chick told me. "But our smaller Friday night get-together - graduates only - at the Blues Jazz Club fell through when a big-shot VIP requested it for a private party, so the club bumped us."

"If someone had sent in our deposit like they were supposed to…" Cliff said, turning to Bernie.

"Hey." Bernie held his hands up like someone was aiming a gun on him. "No one gave me the money. TR was class treasurer." And they all turned to TR, who shrugged.

"That was twenty years ago. I thought Chick was handling the deposit," he said, but Chick shook his head.

"Well, it's too late now." Cindy took a quick sip of her drink - something with orange juice - a screwdriver? - leaving pink lipstick on the straw. "We have a crisis that needs a solution. Let's put our heads together and fix it."

"Mona Lisa owns a restaurant, right?" Bernie said. He looked at me expectantly. "We could have the graduates-only get-together at her place and save a bundle."

Deidre nodded. "Fabulous idea." She smoothed her coif, not that a hair was out of place.

I felt anger biting into me as I realized why I'd been invited tonight. Cliff must have suggested Booty's as a location for the party, at my expense.

I pictured Booty's interior. "It isn't big enough." I glared at Cliff, who looked away, proving to me he was guilty.

"Sure it is." Chick sipped his beer. "Booty's Café? With the boot-shaped sign?" He'd been there? Or was he going by Cliff's description?

"Friday night is for graduates only," TR said. "We're not expecting a big crowd. No spouses. Except Cliff's ex." He elbowed Cliff, who stiffened. "Cliff's the only one I know who married his high school sweetheart."

"Thanks for the reminder." Cliff scowled. "As a matter of fact, Janette just remarried or is about to. Hey, can we stick to the subject?"

I felt sorry for Cliff's being the brunt of TR's ribbing, then I remembered Cliff was in on the plot to use the restaurant.

A waitress glided over to the table and set down a platter of nachos. Apparently, they'd ordered before my arrival. I was tempted to ask the waitress to bring me a salad, but she'd already moved away to help other customers. And I wanted to keep this meeting short.

I placed the menu on the floor between Cliff's and my chairs, but it fell forward under the table. I stretched my arm down to retrieve it and noticed Cindy had slipped off her loafers—her big toe was massaging TR's ankle!

As I sat up straight again, TR's hand shot out, and he dragged a chip through the melted cheese, like nothing unusual was happening. "This looks good." He bit into a mouthful. "Yummy. Delicious."

"Back to Booty's," Cindy said nonchalantly. "How about we put on a spaghetti dinner like the good old days?"

Those days weren't all that good for me. And the spaghetti dinner had been a massive undertaking. No one here at the table had lifted a finger that night; they'd waltzed out the door after dessert and headed for a kegger without helping with the cleanup or inviting me. Then later, they'd taken all the credit for the money earned.

I had to stifle this foolishness. "Booty's serves mostly soup and salad," I said. "We don't even make pasta."

"Throwing spaghetti together is a cinch." Cindy tapped her acrylic nails on the table. She had beautiful hands - the opposite of mine, thanks to my scrubbing them throughout the day at Booty's. "All you need is hot water, noodles, and marinara sauce," she said.

Deidre's grin showed two rows of pearly teeth only an orthodontist could create. "And a Caesar salad and cheesecake for dessert. Or better yet, tiramisu." She didn't mention who would buy the ingredients and spend days in preparation, let alone who would serve and clear the tables.

The thought of tiramisu - Mama's recipe - melting in my mouth made me salivate. But I needed to stay on track. "Cliff said the reunion's in October. Sorry to disappoint everyone, but we might not even own the restaurant in the fall."

"Sell Booty's?" TR rubbed his hands together. "Restaurants are my specialty."

"So I hear. But please keep this to yourself, everyone. I don't want our customers to catch wind of it yet."

"Finding a buyer could take months," TR said. "If we hook a live one, we can write the reunion party into the sales contract, if you choose to list the restaurant with me. I can give you plenty of references. I'll do a good job for you."

The waitress removed Cindy's empty glass and replaced it with a fresh drink. Cindy took a long sip. "I've got a thought," she said. "let's ask Mona Lisa's parents to put on the spaghetti dinner."

My chest tightened. I missed Papa every day since his passing and resented having to speak about his death with people who wanted only to exploit me.

Cliff saved me from having to explain. "Mona's father passed away years ago." My gratitude was short-lived because he went on to say, "But her mother might supervise the dinner."

How dare he? My hands balled into fists, and my frustration set to explode. "Mama lives in a retirement home because she fell and hurt her knee."

"Sorry to hear that," Cliff said. "But when I saw her the other day, she seemed fine - the picture of health. She might enjoy it." Cliff was an expert on old people? He should ask his own mother, not mine.

I turned in my chair to face him. "I think I know Mama better than you do. She's not up to it. And as I said, Booty's is only open for lunch."

"It's a nice little restaurant," Cliff said, glancing at Deidre and then Cindy. Maybe he was trying to flatter me, but his tactic wasn't working. He hadn't bothered to mention our unique paninis or tasty soups of the day.

"Hey, gang, let's all meet at Booty's for lunch tomorrow." Cindy stirred the few remaining ice chips at the bottom of her glass with her straw. "Wouldn't that be fun? Can everyone make it?"

My mouth dropped open. The last thing I wanted were the popular kids - I couldn't help thinking of them that way - seeing me behind the register wearing my white apron. Or getting an eyeful of Joey. That would give them plenty to talk about behind my back.

"Fabulous idea," TR said, and I could see Cindy's knee move, her foot no doubt fondling his under the table. They were both wearing wedding bands. Had I missed something? Were they married to each other? They'd dated in high school, but I'd heard they went their separate ways.

Chick pulled out his iPhone. "My calendar looks free."

"Then it's all agreed." Cindy batted her eyelashes in TR's direction. "We meet at Booty's for lunch tomorrow."

"I'll be there," TR said, and I let out a sigh.

CHAPTER TWENTY-TWO
Cliff

Watching the waitress deliver martinis to the couple at the next table, Cliff raked his hand through his hair. His palm was sweaty, and the top of his head blazed with heat. He could barely fill his lungs with air. His chest felt tight, like a sheet of wet leather left out in the sun to shrink. Bill Swanson would tell Cliff to leave the restaurant immediately before he did something stupid that would send him spiraling down into a cesspool.

Cliff folded his napkin and set it on the table. All evening, he'd tried to appear as if he were having fun without a drink in his hand. Snacking on nachos, he'd watched Chick, Bernie, and TR sip beer, frothy rivers of liquid gold disappearing between their lips. Cindy was discreetly nursing her third screwdriver and Deidre her second margarita. Cliff ran his tongue over his upper lip; he could practically taste the salty rim, the lime, and the tequila.

The restaurant's sound system was playing oldies, which seemed appropriate for the reunion meeting. Cliff recognized singer-songwriter Jim Morrison of the Doors crooning "Light My Fire." The words were muffled below the din of conversation from nearby tables, the clatter of knives and forks, the chink of glasses, but he knew the song by heart. When Cliff was a kid, his mother played the Doors over and over. "Jim Morrison died at age twenty-seven," she'd explained. "What a waste."

Cliff sat back in his chair and crossed his legs at the ankle. Isn't that what Cliff himself had done? Wasted his life?

Another Jim Morrison piece, "Riders on the Storm," started looping through his brain. As a young man, Cliff had sung along to it hundreds of times without analyzing or weighing its message. "His brain is squirmin' like a toad." Cliff could relate. He felt a flood of guilt for his past. He wasn't a murderer, thank the Lord, but he could have been charged with negligent homicide six years ago when he got plastered and piled his pickup into a Toyota Camry, sending an old woman to the hospital for a month. He'd gotten lucky; the lady, in her eighties, wasn't wearing her glasses and suffered from memory problems, and her family hadn't pressed charges. The first cop to arrive at the accident scene was Cliff's former schoolmate Tom Mahoney, who'd neglected to give Cliff a Breathalyzer test and, in his notes, indicated the old woman was driving erratically. Which could be true for all Cliff knew.

He glanced to his right at Mona Lisa, who looked miserable. Did he detect hostility? The corners of her mouth had curved downward ever since Booty's was brought up as a possible site for the Friday night grads-only party. She'd barely touched the nachos or her Diet Coke; the ice was melting, leaving a puddle of water at the top of her glass. If she didn't like soft drinks, why hadn't she ordered wine? Did she have a drinking problem too?

Mona Lisa crossed her arms, which Cliff took to be a defensive gesture. Did she feel as excluded as he did, even though he'd hung out countless times with everyone at the table? Bernie, Chick, and TR had been like brothers and comrades since elementary school, but they didn't know the real him.

Cliff had floated through almost two victorious years without even wanting a drink and had wondered if he really was an alcoholic after all. He bet he could handle just one—a mug of beer or a glass of white wine. It would be like reuniting with a lost love who would treat him better than Janette ever did.

What was he thinking? Bill Swanson would come unglued if

139

he heard Cliff in denial. But Bill had moved to Arizona last year, and Cliff had never sought a replacement. He could call the guy. He still had Bill's number on his cell phone. But he already knew what Bill would say, "Get your butt to an AA meeting, right now." Bill had once told him addiction was unresolved grief and that the only power that could lift it was God. Cliff should admit he was powerless by himself.

TR spoke, his words sliding together and his lips getting sloppy. "Remember the night we got that old codger to buy us a case of Bud at Mini Market and we never paid him?"

Bernie slapped his knee. "Yeah. He asked us for thirty bucks, but Cliff told him we'd already paid and the old man believed him."

Cliff smiled, although he wasn't proud of his antics anymore. He could feel Mona Lisa's disapproving stare cut into him. "That was a long time ago," he said. "When I was young and foolish."

"You're a wise old man now?" Bernie smirked.

"I don't know how wise I am, but you got the old part right," Cliff said. Everyone laughed. Even Mona Lisa, but Cliff couldn't tell if she was amused or just being polite. He felt like a jerk for bringing her here tonight. He should have mentioned the party idea earlier but was afraid she wouldn't come.

"Let's call this meeting to an end," Chick said. "Or should we order dinner?"

"No, it's late. I've got to go," Cliff said.

"Me too." Mona Lisa pushed one arm, then the other into her jacket sleeves.

TR checked his watch. "It's only seven thirty. You two have a curfew?"

Bernie said, "In high school, Cliff's mother never cared when he got home, you lucky dog." Like Cliff's mother's lack of concern was a precious gift. He knew better; his mother wanted privacy.

"I've got my daughter staying with me this week." Cliff needed fresh air. Solitude. But in this topsy-turvy state, did he trust himself to be alone?

"Don't go yet," Deidre told him, reaching across the table and placing her hand on his arm, which seemed like a flirtatious act. "Have something to drink."

Cliff pulled his hand back to the chair's armrest. He was miffed at her for tempting him, but he shouldn't be. Other than Bernie, none of them knew about his struggle to maintain sobriety. How would they? Two years ago, one of his assignments had been to admit to everyone he knew that he was an out-of-control alcoholic, but he figured, why make his friends feel guilty for enjoying themselves?

"How old is your daughter?" Deidre massaged her shoulder, her fingers dipping below the neckline of her sweater.

"Fourteen. Her name's Patricia Ann. But everyone calls her Panda."

"How darling." Cindy aimed her gaze at Cliff. "I bet she's cute."

"Do you have a photo of her on your phone?" Deidre asked.

"Yes, but it was taken years ago." Back when she still smiled at the camera. "She doesn't even look like the same person."

"Bring a recent photo tomorrow to lunch, okay?" Deidre's words came out seductively, like she and Cliff were alone. They had never dated in high school, except that one hot and heavy evening when he and Janette had a spat. He'd never liked being without a girlfriend - what he now saw as neediness and a fear of being alone.

"Panda hates having her picture taken." Cliff walked his chair back from the table. "Last year, she refused to be in her school annual."

"Take one with your cell phone when she's not looking," Cindy suggested. "That's what I do."

"Boys are so much easier," Bernie said. "I should know, I have three of them."

Deidre spoke to Mona Lisa. "How many children do you have?"

Mona Lisa's eyes went blank, and she blinked twice. "None, and I've never been married." She shot to her feet and pushed her chair flush against the table. "I should go."

"Do you need a ride home?" Chick asked. That wolf in sheep's clothing was making a play for her. Over the years, Mona Lisa had matured into a real beauty - a duckling that became an elegant swan. No, she'd never been a duckling, just aloof and indifferent.

"No thanks." She sounded weary. "I have my car."

"I'll walk you out," Chick told her. "It's dark."

Cliff had been so preoccupied that he hadn't noticed the sky turning black. "No, I'll do it. I'm on my way out too." He felt protective of Mona Lisa. In high school, Chick left a string of broken hearts. He'd been married twice but was single again. And she seemed vulnerable - an easy target. Cliff said, "Mona Lisa and I have things to discuss about her mother's house."

"Spoilsport." Chick winked. "But I'll get another chance tomorrow at lunch."

CHAPTER TWENTY-THREE
Mona Lisa

Outside of Duke's, the air hung heavy with moisture from a recent shower. Wandering into the parking lot, Cliff and I approached my Honda, with its door dings and dent in the rear fender - a gift from a fellow shopper at Safeway. My nine-year-old automobile looked like a beater compared to Cliff's sleek Porsche 911, parked several cars ahead of mine. My backseat lay hidden under a jumble of cardboard boxes I was bringing home to use for packing and newspapers were sprawled out on the passenger seat. I hoped he didn't think I was a slob, not that it was any of his business.

A year ago, I would have called anyone predicting that Cliff and I would be spending time together crazy. How had our paths crossed and grown knotted together? As soon as Thomas finished working on Mama's house - he'd painted her bedroom today and would start on the bathroom tomorrow - and the restaurant sold, there would be no earthly reason for Cliff and me to see each other again.

Standing close by, Cliff shifted his weight, waiting for me to unlock my car so he could be on his way. Under the streetlamps, his face looked distorted, his brows shadowing his eyes, his nose elongated, and his mouth sunken. How had I ever found him attractive? He rubbed his hands together. The temperature had dropped, typical of Seattle in the spring. Chilly air was sneaking up my sleeves, but I could feel the heat of anger escaping around my collar.

"Thanks for coming tonight." His words sounded hollow and meaningless. I didn't have the energy to play his head games. At least one question had been answered. I would not attend the reunion party at Booty's or anywhere. If I wanted to get in touch with my old girlfriend Sally, I could look up her number and make a date to get together. I bet Sally, never in with the crowd, wouldn't go to the reunion either.

I dug into my purse, past old receipts, my wallet, and a half-eaten chocolate bar, and fished out my keychain. My car key, Mama's front door key, my apartment key, and Booty's keys were a wad of jingly metal, heavy in my hand. In my foul mood, I felt like hurling them at Cliff's chest, but I never could throw. I imagined missing my target - the keys flipping into the curb and disappearing down the storm drain. Wouldn't that be the pièce de résistance to an imperfect evening?

"Mona Lisa, I'm sorry," Cliff said, drawing me into a conversation.

"For dragging your feet on finishing my mother's house? Or for tricking me into coming tonight?" A pickup approached, headed north, barreling toward the bridge. Cliff moved up against my Honda, invading my space. I had to raise my chin to speak to him. "You and your school chums are trying to use me." My voice sounded hostile.

"You're right," he said. "I should have warned you. It wasn't fair."

"And the spaghetti dinner? How dare you suggest Mama do the bulk of the work?" I remembered Cindy and TR playing footsie under the table. The whole evening had been unreal, a bad dream. "Hey, Cliff, I've got an idea." I exaggerated my soprano voice to sound like phony-baloney Cindy. "Let's call your mother and ask her to put on a spaghetti feed at her house."

"That wouldn't work. Loretta can't even boil eggs."

"You call your mother by her first name?"

"Yeah. She always made me, so people would think she was

younger." He ran a hand through his thick hair, leaving tracks. "And as far as having a get-together at her house, it's a dump."

I was surprised at his candor, if indeed he was being straight with me. Why would he suddenly start telling me the truth?

As I unlocked my car, I relived my humiliation upon entering the restaurant and meeting the exclusive, popular crowd. "I can practically guarantee that Cindy, Deidre, Bernie, TR, and Chick didn't have a clue who I was."

"I bet they did, because of your unusual name. You still look like da Vinci's painting—that unreadable half-smile of yours. And Chick seemed eager to get to know you better."

I guessed Chick and I would be in the sack right now if I'd given him the okay. "He was looking for a one-night quickie," I said. "Should I be flattered?"

"Sorry if he came on too strong." Cliff lingered, not making a move to leave. "TR seemed interested in seeing Booty's."

I shrugged. "He's a realtor hungry for a new listing."

"Well, they all remembered your parents."

I gave him Mama's piercing *look,* the one she used on Joey and me when we weren't being straight with her. "Big deal," I said, "everyone loved my folks."

"Do you want me to tell the committee not to come in for lunch tomorrow?"

"No, it's fine. We can use the business. They'll see for themselves that the space is too small and that will be the end of it. And TR can give the place a once-over. I do need a realtor, but I'm going to check his references like I would anyone else's."

Cliff stroked his square jawline. "If I don't make it tomorrow for lunch, it's because I'm finishing up a kitchen project."

"Hey, give me a break." My hand moved to my hips. "No way you're throwing me into the pool of piranhas without showing up yourself." I sounded like Mama when she'd grounded me for two weeks in high school for sneaking over to Sally's when her parents were out of town.

"Come on," he said, "they're not that awful. I'm behind at

work. Today, I had to drive Panda to school, then turn around midmorning and go back to meet with Mr. Patterson, the middle school director."

He was changing the subject, but my curiosity was tweaked. What had the little imp done? "A command performance?" I imagined her starting a fire in a wastebasket.

"According to Patterson, Panda is 'lippy and impertinent' with her teachers."

In spite of his solemn expression, I couldn't help grinning because that's how she'd acted around me. She was a lippy, impertinent brat.

"But the meeting wasn't all bad," he said. "Mr. Patterson said she's very creative and has potential if she'd turn in her homework."

"Maybe she needs a tutor," I suggested without the slightest idea what I was talking about. As a kid, I would have done anything to gain my parents' approval and graduated from junior high and high school with almost straight As. Like a parrot, I became a master at taking tests and repeating what my teachers taught.

"Mr. Patterson claims Panda should ask her instructors for assistance at lunch or after school. I pay them enough - as much as sending her to college. They should help her."

I pitied her poor teachers. But maybe it was Cliff's fault his daughter had spun out of control. What kind of father was he? He'd divorced Panda's mother. For another woman? Except for Papa, most men I'd met were users and manipulators. Even lovable, benevolent Uncle Vito had ulterior motives - to move me back to Italy in order to marry me off to his aged friend.

"Panda's waiting for me now." Cliff stepped toward his car. Then he turned, moved in on me, and, before I knew what was happening, gave me a clumsy hug.

Stupidly, I sank into his embrace but only because I was cold in my lightweight jacket and I hadn't felt a man's arms around me for too long. I didn't hug him back but stood there, absorbing his warmth, inhaling the aroma of his aftershave, and feeling the strength of his arms across my shoulders. The whooshing sounds of the nearby freeway quieted, and the street traffic vanished.

In the silence, I could hear Papa saying, "How dare he touch my daughter?"

Outrage took hold of me. Most likely, Cliff saw me as an easy target, like Chick had, a pathetic spinster who'd dole out her favors to any guy who gave her the slightest attention. When would a man treat me with the respect Papa had given Mama? I should demand Cliff take his mitts off me and slam him with a cutting remark, but none came to mind. Knowing me, I'd think of something clever on the ride home.

The restaurant's front door swung open. A woman coming outside tittered, and a man chuckled. I assumed they were from the reunion committee. Had they seen us? What would they think?

I gathered my strength, struggled out of Cliff's clasp, and pushed him away. As I did, I heard a sob erupt from his chest and catch in his throat. His arms fell away from me like lifeless appendages.

What was going on? I noticed his eyes were glassy. He couldn't be crying, could he? I remembered sometimes Papa's eyes turned moist when he spoke of the old country, which, for some reason, he refused to visit, or when he'd been laughing. But I never saw actual tears.

The man in front of me looked like he was attending a funeral for someone he didn't like. I saw in his face a mixture of grief and embarrassment.

"Cliff, what's wrong?" My words bulleted out, sounding harsher than I'd meant, because if he were suffering, my natural tendency was to help.

"Sorry," he said, "I don't know what came over me." Then he strode to his car, dove into it, and sped away, gunning his engine, leaving me in the parking lot.

Getting into my automobile, I relived the previous few moments. Had he really hugged me? Maybe, but it wasn't the romantic gesture I longed for.

147

CHAPTER TWENTY-FOUR
Joey

Joey reached under his bed and retrieved the greenish-gray cloth moneybag, which he'd encased in a transparent ziplock bag for cleanliness's sake.

"Why did you take the bag out of the shoebox?" Saint Signore scolded. "And why hide it under your bed? That's the first place Mona Lisa would think to look." The Saint had been in a prickly mood all afternoon, probably because Joey had disobeyed him.

Joey shrugged. "I needed the box for my new rock collection." Honey-colored angular chips of quartz he found on a gravel path. "And I think she's done emptying my room. If not under my bed, then where?" Joey asked out loud, because he was home alone, except for Figaro, who circled him, hoping for another snack. Minutes ago, Joey had fed him a can of Mama's fancy imported Italian tuna, and Figaro gobbled it down.

"Moni should be home any minute," Joey said, hinting that he needed the Saint's help. He still hadn't checked the bag's contents but figured it contained money and charge card receipts. Moni was a thief, no doubt about it. He was shocked she would pilfer Mama's retirement nest egg, but he didn't want his sister to land in jail either, which would upset Mama. Still, if Moni were incarcerated, Joey could continue living here.

"Figaro will warn us when Mona Lisa returns," Saint Signore said in Joey's head.

"Where should I hide this?" Joey rotated, scanning his childhood desk, the straight back chair, and his bureau.

"There are plenty of places in this house you've never thought to look."

"Like, where? I love hiding places." And fooling Moni.

"How about up in the attic?"

"Above Papa's study?" As children, he and Moni had speculated about what lurked in the dead space between the second-floor ceiling and the roof. "*Niente*," Papa had told them. "Nothing but dust, cobwebs, and insulation. Don't you dare go up there and make a mess."

"It's too high." Joey preferred to burrow low, imagining there was space beneath the basement, like the catacombs below Saint Peter's in Vatican City.

"You surprise me," Saint Signore said. "In all these years, you've never crawled up a ladder and pushed the attic's door aside. Aren't you curious?"

"Not really. Maybe there are rats living up there. Or a monster."

"No monsters—not there, anyway. *Allora, andiamo*, we'll go up to the second floor. At least take a look."

Holding the bag, Joey left his room and ascended the stairs to the first floor. With Figaro guarding his back, Joey entered the kitchen. He saw several pairs of his shoes sitting on a folded towel at the door where he always left them. He never wore street shoes in the house.

He looked the room over and considered possible hiding sites. In the bottom drawer behind the measuring cups and the hand mixer Moni never used, up on the highest shelf behind Mama's favorite teapot, or in the pot itself?

"Not there, its opening's too small," Saint Signore said. "You might break it."

Joey remembered its delicate gold and pink ornate pattern. "It was a gift to Mama from Papa. She treasures it."

"She would have taken it with her if she used it." Saint Signore let out a weary sigh. "It's pretty, but too rococo—too

149

flowery for my tastes. And from the British Isles Your papa should have found pottery made in Italy. He purchased it at a garage sale for a mere dollar." Saint Signore didn't approve of many of Papa's choices and sporadically dropped bombshells, telling Joey more than he wanted to know about his father.

Joey left the kitchen and made his way into the front hall. "How about behind the TV in the living room? Or behind the books in the bookcase?"

Saint Signore grumbled, indicating his irritation was escalating.

"*Andiamo*—up to the second floor. Get a move on it."

Joey shuffled up to Papa's study. Sure enough, on the ceiling and painted the color of the room to camouflage it, was the framed board. He felt his heartbeat quicken with excitement. Fear, really.

Saint Signore said, "You're in luck, Jo-Jo. The painter—young Thomas, not a bad fellow—I think he can be trusted—left a stepladder in your mama's room. Go get it."

"Okay." Joey headed to Mama's bedroom. He inflated his lungs and held his breath as he stepped into a toxic cloud of latex paint fumes. Once pink, the walls were now boring beige, which Moni said was more likely to attract typical buyers.

Wearing latex gloves, Joey carried the waist-high stepladder into Papa's study, then let his lungs expand. As he glanced up at the attic's opening, an alarming thought zinged through his mind, followed by a wave of panic. "Is that where Papa's ghost lives?"

"I can't believe what I'm hearing." Saint Signore's voice bristled with impatience. "When will you believe that your father is in heaven?"

"Are you sure he made it?"

"Yes. An example of how our most compassionate God forgives even the worst sinners when they confess and ask for forgiveness. *Capisci*? Do you understand?"

"I guess." But the words, *the sins of the father,* entered Joey's mind, and his shoulders experienced the burden of Papa's lies. "Did Papa confess before his death, or did he proudly hang tight to his deceit? He was a proud man, never asking for help, a man of few friends. A loner."

Saint Signore clucked. "Your papa fashioned his life that way on purpose, first leaving *Italia*, then Garlic Gulch, to avoid people who might correspond with family and friends back home who knew the truth."

Sins of the father zigzagged through Joey's brain like never-ending bootlaces. Joey knew he wasn't without transgressions himself. He'd lied to Moni hundreds of times. He'd lied to his teachers and to Papa often, and now it was too late to set things right, to admit to Papa that as a six-year-old, Joey had listened through his parents' bedroom door when they were arguing about a girl named Teresa. Later, Saint Signore confirmed what Joey learned that day: Teresa, five years older than Moni and living in Rome, was Joey and Moni's older half-sister, a love child, who shared their father's DNA but none of their advantages. Papa never mentioned her existence once. But Saint Signore said she was now in her late thirties.

The Saint was the only one Joey couldn't lie to. Saint Signore could detect falsehoods immediately, as if Joey were hooked up to a polygraph test.

"You always know what I'm thinking…" Joey said.

"And the Lord Almighty," Saint Signore cut in before Joey could finish his sentence. "If I can hear you, don't you think God comprehends your thoughts?"

"Yes, of course he does. Sorry…*Mi dispiace*." Joey feared exasperating Saint Signore so much that he'd desert him forever. Without the Saint, he'd have no one to talk to. Except Figaro, for as long as he was around. The dog's owner - a drug-dealing thug called Sonny, named after former Hells Angels boss Sonny Barger, who'd kept Figaro in his van day and night to guard his drug stash - was hunting for him. In fact, according to Saint Signore, Sonny had heard Figaro was here and planned to appropriate him in the near future.

CHAPTER TWENTY-FIVE
Mona Lisa

When I got home from the reunion meeting, I jogged upstairs to check on the bank deposit bag. On the second floor, I strode into my childhood bedroom and searched the dark cavern of my closet, where, as a girl, I had hidden my Halloween candy so Joey wouldn't steal it. No use complaining to Mama, who'd say, "Now, *cara*, be nice. I'm sure the original Mona Lisa shared with her little brother." It had irked me to no end.

One time, not believing her - I think I was ten - I marched into the living room, opened our book of Italian Renaissance art, flipped to Leonardo da Vinci's famous portrait, and searched the "real" Mona Lisa's face. In spite of her ambiguous expression, she didn't strike me as a woman who'd put up with any guff. "She did not share her candy with her little brother!" I'd yelled, but Mama stepped into the room and said, "You mean she was an only child?"

I supposed I did look like her. We had the same color eyes - amber, green, and hazel all at once - although my brows were bolder; pretty much the same nose, but mine was bulkier, unfortunately; and same mousy-brown hair, but using a net, she'd managed to subdue her curls. That was the day I decided to grow my hair out and part it in the middle. No wonder the kids in junior high thought I was a dweeb. When I got to high school, my friend Sally took a pair of Mama's sewing shears and lopped my bangs, which, when wet, shrank too short. I'd cried and refused to go to school the next day until Mama bought me product to straighten my bangs. I'd worn them on the long side ever since.

As my hand patted the closet's wooden floor, I decided I needed to get out an art book and scrutinize the painting again. I'd studied art history in college and should know more about this unknown lady who lived centuries ago. She and I had a weird connection. In any case, I wanted to break free from her. Maybe I should change my name to Monica.

Down on all fours in the closet, I patted the floor and felt dust bunnies, a hairpin, a plastic bag, and a pair of shoes. I searched my memory and recalled hiding the money where I didn't think anyone would look.

Hey, what were my pumps doing on the floor? Straightening up, I scanned the stack of shoeboxes.

I'd tossed it further than I thought. I wouldn't treat our hard-earned money like that unless I was going bonkers like everyone else in this house.

Papa had always been eccentric with peculiar inventions and jokes that lacked meaningful punchlines when translated into English. And he'd break into an opera aria at the most embarrassing moments - in the produce department at the grocery store or in our backyard while pruning or barbecuing, bringing our neighbors to their windows to gape at him. He could have sung his heart out at church on Sunday mornings, but he refused to set foot in one. He wouldn't even attend funerals unless they took place outside at the graveside. I recalled a fallout with a priest - a terrible argument involving slammed telephones and a visit to our house by a black-suited man wearing a white collar. Mama had flipped out, using words like *repent* and *excommunicate*, but I was too young to remember the details.

I recalled Papa shaking his head when Mama lit candles in the window above the kitchen sink. "You could start a fire," he'd complained, and she'd say, "I hope so, in your heart," or some quip like that. Later, when she wasn't looking, he'd blow out the candles. It occurred to me now that he held onto bitterness toward her religious convictions, which seemed out of character for a man who wore a grin on his face most days. What could he possibly have held resentment about?

Other than continuing to light candles and pray aloud, Mama had seemed stable until lately. I couldn't ignore the fact that she was engaged to Frank DiAngelo. A hideous vision of them in private flashed through my mind's eye, sending creepy feelings across my arms like a colony of ants crawling up my sleeves. Revolting!

I reminded myself that Mama was only sixty-nine. She had more than a few years left. Why wouldn't she wish to remarry? But cranky Frank DiAngelo of all people? He was a codger, mincing along at half her speed, even when she'd injured her knee. He probably needed someone to help him put on his shoes and socks. Would he insist Mama wait on him like his personal servant? Yet he was the same age Papa would have been if he'd lived. If only Papa was still alive. I had so many unanswered questions for him. For instance, why did he break from the Catholic Church? Why wouldn't he visit the Old Country?

I unzipped the bag and peeked in. The cash and receipts seemed out of order. Usually, I stacked the money on top of the receipts, but the bills were underneath. Had someone tampered with the bank deposit? I'd have to recount the money to make sure it was still all there.

From down in the kitchen, Figaro barked, a low warning woof. It was too late for the postal carrier, Amazon, or a UPS delivery. Figaro barked again, adding a threatening growl. He was probably watching a neighbor's cat wander through the backyard. I told myself I didn't need to worry about a prowler. Who would peer into our window, then dare open the door after seeing a dog the size of an Italian mastiff?

As I rezipped the deposit bag, I heard Figaro's nails clicking on the kitchen floor, then I heard him galloping up the stairs. He barged into the room, stopping a few yards from me. His cropped ears pricked, and the guard hairs on his withers stood up, making him grow six inches taller. His menacing glare tunneled into me like I was a stranger.

"Go away, Fang." I'd had enough of sidestepping this unwelcome beast but couldn't mask the fearful tremor in my voice. Because, at a gut level, I was afraid of him. "Bad dog, go downstairs." But he didn't budge.

We stood face-to-face. Was it improper animal etiquette to stare at a dog? Was I challenging him? The last thing I wanted to do was incite a showdown.

He stalked over to me on padded feet and placed his massive jaws around the deposit bag. His canine teeth sank into the greenish cloth like a vice, until he held on to it tighter than I did.

"What are you doing, stupid dog?" I had the end with the zipper, only by a corner. "Why do you want my money?"

He stared back at me, his eyes black marbles, void of compassion.

I reasoned with myself. He was a pack animal juggling for supremacy, vying to become alpha. If I let him win, I'd never be safe alone with him again.

"Let go." But he glared at my hand without blinking.

I heard a noise on the back porch, then the door opened and closed. "Joey?" For once, I was glad my brother was home. "Is that you?"

"Yup."

"Get up here, right now. Please."

In what seemed like five minutes but was probably only thirty seconds, Joey's methodical footsteps ascended the staircase. Finally, his boyish face appeared in the doorway.

His glance came to rest on the moneybag. "Something wrong?"

"This wretched dog is trying to take the deposit bag away from me." I gave it a pull and felt increased tension from Figaro's muscled shoulders and legs as his feet dug into the carpet. "Make him let go."

"What's this money doing here, anyway?" Joey raised his chin. "Are you stealing from Booty's?" Mama had always encouraged him to speak up, but this new confrontational style was the last thing I needed.

"No, I'm not stealing, for heaven's sake. I've done some harebrained things in my life, but I wouldn't rip off my own family. I brought this home because I was running late yesterday, then forgot it this morning."

Figaro inhaled through his nostrils, then let out a raspy breath.

"Joey, please make Figaro let go."

"Leave it, boy," Joey finally said, and the dog unhinged his jaws, loosening his grasp. Joey wandered over and took the bag from us, Figaro letting him. I was too nervous to make a move that might incite the dog. Joey held the bag at arm's length with his thumb and index finger.

"There's something weird going on." I turned my face away from the dog to speak to Joey. "Listen, I hid this money bag yesterday, but when I came back just now, someone had moved it. I'm thinking Figaro did, maybe because it smells like food."

Joey tugged his earlobe. "Dogs' noses are far more sensitive than ours."

"I bet Figaro was just hungry." He always sniffed his kibble with disdain before eating it, like he expected better.

"It was the money Figaro detected, not food."

I chuckled at Joey's wild imagination. "What, he's a trained money-sniffer?"

Joey nodded. "You could say that."

"Whatever." I was relieved when Figaro moseyed out of the room. Once in the hallway, he turned in a circle and sat on his haunches, facing us.

Joey set the moneybag on the corner of my bureau next to three miniature horse statuettes Papa had given me that I couldn't bear to part with. At one time, I'd thought I'd give them to my future daughter, but I should donate the horses to a nonprofit and let the dream of motherhood die.

"Moni, have you noticed how you've gotten rid of all my

stuff, but your room looks exactly like it did twenty years ago?" The corners of his mouth angled down. "Look at this place. It's a museum, frozen in time."

"You're right. When I moved out three apartments ago, I guess I left most everything behind."

Keeping Figaro in my peripheral vision, my gaze traveled to my Canon AE-1. My camera had resided on the bookcase for so long that I rarely noticed it, as if it were transparent. I felt a sense of loss, a hollow void in my chest too painful to explore.

"How is Thomas going to paint this room?" Joey sounded as if we'd switched positions.

"Okay, okay." I let out a puff of air. "I've been so busy taking care of everyone else's problems I've neglected my own."

Where should I start? First, empty the closet of old clothing and shoes. Maybe I'd come across my diary with its little gold lock. I'd hidden the pink leather diary, but where? I didn't want anyone stumbling across it and perusing my inner thoughts and secrets. I'd foolishly recorded the horrific day that changed the orbit of my life. I'd tear those pages out and rip them into a thousand pieces.

CHAPTER TWENTY-SIX
Cliff

"*People are strange*," Cliff sang, his fingers tapping the steering wheel as the Doors' oldie song unraveled in his head. His car's leather interior offered good acoustics, enhancing his tenor voice.

In spite of the poet and psychedelic rock star Jim Morrison's untimely death, Cliff's mother still fondly called Morrison by his nicknames, the Lizard King and Mr. Mojo Risin'. Cliff liked its melody, the drum and bass guitar so familiar to him it was like sinking into the worn corduroy-covered La-Z-Boy in his mother's living room.

No, not there. When sitting on it, he kept his hands on the armrests. He never knew what he might find behind the seat's cushion—a dried-up wedge of pizza or sickening things he couldn't bear to think about.

He stopped singing and grasped the steering wheel with both hands, his vision canvassing the cross street, then following the car in front of him, a Ford Taurus missing a taillight. It occurred to Cliff that driving was like navigating a giant video game. Other players, who might have had too much to drink or were high on meth or heroin, could dart out from darkened shadows and alleyways at any moment, immobilizing his car. At one time, he'd been in their position, but tonight, thankfully, he was in control. Sober, anyway. He had much to be proud of. He hadn't succumbed to temptation. It seemed the straighter Cliff's life became, the more "Evil" set forth temptations, like a fisherman dangling lures in a pond stocked with ravenous trout.

His foot pushed down on the accelerator. He passed the Taurus as it took a right onto a side street. Cliff needed to get back to Panda. Why had he lingered at the meeting in the restaurant and then out on the street with Mona Lisa for so long? As they'd parted, he impulsively gave her a bear hug, the kind he might bestow on his favorite cousin, Angie. He'd never cried in public, not even after Janette left him. But standing with his arms around Mona Lisa, he'd felt a crazy tangle of emotions - sadness, regret, gratitude - erupting up his throat. But he'd successfully stifled the sob. Or had Mona Lisa heard him? She'd stiffened, then shoved him away. Maybe she hated or feared men. Or didn't like him in particular. Either way, it was her problem. He had plenty of his own to worry about.

Cliff needed to maintain his fortitude to be up for the job instead of hoping all obstacles would be removed. Thorns dug into his heart - his failed marriage, his messed-up mother, a father who never loved him, a meager savings account, and no true intimacy. He'd met several women at AA meetings; they were nice enough, but he hadn't felt the buzz of attraction. He'd heard love grew out of friendship. Perhaps he should take the plunge and ask one of them out to dinner and a movie. But he knew from experience that the woman would read too much into it and be disappointed if he didn't ask her out again. Anyway, according to Cliff's AA sponsor, relationship abstinence was encouraged for a year. Which should give Cliff the green light. He'd been dry for two years. But he wasn't ready.

He pulled in behind Mrs. McCloud's elegant old mansion, which still didn't feel like home. He glanced up through the windshield to the second floor and saw a light in his bathroom. Which meant nothing, only that the building hadn't burned down in his absence. He sat for a moment, wondering if Panda had done her homework or if she'd watched one TV show after another.

Panda had been walking in her sleep the other night, and the next morning she told Cliff she didn't remember. He couldn't hold her responsible for what she did in what a sleep-disorder doctor called a somnambulistic trance.

He got out of his car and closed the door quietly so as not to wake anyone. Five other tenants lived there, all of whom were his age or older. And Mrs. McCloud might have trundled into her canopy bed. He'd seen it while replacing a faulty light switch in her room. Earlier, she'd assured him she was a light sleeper and would put her phone on her nightstand in case Panda called.

As Cliff picked his way up the back staircase, he wondered if Panda had spoken to her mother. Had Janette finally called Panda, or had Panda tracked Janette down at a luxury hotel? Either was a good outcome. Then why did Cliff feel his throat strangling his windpipe and his pulse quicken? He was bushed by the time his feet labored to the second floor.

At his door, he slipped his key into the lock and turned the knob, a two-handed maneuver. He was glad to hear the peaceful silence blanketing his apartment. No TV. Had Panda finally buckled down to finish her homework, or had she gone to bed early to avoid doing it?

He stepped into the room and saw a whirlwind of activity. Panda was gyrating about like a pole dancer, hips bumping and grinding.

"I'm home." Cliff spoke, but she took no notice. Earbuds jammed in her ears, she seemed oblivious, near ecstasy, judging from her half-closed eyes and the grin on her face. In fluid movements, she hopped on one foot, then the other, her hips doing some kind of hula, her arms spreading out like a bird taking flight. Her face flushed red, and beads of perspiration dotted her forehead.

What was she listening to? Cliff reminded himself how important music had been to him as a teen. He remembered the words of the O'Jays' song, "I love music." But he knew he didn't like every type. Like most rap music with its hostile sentiments and curse words spewing out, assaulting him.

On the table lay a heap of books. Had they even been opened?

"Panda, honey."

She kept undulating throughout the room, her hips swiveling. Until she twirled around and her hand collided with Cliff's shoulder. Her limbs turned rigid, and her mouth formed an O. She flopped onto the couch and pulled the earbuds out. Panting, she said, "Hi… Daddy, I was… exercising."

"At this time of night? Is your homework done?" A question Cliff's mother had never voiced, but after his conversation with Mr. Patterson, he felt compelled to inquire.

"It's only nine o'clock. I was just about to start." She swung her bare feet to the floor and raised herself to a sitting position. "I finished my reading."

Cliff glanced into the kitchenette and saw dirty plates, a serving spoon, and two pots strewn across the small counter, then he set his gaze on her books. He'd given Panda explicit directions to make a list of every item that needed to be finished before bedtime, and she'd agreed to his terms. Otherwise, he would have stayed home. He felt a floodwater of agitation building in his chest. "Look, honey, do you remember what I told you? Mr. Patterson said you're on probation."

"So? I want him to kick me out. I'd rather go to public school with my girlfriend, Jillian."

Cliff had never met Jillian but had heard the girl's name and assumed she attended school with Panda. "She goes to public school?"

"Yes, she transferred last year. And it doesn't cost her parents a dime. We could go sign me up tomorrow. I could make the switch right away. No more tuition. You'd save a mint."

"You can't run away from your obligations." Although Cliff would be thrilled to shed the monthly payments. It had been Janette who'd insisted Panda attend a private school.

Panda put her feet up on the coffee table, knocking a book to the floor. "I could start afresh, a new beginning."

"How would changing schools guarantee you'd keep up with your homework? You'd have more distractions than ever."

"It would be a lot easier—half the homework. Jillian says she finishes most of hers in study hall."

In the past, Cliff had wondered if Panda's prep school demanded too much. From what she'd described, it was similar to attending a mini-college. An expensive one, at that. But according to Patterson, most of the students thrived on the rigorous academic program, and some parents thought the teachers didn't give the kids enough homework. Cliff had gone to public school, then attended Washington State, but in those days, admission was much easier. His SAT scores and grades had been average, but back then there were no preparatory classes. No one he knew crammed for SATs. Although girls like Mona Lisa Buttaro achieved good grades, she must have gone home every day after school and studied.

"We can't make any changes without your mother's okay." Cliff considered Janette's shock when coming home to find Panda in a new school. "She'd have a royal fit." He felt a smile tugging at the corners of his mouth, prompting Panda to laugh, a girlish hee-hee.

"So? Mom's not here, is she?"

He noticed Panda's cell phone on the coffee table next to her foot. "I don't suppose you've heard from her."

"Not since a couple days ago."

"You talked to her? But you said she hadn't called. Why didn't you tell me?"

"She made me promise not to. She was afraid you'd fly over there and spoil everything."

He couldn't stop his mind from traipsing to Maui, to the newlyweds strolling on the beach, snorkeling, tanning by the pool—all the activities Janette and Cliff once enjoyed together. He reminded himself that there was no turning back now that she was married.

"Did you tell her you'd lied about staying with a friend? That you were camped out at home?" he said. "That you're now staying with me?"

"Look, Daddy-o, if you don't want me here, I can leave.

162

Mom warned me you had a bad temper. She said you threw something at her."

"Not at her, but across the room. On one occasion." The glass candy dish, laden with chocolates from one of Janette's admirers, had shattered magnificently against the kitchen wall. "Losing my temper was wrong, and I've apologized a thousand times." Cliff felt stuck between an avalanche and a snowplow. There was no way he could win.

"Panda, honey, I want you to stay with me, more than anything."

"You sure don't act like it."

"I'm sorry. I guess the chat with Mr. Patterson and then the thought of your mother getting married threw me off balance."

"You didn't think Mom was coming back to you, did you? She hates you."

Panda's words throbbed in his ears like he'd pounded this thumb with a hammer. Even though the landscape of his failed marriage was scarred with potholes, marriage was familiar - what he knew and longed for. He considered the possibility that Janette and Dennis might enjoy a short but tumultuous marriage and then get divorced. She might come running back to Cliff, begging forgiveness - a scene he'd replayed in his mind as he'd tread the waters of living as a single man. A fruitless waste of energy. He needed to focus on the here and now, on Panda. In how many years would she be off to college, leave the Northwest, and possibly live on the other side of the country? But to get into college, she had to graduate from high school.

"Let's get back to your homework." Cliff forced his features to relax. "Mr. Patterson warned me that the school has a waiting list of eager students."

"Perfect, one of them can have my spot, and we'll all be happy."

CHAPTER TWENTY-SEVEN
Joey

When Joey's alarm clock went off, Saint Signore informed him, "I'm sleeping in. You're on your own today."

"What are you talking about?" Since Joey started working at Booty's, his life had been warped out of shape, stretched and twisted to conform to Moni's daily routine. He'd been determined to find a way to squirm out of going to the restaurant ever again - until last night, when his world went topsy-turvy. He'd found Moni had sneaked home a money deposit bag, a sure sign she was pilfering from the restaurant. While Moni was out all evening - she claimed at a class reunion meeting - Saint Signore advised Joey to hide the money in the attic. For the first time, out of paralyzing fear, Joey refused.

"Then you'll have to continue showing up at the restaurant to protect your mother's investment," the Saint had said last night. "Like an undercover spy."

Joey liked that idea. "*Va bene.*" Moni would make him wake up at dawn anyway.

Joey opened his eyes and peered at the daylight basement window to make sure the curtain was closed. He'd turned in early to catch up on much-needed sleep. Days on his feet at the restaurant exhausted him. "How can I go anywhere without you?" he asked the Saint.

"Since you don't need the benefit of my wisdom anymore, it's time you took a solo flight." Saint Signore yawned in Joey's ear. "You'll be fine; you'll have your precious sister with you. *Ciao.*"

"*Per favore*, don't dessert me. I need you."

But the Saint didn't answer.

Joey considered sleeping in, too, like the good old days, back when Mama still lived here. With his mother at Booty's all day, he'd snoozed until sunset. But this morning, the thought of preparing a vat of carrot-ginger soup niggled at his mind. He'd grown proud of his newfound culinary skills. He was actually good at something. He aimed his thoughts at the Saint. "Shouldn't you come into Booty's to encourage me?"

Still no answer.

So Joey showered, dressed, and rode to the restaurant with Moni. He noticed her eyes were swollen from lack of sleep, her brown hair pulled into a sloppy ponytail, and she hadn't bothered with lipstick, indicating to Joey that she'd had a fitful night. He bet guilt was gnawing away at her. Joey could think of a half-dozen things she should feel remorseful about. Not to mention the stolen money. If Saint Signore were traveling to the restaurant with them, he'd list her blunders out in detail. Joey wondered if Saint Signore was playing a joke on him if he'd suddenly speak up and say, "*È una bella giornata,*" it's a beautiful day - even though the inky sky was heavy with clouds.

"Saint Signore, where are you?" Joey hoped the Saint wasn't punishing him for his disobedience last night.

Several hours later, in Booty's kitchen, Joey finished his soup preparation. He brought out the step stool. Thanks to Ramon and Annie's guidance, he now knew where most everything was. He liked Annie, a soft-spoken young-twenties brunette. Saint Signore had called her *una bella ragazza*, a pretty girl. Sadly, this was her last week as waitress and busboy; she was apparently moving somewhere to be with her boyfriend. Moni had mentioned a goodbye party for her on her last day, a seemingly generous gesture, but Joey wondered if Moni had fired Annie out of spite.

Had Annie caught Moni stealing money from Booty's? Or was Annie fleeing from the law? He was used to Saint Signore refuting or substantiating his musings, but the air between his ears lay flat, like on the prairie when even a blade of grass doesn't move.

Joey positioned the stool next to the cash register under the chalkboard and climbed up. After cleaning the previous day's soup off the board with a damp rag, he wrote Carrot Ginger Vegetarian Soup below Minestrone, printing like a second-grade schoolteacher, using his right hand - he was left-handed - so a handwriting expert couldn't analyze his personality.

They'd run out of minestrone soup yesterday afternoon, and Moni was hurriedly preparing a new batch. She brought a spoonful to her mouth and frowned. "What's missing?" she asked Ramon, who stood in the kitchen area prepping for lunch, filling the aluminum containers with sliced onions, tomatoes, and avocado. His shirtsleeves were rolled up, and his shoulder-length black hair was tied back. He was humming a salsa beat. The restaurant's sound system wasn't turned on yet. Did Ramon hear voices in his head, too, or only music?

Ramon and Annie ambled over to Moni. Both sampled a mouthful.

"It doesn't taste like your mother's," Annie said.

"My guess is it needs more basil and salt," Ramon said. "And a couple hours to simmer."

"Yes, the soup always tastes better the next day," Moni. "I should have stayed late yesterday to make it. At least Joey's is finished. How did I manage before he started coming in?"

Joey pretended he hadn't heard them. Were they trying to manipulate him through flattery? Without the Saint to filter their conversation, how could Joey know what to believe?

"He's especially valuable with Annie leaving," Ramon said.

"I'm going to miss you," Moni told Annie, hugging her. They stood embracing each other for a moment, then stepped apart. The scene - two women so close together, particles of their exhaled air intermingling - made Joey shudder. Then a lonely void deep inside caused his hands to wrap around his upper arms for comfort. Mama still insisted on a hug, but no one else got within a three-foot perimeter of him because he wouldn't let them for fear of picking up an infection or a virus. Sometimes people with strong immune systems carried illness without showing symptoms, and sometimes others with sniffly noses claimed they suffered allergies but were really sick. Joey couldn't take a chance with any of them.

Still, he missed the warmth of another human's touch.

"I'll miss you, too, Mona, and this place." Annie blinked away a tear. "I need to say goodbye to your mother. She was so kind. I'd never worked in a restaurant in my life, but she hired me anyway."

"Mama has always been a good judge of character," Moni said. "I'll call and ask her to stop by for lunch today or tomorrow."

"Isn't she out of town?" Ramon said, then pressed his lips together in a way that told Joey he had said something he regretted.

"I haven't heard from her for a few days," Moni said, "but she wouldn't take a trip without informing me. Where would she go?"

"Please, don't tell her I said anything." Ramon raised a hand like he was stopping traffic. "I promised not to."

"What? She told you something she wouldn't tell me? Mama and I don't keep secrets."

Even without the Saint's input, Moni's statement rang false. His sister had plenty to hide. And so did Mama. Where was she?

"I'll call her right now." Moni dug through her purse for her cell phone and called but got no answer. She left a message, "Mama, come into Booty's. Annie wants to say goodbye to you in person." She folded the phone and slipped it into her purse. "Joey, do you know where she is?"

"No." Saint Signore would have informed him if Mama was taking a trip. "She's probably getting her hair done. Or with Mr. DiAngelo."

"There's a gruesome thought."

"I agree. I don't want him for a stepfather." Joey remembered Mama's tittering over her engagement ring. What was Frank DiAngelo's motive for taking over Papa's place? Did he have some plot brewing?

"Hey, everyone, I'm expecting friends from high school to come in for lunch." When she said *friends*, Moni made air-quotes. "We weren't actually friends in school… it's a long story. My plan is to get them in and out of here as quickly as possible. Ramon, don't you dare flirt with the two women."

"Me? When do I flirt?"

"When don't you?" Moni asked, and Annie chuckled.

"Please, Ramon, contain your manly self for one day." Moni said.

"How will I know which ones are from your high school?"

"They'll be my age." Moni paused as if she regretted bringing up the subject. "Annie and Joey, serve them as quickly as possible. If they ask for me, tell them I'm too busy to come out from behind the register."

Joey detected anxiety in her voice. What was she covering up now? "Is Kavi coming in at noon to wash dishes?" Joey asked. Kavi and his brother recently emigrated to America from Thailand and spoke little English. Usually, Saint Signore translated for him. How would Joey communicate with Kavi today?

Moni retied and straightened her apron. "Yes, Kavi will be here. Everything will run smoothly. Better than normal. Let's hope."

Joey returned to his soup to make sure the burner was at the correct temperature - warm enough to heat but cool enough not to burn. He gave the creamy orange liquid a stir and inhaled the blend of warmed ginger, nutmeg, garlic, and carrots. Moni seemed doubtful customers would like the soup, but Joey insisted. Now he wondered if he'd made a mistake; he wished the Saint would speak words of assurance in his ear.

Abruptly, a female voice sliced through the air, startling Joey and making him drop the ladle into the soup.

"Hi, there, honey," Gloria drawled.

He recognized the woman's southern accent from years ago,

before Saint Signore banished other voices from his head. Joey checked over his shoulder and saw Moni at the register counting the change, Ramon leaning into the cooler, and Annie swiping the bar with a damp cloth.

"Long time no see, honeybunch," Gloria said.

"What are you doing here?" Joey asked, and Moni turned to look at him.

"What do you mean, little brother? I'm not here to get my nails done."

"Uh, never mind," Joey said.

Gloria cooed in Joey's ear. "Honeybunch, have you missed me?" she said, but this time Joey knew better than to answer aloud. In the past, Gloria had nagged and pestered him, but he thought she was *morta* - dead and buried.

Joey held his lips together to keep his words from blurting out. "Go away!" he screamed in his mind. Happily, Moni appeared not to hear him. She put a dollar bill in the tip jar as an incentive for customers.

Joey got an idea that would scare Gloria away. "I'll call the Saint," he threatened, careful not to move his lips.

She let loose bubbles of laughter that echoed in his head. "How is that old rascal?" she asked. "Last thing I heard, your illustrious friend was on his way to have an audience with the Pope."

He wasn't sleeping in?

"No, he's gone to the Vatican, for good," Gloria said, picking up on Joey's thoughts. "Or bad, depending how you look at it." She cackled.

Joey's mind reeled with worry. How would he cope? The Saint would tell Joey to ignore Gloria. Saint Signore once said, "That cunning vixen's only a figment of your imagination." Meaning the Saint wasn't?

"Saint Signore has loved me from afar for over a century," Gloria said. Her sigh spanned an octave. "Unrequited love."

Joey didn't believe her. In the past, she'd told him a

169

cornucopia of falsehoods - that Russia had invaded Alaska and troops were working their way down to the state of Washington, that Elvis lived in a Podunk town in Texas using a pseudonym, and that Papa wasn't really Joey's biological father.

Joey needed to pull the ladle out of the vat of soup, but first he had to change his latex gloves. He peeled off his used ones, discarded them in the trashcan, and replaced them with a clean pair from the box he'd brought from home yesterday.

"When are you going to get yourself a girlfriend?" Gloria asked him.

"None of your beeswax." Joey liked girls but was afraid to speak to them, except for relatives and Annie, who had a boyfriend and wouldn't be interested in him anyway. Even if he met a woman he liked, where could he take her on a date? Not to a darkened movie theater filled with strangers. Who knew how many slovenly people had sat in the seats before? Not to mention an infestation of bedbugs. The sound system at theaters blared, making him plug his ears; the images were too violent, even the trailers. He hadn't entered one for twenty years.

"If not a movie, how about you and I have a night out on the town?" Gloria suggested. "A few drinks. Live music and dancing."

Pretending he couldn't hear her, Joey brought the ladle to the sink and flushed hot water over it.

"You can't ignore me, honeybunch," Gloria said.

What should he do? He knew he wasn't strong enough to bluff his way through the rest of the day.

CHAPTER TWENTY-EIGHT
Mona Lisa

I stepped outside Booty's, lugging our sandwich board, and saw lanky TR Wincheimer exiting a black sedan parked at the curb. Then he strode my way.

"Let me help you with that." He lifted the hinged boards from my hands and faced them so pedestrians could read the restaurant's name and hours from both directions. At the moment, we were the only two people on our side of the street.

"This okay?" He was dressed in a sports jacket, an open-collar shirt, and jeans.

"Yes, thanks." I was grateful for the help, but he seemed overly eager.

"Anytime. I came early to look the place over. I'll compare Booty's with other recently sold restaurants and put together a market analysis."

"Okay, good." It occurred to me that Papa would demand a second and third opinion. And he might insist the listing agent be of Italian heritage. Even though he'd moved our family out of Garlic Gulch, his Italian roots ran deep. But they stopped with me. I considered myself an all-American gal. I hated when people asked where my parents were from because I wanted to blend in.

I turned and gave the building's edifice a once-over. Under a cloudy sky, Booty's stucco exterior looked drab, and several cracks needed patching. The front window begged for a thorough washing. At least it wasn't raining. No. Wrong. A droplet of moisture landed on my forehead. If we hired TR, he'd find out the flat roof needed repair. We had a bucket beneath the leak in the back storage room.

"You own the building?" he asked.

"I don't know if we own it outright. I think my mother still makes payments to a bank." I felt foolish. "I have no idea how much my folks spent on Booty's—it was once a hardware store—or anything about the mortgage. I'll get that information."

He assessed the low structures across the street, mostly residential except for the small mom-and-pop grocery store, a shoe repair shop, and the bike shop. "Nice neighborhood," he said. "But not much foot traffic."

"We get our fair share. Folks working up on Forty-Fifth, down at the Bastyr clinic, and in that retirement community, University House." Why was I self-conscious about the funky one- or two-story houses and shops dotting the street that I ordinarily thought were quaint?

"I should get back inside." Another drop of rain landed on my scalp. "Look, TR, my customers don't know we're selling yet. And I need to tell my staff, but not this morning because we're twenty minutes away from the lunch rush."

"Okay, we'll say I'm a childhood friend coming in to talk about the good old days." His domed forehead shined like old man Hitchers, our sophomore biology teacher, who in high school seemed ancient. I realized we were now Mr. Hitcher's age. At least TR had something to show for his life - a wife, kids, and a career. And a woman on the side? I hadn't imagined Cindy's toe nudging TR's under the table.

He followed me into the restaurant. "Your sandwich board says you're open for lunch six days a week." His vision canvassed the walls and the framed prints of Positano and the Amalfi Coast, but he didn't ask about them. "Have you considered serving dinner and opening on Sundays?"

"Yes, but I decided it's too much work." I backed into the

---

restaurant, away from the front door, in case customers arrived. "I inherited this place without much experience. None, in fact. And I already work six days a week."

He paid me no heed. "You should seriously think about opening for dinner. Offer imported bottled wine and mixed drinks, good income producers. Happy hour and serving dinner could double the restaurant's revenue. And consider Sunday brunch."

"Hush. Please, keep your voice down so the whole world doesn't hear you." I felt myself bristle with annoyance. "I'd have to hire a new cook and more waitstaff. I'd need to put a cot in the back room and spend my nights here."

"No, you wouldn't. Find an assistant manager." He glanced into the kitchen at Ramon, who was watching us through the long, narrow space above his workstation. He'd probably heard every word TR said. I owed Ramon an explanation. I wouldn't blame him if he started a job search today.

Ramon got back to work, his hands out of sight. TR stood eyeing Ramon, a man who could pass for a movie star. Was TR wondering if I had something going on with him?

TR turned back to me. "I'll make a list of my suggestions. You want to make a tidy profit, don't you?" He seemed a bit pushy, verging on aggressive. Could I trust him? Papa once said, *"Fidarsi è bene; non fidarsi è meglio."* To trust is good; not to trust is better.

I put my finger to my lips, a signal for TR to lower his volume. "Yes, I do." I spoke one notch above a whisper. "Enough to see my mother through her senior years." Mostly I wanted to rid myself of this albatross. Should I admit I didn't like cooking the way a real chef relished preparing gourmet meals? And I wasn't crazy about waiting on customers either. No, the less TR knew, the better. "I think I'll leave serving dinner up to the next owner, if we can find one."

"You're missing out on great opportunities." He meandered into the dining area and counted the tables and the stools lining one side of the bar, then moved to the passway between the cash register and the counter, where the coffee urn stood. "How about a cup of java?"

"Okay." I poured him a mug of steaming Italian roast; we brewed it strong, the way Papa liked. "Cream or sugar?"

He stared at the syrupy liquid. "Half-and-half, if you have it."

Annie, who'd been emptying the dishwasher, must have overheard our conversation. She whisked out of the kitchen with a pint of cream and dribbled some atop the coffee. "Thanks," I said, then passed the cup to TR. "You having lunch?" I asked.

"A cheeseburger and fries sounds good."

"Sorry, we don't serve them. But we have assorted sandwiches, delicious paninis, several salads, and two homemade soups."

His brows furrowed. "I'll wait for the others to arrive and see what they're having." He made no move to pay for the coffee. I may sound cheap, but the price had escalated. "Over the course of the day, if we gave everyone free coffee, we'd be in the red, losing money."

With his other hand, he took the unopened *Seattle Times* off the bar and wandered to a table against the wall, his chair facing the front door.

Only minutes before opening, I still had plenty to keep me busy. I checked the restrooms to make sure the cleaning service - a woman who came in after hours - had replenished toilet paper and towels. Then I straightened the pictures; our cleaning lady liked to leave them at a slant to indicate she'd dusted.

Next, I counted the stock in our beverage cooler. Plenty of Italian colas - rarely sold but stocked to make Mama happy. Curtis, our beer and wine deliveryman, hadn't come in yet. What was keeping him? Was he gabbing with the owner of our chief competitor several blocks away? Curtis's arrival during the lunch rush always caused a commotion. I peered through the glass door of the cooler and saw we had plenty in stock. In spite of TR's prediction, we didn't sell much alcohol - only a few glasses of wine or bottled beers per day. I had stopped drinking when I'd gotten pregnant, and after losing my precious child, I never took another sip. Why? So my body would be prepared should it happen again? With no husband, no boyfriend? Well, not drinking had cut down on my caloric consumption. Over the last few months, I'd trimmed down to my college weight.

Nearing the cash register, I noticed a man talking to Annie. The light flooding in from the front window darkened his face until I was within yards of him.

"Hello there, Mona," Kevin Shaughnessy said in his low, sexy voice. I hadn't set eyes on my former beau for months. He seemed taller, almost as tall as Cliff, and he'd grown more muscular, his shoulders and chest filling out his navy-blue jacket like he'd been working out and lifting weights. He was wearing the ebony tortoiseshell glasses I'd sold him that enhanced his smoky blue eyes.

"What brings you in here?" I figured he'd fallen head-over-heels in love with a bombshell ten years my junior who'd won triathlons and earned her PhD in physics. He was about to bestow me with an invitation to their upcoming opulent wedding of the-year? I would simply refuse to take it from him because there was no way I'd attend.

"You didn't return my email," he said, ignoring Annie behind the register. She'd worked here long enough to know him and remember our breakup. She raised her brows in my direction as if to ask me what I needed from her. Should I tell her to stab him with a fork? I wished we still served marinara sauce so she could splat a cupful across the front of his jacket and slacks. Or would I rather savor those acts myself?

"I meant to get back to you." I spoke as nonchalantly as I could muster. "I guess I forgot." Not true, his email had plagued me since its arrival, like an itch I'd managed to ignore by keeping occupied. "I've been extremely busy."

"Yes, I heard through the grapevine how you stepped in to run Booty's."

Seattle was a big, small town. Dr. Kamahuri, my former boss, had been in for lunch last week. Was he the culprit who'd told Kevin? Or my friend Shirley, whom I'd met at the health club I no longer belonged to. Thanks to my recommendation, she was Kevin's patient.

"Very impressive." Kevin seemed sincere in his praise. "Not many women could switch professions so capably. Congratulations."

"Thanks." I considered his words. It never occurred to me that managing the restaurant would elevate my stature in his eyes. Maybe other men now saw me as an eligible bachelorette? For a dizzying moment, I wondered if I was making a mistake in selling Booty's. What would I do next? I had no job prospects and few skills. And Joey? Who would hire him? When both Mama's house and Booty's were sold, would all traces of Papa evaporate?

"Can we talk?" Kevin asked.

"Not now. In fact, I see no point in further conversation." Maddening as it was, I felt my heart flutter like the first time I saw Kevin entering the optometrist's office looking for glasses. Had I no pride?

"Please," he said.

The logical side of my brain despised him, but a chunk of me found him as attractive as ever. My hand automatically reached to smooth my hair. I remembered washing my face earlier, but had I applied cream, foundation, and mascara? Well, what did it matter? This was the man who dumped me. I owed him nothing.

"Seriously, I don't have time. I'm swamped." I couldn't risk a tantrum or a crying jag in front of my employees and TR, who sat doing a crossword puzzle.

"I can wait." He glanced at a copy of our printed menu, then up at the chalkboard. "A grilled chicken and mozzarella panini and a bowl of minestrone," he told Annie. He handed her a twenty-dollar bill. "Keep the change."

"Thank you, sir. I'll bring it to your table." She was polite but formal.

"Is that your brother in there?" Kevin leaned forward to peer into the kitchen. Joey, speaking to Ramon, was smocked in two white aprons, their strings strung tightly around his waist. I felt a flush of embarrassment. I'd told Kevin about my brother's oddities - how he collected papers and bits of tin foil, and how he slept most of the day to avoid people - and now wished I hadn't.

"Yes, Joey works here." I forced the corners of my mouth to curve up a smidge, like the real Mona Lisa. "It's a family affair." I refused to add more details.

A moment later, Cindy Fenning and Deidre Elstrom entered through the front door and sashayed up to the cash register, snickering and chatting. I imagined Booty's through their discriminating eyes. They probably thought it was a hole-in-the-wall compared to Seattle's classy restaurants like The Pink Door or Daniel's. But wasn't that my aim - to make the reunion committee choose another venue for the graduates-only party?

The two women stopped short when they noticed Kevin. While dating him, I'd grown used to women looking him over because he was drop-dead gorgeous - strong chin and short, straight nose - the opposite of the Buttaro schnozzola. Don't get me wrong, I adored Papa. But I didn't want my future children, should I have them, plagued with bulbous noses.

"Well, hello, there." Cindy's auburn hair was drawn back into a flirty ponytail and her emerald-colored turtleneck made her green eyes flash.

"Good morning." He smiled graciously, as if she might be one of his patients.

"You look our age." Deidre's frosted mauve lipstick echoed her quilted jacket, worn over black corduroy slacks. "Are you joining us for the meeting?"

"What kind of get-together is it?" he asked.

"A high school reunion committee," both women answered, then tittered.

"We'd love to get your input," Cindy said.

"If you think I could help...."

"I bet you could do anything you put your mind to." Cindy reminded me of a she-cat about to stretch up against his long legs.

"Where did you go to high school?" Deidre asked him.

"I grew up in Chicago."

"That doesn't matter," Cindy said. "We'd love to have you join us."

177

Did I mention Kevin was a lady's man? Silver-tongued is how I described him after we broke up. He had a way of looking at you with those dreamy eyes like you were the only woman on Earth. He might have learned that from his profession as a dentist specializing in TMJ, or maybe he was born with the skill.

"I came in to speak to our proprietress." He glanced my way. Both women seemed to visibly deflate with disappointment.

"What a shame," Deidre said.

Grazie, Dio, I thought, because I didn't want those two and Kevin getting chummy and exchanging information about me. It would be like two worlds colliding, spattering debris all over me.

As I ushered Kevin into the dining area, I said to Annie, "Would you please take these ladies' orders?"

"All right." Annie sounded less than hospitable. She must have picked up on my anxiety. I should have warned her that I wanted the reunion committee to hate Booty's. No - not hate the place, just find it unsuitable for their event.

Kevin positioned himself on the first bar stool, one elbow supporting him. "Can we chat for a minute?" Sitting, he and I were the same height.

"I'm too busy." I let impatience harden my voice. I stepped to the side to scope out the area behind the bar. The stainless-steel counter and two sinks were used only for washing beer glasses, so the suds would hang to the glass just right. Behind it stretched a wide mirror with a smudgy streak across its surface. "Kevin, is this something you can tell me in one sentence or less? Because I've got to get back to work."

"Well... I brought you something." He patted his jacket pocket.

Feeling weak in the knee, my imagination sprang to life. An engagement ring? Had he gone to Fox's Jeweler or Ben Bridge? Was he about to ask for forgiveness, then get down on his knees right here in Booty's in front of the reunion committee and ask me to be his wife? I couldn't help feeling boosted by Cindy and Deidre's inevitable envy. They'd obviously found Kevin delectable.

No, that was crazy thinking. He had a wedding invitation in his pocket. He didn't love me - never had - and who cared what Cindy and Deidre thought?

"Whatever it is will have to wait." I realized I hadn't turned the sound system on. "Kevin, you picked the worst moment to come in."

"Then I'll hang out until you're free. I'm on my lunch break." Which meant he had two hours at leisure. It was a time he and I used to meet. But that was before he tossed me under the Monorail and before I was saddled with Booty's.

I heard Bernie's bass voice at the cash register, then Chick's laughter.

"I've got to go," I told Kevin.

Like a little kid at Christmas, I gave in, glanced down at his jacket pocket, and saw the outline of a small box.

179

CHAPTER TWENTY-NINE
Cliff

When Cliff entered Booty's, he spotted Bernie, Chick, TR, Deidre, and Cindy at a table, all chairs taken. Had they finished their meals and given up on him?

He checked his watch. He was forty-five minutes late because he'd been finishing his kitchen remodel, putting the icing on the cake by hanging the chandelier over the table at just the right height and screwing in flame-shaped light bulbs.

His mind flipped back to childhood. His parents were late to everything, you name it. And his mom hadn't served dinner at a special time - she'd never roasted a turkey or a ham for Christmas. His teachers learned not to expect them to show up for parent-teacher meetings and open houses. As a kid, Cliff swore he'd break his parents' pattern of tardiness and arrive early for every occasion. But for the most part, punctuality escaped his grasp. Was he turning into his parents?

Cut the negative self-talk, he warned himself. One day at a time.

The reunion committee still hadn't noticed Cliff. He was tempted to duck out, dive back into his car, and head to Dick's Drive-In. Not great food, but a favorite lunchtime haunt since high school. He'd treat himself to a strawberry milkshake. Since finishing his kitchen remodel, he felt like celebrating, not apologizing. And he needed to check on Thomas, who'd found crumbling grout behind the tub in one of Mrs. Buttaro's bathrooms. You never knew what you'd unearth in these old homes.

He saw Mona Lisa at the cash register, chatting with a waitress. Then Mona Lisa greeted a couple who seemed like regulars and rang up their orders.

If Cliff spoke to Mona Lisa now, she might ask how her mother's project was moving along. Instead of waiting for a private venue, he'd feel compelled to tell her about the bathroom and that she might have to sink another thousand dollars into it. Honesty was key to his recovery. No more white lies.

Cliff recalled The Hug, as he now labeled his and Mona Lisa's quick one-sided embrace. What on earth had inspired him to reach out to her? Facing Mona Lisa today was worse than recovering from a hangover. Since getting sober, he thought he'd rid himself of next-morning regrets.

She glanced past her customers and gave him an unexpected smile - a real one. Maybe she'd forgiven Cliff for his impulsive act. Or forgotten it.

He moved forward, following several college-aged youths, past busy Ramon in the kitchen prep area. Nearing Mona Lisa, Cliff found himself comparing her to Janette. The women were opposites. Janette wouldn't be caught dead in public without makeup and a figure-flattering outfit. Some days she'd try on half a dozen to achieve the desired look. But there stood a fresh-faced Mona Lisa with her hair clipped back at the temples, wispy bangs framing her face, wearing a long-sleeved teal-colored T-shirt and denim slacks, looking younger than her age.

When it was his turn to order, Cliff asked for exactly what he had before. "The soup-and-sandwich special - roast beef on white, heavy on the mayo."

"A creature of habit?" Mona Lisa asked.

"You could say that." Growing up in an alcoholic household had trained Cliff not to make waves and to blend into the woodwork.

He brought out his wallet. "The lunch I had here last time was so good, I thought I'd have it again. No, wait a minute. Instead of a sandwich, make that the Mediterranean salad and a cup of soup. At a recent health fair, I discovered my cholesterol's slightly elevated, and my blood pressure is borderline high."

Mona Lisa shot him a quizzical look, her sculpted brows raised. "Okay, the Mediterranean and a cup of soup." She changed his order. Now she'd think he was wishy-washy, and on the verge of a heart attack.

Cliff could see Joey hovering in the kitchen, listening to Mona Lisa but not making eye contact with him. Around Joey's waist hung two white aprons, one knotted in front and the other in the back. And latex gloves, one size too big.

"I'd better warn you, the soup of the day is carrot ginger," she told Cliff. "I could substitute minestrone instead."

"No, I'll try the carrot. It sounds healthy."

At this, Joey came to stand at her elbow and grinned, the first sign of happiness Cliff had witnessed.

"See, I told you," Joey said to Mona Lisa. "You should take a poll of all the customers today. See if they like carrot-ginger soup enough to have it again in a couple weeks.

"Joey, please help Annie clear up the seating area. If you want to ask customers for feedback, you'll have to do it yourself."

Joey's face turned pale. "All right, I'll do it." He gathered a pencil and pad of paper and inched over to the nearest table.

Cliff thought the Buttaro's might be a quirky family, but they were saints compared to his own. He'd always wanted siblings. Growing up as an only child had been a nightmare. Now, with his parents aging, he had no one to help shoulder the burden. He hadn't seen his father in years, but that didn't mean Cliff wouldn't receive a call some late night informing him his dad had suffered a stroke, carried no health insurance, and needed round-the-clock medical attention. And who knew what kind of trouble he'd have to bail his mother out of next time? If only he'd had a mother like Barbara Buttaro.

"Is your mother here today?" Cliff asked Mona Lisa. "I always enjoy talking to her."

"No. She's flown the coop. I have no idea where she is." Mona Lisa pursed her da Vinci lips. "In fact, if you hear from her, would you let me know?"

"Sure, I'll ask Thomas if she's been by the house." Cliff scanned the room. "It looks like the reunion committee finished their meeting without me. I could sit at the bar."

"No, not there." Her gaze cut to her left. A man who resembled a forty-year-old movie star perched on the nearest stool was intently watching her.

She gave her head a shake, as if trying to rid herself of an unwanted thought.

"Please, help me out," she said to Cliff. "Convince your high school comrades this place is too small for the reunion party."

"If you don't want the party here, just say so."

"I tried last night, but they wouldn't listen."

She didn't strike Cliff as a helpless coward, but he said, "Sure, I'll talk to them. No problem."

At that moment, TR and Bernie stood and made their way toward the front door.

"There you are, old man," Bernie said, moving to Cliff's side. "Running behind, as usual."

"I was putting the finishing touches on a remodel. I figured you didn't need me here."

Cindy shot to her feet in stiletto heels as high as Cliff's mother's favorite red party shoes and clicked toward the exit, brandishing a cigarette. "I need a smoke," she said, and TR fell in next to her. He opened the door with a flourish, then followed her outside.

Cliff and Bernie stepped away from the register toward the front door, leaving Mona Lisa to deal with a young man who wanted to order his meal in Italian because he was studying the language in preparation for a trip.

"*Mi dispiace. Non parlo Italiano*," Mona Lisa said like a native-born Italian. "What can I get you?"

"*Un'insalata di tonno e una ciotola di... minestra,*" the young man persisted, his words staggered and his pronunciation doubtful.

"Anything else?" she asked.

"*Sì. Una birra, per favore.*" He didn't roll his *R*s - even Cliff could do that.

"We have imported and domestic beer." In other words, she understood her customer but refused to speak the language. Why? If Cliff knew Italian, he'd be delighted. Even though he didn't carry a drop of Italian blood, maybe he should take up Italian. Someday, he and Panda might travel together to Venice. After reading a book about a Venetian girl Panda had said she wanted to visit the city of islands and waterways, and ride in a gondola. At least he could buy a CD to play in his car, practice up, and surprise Mona Lisa - better make that her mother, Barbara.

Bernie looked out the window at TR and Cindy, who hadn't lit her cigarette. "What are those two up to?" Bernie made no attempt to mask his disapproval. "They're playing with fire."

"Yeah, the words *thick as thieves* come to mind," Cliff said. "But I'm no one to judge others until I get the log out of my own eye."

"What have you done wrong? Your wife left you out of the blue, and you haven't been on a date since the divorce. Am I right?"

"Yeah, well, I will, when I meet the right woman. And when I can afford to take her somewhere nice. Besides, you know about my drinking."

"But you're dealing with your problem, more than most people." Bernie was aware of Cliff's struggle after a phone call two years ago, but Bernie didn't understand the depths of Cliff's cravings and past erratic behavior. Bernie didn't appear to need alcohol at all. He could take it or leave it, which didn't seem fair. But Cliff knew comparing himself to Bernie or anyone else would only cause resentment and make him more likely to fall off the wagon.

Bernie observed Mona Lisa, then looked back to Cliff. "Hey, brother, tell me all. You and Mona Lisa left together last night…"

"There's nothing to tell. She went her way, and I went mine."

"Are you nuts? You'd have to be blind not to notice she's turned into a fox."

"Better not let your wife hear you talking like that." Cliff figured his reprimand would shut Bernie up.

But he bounced back with, "Are you kidding? Sharon prides herself on her matchmaking skills. She'd agree with me. Mona Lisa's got a beautiful, mysterious face, that luscious dark hair, and a slim figure Sharon would kill for. And how many women own their own restaurant?"

"Technically, Booty's belongs to her mother."

"You're splitting hairs." Bernie tipped his head toward the seating area at the bar that stretched out on the other side of the cash register. "That guy sitting on a stool's been trying to snag Mona Lisa's attention for an hour. I wonder what that's all about. If Sharon were here, she'd find out…"

"Cliff, your order's up," Mona Lisa called. "Where should Annie put it?"

He looked into the dining area and saw Joey speaking with timidity to Chick and Deidre.

"I'm headed over to the table against the wall," Cliff told her.

At that moment, the guy sitting atop a stool - the guy Cliff had noticed earlier - held up an empty coffee mug in Mona Lisa's direction. His pretty-boy face wore a pleading expression, but she paid no attention. When she'd finished taking a customer's order, she carried the coffee urn right past the man, who said, "Mona?"

Minutes later, she returned to the kitchen, not stopping. "Hey, I need coffee," he said. Finally, Annie refilled his cup without ceremony.

The man kept his gaze fixed on Mona Lisa, who was now at the register. When she glanced his way, a strained electrical tension filled the air between them. Cliff was tempted to play the detective and find out who he was.

185

CHAPTER THIRTY
Mona Lisa

I looked out Booty's front window as Bernie and TR departed. Cindy was returning, her unlit cigarette still clamped between her first two fingers. Most likely she was trying to give up smoking, a bad habit I'd avoided because I never started. Papa would have killed me. But I wasn't free from dependencies. Kevin, for example. Did he have a barbed hook planted firmly in me? Why was he here at Booty's? His office was miles away on University Way.

The lunch rush was winding down, and customers were hustling back to work or to class. Several took the time to say goodbye to me. "Thanks so much for coming in." I couldn't contain my grin. I felt comfortable working at Booty's and was beginning to understand what my parents felt when their regulars arrived like friends each day. I'd begun to like the place now that I knew the routine.

Annie tidied up the seating area. I should wander around and ask people if they wanted dessert. I'd make up a dessert tray tomorrow and tempt our patrons to indulge in high-calorie, high-profit items like our scrumptious tiramisu. TR was right. I should make every effort to build sales, even if it meant opening for brunch on Sundays. A dozen questions swirled through my mind. Was our kitchen set up to produce dinner and breakfast items like waffles and French toast? Who would do the prep work, cooking, and serving? I couldn't ask Ramon to work more hours. He might get fed up and quit his job altogether. Annie was leaving me, and I needed to find her replacement, pronto. Could I talk Mama into coming back to work just one day a week? No, she maintained that Sunday was a day of rest.

It occurred to me that I should spend more time scoping out our competition. On Sunday it wouldn't hurt me to cruise by our nearest competitor, Dawn to Dusk Bakery, to see what kind of business they did.

"Mona, please come over here and talk to me." Kevin had a melodious way of speaking when he wanted something.

Steeling myself, I crossed my arms and leaned against the stool next to him while keeping my eyes on the cash register. "What's up?" My words were clipped. Then anger took hold of me. "Let me guess, Kevin, you're getting married and want me to cater the meal." Hey, catering was a money-making option I hadn't thought of before. Not a bad idea. But again, I'd need more staff, and my workday would increase. It didn't look like I'd get a vacation this year. I recalled Uncle Vito's invitation to visit him in Rome, all expenses paid. Once we sold Booty's, I'd be a dummy to pass up a chance like that, even if the trip included an introduction to a rich *paesano*. Ever since my teens, I'd sworn never to marry an Italian because I didn't want a long —iano last name connected to mine. I wanted to fit in, to be like the popular girls, an impossibility growing up with my parents in our mostly Germanic-Nordic neighborhood.

Mona Lisa Smith or Jones had a nice ring to it. Or Mona Lisa Shaughnessy? No, what was I thinking? I despised Kevin.

As if hearing my thoughts, he said, "I want to talk about you and me."

"Huh?" My face swung around to take in his expression, thinking he'd be guffawing. But he looked straight-faced.

"Is this some sick joke?"

"Not at all." He reached for my hand, and I felt the warmth of his smooth skin on the top of my fingers. I'd dreamed of this moment and replayed this scene over and over—Kevin wanting me so I could be the one in control and tell him to drop dead because I was over him. At least, I thought I was.

I pulled my hand away, pretending the weight of his was crushing mine. "I can't believe you have the nerve to show up here." My words bulleted out, filling the dining area and stopping conversation at the nearest table. Even Cliff, now seated with Chick, Deidre, and Cindy, glanced over.

"Maybe now is not the time." Kevin's voice sounded subdued. "But when I woke up this morning, everything was crystal clear. What a fool I've been."

I forced my gaze away from Kevin, into the kitchen, and saw Joey talking to himself, shaking his head, and apparently not caring who saw or heard him. I should call Mrs. Landis. Mama was still paying rent at The Home. I should get Joey moved back there.

Where was my mother? Never in my life had she disappeared; she'd always been a mama bird, circling her two chicks. I told myself to stop fretting. She was probably at the beauty parlor. She certainly was spending more time on her appearance than she used to.

"Mona, please." Kevin stood and moved closer. "May I take you out to dinner tonight?"

I narrowed my eyes at him. "I don't know what kind of game you're playing, but I have work to do." Papa would be proud of me. But if I sent Kevin away, would I ever see him again? I got a lousy sinking feeling in my chest, but I straightened my posture the way Mama had instructed when I was a slouchy teen.

"Don't you have a girlfriend?" I asked.

"I was dating someone, but she was too young. She didn't even know who the Beatles were."

I felt a grin spreading across my face. I wanted to laugh out loud. But at the same time, I wondered what he'd found unfavorable about me. He and I liked the same music. I'd pretended to appreciate his favorite sports teams and even made a big deal about the Seahawks and the Mariners.

I noticed movement across the room. Chick was waving to me, beckoning me to their table. I couldn't ignore what was left of the reunion committee any longer.

"I have a meeting," I told Kevin. I paused for a moment to survey the cube-like shape in his jacket pocket and played Twenty Questions with myself, a game Mama used years ago to keep Joey and me out of her hair when she was preparing dinner. "I spy with my little eye," she'd say.

"Smaller than a breadbox?" one of us would chime in. Yes.

"Animal or vegetable?" No.

"Flat? The shape of a wedding invitation?" No.

"The size of a ring box?" Yes!

Or a free sample of dental floss? Was he worried about my oral hygiene? In which case, I might go insane and strangle him on the spot. I spun away from him too quickly, tripping on my own two feet.

His hand swung out to grab hold of my elbow and steady me. "Are you all right?"

"Of course, I'm fine." I retied my apron.

"About tonight -"

"Haven't we said all there is to say?" Sick as it seemed, I was dying to know what he'd brought me. But I also wanted to let him have it with both barrels. Who cared if he didn't like my Buttaro nose? Or if my boobs weren't the size of ripe melons?

"Where are you living now?" he asked.

"At my mother's."

As I strode across the room, Chick got to his feet and pulled out the chair TR had vacated, putting me between Chick and Deidre.

"This place rocks," Chick said. "Good grub."

"Thanks." I sat, not scooting my chair in. "I can stay only until another customer comes in." Which I hoped would be any minute.

"Who's the hunk at the counter?" Deidre turned her majestic head to watch Kevin scan his iPhone for texts. He was always examining it, even when driving. He'd told me he wanted to be available for patients with jaw pain. Later, I realized I had no idea how many text messages came from women requiring his personal attention in the back room of his office, with its foldout couch.

"He's a blast from the past." I was joking, quoting the reunion party's ridiculous name.

"Your conversation seemed pretty intense." Chick proved they'd been spying on me. "You sure he knows it's over?" Chick wiggled his eyebrows à la Groucho Marx.

A sliver of my insecure self was glad they'd witnessed Kevin's groveling for attention.

I glanced over my shoulder to make sure no customers were waiting at the cash register and to see Kevin getting to his feet. I turned away from him, trying to shut him out of my thoughts.

"Let's talk about the reunion party." I gathered Cliff, Deidre, Cindy, and Chick's attention. "You do understand Booty's is too small?"

"The space between here and the front door is wide open," Chick said. "We could rent a pool table for the night and set it up in that area."

"How would that add more square footage?" I shook my head. "The fire inspector wouldn't appreciate our blocking the exit."

"We could erect an awning out front and rent café tables, like in Paris," he persisted.

"Please, let's agree to find somewhere else."

"Okay, you win," Chick said. "We came up with a couple other ideas. An art gallery or a tavern that would let us have the place exclusively for the night."

"I like the art gallery idea," Deidre said, surprising me. She was interested in the arts? Maybe there was more to her than met the eye.

"Nah, that sounds too refined." Cindy picked at her salad. Her cup of carrot ginger soup looked untouched. "We need a DJ playing oldies and a dance floor."

"Get down and funky without your husband?" Deidre asked. "No, he hates dancing." Cindy wrinkled her pert nose. "He doesn't mind my dancing with other men, as long as he doesn't have to make a fool of himself."

"I like the tavern idea," Chick said. "Casual atmosphere. Pool tables, video games, and a sound system."

"I doubt any taverns would shut all their regular patrons out on a Friday night," I said.

"That's what's so great about this place," Chick said. "It's closed in the evenings. And we're in tight with the owner." Amazing how I was now included in their elite clique. Once they found another party venue, none of them would recognize me again.

"We're not any closer to choosing a place than we were before," Deidre said with a huff. "And, no, I'm not roller-skating, as TR suggested."

"How about a bowling alley?" Cindy said.

Deidre made a face. "Ugh, I hate bowling."

"Here's an idea," I said. "Rent half of a restaurant or pool hall. Some less popular establishments would be thrilled to have the extra business."

"But where?" Deidre asked.

"Mona Lisa, will you come with me to check them out?" Chick asked. "You'd know all the right questions."

"I don't have much spare time."

"Who does?" Cindy asked.

"You do." Chick raised a hand. "When you're not at the mall or having your hair done. And I don't trust your judgment."

"You should talk," she spit back. "I'm tempted to tell Mona Lisa everything I know about you."

"Truce," he said. "In all honesty I'm waving the white flag."

I stood and pushed my chair against the table.

"Do we have a date?" Chick asked me.

"Okay, how about brunch Sunday at a place north of here, the Dawn to Dusk Bakery." I hated eating alone.

191

"You bet." Chick grinned.

I saw movement up at the register - a good excuse to leave. Annie waited for me when I arrived at her side. A small, gift-wrapped box sat on her palm. "Looks like a certain somebody left you a gift," she said.

CHAPTER THIRTY-ONE
Joey

Gloria had tormented Joey incessantly since he went to bed, robbing him of much-needed sleep after a long day at Booty's. She'd scolded, poked fun at him, and snickered at her own sarcastic humor. "You might as well get up," she'd said several times. "You'll never fall asleep. Your circadian rhythm's out of whack. Making you whacky. A whack-job." The few times Joey drifted off, she made his feet jerk, rousing him into consciousness. "If your legs are itchy-crawly," she'd said. "There's a spider in the bed."

"Shut up and leave me alone!" He'd wanted to yell full force, but then she'd know he could hear her. He was determined to ignore Gloria until Saint Signore returned, and he must not wake Moni, who still wanted to move Joey back to The Home. He'd listened in on his sister's phone conversations with Mrs. Landis; the two women were plotting against him. Without the Saint, Joey had to protect himself. He had to be an army of one.

Where was the Saint? Joey had called out to him over and over, then pleaded with God the Almighty. First in English, then Italian, and then Latin. The Maker of the universe and every creature upon its craggy surface or dwelling in its salty oceans must understand all languages. And thoughts.

Joey pounded his feather pillow into a ball. He envisioned the domed ceiling of the Sistine Chapel. Was the Saint really visiting the Vatican? "Saint Signore doesn't exist," Gloria had repeated, plugging that thought into Joey's brain. She was making him question everything. Should Joey fly to the Vatican and find the Saint? Joey had never been on a commercial jet. He wondered which was preferable, safer, and cleaner. An Airbus or a Boeing 767?

He realized Gloria wasn't correcting or advising him. The air in his bedroom lay as smooth as Mama's satin pillowcase. Had Gloria finally fallen asleep?

He cracked open his eyes and checked his clock. Five thirty. In thirty minutes, Moni would yell down the stairs to make sure he was up. At least she hadn't barged into his room again. She'd rouse Gloria, too, and Joey's head would be filled with her Southern-drawl chatter for the rest of the day.

Joey listened to his own shallow breathing and the sound of the furnace kicking on.

Still no Gloria jabbering in his ears. Normally, when she ran out of words, she'd hum or sing "My Old Kentucky Home" with a wobbly vibrato, like she was sitting in the stands at Churchill Downs wearing a wide-brimmed hat smothered with fake flowers. Had she packed her bags and traipsed off to plague someone else? Unlikely. She would have made a grand finale exit, threatening a return visit.

As he lay in the darkness, an idea shaped like rotini pasta uncoiled in the back of his mind. If he slipped out of the house, Gloria might not notice his exit. He might rid himself of her pestering for a day. He could walk to work in fifteen to twenty minutes; it was too early for the bus. By the time he reached Booty's front door, Moni would arrive with the key.

As quietly as he could, he pushed the top sheet and blanket away and swung his legs over the side of the bed. He stepped into the clean underwear and clothes he'd set out on his dresser the night before—earlier, he'd sanitized the bureau's surface with Lysol. He poked his feet into white socks and tied on his faded black Gore-Tex shoes that had been laundered and bleached in the washing machine. There was no time for breakfast or his usual good-morning shower.

No shower? He hesitated for a moment as a surge of panic scratched over him, prickling the skin on his forearms and drying the inside of his mouth. But the sensation passed, melting away like butter on Mama's homemade bread.

He tiptoed up the stairs and into the kitchen, passing Figaro, who opened one eye, then returned to his dream, Joey guessed, of chasing the neighbor's orange tabby. Saint Signore had told Joey that a recurring nightmare haunted Figaro. Joey was glad the dog was enjoying an entertaining dream rather than fretting about the dangers lurking ahead.

He left through the kitchen door. Out on the sidewalk, Joey heard a robin's trill climbing an operatic scale with his springtime mating call, then a wren. Water trickled in the storm drain under his feet. Rain must have fallen during the night, with gravity pulling the clear liquid down to Lake Union and then to Puget Sound. Immersed in predawn murkiness, the streetlamps still glowed. Low, gray clouds hovered overhead.

He should have worn a warmer jacket, and he should have left Moni a note. But too late. Gloria would be all over him like a relentless case of chicken pox.

He headed up the street, his eyes scanning the yards and bushes. A complex nocturnal community explored the neighborhood at night. A raccoon he'd named Wily hustled across the street toward the neighbor's garbage can. Joey thought Wily was the cleverest fellow in the neighborhood. The masked creature knew who left cat food out on their back porch and where all the movement-activated spotlighting systems were set up.

There was no time to watch Wily dig through the neighbor's trash. Joey needed to keep on the move. In a few minutes, Wily and his mate would retreat into their lair, tucking themselves away to avoid daylight creatures like dogs and humans. Joey thought it ironic that people considered nighttime dangerous when, in fact, the true perils ruled under daylight.

Joey zigzagged toward Booty's, afraid to take the quickest route lest Gloria locate him. As he traveled south, his eyes inspected the parked cars, and he read their license plate numbers. He liked to memorize them, especially if they were out of state. Who knew when he might need the information? He noticed a four-door Buick from Florida. Someone had driven that far? Were they visiting relatives, or was this a stolen vehicle?

A jogger sprinted his way, moving quickly, so Joey stepped to the side, behind a tree, until the man passed by.

Several minutes into his trek, Joey's nostrils picked up the odor of singed wood, paper, and melted plastic - an ugly smell, reminding him of the day his neighbor's garage had burned to the ground. According to Papa, kids had been smoking or lighting matches. Papa had asked Joey, then eight years old, "It wasn't you, was it?" "No, Papa, I promise and hope to die." And his father had been satisfied.

Joey had a pretty good idea who had started that burning inferno: Moni. But Joey kept the secret to himself. He couldn't blame her; as a kid, he'd been fascinated by fire. He'd loved gazing at the flames from the barbecue pit undulating like exotic dancers in his parent's backyard on summer nights. He'd begged Papa to let him put a match to the crumpled newspaper, and finally, at age twelve, he had been given the honor of being the fire starter. By then, Moni had lost interest in anything other than tanning her legs and chasing after boys.

The breeze picked up, wafting out of the southwest. The smell worsened, making Joey's nasal passages sting and his eyes water. He considered turning around and retreating to the safety of Mama's house, but Gloria waited for him there, like a cat beside a birdcage.

He slipped a facemask out of his pocket, placed it over his mouth and nose to protect his lungs, and tightened the elastic strings.

Finally reaching the main drag, NE Forty-Fifth, a street lined with still closed shops and restaurants, he turned his head to the right. His eyes were bombarded with blinding lights flashing from three huge fire engines.

In Joey's mind, he saw men and women jolted awake by an ear-splitting alarm, half asleep, jumping into fire-retardant overalls and jackets. He imagined sirens wailing and horns blaring.

He saw the destruction several buildings down: the two-story clapboard structure, once the Dawn to Dusk Bakery, was now a blackened shell.

He rounded the corner and walked closer, drawn to the sight of a half dozen tired-looking firemen unhooking the hydrant and rewinding flattened hoses.

"Good thinking," Gloria said in Joey's ear, startling him. Had she been trailing him the whole time? "Knocking out the competition?" she said, laughing. "Way to go, Little Joe. Hey, I'm a poet and don't know it."

"I didn't do this!" Joey was outraged by her accusation.

"What was that you said?" a policeman asked Joey. The man, a mean-looking fellow with a wrestler's build, reached into his breast pocket, then displayed his badge. Joey gave it a cursory glance. He distrusted anyone wearing a uniform; a person could buy a phony uniform over the internet. And without his reading glasses, he couldn't see the badge clearly.

"I was talking to myself." Joey hid his hands in his pockets and took a step, but the policeman blocked his path.

"You know anything about this fire?" The officer's voice was gruff, like when Papa had drunk too much Chianti.

Joey shook his head. "No, I just got here."

"What are you doing out on the street at this hour?"

"Coming back to the scene of the crime to see your handiwork?" Gloria chimed in. "I'm proud of you. I couldn't have done better myself."

"I'm on my way to work." Joey ignored her words. "Down the street. Four blocks away. Booty's Café."

"By yourself, on foot?" the policeman said. "Let's see your driver's license."

"I don't drive."

"Got a DWI?"

"No, sir, I never learned how."

"Then your ID card?"

Joey's palms were growing moist. "I left it at home."

"Take that mask off." The officer put out his hand. Joey removed the mask and gave it to him.

Another policeman hulked over to them. "Who's this guy?"

"Claims he's on his way to work," the first policeman said.

"Where's that?"

"Booty's Café." Feeling heat rising up his chest, Joey unzipped his jacket.

"How long have you worked there?" the first policeman said.

"Not very long. It's my mother's, but my sister runs it now. She's going to sell it as soon as business picks up."

"I'm guessing it will, with your chief competitor out of the race," the second cop said. "I bet the two restaurants had a rivalry going."

"I never thought about it."

"Yeah, right." The second cop tipped his head at the harried-looking man talking to the firemen. "Jim O'Hara's customers will need a new place to eat, won't they?"

The first cop brought out a small pad and pen. "What's your first and last name? Address?"

Joey gave his name and address. "I was trying to slip out of my mama's house without waking anyone," he explained.

"What were you running from?" the second cop asked.

"Nothing. I—"

Gloria interrupted him. "Hold on, our illustrious policemen haven't read you your rights. Even if you're guilty, they can't detain you just because you're walking down the street."

"Uh, sir." Joey stared at the second policeman's soot-covered shoes. They were heavy and cumbersome, like the cop himself.

"A guy could torch his competitor's establishment," the first policeman said.

"Then in a week, burn down his own place and collect the insurance?" The second policeman snickered.

Joey ran his fingers around the neckline of his T-shirt. "We'd never do that." Or would Moni stoop to that level to rid herself of Booty's? "Are you sure it was arson?"

"We found rags dipped in paint thinner out back." The second policeman's glare bore into Joey. "Let's see those hands, buddy."

Joey brought them out and was glad they were clean; his nails were clipped short and rounded. "Sir, are you done with me? Is there anything else?"

"I guess not. For now. Did you notice anyone running up the street or acting suspiciously?"

Other than Gloria? he thought.

"No. When did the fire start? I got here only five minutes ago."

At that moment, he noticed Moni's car heading in their direction.

CHAPTER THIRTY-TWO
Mona Lisa

Steering my Toyota toward Booty's in the early morning hours, I drove alone, fuming and feeling sorry for myself. It appeared I'd be working the early shift solo until Ramon arrived.

Where was Joey? I'd looked everywhere, even in Mama's car, but he was gone. My thoughts turned to my mother, lounging in bed. The least she could do was come in and help me a few hours a day, but so far she'd refused, fabricating one lightweight excuse after another. Anyway, she didn't appear to be in Seattle. I'd called her repeatedly over the last few days and got no answer. I finally checked with the front desk at her assisted living facility. The lady answering the phone advised me Mama was on vacation. First Mama saddled me with Booty's, and then her house and son. Now she left town without telling me. Should I be worried for her safety? I felt like a mother whose teenage daughter was out on a date and hadn't bothered coming home.

I reached the main arterial and took a right. The traffic in front of me crawled along, bumper-to-bumper, a rarity at six in the morning. A smoky stench seeped into the car through the ventilation system, smelling like a soggy, extinguished campfire. Inhaling through my nostrils, I wondered if my car's motor was having problems, something I knew zilch about. A slipping fan belt? When was the last time I checked the oil level? If only Papa were here to help me, he could fix almost anything.

A half block farther, I noticed three massive fire engines, one partially blocking traffic, another positioned at an angle, its right front tire on the sidewalk. Several firemen stood stowing their hoses and gear into their trucks.

In the dull morning light, my bleary eyes focused on a burned-out structure—a charred and blackened building. Once white with cheery yellow awnings over its three front windows, the Dawn to Dusk Bakery—where I'd planned to meet Chick for brunch on Sunday—had been gutted by fire. Its windows were broken, chards of glass spiking out like knife blades, walls sagging, the sidewalk and street out front waterlogged, and puddles accumulating in the gutter.

Was I nuts, or was that Joey with two policemen interrogating him, one taking notes with a pen and pad? What was Joey doing here?

The driver in the sedan in front of me slowed to a halt to gawk for a moment, then he rolled forward, giving me room to swerve my car to the curb.

I jumped out. "Joey?" I jogged over to him. Both policemen turned to me. It seemed I was about to be questioned myself.

"Do you know this man?" one policeman said, a harsh edge to his voice, like he'd been up all night and was in no mood for delay. He was wide-shouldered and tall, well over six feet, a don't-mess-with-me guy, who would ordinarily be exactly the kind of officer I'd like protecting me. But today he seemed aggressive and frightening. I could see Joey was intimidated; his head bent forward and his weight shifted from foot to foot, like he was ready to take flight.

"He's my brother." But Joey, his lips sucked in, stared at the ground like he hadn't heard me. Was he involved with this fire? He always loved playing with matches.

"Can you think of a reason he'd be here?" the other policeman demanded.

"He goes out walking at night sometimes." I glanced at Joey, who seemed to be shivering in his lightweight jacket. Or had fear brought on his trembling?

"Joey, what are you doing here?" I tried to camouflage my annoyance and worry.

"I was on my way to work." He sounded timid, his voice a mere sliver. More cars were slowing to get an eyeful of the burned-out restaurant, and us, two civilians, being questioned by the police. I hoped no one I knew was passing by.

"Does he ordinarily walk to work at this early hour?" the first officer asked.

Should I lie and answer yes when, in fact, I always drove Joey in the morning? Mama would expect me to protect him. What would Papa say? He was strict about telling the truth.

"It's not out of the question." I looked the officer in the eye as though we had nothing to hide, when in fact Joey was an enigma—a puzzle. "Booty's Café is only a few blocks away. I'm on my way there right now."

"May we have your name and contact information? In case we have further questions," the officer asked.

"But I – we - had nothing to do with this." I hoped I was right, but my mind explored the possibilities. I recalled clearing out Joey's bedroom several months ago when we'd moved him into The Home, particularly the mason jar crammed full of matchbooks and discarded lighters. My thoughts flew back to the Fourth of July when we were kids. Joey loved shooting off bottle rockets and twirling sparklers in the dark. But most of the boys in the area had gotten into mischief. And I couldn't blame the neighbors' garage fire on him. The source of that inferno had been a much-speculated mystery since we were kids. I'm sure our parents talked about it at many local gatherings.

Only I knew the truth. Because I was the guilty culprit. I was the ten-year-old idiot who'd huddled in the corner of the empty garage that summer afternoon, ripping up and then burning poison-pen letters from my nemesis, Cynthia Wilson.

I could still see the fire spreading to a stack of old newspapers, leaping to the gas mower, then engulfing the paint cans. I should have run directly to my parents and screamed for help, but I stood there, mesmerized, watching the flames lick their way up the walls to the rafters. Then I fled out the side door and ran.

Was I afraid of Papa's wrath? Not really, because he was the fair-minded head of the household. He had dealt out punishment according to our crimes. I'm sure I would have been grounded and forced to mow the neighbor's lawn for the next ten years, the least I could do. My parents might have been held financially responsible for rebuilding the garage, which fortunately was not attached to The Home. Mostly, I saw myself disappointing Papa. Losing his admiration. On top of starting the fire, I would have had to admit that the most popular girl in my class sent me hate letters, warning me to keep away from her friends. Why the queen bee had targeted me, I never understood. She called me a stupid *wop*. Was carrying Italian DNA my only transgression? My father would have been furious and demanded to meet with her parents. Then Cynthia would have ramped up her hatred and talked about him at school.

As for the fire, I never told a soul what I'd done. But now, standing in the street in front of the incinerated bakery, I had the crazy notion of confessing to these two policemen just to get the burden off my back. But then they'd think they'd happened upon a family of pyromaniacs, and we'd both end up in jail.

Glancing past the policemen, I recognized the restaurant's owner, Jim O'Hara, mid-fifties, wrapped in a bathrobe over jogging pants, talking to his wife, her hands hugging her arms for warmth. They both appeared devastated.

Part of me wished Booty's had burned down instead. Half my problems would be solved. Or would they? I was becoming attached to that stupid place, its rhythm, and the customers who called me by name like I was someone important. And I was keeping my parents' dream alive.

"Any idea what started the fire?" I asked the officers. "A stove or fry pan left on?"

"We're ninety-nine percent sure it was arson," the first policeman said, brandishing a rag emitting the fumes of paint thinner, an odor I recognized from Papa's workbench. When I got home later, I'd check to make sure Papa's tin of paint thinner was still there. If it was gone, then what? I couldn't turn in Joey, when I, in fact, was responsible for burning down the neighbor's garage. Honestly, it was an accident - a horrifying scene. I could have suffocated in the garage mushroomed with smoke. In the hubbub - fire trucks, water spraying, neighbors praying the house didn't burn down too - I stood off in the distance, in a daze. The moment to step forward and confess flashed by.

Even today, I've considered going to confession to tell it all to a priest behind a screen. Would spilling my guts ease my guilt? My folks never suspected their sweet little Mona Lisa would harbor such an ugly secret, but I've always had the feeling that Joey knew. Would he tell these two officers about me right now?

An endless stream of cars took their time passing by us, not that I could blame them. This was a big event for this usually peaceful stretch of road.

"Are you done with us?" I asked the policemen. They both gave Joey another looking over. His jeans hung a couple inches too short, his white socks brightly showing themselves, but his pant legs and shoes were clean.

"We should get to work," I said.

The two policemen conferred, then one said, "Go ahead. "Someone may come by your restaurant later with more questions."

A blue-white flash filled the air. Joey and I spun around to stare into a reporter's camera. Another flash went off. Oh no. Would our faces appear on the front page of the newspaper?

A KOMO TV News van pulled in behind my car, and four people hopped out carrying camera equipment. I recognized a newswoman from another local station striding over to me, tailed by a cameraman. The smiling woman pushed a microphone in my face and introduced herself. I'd always wanted to be on TV, but not like this.

I held a hand up to cover my face. "We were just passing by

on our way to work." I grabbed hold of Joey's arm, hurried him to my car, and we both dove in.

I gave the Dawn to Dusk Bakery a final glance, and my heart sank. I'd met the proprietors, Jim and Bessy O'Hara, on several occasions. Both were kind people who loved serving the public. In fact, I'd often seen policemen in their establishment buying coffee or having breakfast or lunch. Who would want to harm the O'Haras?

I noticed the reporter had followed us to the car. I locked the doors and gunned the engine. As I drove to Booty's, I smelled the rancid smoky odor on Joey's and my clothing. I hoped it would dissipate once we got the vegetables sautéing for the soup. I would use plenty of garlic today.

"Joey, do you know anything about the fire?" I was not sure if I wanted an honest answer. He was looking over his shoulder like we were being trailed. "Well, do you?" I asked.

"No. But it reminded me of a dream from when we were kids. Was there a fire in our neighborhood?"

I got an uneasy feeling in my gut. "A long time ago, across the street and down two houses, a garage burned."

"Oh yeah, they say kids were playing with matches. I remember the fire engines."

"Joey, you wouldn't intentionally burn down the Dawn to Dusk Bakery, would you?"

"No, I don't think so." His voice came out with little conviction, more like a mystery he was already pondering.

CHAPTER THIRTY-THREE
Cliff

From the second floor, Cliff heard Barbara Buttaro enter her house and call out, "*Ciao*, anyone home?" in her elegant alto voice.

"I'm upstairs in the second bathroom." Cliff stepped out of the shower stall Mona Lisa must have used as a child. Towels hung neatly folded, and toiletries sat outside a clear zippered bag, indicating she was here for a short stay. She'd made it clear she planned to move back to her apartment as soon as possible.

As Cliff wiped his hands and tossed the rag in an empty bucket, he listened to Barbara scale the stairs. She rounded the corner with a jaunty step. Wearing a caftan and slim slacks, she looked younger than the last time he'd seen her. She was probably his mother's age but could pass for her early fifties. Barbara's dark hair was newly fashioned, shorter and highlighted. Her full lips were tinted with deep coral red lipstick.

"The tiles look wonderful." She stepped closer to appraise the shower stall.

"I thought I'd better take this job on myself. It's too difficult for Thomas, and I didn't want to outsource it. My next remodeling project is weeks away." He surprised himself with his candor. Barbara was easy to talk to.

"Are you good at everything?" Her head tilted so her dangly earrings swung in small circles.

"In my business I've learned to be a jack-of-all-trades."

"You'll make some woman a wonderful husband."

"I tried that once, but it didn't work out."

"It's never too late to try again."

"Nah, I'm an old dog who can't learn new tricks."

She shook her head and laughed. "Not compared to me." Was she flirting with him or referring to her perpetually single daughter? Most likely, the latter.

"I'm almost done with the grouting, then Thomas will paint the woodwork in here, and I'll hang the light fixture," he said. Cliff had found a small Venetian chandelier in the basement in a giveaway/garage sale box.

"I should have done this years ago." Her brows lifted. "After my husband died, I let the house go." She moved toward the hallway. "The creamy beige Thomas painted the front hall and staircase was a good choice - yours I assume. It ties the interior of the house together."

"I'm glad you approve. Do you regret leaving? If I'm not being too nosy."

"*Mezza mezza.* Yes and no." She tipped her flattened hand, and Cliff noticed she was wearing a bulky ruby surrounded by diamonds.

"I can't picture you in a retirement community when you have this lovely house to live in." He glanced out the window. "And now that your knee is on the mend, you seem fit, capable of climbing stairs and keeping-up the garden."

"I do enjoy gardening and growing fresh tomatoes and basil - but I have reasons for not moving home, big changes in my life. Even my children don't know about them yet."

"Sounds intriguing." Cliff felt complimented to be included in a private conversation with a woman of her caliber. Did he have a crush on Barbara? No, more likely he had one on her beautiful daughter, Mona Lisa. What man wouldn't? He was amazed no guy had pursued her with fervor. Maybe she'd turned them all down.

He and Barbara strolled the second floor, discussing the repairs Thomas had accomplished. One bedroom door stood closed. It was closed when Mona Lisa gave him his first tour and had been ever since. He wondered about her taste in furniture. He doubted she went in for frilly bedspreads and chintz. Not that she wasn't feminine. She was.

"Mona Lisa's room?" Cliff asked, and she nodded. "Does it need painting?" His hand moved to the knob.

"We'd better wait until Mona Lisa's home. She tends to be private. Which is not necessarily a bad trait."

"I suppose you're right."

He and Barbara entered her late husband's study. "This is where my Carlo worked on his designs." She eyed the bookcase that still housed hardbacks and oddly shaped objects.

"Mona Lisa said her father was an inventor."

"Yes, a brilliant man. Not that he didn't have his faults. All men seem to."

Cliff wanted to point out that women had plenty of faults as well, but he kept quiet.

She closed in on the desk, a squat utilitarian piece of furniture littered with papers and surrounded by cardboard boxes. "It looks like someone's been going through his files. Mona Lisa, no doubt. She'd better not throw anything important away. I need to speak to her." Barbara reached into an opened box and pulled out a file marked Stink and Think.

Cliff let out a chuckle. "What in the world could that be?"

"I have no idea." She tucked the file under her elbow. "I should have paid better attention. But you know how it is when you're married—you take your spouse for granted."

"Yes, I was guilty of that, until my former wife kicked me out and I pretty much lost touch with my daughter—you've met her—Panda. That's why this past week has been so special. She's been living with me while her mother is getting married." He had trouble getting the word *married* out of his mouth and wondered if Barbara noticed. "Panda and I have been a little cramped in my apartment. And the furnace for the house I live in conked out this morning, so my place is freezing. I'm sure Panda can't wait to get home to her own room."

"I'll bet she's enjoyed spending time with you. Teenage girls don't always show their true emotions. I rarely knew what Mona Lisa was thinking. She was a moody girl."

That fact didn't surprise Cliff. Mona Lisa still seemed temperamental.

Barbara's face grew animated, her brown eyes alive. "Cliff, I have an idea. What are you doing tonight? We're throwing a dinner party—a special occasion—and would like to include you."

"I'd love it, but I need to pick up Panda after school, then bring her to her mother's this evening. Her mother's plane lands around ten tonight." Cliff would have to face his former wife, remarried, a scenario that made his insides twist like he'd eaten a bag of green apples.

"The timing sounds perfect." Barbara apparently did not sense Cliff's apprehension. "Bring Panda with you, then take her to her mother's after dessert."

"That's a kind invitation." His thoughts turned to the dinner. He feared his daughter would make a scene at the table and flirt with Joey if he were there. Cliff hoped he wouldn't be. On the other hand, he hated facing a whole evening waiting for Janette and Dennis's triumphant return as man and wife. Would he be forced to plaster on a phony smile and congratulate them? He couldn't sulk in the car while Panda lugged her gear into the house. He hoped the day would come when he felt nothing toward Janette. A big fat nothing instead of a festering, twisted resentment.

It would do Panda good to be around Barbara Buttaro, a charitable woman unlike Janette's cool and aloof parents. Some grandparents they were - not to mention Cliff's own mother, usually stewed and foulmouthed. Janette had never allowed her to babysit Panda. Cliff and Janette agreed there.

"We'd like to come, thank you," Cliff said. "I look forward to a home-cooked meal."

"Wonderful. The more, the merrier. But the dinner's not here. It's at Canlis, on the north end of Queen Ann Hill. Not an Italian restaurant, but we've known the family for years. Now, you promise to come, please? My treat. I won't take no for an answer."

"All right, thank you." He was overcome by her generosity. Canlis was one of the most exclusive and respected restaurants in Seattle. He'd never set foot in it; he'd have to call the restaurant and ask if they had a dress code.

"*Bravo.*" Her smile was warm.

Was there a delicate way to ask for the guest list? He assumed Mona Lisa would be included. Was it her idea to invite Cliff? Unlikely. "Is it a large party?"

"No, just Frank and me and a small handful. We're planning to have dinner with his family tomorrow - over two dozen people. Most of our casual friends don't go out at night anymore and several are on vacation. They talk about the same things over and over, like broken records. That's why it's important you and Panda attend to liven things up."

* * *

Ever since Barbara's dinner invitation, Cliff had been pondering the evening ahead. He didn't know her very well. Why had she invited him? And how would Panda conduct herself? Her table manners were iffy at best and she wore too much eye makeup, not to mention the provocative way she dressed.

Standing in the spare bedroom, what he now called *Panda's room*, he listened to her gripe about his apartment's frigid temperature; the furnace had conked out several hours ago before he'd picked her up from school.

"I'm glad I don't have to spend another night here. I'd freeze to death." She stuffed dirty clothing into her suitcase that yawned open on one of the two twin beds.

"I hate to give you up," Cliff said, "but I'm grateful for the time we've shared."

She jimmied a pair of shoes next to her lingerie. "I still think I could have stayed at Mom's by myself. In some countries, I'm x after all. Cliff checked himself out in the mirror. He wore a navy-blue sports jacket over slacks with a red tie. He looked good, as far as he could tell.

Twenty minutes later, exiting Highway 99, Cliff steered his Porsche to the restaurant, a sleek building in the Frank Lloyd Wright style. Cliff pulled under a roofed entrance, past sand-colored rough rock columns.

He gave his keys to the valet parking attendant—he'd be expected to tip the young man later. Cliff wished a few dollars didn't matter to him, but every penny was important.

As they entered the one-story building, with its tall, sloping ceiling and unique chandelier Panda said, within earshot of the hostess, "Are you sure we can afford to eat here?"

He spoke above a whisper. "Yes, honey. Mrs. Buttaro is treating us."

"I bet Dennis has enough money to eat anywhere. He's loaded, with a capital *L*."

"Let's leave what's-his-name out of the conversation for the evening, okay?"

"Fine by me. Now I'll have to face his smarmy smile every morning at breakfast. I don't understand what Mom sees in him other than his fat wallet."

Cliff felt like saying that made two of them, but he didn't want to divulge anything that could be repeated to Janette. He hadn't untangled his ill feelings toward Dennis but knew a thick strand of jealousy ran through them.

Panda looked up at Cliff. "I won't have to call him Dad, will I?"

"Of course not, honey. I'm your father. Call him what you do now."

"You mean *Mr. Toad Head*?"

Cliff laughed out loud. Then a thought hit him—she was funny, but would Barbara appreciate her brand of humor? "Panda, as a favor to me, please be extra polite to Mrs. Buttaro, okay?"

Her hands moved to her narrow hips. "Like, when aren't I polite?"

He could rattle off a dozen instances in the last week alone. "Most of the time you're a perfect angel." Cliff looked into the restaurant. His mother would call it ritzy, but he knew it to be refined elegance.

"Buttaro party," he told the hostess.

"This way, please." She led them to a table that offered a magnificent view of Union Bay and the Cascade Mountains. Barbara and Frank DiAngelo were sitting with their backs against the wall, thick in conversation. Frank brought Barbara's fingertips to his lips and kissed them. Their age difference seemed to have expanded, perhaps due to Barbara's new, younger look. Her shortened hair swept away from her face to accentuate her high cheekbones, and a silk dress showed off her shapely figure. Another contrast to his own dumpy mother.

When Frank saw them, he rose to his feet with a flourish. "Welcome! We're so glad you could join us. Cliff, isn't it?" He reached out his hand to shake Cliff's.

"Yes, Mr. DiAngelo."

"Please call me Frank. What did you say your last name was?"

"He's trying to find out if you're Italian," Barbara cut in.

"And what's wrong with that?" Frank asked.

She rested her hand on his forearm. "Not a thing, darling."

Cliff said, "My last name is McFarlane, and this is my daughter, Panda." He was pleased Panda put her hand out to shake Frank's.

"*Molto piacere, bellissima ragazza,*" Frank said. "Please have a seat."

There were only four vacant chairs, not what Cliff expected. He moved to the far end of the table, and Panda lowered herself into the seat next to him, across from Barbara.

Cliff saw the hostess greet Mona Lisa at the restaurant's front door. Then Cliff's attention was drawn to a tall man with sandy hair striding into the lounge area and sitting before a grand piano.

With ease and unique embellishment, the pianist commenced playing a medley of tunes from modern musicals. Panda swiveled in her chair to watch him. "I love that tune," she said, as a piece from *Les Misérables* rippled through the room. Then, without warning, she left her seat and went to speak to the pianist, who continued playing softly as they chatted. A moment later, much to Cliff's astonishment, Panda began to sing, "There is a castle in the clouds." She wasn't using a microphone, but her pure soprano voice floated above the chatter until most of the diners stopped talking and were listening to her in admiration. Cliff hadn't heard her sing since she was a child, and then only at birthday parties.

Panda stood as poised as a pro, her elbow on the piano, and finished the song about a girl living in a make-believe world where no one shouted or talked too loud. The tale forced Cliff to remember Janette's and his verbal battles, their words aimed at each other like shrapnel. They'd wounded their daughter in the crossfire, no doubt. Cliff vowed to find a way to make it up to Panda. But how?

When Panda sang her last word and the pianist finished the piece, a surge of applause erupted. Panda smiled and made a small bow. Cliff's heart swelled with pride, and he felt a new fierce loyalty for his daughter. He loved her more than anything, including her green bangs and her bodacious attitude.

When she returned to her seat Frank clapped and Barbara said, "*Bravissima.*"

"Your voice is beautiful," Cliff said. "When - where did you learn to sing like that? And how did you have the guts to stand up in front of an audience?"

"Mom owns the CD, and I've been practicing for auditions at school for the annual musical. Which I got into, by the way."

"You're going to sing in a musical? That's wonderful." He felt like he hardly knew her, and it was no one's fault but his own.

"Here's our Mona Lisa." Frank waved his hand across the room. "I hope she heard Panda's singing."

As Mona Lisa reached the table, her gaze zeroed in on Cliff.

213

"This is a surprise," she said in a less-than-cordial tone. "I wasn't expecting to see you here tonight."

"I invited him," Barbara said. "And he was kind enough to bring his charming and talented daughter. Did you hear her sing?"

"Yes. Beautiful voice." Mona Lisa glanced at the two remaining chairs. She looked striking in a chocolate-brown wraparound dress that accented her eyes and hair, but her demeanor revealed displeasure.

Cliff spoke to Barbara. "If our being here's a problem, we can leave."

"No, Daddy." Panda elbowed him. "We were here first. Let Mona Lisa leave."

Mona Lisa set her attention on Barbara. "Where have you been for the last few days, Mama? I've been worried sick."

"*Un momento*, please take a seat." Frank said. "Your mother and I have an announcement. Wonderful news. Shall we wait for Joey to get here?"

"Joey refused to come with me," Mona Lisa said. "No surprise. He won't eat at restaurants, except Booty's, where he prepares the food. Mama, you won't believe what happened on the way to work today—" She pursed her lips as she sat down across from Frank. "Never mind. I'll tell you later. When it's just family."

"This is family," Barbara said.

"No, it's not." She accepted a menu from the waitress. "So what's the good news? Someone win the lottery?"

"Even better." Frank took hold of Barbara's hand and held his and hers up in a show of unity. "Say hello to Mr. and Mrs. DiAngelo."

Mona Lisa's eyes bulged. "Don't tell me you two got married?"

"*Cara*, you knew we were engaged." Barbara wiggled her ring finger.

"Have you forgotten about Papa?"

"Not any more than Frank has forgotten about his dear Cecelia. I'm sure both are smiling down from heaven, glad to see us happy."

"But Frank, of all people?"

Panda turned to Cliff and whispered, "And you were worried about my bad manners?"

Cliff felt heat creeping up his shirt collar; he loosened his tie. "Maybe it would be better if we left," he told Barbara.

"No Cliff, not until someone has toasted us, the newlyweds. Would you mind?"

"I'd be honored."

"Waiter," Frank said. "A bottle of champagne. In fact, champagne for everyone in the house."

"Yes, sir. Right away." Minutes later, the staff busily distributed trays of fluted stemware around the dining room, and heads were turning to the Buttaro table. Cliff had never been shy, but his mind spun as he tried to think of an appropriate toast. Was a clever remark required? He and Janette's wedding had been the bash of the year with a dozen witty toasts, not to mention caviar and a feast for three hundred—her parents had insisted. And look where the two of them ended up. In divorce court.

With his water glass in hand—he didn't dare take a sip of champagne—he stood and found he had the attention of everyone in the restaurant. "I'd like to introduce you to the newly wedded DiAngelos," he said. "May the Lord bless their marriage and may their love for each other continue to grow."

"Here, here!" people at surrounding tables said.

"Salute!" Frank clinked Barbara's glass, then Cliff's and Panda's glasses.

Everyone except Mona Lisa was grinning and sipping their drinks. She was too far away from him to tap her glass with his, so he clinked Panda's, who then sipped her coke with maraschino cherries through a straw. Finally, Barbara reached across the table and clinked Mona Lisa's glass. "Are you all right?" Barbara asked Mona Lisa, who looked dazed.

"Just surprised. Mama, you changed your last name?" Mona Lisa's usual olive complexion had turned pale.

"Yes, of course. I'm now Barbara DiAngelo."

"Then you and I won't have the same last name."

"Mona Lisa, when you marry—it's sure to happen—you'll take on your husband's name too."

"But have you forgotten?" Mona's brows furrowed. "Booty's is a play on our last name."

"I have a wonderful idea," Frank said, positioning his glass next to Barbara's. He wrapped an arm around her shoulder. "We should change Booty's name to DiAngelo's. Then there's no inconsistency."

"How dare you?" Mona reminded Cliff of the yellow jacket he'd stirred up behind his landlady's back porch.

"*Cara*, I thought you hated working at the restaurant." Barbara sipped her champagne. "If we sell it - that's your plan, isn't it? The new owners will likely change the name."

CHAPTER THIRTY-FOUR
Mona Lisa

"Congratulations!" said a mid-fifties couple at the next table. "We've been married twenty years and couldn't be happier."

"Thank you," Mama and Frank said in unison and clinked their champagne glasses with the couple's. The entire restaurant bubbled with contagious gaiety, while the pianist played the wedding march with a profusion of ornate chords and embellishments.

As Mama and Frank shared a brief kiss, I brought a crystal glass to my lips and took the tiniest sip, just enough to make a polite toast, then settled back into my chair and tried to calm my nerves with a breathing exercise I'd learned from reading an Andrew Weil book. Clinging to my appearance of decorum, all I could muster was a placid smile. I felt raw emotions—betrayal, resentment, loneliness—swirling through my mind, threatening to spew out my mouth. I pushed the champagne glass further away. The last thing I needed was alcohol to loosen my tongue.

Distressed and distracted as I felt, I vowed not to allow myself to pout and put a damper on the festive occasion. What kind of selfish daughter would hurt her mother, a woman who'd grieved for more than ten years over the loss of her husband? I had thought she was still a brokenhearted widow, but apparently not. If only Papa would walk in this room right now and save the day.

Thinking about him ignited a fresh round of sadness. I missed my father more than ever.

Mama sent me a lopsided smile. I knew from experience there was a question attached to it. I needed to act ecstatic for her, not behave like a spoiled brat who threatened to demand an annulment - was it too late for that? As far as I was concerned, Frank was an old coot with four grown children, none of whom I'd ever liked. But I reminded myself that few women remarried at Mama's age. In fact, how many women find commitment material in the dating world? I should be so lucky. At this moment, I felt myself wilting into spinsterhood. Even Cliff, sitting at the far end of the table and looking appealing in his blazer and red tie, hadn't made eye contact with me or said hello. Did I still have a pathetic crush on him left over from high school?

Mama, sitting on the other side of Frank, placed her left hand on the table. The faceted diamonds surrounding her magnificent ruby captured sparkles from the votive candles, the overhead lights, and the setting sun reflecting off the distant Cascade Mountains. I had to give it to Frank. He had good taste in jewelry and women. Was he as wealthy as he acted? As far as I knew, he owned an importing business, specializing in Italian canned goods, olives, and olive oil, that his two sons now operated, and he resided in a three-story mansion on the shore of Lake Washington near Madison Park. Had Mama already moved in with him without telling me?

"Where will you two be living?" I asked.

"At my place." The way Frank answered - stressing the word *my* - made me wonder if his children had insisted Mama sign a prenuptial agreement, like Kevin had hinted at - a fact I hadn't shared with Mama or anyone because I was too embarrassed.

My thoughts shifted to Kevin. I'd dwelled in the land of confusion since he'd come into Booty's. I'd opened his gift - a gold charm in the shape of a boot. In the bottom of the box lay a slippery gold chain. It was a thoughtful gift, but why buy it for me? A consolation prize? What was his motive? And why should I care? If I had any brains, I'd give up men forever. Unless I could find a guy exactly like Papa.

"Mona Lisa?" Mama reached past Frank and patted the back of my hand. "Is something wrong? You look sad."

"No, I'm happy for you - I really am. I've been shaky ever since this morning when I saw the O'Hara's restaurant had burned down." Although, that was only one of the reasons for my conflicted emotions.

"The Dawn to Dusk *è finito?*" Frank said.

"Yes." It felt good to allow the corners of my mouth to sag. "The police think it was arson. The restaurant probably won't reopen for six months."

"*Mio Dio,*" Mama said. "I'll have to call the O'Haras and offer my condolences."

"If their phone works." I opened my napkin and dropped it in my lap. "The second floor looked okay, but it might be ruined by smoke."

"Then I'll stop by tomorrow."

"Too bad they're not Italian, or I could help them." Frank's remark irked me. What kind of bigot had Mama married? Papa was all gung ho Italian, but he never would have made such a statement. Wadding my napkin in my lap, I didn't lash out; there was no use digging a wider trench between Frank and me.

"It can't hurt to have our competition out of commission," he said.

Did I hear the word *our*? Frank was planning to take over Booty's?

"We were swamped all day," I said. "At their expense, which doesn't seem fair. Mama, I'm sure the O'Haras would appreciate any assistance they can get. They looked devastated."

"You actually saw them?" With her elbows on the table, she cupped her chin in her hands.

"From a distance, on the way to work this morning with Joey."

"I'm sorry our Joey had to witness that," she said. "You know how sensitive he is."

Mama always protected Joey when, in fact, he could have started the fire. When I asked him about it this morning, he'd acted as though he didn't have a clue. I considered my little brother harmless, but what did I really know about him?

But who was I to point fingers? Mona Lisa Buttaro was an arsonist. Now that I thought about it, my life was forever changed after lighting the garage afire. I separated myself from my closest friends for fear of mentioning the incident by mistake. Even today, the smell of smoke or sulfur from a lit match hurled me back to the past, to my criminal deed.

I heard Cliff speak and looked down at the table to see him giving the waitress his dinner order. Glancing at Panda, he pointed to the menu, and she shook her head. I had to admit, Panda's singing voice was magnificent. Who would have thought? But how on earth did she land in the spotlight, entertaining everyone in the restaurant?

I leaned closer to Mama, speaking past Frank's extensive paunch. "It's your party," I said, "but I have to wonder why you invited those two to dinner."

"Cliff was at the house today, and the invitation seemed natural enough. I've grown fond of him. He's restoring the house beautifully."

"As you've hired him to do, Mama, don't forget that."

"Sure, I pay him. But it's apparent he loves the integrity of old homes."

He did seem to appreciate her house, both architecturally and structurally. He even admired the cracked lath and plaster walls. But the bottom line was that Mama was shelling out his salary.

"If I'm not mistaken, the job has grown." I flattened my napkin on my lap. "I shudder to think what the bill will be."

"Don't worry about it," Frank advised me. "I'll take care of everything."

"Still, Cliff's not a person I would have invited tonight." I felt vulnerable. Because he reminded me of high school, or because Mama was so taken with him? I couldn't help noticing a growing attachment between Mama and Cliff. Were Cliff and Panda in the process of replacing me? Was I even needed here?

As my thoughts zigzagged, a headache enveloped my skull, like I'd swallowed ice cream too quickly. The pain was enough to make me lose my appetite. But as I inhaled the tantalizing aromas wafting from the kitchen and nearby tables, my stomach growled with anticipation.

"Anything else on your mind?" Mama asked me. "Besides getting used to having a new stepfather?" She placed her hand on Frank's, and he nuzzled her cheek, making me cringe.

I tried to detangle my warring emotions and had a flashback to childhood. In elementary school there had been a popular girl's birthday party I wasn't invited to - had it been after the garage fire? I'd sulked on the perimeter, like looking through a picket fence at others having fun. I felt excluded again tonight. Why hadn't Mama included me in her plans?

"I don't understand the secrecy," I said. "You and I used to be so close. The best mother-daughter combo I knew." Until Mama hurt her knee and then forced me to run Booty's. Or did the fissure between us open up earlier, and I hadn't noticed?

"For several reasons, we wanted to elope." She sent me a smile.

Frank's face beamed. "Like Romeo and Juliet."

The thought of them on their wedding night filled me with revulsion. I didn't want to know the details. "At least tell me where you tied the knot. At city hall?"

"No." Her lips gathered into a smile. "Las Vegas."

Papa didn't approve of gambling. He'd refused to go to what he called Sin City, and she knew it. "You used one of those phony chapels?" I asked.

"Yes. We had a ball." Frank's grin widened. "We stayed up late, took in a few shows, and sat by the pool."

"I wish you two had had a real wedding," I said. "One I'd been invited to." With a bridal bouquet I might have caught.

"We were afraid if we included all my family members it would have taken months to organize." Frank took out a cigar. "You know my eldest daughter, Lola. She would have turned the wedding reception into a three-ring circus. She means well." He twirled his cigar but made no move to light it.

I could picture his boisterous family, all jabbering at once, half in English, half in Italian. "I guess you're right." I had no idea how many grandkids Frank had but figured at least a half dozen little girls would have been demanding to be flower girls.

"I guess I'm just in shock, Mama. I'll get over it." Given enough time. I would stuff my disappointments in the recycle bin in the back of my mind along with my other letdowns.

Frank raised his volume and directed his words to Panda and Cliff. "Order anything you like. I'll cover the bill."

"Even lobster?" Panda's face grew animated with excitement. "I've never eaten it before."

"Yes, *certo*. No matter the cost."

Cliff pulled out his iPhone and frowned at the screen. "Sorry, everyone. I just got a text message from Janette. Her flight's been cancelled. There's a problem with the aircraft, and the airline doesn't have the parts to repair it. She and Dennis won't be home until tomorrow." His hand lightly massaged Panda's shoulder. "Looks like we're headed back to my place tonight."

She squirmed out of his reach. "No way, it's freezing over there. I'll catch pneumonia. Just take me to Mom's so I can sleep in my own room."

Cliff stuffed his phone back into his pocket. "I can't leave you alone by yourself. And I refuse to spend the night at your mother's."

"Then we'll stay at a hotel and order room service." She clapped. "Goody, I'm already packed."

"I have the solution," Mama said, capturing everyone's attention. "You two come stay at my old house tonight."

My jaw dropped open in silent protest.

"We couldn't impose," Cliff said.

"The house is almost empty," Mama said. "Cliff, you said you were planning to be there first thing in the morning anyway. Panda can sleep in my room. My king-size bed is still made up. What do you think, Mona Lisa?"

Everyone at our table fell silent, all eyes on me. Mama was being unfair. "Doesn't Panda have a girlfriend she could stay with?" I asked.

"It's too late to call anyone on a weeknight." Panda placed her hands in a pretty-please praying position, not her usual style. Instead of a bossy brat, I saw, for the first time, a little girl who'd been passed between her parents at their convenience.

I checked my wristwatch. "I guess you're right."

"Does that mean I can stay?" She gave me a saccharine smile. "I'll take Figaro out for a walk before school. And I won't make a mess in the kitchen, I promise."

"Okay."

"But Joey…" Cliff's hand tightened into a fist. "With him there, I'd worry."

"Mona Lisa will be home," Mama said. "Joey sleeps way down in the basement. He's so shy, he wouldn't hurt a flea."

Cliff didn't look convinced, and I couldn't blame him. Just minutes ago I was wondering if Joey was an arsonist. Who knew what he did all night? And I remembered Joey's and Panda's connection of some sort in our yard when they'd first met and then again at Booty's.

"I understand Cliff's reservations," I said. "Mama, remember how protective you used to be of me?"

"Then Cliff will stay too," she said. "We have a cot you can set up in the study. There's plenty of space."

"I suppose I could," Cliff said.

"Can Figaro sleep in my room?" Panda asked.

Cliff swiped his mouth with his hand. "If it's all right with Mona Lisa."

I stiffened in my chair. The rules of the game were changing faster than I could keep up with them. Cliff glanced at me, and I got the feeling he wanted me to turn him down. I'd noticed he hated saying no to Panda. As a rule, I felt sorry for divorced dads; I really did. But I didn't want to be the bad guy either.

"It's okay with me." What else could I do? The word *rail-*

roaded came to mind. But it wasn't anyone's fault that Janette's flight was cancelled, and here was a chance to demonstrate more generosity than I felt.

"Then it's all settled." Mama sent me another smile.

I scrutinized Panda from across the table. Dressed modestly as she was tonight, if you ignored her green bangs and owl eyes - too much black liner and mascara - she looked like an ordinary teenage girl who adored her father. And Cliff was smitten with her, which meant he had a kind heart.

"I need work done on my house," Frank declared. "My new bride, she wants to redo everything. Cliff, how are you at remodeling kitchens?"

"My specialty." Cliff sat taller.

"*Va bene.* Okay. While Panda's in school tomorrow, I'll swing by, pick you up, and give you a tour of my home."

"*Un momento,*" I said to Frank, joking. "You'd hire Cliff? He's not Italian."

"*Non c'è problema,* not a problem." Frank winked. "I'll make an exception in his case.

CHAPTER THIRTY-FIVE
Cliff

While Cliff dashed into his apartment to change into casual clothes, Panda waited in his car, listening to the radio. He figured she wasn't taking any chances of being talked into sleeping at his chilly apartment, what with an adventure at Barbara's ahead.

Cliff had reservations about staying at the Buttaros'. His gut told him Joey was a man he didn't want anywhere near his daughter. But Cliff reminded himself that everyone had an odd uncle. Except in his family. His mother's brother was a respectable engineer at Boeing, and her sister was a nurse at Children's Hospital. Cliff's mother served as the no-good misfit.

Minutes later, Cliff trotted down the back steps, carrying his duffle bag, and opened the car door. "Here I am."

"Obviously," she said.

He tossed the canvas bag behind the driver's seat next to hers.

As he steered his car north, leaving Capitol Hill, he wondered if Frank DiAngelo would make good on his promise to take Cliff to his house, described by Barbara as a mansion. From what Frank had said, he could keep Cliff busy for months.

Ten minutes later, he pulled his car up front of the Buttaros' and saw Mona Lisa's automobile parked in the driveway. Cliff dreaded the awkward scene that awaited him. Mona Lisa seemed to harbor a grudge toward him, probably left over from high school. He'd thought inviting her to the reunion meeting would negate his former snobbish attitude, but he'd flubbed up big time with his bear hug outside of Dukes. At that moment, he'd felt so desperately alone that he might have hugged a lamppost. At Twelve-Step meetings, attendees sometimes shared hugs of support, meaning nothing more than, "I'm with you. Hang in there."

As Cliff set his parking brake, Panda jumped out of the car, trotted to the back porch, and bopped up the steps. The bounce in her stride told him he was doing the right thing. Sure, spending the night here was inconvenient, but it was a chance to have his daughter another night. Once Janette got home, he might not see Panda again for weeks. Even months.

Panda pushed the bell. The back door swung open, and Mona Lisa said, "Come on in." Her mood seemed elevated. She stepped out onto the porch with Figaro at her side. Panda put her hand out to scratch Figaro behind the ear, and he basked in her attention, leaning his massive body against her legs.

As Cliff neared the house with the bags, Figaro woofed in his direction. Cliff had never been afraid of dogs but felt a healthy respect for an animal this size and wasn't about to climb the steps until the dog relaxed.

"Good boy," Panda said, and the dog turned his head and greeted her with a show of his front teeth, canine teeth as big as a mountain lion's.

"It's okay," Mona Lisa told Cliff. "He looks scary, but he's smiling. It took a while for me to get used to it."

"If you say so."

"I wish I had a dog," Panda said. Cliff realized if he bought a puppy, she'd be begging to come visit him. But how could he manage? He wasn't home enough to take care of a guinea pig or a goldfish. Which wasn't how he meant to live his life. He wanted to return to the life he'd led prior to the divorce. No, one of the reasons his marriage crumbled was because he worked too much. At least the long expanse of hours spent at bars was behind him. It was amazing how much more time he had now that he didn't drink.

"Figaro likes you," Mona Lisa told Panda. "He doesn't trust everyone."

"Mona Lisa, are you sure our staying here is okay?" Cliff asked.

"Not a problem."

But Cliff wasn't convinced. She seemed ill at ease, her features tense. Every time he came to this house, she acted standoffish. Well, what woman wouldn't be a tad bit nervous when alone with a man? Afterall, he knew how protective of Panda he felt. Why, oh why, had he hugged Mona Lisa? Now her antennae were up, waiting for him to make a pass at her. He felt like promising her right here and now to never again come within a foot of her - make that a yard. After Panda was tucked in bed, Mona Lisa might worry about her own safety. He hoped she had a lock on her bedroom door to give her a sense of security. She didn't need to worry. Not that he didn't find her extremely attractive.

"I was glad for an excuse to leave the dinner party." She paused for a moment and gave her head a small shake. "Let the newlyweds celebrate into the wee hours. I need to get up early in the morning." Her shoulders slumped.

"So do we," Cliff said. "Panda has school."

"You can go up to Mama's room," she told Panda. "At the top of the stairs, first door." Panda lugged her bag off the chair and climbed the stairs with Figaro tailing her.

Mona Lisa yanked at her hair. "I can't believe Mama got married."

"I can't believe my ex got married," Cliff said, then wished he hadn't. "Sorry. The last thing I want to do is make you or Panda feel uncomfortable."

"No sweat. I had an ex of sorts lurking around the restaurant."

"The guy at the counter? Yeah, I saw him." It looked as if she'd done her best to ignore him. Deidre and Cindy had made no bones about appreciating his smooth good looks. Cliff's assessment? Mona Lisa shunned attractive men; she'd been burned.

She lifted a small box off the table, opened the lid, and extracted a miniature gold boot. "He gave me this."

"He wants to get back together?" Cliff asked. Was he getting too personal? Too late. He'd already spoken.

Her cheeks flushed. "Apparently."

"And you? What do you want?"

"What every other woman in the world wants. A life like her old-fashioned parents."

Cliff could not relate, except from watching sitcoms as a kid. He'd never experienced a loving family. "You were lucky to have grown up with such wonderful parents."

"I can't help noticing you and Mama get along awfully well."

"Is that a problem? You looked less than thrilled to see me at dinner tonight."

"Sorry, was I acting like a pill?" She raked her hand through her wavy hair, her fingers snagging a tangle. "Yes, of course I was. I was in denial—shocked and horrified. I almost turned around and left the restaurant. I should have, instead of taking my lousy mood out on everyone, including you."

He remembered how striking she'd looked and how the cut of her wraparound dress clung to her slim waist. "You weren't that bad."

Her lips parted the tiniest bit. Had he said the wrong thing again? What was it about her that made him second-guess every word, like he had foot-in-mouth disease?

She stared at him, waiting.

"If it makes you feel any better, I would have been dumbfounded to have you show up at a family function too. Not that we have them."

"None?"

"Not since I've been single." He stroked the side of his face.

"How about your folks? Do they still live around here?" she asked.

"Yeah, but on opposite sides of town from each other."

"I've got to wonder why you aren't staying with one of them tonight."

"I called my mother yesterday, and her voice message said

she'd flown to Paris to visit Jim Morrison's gravesite." When Mona Lisa showed no sign of recognition, he said, "He was a rock singer who died decades ago. My mother still has a crush on him and plays his music all the time." Cliff wouldn't allow Panda to spend the night at his mother's anyway.

"The going to Paris part sounds fun," she said.

"Knowing my mother, the whole thing is a scam. No way could she afford the trip, unless someone else is paying, in which case she's kooky enough to go." He chuckled, as if he found her antics amusing.

"And your father?" Mona Lisa asked.

"Missing in action." He felt a lump expanding in his throat. "Last I heard, my dad was living in Ballard." A fifteen-minute drive. "I gave up trying to keep in touch with him." Why had Cliff shared so much personal data? The last thing he wanted was to be the object of Mona Lisa's pity. He needed to change topics before he blabbed anymore about his messed-up family. "Want to show me that bed upstairs?" He remembered seeing a low single bed, its faded paisley spread covered with stacked magazines, books, and old newspaper clippings.

She checked out the length of his torso. "I think it's too short for a man your stature. We should make a switch, give it to Panda, and put you on Mama's king-size."

"I'd rather not move her if she's already settled in." Panda was tired and might throw a fit. He didn't want Mona Lisa to see his daughter at her worst.

"Here's another thought," she said. "We have a cot in the basement we could bring upstairs. But I can't imagine it would be very comfortable unless you like camping."

"It's been a few years."

"Not since Boy Scouts?"

It felt good to have the tension between them lessening, his shoulders relaxing.

"Chick and Bernie and I went out one time in high school, up near Mount Baker. We brought beer, salsa, and chips. We remembered a tent but forgot sleeping bags. City boys. My dad had already taken off. I was such a stooge back then."

"But you've changed." Her pronouncement startled him. "You seem more sincere and caring. Humble." The last thing he thought she'd say.

"Having a teenager can do that for you." He shifted his weight. "And a botched marriage. It's like a banner waving across the sky saying Cliff's a failure."

"But at least you got married."

Meaning what?

"Sometimes remaining single seems the safest route. But then I wouldn't have my Panda."

As if they'd been discussing the weather, she let the subject evaporate. "Let's look at the cot, okay?" She led Cliff down a narrow staircase with low-wattage light bulbs. At the bottom and around a corner stood a workbench, a paradise for a tinkering man - a profusion of drills, bits, glue guns, power saws, you name it. Several chests of labeled drawers housed nails, screws, and bolts. His nostrils picked up the familiar scent of paint thinner and WD-40.

"It's been years, but I can't bring myself to disassemble Papa's work area." She canvassed the neatly arranged tools that appeared as if they'd been preserved as a monument. She picked up a tin of paint thinner and gave it a shake - its sloshy contents sounded half empty - then she returned it to the shelf, next to several others. "Maybe next week. I should hire someone to put on an estate sale."

"If I had the extra money and space, I'd take these tools off your hands. One more reason to buy or lease a home of my own with a double-car garage - half for my Porsche and half for a work area."

"It's a beautiful car," she said. So she'd noticed his Porsche, but it was impossible to know what she thought of it. A feast for her eyes, or too showy?

"I should get rid of it," he said. "I can barely afford the

monthly payments. But that would mean arriving at Canlis and taking Panda to school in my pickup."

"She wouldn't like that?"

He was pretty sure Panda couldn't hear him from the second floor, but he lowered his volume. "When I drive the pickup, she makes me drop her off one block from school."

"Walking is good exercise." She smiled her half-smile. "I was the same way when I was Panda's age. Everything my parents did was a giant embarrassment."

"When do kids outgrow that?" Cliff still hadn't and wished he could mature to the point where he didn't think about either one of them.

"This isn't a good day to ask me," she said. "Maybe when I turn forty?"

They passed a closed door. "That's Joey's bedroom." She cracked the door and flicked on the light. "He doesn't appear to be home."

"Does he know Panda and I are staying here?"

"Not yet. I'll leave him a note on the kitchen counter."

She pointed to a corner near a washer and dryer. "There's the cot. I don't think it's been used in twenty years, not since Joey and I had friends spend the night." The folded cot of yellowing fabric and six-foot two-by-twos tied together with twine leaned where two walls met amidst cardboard boxes.

Cliff brushed away a cobweb. "It looks like it's left over from World War II. And the fabric's ripped."

"There's the couch in the living room," she said.

"No, I'd rather sleep upstairs, thanks." What if Panda walked in her sleep? She hadn't for several nights, and Cliff prayed she'd remain tucked into Barbara's bed until morning.

As he followed Mona Lisa to the second floor, he couldn't help watching her hem sway across the backs of her knees and her narrow ankles. He averted his eyes and lagged back to gain distance. He must not reach out to her again.

Entering the study, Cliff said, "I forgot how small the bed

is." Five feet long, max; the paisley cotton spread covered with magazines, books, and news clippings.

Mona Lisa pushed down on a squishy corner. "Joey moved into the basement around age twelve when Papa took over this room for his study. Our folks bought Joey a longer bed. This one has been serving as a horizontal bookcase ever since." Her gaze followed him head to foot. "It doesn't look long enough for a tall man like yourself."

He wondered what she saw when she looked at him. He hoped she found him handsome and, more importantly, a man of integrity. He couldn't be anything like her papa. He summoned up his own father's image - a man with a pointy chin and straight black hair who was short enough to fit on this little bed. Cliff's chin was square, he stood a couple inches over six feet, and his hair had a slight wave to it. Did he and his father share any features in common? People always said Cliff took after his mother and at one time that remark had been a compliment.

A thought hit him full force, like a robin flying into a windowpane. Was the man he called Dad his real biological father? Is that why his father moved to the other side of town and never returned Cliff's calls? There was no use asking his mother. She might not remember or have known in the first place.

What was wrong with Cliff tonight? Why was he questioning everything? He wished he had a drink in his hand. One smooth shot of Bourbon would warm him down to his stomach, settling his scattered thoughts.

No, he admonished himself, he must not contemplate drinking ever again.

"This bed will be fine." He'd probably curl into the fetal position and wake up stiff.

"Okay." She gathered an armload of magazines off the bed and set them on the floor next to the desk. "We'll get this cleared off, then I'll find you clean sheets."

As she set down another batch of magazines, Mona Lisa's vision landed on the desk. "Hey, I left a check sitting on the corner, right there." She got on all fours and looked under the desk.

She seemed so distressed at its absence that Cliff said, "I saw a check earlier today, when I was speaking with your mother. She tore it up and dropped it in the wastebasket."

Mona Lisa sprang to her feet and peered into the wicker wastebasket. "Why would she do that?"

"I have no idea." Barbara had ripped the check fiercely, obliterating it.

"This is getting stranger and stranger," Mona Lisa said. "The check was written to a woman I've never heard of. I wonder who she is."

In a swift movement, she dove into a cardboard box, one filled with bank statements, pulled out an envelope, and removed a cancelled check. "Here's another, written fifteen years ago. Same woman: Anna Maria Moretti." She pawed through more envelopes and extracted a check from each until she fanned a dozen, all made out to the same woman. "Who is she? I'm going to get to the bottom of this."

"You could try Googling her," Cliff suggested. "If she's still alive, she may be on Facebook."

CHAPTER THIRTY-SIX
Mona Lisa

"Let's get your bed made up." Clasping the checks in my hand - I wouldn't take the chance of leaving them in Papa's study - I guided Cliff to the hall closet. I opened the door to see neatly folded sheets left over from Joey's and my childhood, still in good shape. At one time, I'd expected to use the softened fabric on my own child's bed, especially the set with the jungle animal print.

"It looks like the singles and pillowcases are on this shelf." Cliff reached in. "Your mother's quite organized." He selected red-white-and-blue sheets and then a blanket from the top shelf.

"She's organized about some things, but you'll notice she's left me with this house full of stuff. And my little brother. And a Doberman pinscher." I reminded myself I was glad Mama hadn't thrown the boxes of checks away. If only Papa were alive, he'd tell me who Anna Maria was. He'd never once mentioned her name.

I could hear Panda speaking to someone behind Mama's closed door. Was she on her cell phone or talking to Figaro?

"I bet there's an extra pillow in Panda's room," I said.

"Okay, I'll get it." He was hesitating to avoid meeting up with Figaro.

"Would you rather I did? I could make Figaro sleep in the kitchen so neither one of us stumbles over him in the middle of the night."

Cliff's eyes met mine. Was he considering the possibility of our bumping into each other on the way to the bathroom? I felt a girlish blush spreading across my cheeks. So what if it happened? Would we melt into each other's arms?

"I'm fine with Figaro in Panda's room," Cliff said. "Her own personal bodyguard."

While Cliff deposited the bedding in Papa's study, I went into my room. The checks felt alive in my hand, as if the ink was so fresh it might smudge. I glanced down at them as I walked. Papa's handwriting was formal - much neater than his usual scrawl, which I always had to decipher for my teachers when he wrote absentee notes. "Mona Lisa has a dental appointment this afternoon at 1:00," I'd read aloud, when in reality I could have been skipping away to any destination and taken the afternoon off.

No, not me. I walked the straight and narrow. All for nothing, really, when I looked at the way my life turned out. While Cliff was carousing with his friends, I spent afternoons laboring on homework or in the darkroom at school. As teenagers, Cliff and I couldn't have been more different. Yet his temperament had mellowed. Sweetened, really. I was awed by his honesty and the way he spoke of his childhood and parents. Who would have guessed he hadn't grown up in a perfect household?

As if listening in on my thoughts, he knocked on my doorjamb. "Need any help locating that woman?"

"Sure, okay," I said, and he stepped into my room empty-handed.

"Find a pillow?" I asked.

"Panda's still on her phone. I'll wait another five minutes."

I set the checks on my desk. "As you'll see, I'm not very tech-savvy." I sat, rolled my chair in, and opened my screen.

"First let's Google her." He reached around me and looked up Anna Maria Moretti. A page of Anna Marias appeared, with several captions written in Italian. "If you don't find her here, I'll log into Facebook," he said. "And Instagram."

"There could be one thousand Anna Maria Morettis." I

crossed my legs at the ankles, then uncrossed them. "How will I know which one I'm looking for?"

"Ask your mother?"

"That's the most logical route. But it's too late tonight." As I visualized Mama's tearing up the check, I got an itchy-crawly feeling, making me rub my upper arms. I wondered if she was trying to hide something or if she wanted to protect Joey and me. But from what? "Cliff, you saw Mama tear up the check. What was her facial expression?"

"Determined." He shifted his weight. "Angry? I don't know. You should ask her yourself. I've never been good at reading women."

"I find that hard to believe." I turned toward him and found him gazing over my shoulder into my computer screen, his cheek only inches from mine.

"Shall I log onto Facebook?" His hand rested on the back of my chair.

"No, thanks. Maybe tomorrow." I felt an unexpected dizzying buzz of - attraction.

"Chances are, Anna Maria was a distant relative." I let my imagination wander. "A widow lady, who died years ago."

"Makes sense. Your father might have helped her out."

"But then why would Mama rip up the check?" I clicked on my email account.

Cliff stood there for a moment, then turned away. "I'll run downstairs and get my bag, then check on Panda." He left the room.

My attention landed on the computer screen. I saw what my uncle Vito had written. I should have gotten back to him by now. I also noticed an email from Kevin, subject: Dinner Tomorrow Night? And a dozen pieces of spam I deleted right away. I should do the same with Kevin's note. Trash it, but I was curious. Good manners dictated that I write him a thank-you note for his gift. But I had no intention of wearing a miniature boot around my neck just because he gave it to me.

It felt good to have the upper hand. Finally. Or was he toying with me?

I decided to read Uncle Vito's email first. Subject: *Una vacanza*, which I figured would be another invitation to visit him. *Dearest Mona Lisa, Rome is glorious. The weather is perfetto this time of year. As I told you, I have a gentleman who wishes to make your acquaintance.*

I pressed reply. *Dear Uncle Vito, did Mama tell you she married Papa's long-time friend Frank DiAngelo? Do you remember him? Also, do you know an Anna Maria Moretti?*

I received a reply from Uncle Vito before I could even scroll to Kevin's message. What time was it in Rome? Nine hours later? I didn't envision Uncle Vito an early riser. I was surprised he didn't remark about Mama's dreadful marriage to Frank but rather chose to speak of Anna Maria Moretti.

Anna Maria's been asking about you too, he wrote. *May I give her your email address? Or you two could meet when you visit me. I hope soon.*

Huh? Anna Maria had been asking about me? Maybe she was my great-great-aunt? Why would Mama tear the check into shreds? I felt my heart beat faster and my adrenaline kick in, making my fingers tingle.

How do you know her? I wrote my uncle. *How old is she? Is she a relative?* I typed as quickly as I could, but he didn't reply. Had he closed his computer, or was he ignoring my queries? Should I pick up the phone and call him? No, I couldn't. Mama had her personal telephone book with her; I didn't know his number.

I heard Cliff's voice coming from Panda's room. Thinking I should act like a proper hostess and check on Figaro in case the dog got rambunctious, I got to my feet. Not that I had much control over him.

I hoped I'd get rid of Figaro soon. Tomorrow would be nice.

I found Panda lounging in bed, leaning against the headboard, surrounded by Mama's many pillows, and Cliff sitting on the end of the bed talking to her. Figaro lay near the nightstand, his head raised and ears pricked, like he was listening to something far away. The dog carried with him an undercurrent of anxiety. But maybe it was I who was anxious—to get rid of him. I'd contacted the animal rescue group last week, but apparently no one had called asking for him. When I mentioned I was planning to sell this house and needed to find the dog a new home, they didn't seem keen on taking him.

"I just had a brilliant idea." I should have thought of it earlier. "Figaro can move in with Mama and Frank."

"Does Mr. DiAngelo even like dogs?" Panda asked.

"I don't have a clue. I've never been to his house."

"I have a better idea." Panda raised her chin. "I want Figaro to come home with me."

"We can ask your mother." Cliff shook his head. "But your mom's a neat freak. She'd have to vacuum every day."

"We could leave Figaro out in the yard while I'm at school."

"What if he dug up her flowerbed?" he asked.

"He wouldn't do that. He's a good boy. Isn't he?" She looked to me for confirmation, and I shrugged.

"Honestly, we don't know much about him. How my mother got talked into adopting him is beyond me."

"No use discussing this until your mom gets home." Cliff crossed his arms. "Panda, did she mention when she'd return?"

"No, she said next morning's flight was sold out. She didn't know when they'd be home."

I wasn't sure why this pleased me. "Panda, you can spend tomorrow night here, too, if need be. Although your dad's heat will probably be working by then."

"I'd rather stay here with Figaro. He could help me do my homework."

"Which I assume didn't get finished today," Cliff said.

"I could help you tomorrow," I said, "after I get home from work. I was a pretty good student."

"Practically straight As," Cliff said.

Hugging a pillow, she stared at me with intensity. I felt a

connection forming between us. My guess was that she wasn't popular at school either. We had something in common.

"I certainly wasn't as talented as you," I told her, recalling her stellar performance. "I still can't sing, except in the shower."

"You were a fine photographer," Cliff said.

I was surprised he'd noticed. "That was a long time ago. Although my uncle in Italy sent me a digital camera last week. I don't have a clue how to use it."

"First step, charge the battery," Panda said. "I could do that for you."

"That would be great. Thanks. I'll get it out of its box and maybe tomorrow before school—"

Figaro's head jerked, and he woofed. In a burst, his legs scrambling, he raced out of the room as the front doorbell rang. I checked my watch: 9:55.

Panda remained nestled in Mama's bed as Cliff and I trotted down the stairs to the front door. The bell rang again - a long, persistent shrilling sound - and Figaro barked several times.

Cliff reached the door before me and opened it. Mama's elderly and often meddlesome neighbor said, "Who are you?"

"I could ask you the same question," he shot back easily.

"I'm Mrs. Warwick. I live next door. I promised Barbara I'd keep an eye on the house."

I moved alongside Cliff to see the mid-eighties woman was wielding a fireplace poker and was dressed in a raincoat over a floor-length flannel nightgown and red satin bedroom slippers. Her first name was Virginia, but Joey and I never dared address her informally.

"Everything's okay." I thought she'd shrunk since I'd seen her last.

"What's going on?" Her short pinkish-white hair frizzed under the porch light like cotton candy. "Are you throwing a party in your mother's absence?" Not wearing her usual lavender-tinted plastic glasses, she squinted at Cliff, chiseling a map of fine lines across her prunish face, then glared up at me.

"It's not what you think," I said. "A family friend and his

daughter are spending the night. Mama knows all about it. In fact, she invited them."

"Humph. Five minutes ago, I saw a man in your yard. I assumed he was a party-crasher." She peered around me, through the front hall, toward the living room.

Figaro stalked out onto the porch, circling Mrs. Warwick and sniffing the hem of her nightgown. She tapped his nose with the poker, and he backed away, then lumbered down the steps. Nose to the ground, he examined the parking strip, the driveway, and the backyard gate, illuminated by the light fixture on the side of the house. The gate was cracked open.

"You probably saw my brother, Joey," I said. "He normally shuts the gate carefully." My hunch was that he entered through the kitchen door and scurried down into the basement.

"It wasn't Joey," Mrs. Warwick said, all huffy. "I've lived next door for thirty-three years. I'd know Joey if I saw him. This guy - he was a rough-looking character - drove up in a van, and he was twice Joey's size."

I'd grown weary of her know-it-all tone, an attitude I wouldn't miss when selling the house. "Even bigger than Cliff here?"

"I tell you, this guy was a hulk," Mrs. Warwick said. "He was sneaking around the perimeter of your house, peeking in your windows. I should have called the police."

I wanted to get rid of my pesky neighbor, dive back onto my computer, and reconnect with Uncle Vito.

Mrs. Warwick didn't budge. "I think I'd better call your mother."

I noticed across the street that Tom Kanazawa was watching us through his window. I gave him a small wave to indicate everything was all right.

I tried to keep my volume down. "Mrs. Warwick, Mama moved."

"What did you say? Speak up. How do you expect me to hear you?"

"She moved." I said, full force.

"Without letting me know?"

"She eloped," Panda said, strolling out the front door in a knee-length, hot-pink bathrobe made of slinky knit fabric. "She ran off and got married."

Gawking at Panda - they were almost the same height - Mrs. Warwick's mouth fell open. "Who are you, little girl?"

"I'm not a little girl. I'm fourteen."

"I don't care if you're one hundred and fourteen, I don't believe a word of it. I have Barbara's cell phone number. I'll call her."

"Please, don't bother Mama tonight." I tried to banish visions of my mother in Frank's arms from my mind. "I'll ask her to call you in the morning and explain. Honestly, everything is copacetic." I looked up and down the street. "Mrs. Warwick, where's the van you were talking about?"

"When the man noticed me standing at my window, he hustled back to it and sped away."

Panda scanned the street. "There was a man out here?" She sounded pleased.

"I don't recall hearing a car door slam or tires peeling," Cliff said. I was glad he was here to offset Mrs. Warwick's hysteria.

"I didn't hear anything either." I moved to the edge of the porch and scrutinized the grassy yard in need of mowing. In spots under the living room window, the grass lay on its side, flattened. On closer inspection, I could make out the shape of large footprints. I felt a chill creeping up my legs and a shiver encircling my arms.

"Mrs. Warwick, were you standing in the yard over there?" I pointed and found my hand shaking.

"In these slippers? No, I used the sidewalk, then your mother's walkway." She surveyed the grass beneath the window. "Aha, I was right. Someone was looking in your house. I told you so."

"They're man-size footprints," Panda said. "As big as Dad's."

"We could have had a prowler." I turned to Cliff. "But wouldn't Figaro have warned us?"

The corners of Cliff's mouth drew back. "In any case, we're all fine now, and we'll be sure to lock the doors. Mrs. Warwick, you should do the same."

Holding the poker like a weapon, she stood for a moment, staring up at him.

"Time to get back inside," Cliff told Panda. "In fact, I don't want you dressed like that below the second floor again."

"I just wanted to see who was at the door."

Mrs. Warwick's mouth twisted with disapproval. "In that skimpy bathrobe? My father wouldn't have allowed me to own such a flimsy garment."

"It's not like I'm naked or anything." Panda clasped her hips. "You're dressed in your nightgown too."

"Plus a wool-lined coat. And I'm twice your age."

I had to smile. Mrs. Warwick was far older than twice Panda's age. But she did have a point; Panda was dressed provocatively, and I was glad Joey wasn't home.

"Thanks for your concern," I told Mrs. Warwick. "Next time, why don't you call us and save yourself the trouble of coming over? If there was someone out here, you wouldn't want to meet up with him."

"May I walk you to your door?" Cliff asked her.

She brandished the poker. "No, young man. I'm not afraid of anyone."

"I believe you."

She extracted her house key from her raincoat and marched down our steps.

"Come here, Figaro," Panda said. His nose inches above the grass, he paced under the front window, stopping several times to inhale deeply, then he moseyed back to the porch.

"If someone was out there, you should be thankful to have a neighbor watching out for you, even if she is a bit pushy," Cliff said.

"She was always on Joey's and my case when we were kids, accusing us of picking her prized peonies," I said.

"And were you?" He chuckled. "I wouldn't want to meet up with her in a dark alley." He turned to Panda. "Did you hear me tell you to get back in the house?" But she didn't move.

"You silly boy." She rubbed Figaro's arched neck. "Who was out there? If only you could talk, you'd tell us, wouldn't you?" The dog yawned.

I spotted Joey ambling down the block, carrying a lunch-size paper bag. His lips were moving. Great, he was talking to himself. He paused when he saw us, then kept approaching and was soon at the corner of our property.

Cliff made a beeline for Joey, who was now on our walkway. Cliff put out a hand to shake Joey's, but Joey sidestepped him and sauntered up onto the porch. In a flash, Cliff was on his heels, taking the steps two at a time. He draped his arm over Panda's shoulder protectively.

"Hey, Joey," she said. "What's up?"

He glanced down at her bare feet, then inched toward the front door. "Nothing much. Going to bed early."

"Where have you been?" I blocked his entrance. "You missed the celebration."

"You asked old lady Warwick over for dinner?"

I wouldn't mention we suspected a prowler, which would fuel Joey's paranoia. "You know exactly what I'm talking about." I wagged my finger at him. "Mama and Frank's big fat announcement party at Canlis I'm sure Mama invited you and even begged you to attend. Am I right?"

"She left a note taped to the inside of the back door. But—"

"Skip the excuses, little brother. I'm too tired and rattled to be polite." I wanted to get Panda back into the house and bolt the door. And Uncle Vito's email was still gnawing at me. Not to mention Kevin's email.

"Your mother and Frank flew to Vegas and got married," Panda said. "At their announcement party at Canlis - that fancy restaurant - I sang a solo accompanied by a pianist and everyone clapped."

I nodded but wasn't echoing her exuberance. "Frank is officially our stepfather."

"Mr. DiAngelo's moving in with us?" Joey said with a gasp. He was gripping the paper bag so tightly the top was fraying.

"No," I said. "Mama says he owns a palatial mansion on Lake Washington. Cliff can tell us all about it. He's going over there tomorrow."

Joey lowered his eyebrows. "What's Cliff doing here now? Working late?"

"Panda and I are spending the night," Cliff's voice grew stern. "My daughter's sleeping in your mother's room. I don't want you anywhere on the second floor while she's here. Have I made myself clear?"

I crossed my arms. "Hey, you knew Joey lived here when you invited yourself over."

"Wait a minute. Your mother invited us. And you mentioned Joey was supposed to be living in a group home. I'd be happy to drive him there right now."

"Really? Would you be my hero and return Joey to The Home?" I checked my watch. "Mrs. Landis shut her doors at ten sharp a few minutes ago, so we may be too late. I'll run inside and call her."

"No way." Joey grasped the bag to his chest. "I have more right to be here than Cliff does." He took off for the front door and dashed inside.

CHAPTER THIRTY-SEVEN
Joey

"Run, run, as fast as you can, you can't catch me, I'm the gingerbread man," Gloria chanted into Joey's ear as he bolted through the front hall on the way to the kitchen.

"*Basta!*" Joey said. "Enough, already! Can't you shut your trap for two minutes?"

"Ya'll should be glad I'm here to protect you, or your ole pal Domino would break back into your gray matter, bouncing around like a ping-pong. Even I found him annoying."

Joey's hands covered his ears - always a futile act because Gloria resided in his head. Five years ago - or was it ten? - the Saint had booted Gloria and Domino out at the same time, banishing them both from Joey's mind. He'd almost forgotten Domino's grating voice. Joey would go crazy if Domino returned. Before Gloria and Domino, other lesser voices had muttered their negative opinions in Joey's mind - it was near impossible to ignore them. In Saint Signore's absence, would they all swarm back like bees seeking their old hive?

Where was the Saint when Joey needed him so desperately?

"Gone with the wind." Gloria's southern drawl expanded her words. "Fiddledeedee, it's just you and me, darlin'. You better dive into the basement before Cliff tosses a gunnysack over your head, binds your arms and legs like a rodeo calf, and transports you back to The Home."

Joey couldn't recall what a gunnysack was, but it sounded suffocating. He could see the basement door yawning open, inviting him, but he didn't trust Gloria's advice. She'd kept him from attending Mama's party earlier tonight. Joey had planned to duck into Canlis long enough to congratulate Mama and Frank. Joey had never liked Frank, the self-important blowhard, but Joey had planned to make an appearance at Canlis and stay for a few minutes, taking great care not to touch or eat anything.

On the way to the restaurant, the Metro bus had trundled south, traversing the towering expanse of the Aurora Bridge, a terrifying ordeal. Joey had held his breath, as he always did when crossing bridges. He'd felt so dizzy and disoriented by the time the bus finally made contact with terra firma Joey physically couldn't get off. It was as if his pants were glued to the seat and his legs had turned to Jell-O. Had Gloria been playing a practical joke? In his ear, she'd assured him, "I'm doing you a favor. Someone in that restaurant might have swine flu. One day you'll thank me."

In a way, he was relieved to miss the so-called celebration but said, "I don't trust you as far as I can throw you."

She'd cackled. "You crack me up. How are you going to toss me anywhere without having a lobotomy?"

He was determined to escape her. At the next stop, he hurried off the bus and transferred to another and then another for hours, until finally one brought him within a couple blocks of the house, only to find Cliff and Panda had invaded it. Actually, he didn't mind Panda's being here because she was a sweet, straightforward girl, and Figaro liked her. Cliff was a different matter.

Moni strode into the kitchen. "We need to talk, Joey." She sounded exasperated, like Mama when she'd overcooked the pasta.

"Keep your sister gabbing until we're sure The Home is closed for the night," Gloria said.

"If you take me to The Home tonight, I'll run away." Joey pulled out a chair, sat, and scooted its arms against the table for protection. "I'll tell Mama you forced me out onto the street. Some wedding present."

Moni's shoulders rounded. "Do you think she'll be happy with Frank?"

"Not if you force me to live under the freeway."

Looking defeated, she leaned her hip against the counter. Joey figured she had more on her mind than Mama and Frank, but without Saint Signore's input he wouldn't dare ask personal questions.

"Okay, you win for now," she finally said.

"Whoopee!" Gloria hooted. "She's giving up."

Joey felt a fresh round of energy. "If Frank's stinking rich, maybe I can stay in this house. Mama likes me here, taking care of Figaro."

"We'll talk to her tomorrow, have a family meeting at Booty's." Moni pushed herself away from the counter.

"Brilliant idea," Gloria said. "Tell her you quit as of this moment."

No, he wouldn't do that. Unexpectedly, he'd started to enjoy working at the restaurant and had recently found several vegetarian soup recipes he wanted to offer their customers. "I won't flake out on you," he said. "I'll work as long as you need me. Until you sell the place."

"How did you know I was selling Booty's?" She huffed. "Never mind, I've got other worries." She sat at the table across from him. Her chin rested on her knuckles, as if her neck didn't have the strength to hold it upright. "Remember that check to Anna Maria I found upstairs? I discovered a dozen more checks, all written to this same woman. Do you know anything about her?"

Gloria jabbed Joey in the ribs, so to speak. "Don't you dare tell your sister anything about Anna Maria." But Joey couldn't help his head from nodding, his body refusing to obey.

"Who is she?" Moni's voice reminded Joey of a bleating lamb. "Please tell me."

"I found out by mistake," he said. "Decades ago. But I promised Papa never to tell anyone. Or to talk about Anna Maria with Mama."

247

"Now you've done it," Gloria said. "Opened Pandora's box and out jump the family skeletons."

"Papa's gone." Moni blinked. "It's okay to tell me. I'll find out anyway."

"How?" He glanced up at the ceiling. "Are you in contact with Papa's spirit?"

"No, I wish I were." Her lungs seemed to collapse. "Uncle Vito knows Anna Maria. In fact - and this is odd - he said she's been asking about me and wants to meet. Why me?"

"You've got to snuff this conversation," Gloria said so loudly that Joey was amazed Moni couldn't hear her. But his sister showed no sign of noticing Gloria.

"Uncle Vito lives far, far away," Joey said. "In Rome now, not Naples anymore."

"Yes, we correspond by email. You must know that. For some reason, he didn't answer my last email. I'll try reaching him again in a few minutes, once you agree not to go up to the second floor with Panda here."

"I have no intention of getting anywhere near her or her domineering, freaky father. I didn't invite them over.

"Moni, don't go poking around about Anna Maria. Mama wouldn't want you involved. And you won't like what you find."

She bolted to her feet. "Why not? What do you know about her? I'm getting this eerie feeling, like there's a conspiracy, as if I'm the only person who doesn't know what's going on." Her expression suddenly changed from anger to excitement, her brown eyes brightening, resembling Papa's.

"If Uncle Vito doesn't answer me, I might surprise him and hop on a plane and go speak to him in person," she said.

"No!" Gloria shrieked. "Talk her out of it."

"It had better be soon," Moni said, "before Annie leaves."

"You can't go anywhere," Joey said. "Who would run Booty's?"

"Ramon can handle it with Annie's and your help."

Gloria hissed. "She's bluffing. Your sister moves at a snail's pace. She never does anything spontaneously." But Gloria's statement didn't ring true. Moni had catapulted off course before. For example, she'd put her beloved camera out to pasture. According to Saint Signore, she'd tossed away a brilliant career. Then later, she humiliated her parents by moving in with Kevin. Saint Signore could see right through that phony guy.

"Moni, we can't run Booty's without you," Joey said. "Now that the Dawn to Dusk is closed, business is booming."

"Good, keep her talking," Gloria said. "Warn her about the perils of traveling abroad. Pickpockets and gypsies and what if the police arrest you for arson? You're their number one suspect."

Before Joey could speak, Moni said, "Get Mama to come in and lend a hand. You're the only person who could cajole her into it."

"The police might put me in jail," Joey said—a genuine fear. "They came in yesterday while you were at the bank. They suspect me of starting the fire."

"Why didn't you tell me?" Her features went horizontal, her mouth a pencil-thin line. "Since we're talking straight talk, Joey, did you or didn't you burn the Dawn to Dusk down? I want to believe you're innocent. But you loved playing with matches when we were kids, and you've got a match collection. Which makes me wonder, what's in that paper bag?"

Did she have X-ray vision? He would stop in several places during the evening and ask for matchbooks, and he had found an almost-new lighter in a gutter.

"I'm not the arsonist in the family, big sister."

Her cheeks turned visibly paler; Joey had never seen her look so stunned. Which gave him the courage to go on. "You lit a fire when we were kids, didn't you? Every time I hear Johnny Cash's "Ring of Fire" I remember it." With Gloria's prompting, Joey sang, "And the flames went higher…."

Moni shook her head, like he was speaking Pig Latin.

Gloria encouraged Joey to continue singing. "It's ten thirty," she said. "The Home is closed for the night."

But Joey didn't have the heart to sing the next line. He knew Saint Signore would not approve of this song. "You're fanning the Buttaro Curse," the Saint would say. He'd warned Joey not to goad or taunt Moni about the garage fire. Joey recalled parts of the incident with clarity - he'd been spying on his sister through the garage's window. When the flames first took off, Joey could have rushed for help, but he didn't. He'd watched the fire come to life, listening and waiting for the moaning of sirens. Which made him feel guilty because he should have helped her put it out.

"I refuse to talk about this," she said. "I don't know what you think you remember -"

"Moni, you can be honest with me. I won't tell Mama."

Her hand swiped her eyes, smudging her mascara.

"There's nothing to tell."

But Joey wondered if she was on the verge of confessing.

Above them, up in Mama's bedroom, floorboards creaked the way they always did when Mama settled into bed, and then Joey heard Cliff lecturing Panda.

"I'd hate a dad like him," Joey said. A horrendous thought hit Joey. What if Moni married Cliff, making him a household fixture?

Joey's words bobbled out. "I hope you don't marry him."

"No one other than Mama's getting married around here."

"It's part of the Buttaro Curse," Gloria told Joey. "Remember, the sins of the father... Neither you nor your sister will ever be wed."

"I guess Mama will never have grandkids," Joey said. This fact saddened him, for Mama's sake. "I couldn't take care of a wife and child. I can't even look after myself. She was counting on you to provide her with grandchildren."

"I was counting on me too," Moni said. "Never mind, it's late, and this is the last thing I want to talk about. I need to get upstairs and see if Uncle Vito replied to my email." She yawned. "I think it's tomorrow morning in Rome."

She left the room. Joey could hear her trudging up the stairs.

"She's going to learn the truth if you don't do something fast," Gloria said.

Joey knew Moni's childhood fantasies about her perfect father would forever crumble. And what tricks did Anna Maria have up her sleeve? But there was nothing he could do to stop her.

Yes, there was, Joey thought - before Gloria could echo the same idea. This time, Joey was way ahead of her.

CHAPTER THIRTY-EIGHT
Cliff

Exhausted as he was, Cliff knew he wouldn't find restful sleep on the twin bed in Mr. Buttaro's old study unless he shrank six inches. He thought about the expansive eight-foot couch luxuriating in the living room but discounted the notion; he needed to stick close to Panda.

He set to work removing the remaining stacks of books and magazines from the bed's sagging surface, noticing the magazines' dates—over a decade old—and the titles, all dealing with scientific study, physics, and the environment. No wonder Mona Lisa held her father in such high esteem; he must have been a brain. But had he actually patented any usable devices with his research?

Earlier today, Cliff rewired Barbara's garage door opener. Apparently, it hadn't functioned right since Mr. Buttaro monkeyed with it. When Cliff made a repair or designed a new kitchen layout, he liked to think he was being creative, akin to an inventor, using both sides of his brain, always on the lookout for new and better ideas. Over dinner, he'd been wowed by the interior of Canlis—the use of space, the fabric textures, the windows, the lighting—and had made notes in his small pad to use later. He'd noticed Mona Lisa fit into the elegant setting. Cliff must have worn blinders in high school to miss her.

He grabbed hold of the edge of Mr. Buttaro's desk and

muscled it a couple feet toward the wall to give himself more space. Then he tugged the mattress off its frame, and it flopped to the floor.

He thought about Panda, tucked in bed in the next room. "Please, Daddy, let me stay with you forever," she'd said as he'd kissed her goodnight. Words he'd longed to hear, but now that she'd asked to live with him, could he manage? He'd been sober for two years and was working steadily at a job that gave him the flexibility to drive her to school and then pick her up. Or was custody a fantasy he couldn't handle? Inadvertently, Janette had given him a week's trial, and he'd come through with what he thought were flying colors. He'd succeeded, even with a few glitches, like Panda's homework debacle that in reality sprouted roots before Janette flitted off without informing Cliff. Janette was the irresponsible parent.

"If you're serious," he'd told Panda, holding her hand and noticing eggplant-colored fingernail polish, which he now found cute. "I'll call my attorney in the morning and see what our options are. But your mother's going to fight us."

"No, she won't. Everything's about Dennis now. He pretends to like me, but it's an act."

Hugging her narrow shoulders, Cliff wondered how it was possible to love anyone as much as he loved Panda. They'd lost years together, and he intended to make it up to her and be two dads in one, if necessary.

He kneeled, unfolded the bottom sheet, and spread it over the stamp-size mattress on the floor. Mona Lisa walked by the open door and stopped to watch him. She was still dressed, minus her shoes. "You need help?"

"I can get it." Knowing how touchy she was, he added, "I hope you don't mind. I should have asked for permission to move the desk. I figure I'll be more comfortable without the box springs."

She leaned against the doorjamb, her weight on one leg. "I still think we should have put Panda in here and given you Mama's bed."

"If you think I spoil her, you're right. I get so few chances to spend time with her -"

"You don't need to apologize to me, Cliff. You're a good dad. If she were my daughter, I'd probably do the same thing. As far as Joey goes, he's harmless. He talks to himself and must be OCD the way he collects things like bottle caps and envelopes, but he's never shown a preference for teenage girls. And I've never seen him commit an unkind act."

"That's good news." That is, if he could believe her. A sister might be blind to her brother's faults and try to protect him.

Cliff pictured Joey's face - nice-looking features, even if he tended to squint when he looked at Cliff. In conversation, Joey often gazed at the ground or an unseen speck on Cliff's shoulder to avoid eye contact. A sign he was introverted. Being shy wasn't a crime. Joey's wavy brown hair, lighter in color than Mona Lisa's, needed a visit to the barbershop for a professional trim, but he kept it clean and his face shaved. Cliff envisioned Joey dressed in a Polo shirt and new Levi's. Maybe Cliff had misjudged him. But then Cliff considered Joey's panhandling on the freeway and his sleeping in the back seat of Barbara's Cadillac. There's nothing conventional there. Was Joey's night in the garage a brotherly ploy to irk Mona Lisa? Had Cliff mistaken Joey for that grubby panhandler? He hadn't seen Joey at the freeway entrance again.

As Cliff spread out the top sheet, he felt a pinch of guilt. He should feel sorry for the guy. Why hadn't he noticed earlier that Joey had mental challenges? Last year, Cliff read an article about a young woman who, midway through college, became terrified her professors were following her; then she tumbled into a schizophrenic nightmare, dropped out of school, and had to move home with her parents. Cliff had learned at his Twelve Step meetings that he must not judge others, but that's exactly what he'd done with Joey.

Cliff turned to face Mona Lisa and noticed dark circles under her eyes. What did she think about his sleeping here? Her opinion was becoming all-important. Was it a sign he was falling in love with her? The phrase *on the rebound* came to mind because, pitifully, he wasn't entirely over Janette. Although his contempt toward her was fading to passivity. Who cared if she remarried or moved to Mars, as long as she didn't take Panda with her? Here stood barefooted Mona Lisas - he had beautiful, slender feet - and his every fiber felt drawn to her. He wondered if she felt an ounce of attraction toward him.

He didn't want her to leave. "I should have warned you earlier." He smoothed the top sheet. "Panda walks in her sleep."

"Seriously?" She stepped closer. "What does she do?"

"She usually wanders from room to room, sometimes grazes through the freezer, and brings out ice cream. I hope you don't mind. Nothing drastic. I'll sleep with my door ajar." He'd be amazed if he slept at all.

"But you're worried she'll meet up with Joey? No wonder you're nervous about his sleeping downstairs." She perched on the corner of her father's desk.

"Yes, that's why I offered to take Joey to the group home."

"Whatever your motive, I appreciate your suggestion."

Cliff draped a plaid blanket over the mattress, then sat on its corner, his long legs stretched out. He felt the hard wood floor beneath him.

"I still feel badly about making you sleep in here," she said.

"Don't give it another thought. I like this house. Everything about it reminds me of the home I never had. Say, do you think your mother would consider renting it to me?"

Using one hand, she massaged the back of her neck. "A week ago, I would have said no, because Mama needed to sell. But now I have no idea."

"I'll ask her, if it's okay with you. You said you wanted to move back to your apartment."

"I do." She stood and crossed her arms. "At least, I thought I did. But in a few months, it'll be summer, and my one-bedroom is on the south side of the building. No air conditioner. And my neighbor above me makes too much noise."

255

"Meaning you might want to stay right here?" With him? No, she'd never go for it.

"I don't know anything, anymore," she said. "This whole night has made me rethink everything. And now I can't get on the internet."

"You want my help?"

"Not now. I'm too tired. But I'll take you up on that offer in the morning." She raked her hand through her hair. "I came up with an idea. I may be taking a short trip. I don't know. It may be out of the question."

Cliff stood. He wasn't surprised by her revelation. Earlier, fifteen minutes ago, he'd intended to chat with Joey and her in the kitchen, but from the front hall, he'd overheard parts of their conversation. Mona Lisa declared she might travel to see their uncle in Rome. But their voices had seemed combative and strained, so Cliff had backed off and retreated upstairs.

"Here's a thought." Mona Lisa grinned, bringing playfulness to her face. "You stay here and look after the house and feed Figaro while I'm gone."

He grimaced at the thought of the dog baring his teeth at him. He didn't buy Barbara's explanation that the Doberman was smiling.

"Figaro's well-behaved, for the most part," she said. "He'll get used to you."

But would Cliff get used to Figaro? "Does that mean he doesn't eat hand sandwiches for breakfast?"

She laughed a girlish laugh, smile lines framing her mouth.

"I'm tempted," he said. "But what about Joey? Panda said she wants to live with me, but that could all change when her mother gets home." Most likely, Panda would move back with Janette tomorrow.

"Maybe by the time I return from my excursion - if I go, that is - you will have found a new owner for Figaro and moved Joey into The Home."

He sputtered a laugh. "You think I'm a miracle worker?"

"I'll make you a deal, Cliff. If you can manage both, you can stay here rent-free as long as you like."

Was she for real? She'd given him a lot to ponder when he should be going to sleep.

* * *

For an hour, Cliff tried to shut off his mind. He lay on his back, staring at the darkened ceiling, his head resting on a feather pillow he'd bet was thirty years old, judging from the lumps. His nostrils picked up the trace aromas of shampoo and perfume—a hint of rose. Had the pillow come from Mona Lisa's bed? He remembered the wallpaper in her childhood room—twines of roses, the hue of cherry blossoms. He couldn't help himself; he wished she were in his arms right now. He'd been lonely for too long.

His thoughts started playing hopscotch, his feet first landing on the splendid possibility of his moving here, if only for a week. Or would Mona Lisa throw a wrench in the works? If he moved here, would he become Joey's designated caretaker? If so, he'd insist Joey see a psychiatrist.

Cliff flipped onto his side and bent his knees.

An idea leapfrogged to another. If Panda returned to Janette's house, Cliff would not allow Janette to usurp his weekends with his daughter anymore.

His thoughts jumped again. Panda had school tomorrow and hadn't done her homework. Would Cliff receive another call from Mr. Patterson? Cliff reached for his iPhone and set his alarm so he'd wake up in time to get her to school, although he figured he'd hear Mona Lisa and Joey leaving for work in the morning.

A dog barked in the distance, reminding him that a prowler had circled the house earlier tonight. Still not comfortable, Cliff bunched up the pillow and turned to his other side. He envisioned Figaro's sniffing the grass under the front window. Cliff was glad he was here to protect Panda and Mona-Lisa.

What had Cliff gotten himself into? Mona Lisa couldn't possibly expect him to both get rid of Figaro and take Joey back to the group home. Was this her idea of a joke?

257

CHAPTER THIRTY-NINE
Mona Lisa

Unable to fall asleep, around midnight I roused myself out of bed and inspected my computer to discover the Comcast cable was unplugged and the wire wound into a ball stuffed behind the desk. Who would do such a thing? In any case, I got online, reconnected with Uncle Vito, and quizzed him about Anna Maria. Who was this woman who'd been asking about me?

My uncle seemed reluctant to answer my inquiries, begging me to talk to Mama. But he finally wrote, *I thought you knew by now, cara mia. Anna Maria Moretti is your half-sister. Your father's first child was born out of wedlock before he married your mother. I'm sorry to be the one to tell you.*

I sat stunned, unable to expand my lungs, feeling like I was drowning—suffocating. I didn't believe my uncle because Papa was the most honest man who ever lived. Uncle Vito was either lying or suffering from dementia. When corresponding with him, he always seemed lucid. He even remembered my former love of photography and sent me a camera. But he was wrong about Papa. My father loved family above all else; he'd never forsake his own daughter. That would be tantamount to disowning me.

Wait a minute, just because someone sent me an email from across the other side of the world didn't make it true. I verified my uncle's email address and found it correct. Still, anyone could be using his computer.

Hoping I'd outsmart an imposter, I asked him a question I figured only Uncle Vito would know - Mama's birthday, including the year, because she often lied about her age.

He - whoever it was - responded with the correct data. *Our parents had a terrible disagreement over her name*, he wrote. *I was four at the time, but I still remember the day they brought her home.* He must have known what I was up to—testing his authenticity because he added the hospital's name and location.

Elbows on my desk, my head fell forward into my hands. I rubbed my eyes. If Uncle Vito was correct, Papa had masterminded a cover-up my entire life. I thought about Papa's words of wisdom, Italian sayings I clung to as truths. Because he'd said them. *Il bugiardo deve avere una buona memoria*—a liar must have a good memory—and other proverbs that admonished one to speak honestly.

I felt the foundation of my life shift off-kilter. Was an earthquake rocking the house, the way my chair rolled a couple inches from the desk? No, nothing else in my room was swaying, and the air was quiet, except for my own voice in my head, questioning everything Papa ever told me.

Another thought hit me like a tornado, practically picking me up and slamming me against the wall. Was Mama in on this conspiracy? She must have known Papa had fathered another child. She'd seen the checks and the monthly shut-up money. They'd deprived me of a sister. I'd always wanted a big sister, but not like this.

CHAPTER FORTY
Cliff

Amid his skittering thoughts, Cliff finally drifted to sleep and woke up rested and refreshed, even with his feet hanging over the end of the mattress. He'd been dreaming about Mona Lisa. They were sitting on a low dock on Lake Washington. She was dipping her bare feet into the water and laughing.

He didn't want to wake up but heard a fierce rapping on the door. He opened his eyes to see Mona Lisa barge into the room.

Her voice was shrill. "Joey and Panda are gone!"

CHAPTER FORTY-ONE
Mona Lisa

I watched Cliff's legs come alive and propel him to his feet. The plaid blanket and top sheet swirled onto the floor, landing in a puddle. He was wearing a T-shirt and boxers.

"Are you sure?" He grabbed his jeans off the chair.

"When I woke up, I heard Figaro in the backyard, begging for breakfast," I said. "He was in Mama's bedroom with Panda when she went to bed. A few minutes ago, I went to get Joey, to give him a ride to work, but couldn't find him." I was dressed in work clothes, a long-sleeve T-shirt and slacks, ready for a day at Booty's.

Cliff stepped into his jeans, zipped them up, and raced for Mama's room while fastening the top button. I followed him through the open doorway and examined the bed—mussed sheets and quilt, pillow dented in the center. Panda's bathrobe and nightgown were draped on the end of the bed. Clothes lay strewn helter-skelter across the floor, like she'd tugged them out of her bag looking for something to put on in a hurry.

"I peeked in a minute ago, when I noticed Panda's door was ajar - the bed was empty."

"Could she be in the kitchen?" His limbs were taut, as if ready to start a marathon. "She loves ice cream."

I shook my head. "I was just down there."

He pulled the curtains aside and looked out the front window, then the side. "Both your and my cars are there." He turned to the doorway. "Panda!" His voice echoed against the walls and ceiling.

"Maybe she's in the living room." I tugged my hair out of the rubber band. "She might have fallen asleep on the couch."

I tailed him as he loped down the stairs. The couch's pillows were out of place. An open bag of chips and a can of Coke sat on the coffee table. "Someone's been in here." He picked up the can. "It's lukewarm."

I doubted Joey would drink pop - only filtered water - let alone eat chips, but I wouldn't mention it to Cliff.

"Where else could she be?" he asked. "Did you check the upstairs bathrooms?"

"Yes. I even pulled the shower curtain aside."

Cliff spun around and thundered down into the basement. I followed, afraid of what he might find. He came out of Joey's room. "No one there."

"Good," I uttered under my breath. I couldn't picture Panda in bed with Joey - he'd never take advantage of a teenage girl - but my imagination was weighing every worst-case scenario through Cliff's mind. Louder, I said, "There's no reason to think they're together." I sounded like codependent Mama, defending Joey.

Cliff tossed me a look of contempt, his eyes fierce and the veins on his neck coiling. "If anything's happened to Panda, I hold you responsible."

"How dare you? Joey could have taken off for work on foot an hour ago. Sometimes he does." Once, anyway, the night the Dawn to Dusk burned. "Panda could be somewhere in the house. Would she hide in a closet?"

"You think she's playing hide-and-seek? She's not a three-year-old." He aimed his finger at me. "I'm calling the police."

"Okay, but I think we should search the house first. You take the second floor. I'll look down here."

He dashed up the stairs. A moment later, I heard him opening and slamming closet doors on the second floor.

I rechecked Joey's room and found it vacant. I was glad he'd been able to keep his compulsive accumulating under control. I opened his closet door and out tumbled a mountain of Papa's old clothes and shoes - time to straighten up. I left Joey's room and passed Papa's workbench.

My thoughts whirred like a hummingbird's wings. Panda seemed content when she went to bed. But during the shadowy recesses of the night had her heart turned despondent with the reality of her mother's returning with a new stepfather? I tried to put myself in her shoes. Well, in a way, I was. My mother just remarried without my approval, and I didn't like my stepfather. But at least I didn't have to live with them.

"Panda, honey, are you down here?" I hastened to the laundry area. I pulled the string, and a bare light bulb illuminated the small space. I was relieved she wasn't there; my imagination had pictured disaster.

The room was crowded with years of Buttaro heritage: wooden shelves stacked with dishes, glasses, and pitchers from the Old Country that never got used. Mama couldn't bring herself to give away family relics. I'd been ignoring them, too, but after what Uncle Vito dumped on me only hours ago, I felt like sending the clutter to him. And changing my last name.

I heard Cliff's footsteps stomping to the front hall, then lumbering down the basement stairs. "Any luck?" he asked.

"No." As I stepped out of the backroom, I heard an automobile's engine igniting. "It must be the newspaper delivery guy," I said. "Although that kinda sounded like Papa's Alfa Romeo, but after all these years it doesn't run."

"Hold on," Cliff said. "When I asked your mother if I could tinker with it, she was delighted and asked me to work on it when I had time. She said you'd want to sell it."

"Why wouldn't Mama want to unload her gas-guzzling Cadillac?" Was she trying to erase all traces of Papa?

CHAPTER FORTY-TWO
Joey

As Joey perched on the driver's seat of Papa's red 1966 Alfa Romeo Spider, regret and fear sloshed through his brain as if a hand were shaking a bottle of oil and vinegar that refused to mix. How had he let Panda talk him into this expedition to visit her friend?

Gloria hissed in his ear, "What kind of freak would be awake this time of day? Panda is playing you for a fool." Her nattering made him determined to do the opposite of what she'd said, to rid his brain of her harassment.

"This is such a cool car." Panda stroked the black leather seat. "Can we put the top down?"

"Maybe later, if the sun comes out." Joey hadn't been in Papa's car since he died and never in the driver's seat. Five minutes ago, when he glided the Alfa's key into the ignition, the cool metal slipped right into place, like the car was aching to leave the claustrophobic confines of the garage.

"This car has a manual transmission, like Dad's Porsche." Panda located the garage door opener on the visor and pressed it. The door shimmied open. "Do you know how to change gears?"

"No, I told you, I can't drive, period." He glanced over to see her wide expectant eyes - even in the darkened garage, her green irises echoed the swatch of hair in her bangs. She reminded him of a pixie and of the little sister he never had - the opposite of Moni.

"It's time you learned." Her youthful voice gushed with enthusiasm, unlike Gloria's. "You start in first gear, then once you get going, use your left foot on the clutch and ease this knob into second gear, then third. It's a cinch."

Joey had watched Papa drive hundreds of times and marveled at his father's skill and confidence. Papa had offered to teach him, but Joey had been afraid the gas pedal would get stuck and he'd run into something. Or plunge off the side of a bridge.

"Okay." Panda released the hand brake. "Push your left foot on the clutch - all the way down to the floor. That's right. At the same time, press your right foot on the gas pedal. No, that's the brakes."

Feeling clumsy, Joey moved his right foot and tapped what he now knew was the gas pedal. The engine revved, filling the garage with rumbling vibrations and exhaust. But the car went nowhere.

"You have to disengage the clutch at the same time," she said. "Both feet need to work at once."

"Like juggling? I can't even juggle with my hands."

"Don't give up now." She giggled. "You'll get the hang of it."

"You'll hang yourself, is more like it," Gloria said.

"For once, will you shut up?" he asked.

Panda turned in her seat to face him. "Huh? I didn't say anything."

"Sorry, I wasn't talking to you." Using every ounce of concentration, Joey eased up on the clutch with his left foot while feeding the engine gas. The Alfa grumbled, sputtered forward a couple feet, then died.

"Hurry up, try again," Panda said.

After several more attempts, Joey jerked the Alfa past Mama's Cadillac, out of the garage, and onto the driveway, which slanted down to the street. The sun was rising behind a bank of murky clouds, and the sky was the color of soot.

"Luckily, Papa backed it in the last time he drove," Joey said as they rolled forward, gravity luring the car toward the street.

"Luckily, my dad fixed the garage door opener," Panda said. Joey detected pride in her voice.

"Luckily?" Gloria said with scorn. "There's nothing lucky going on here. Joey, get out of the car this instant. Go back to the house. You're nuts! You're going to kill us all."

"Panda, we could take the bus." Joey's heart beat triple-time, flapping against his ribs, like Desi Arnaz's hands playing the congas on *I Love Lucy* reruns, making it nearly impossible to breathe.

"I wouldn't be caught dead riding a bus." Panda crossed her arms. "If you don't drive me, I'll hitchhike."

"No, that's too dangerous."

As the Alfa crept to the street, Panda grabbed hold of the steering wheel and yanked it to the right. "Turn, turn, turn."

Joey helped her – it was hard work. The car's front tires turned onto the street.

"That's enough, let it straighten out." Panda tittered, her shoulders shaking. The Alfa turned the corner and slowed to a halt. "Feed the engine more gas," she said.

With his left foot easing off the clutch, he pushed his right foot on the gas pedal. The Alfa staggered forward, clearing the neighbor's parked SUV by inches. And she kept going, almost to the end of the block.

"Slow down," Panda said. "We need to take a right."

Joey let up on the gas pedal, switched to the brakes, and the car halted, the engine faltering, then lifeless again.

Panda laughed so hard she bent at the waist. Joey felt his face crumple, the corners of his mouth turning up, and he erupted into laughter too. He hadn't laughed since - forever. Not since childhood. He remembered that, as a kid, he and Moni fell into uncontrollable giggling sprees. He'd played like a normal boy. He'd been normal then.

"Ya'll were never normal," Gloria declared, but Joey ignored her.

"How do you know so much about cars?" he asked Panda.

"The boy next door - he's seventeen - gave me a lesson."

"Maybe you should drive."

"Duh, I'm too young. A cop would stop us." Panda took Joey's right hand and placed it on the stick shift. "Try again." Her voice was still upbeat, like they were playing a game. "Get ready to shift."

Left hand gripping the steering wheel, Joey took one foot off the clutch while pressing his other foot on the pedal - what he now knew was for gasoline. He imagined the clear liquid entering the engine, but then what? He contemplated checking books out of the library to study combustible engines. Papa would have been able to tell him how the car's motor worked. There were so many things Joey wished he'd asked Papa before he died.

"Take another right," Panda said.

As the car gained momentum, they worked the steering wheel. He gunned the engine, and in a burst, the car swerved and clipped the sidewalk, bouncing them several inches up. A moment later, the front tires thumped down and then the rear tires landed hard on the cross street.

"Phew," said Panda. "I thought we were going to bottom out."

"That's it, I'm leaving." Gloria snorted. "You're on your own."

"Good riddance," Joey said.

"Do you always talk to yourself?" Panda asked him.

"Sorry, I don't mean to." But Gloria was right. He was in over his head.

"You bet your bippy I'm right," Gloria said. "I always am."

Joey guided the car at ten miles an hour, anticipating another cross street so he could turn around. "We need to drive you back home before your dad gets up. He's going to kill me, not to mention Moni."

"Or worse," Gloria said with glee. "A mental institution like in *One Flew Over the Cuckoo's Nest*. They'll strap you in a straightjacket."

"You promised to drive me," Panda said. "My friend Dirk

told me to come by any time." She rubbed her hands together for warmth.

"You want to visit a man?" Joey was afraid to take his eyes off the road. They were now on NE Forty-Fifth Street, headed east; to go home, they should be going in the other direction. "You mean a boy from school?"

"No, a guy I met at the grocery store on Capitol Hill near Dad's place."

"How old is he?"

"I don't know. Mid-twenties?"

Joey punched the brakes, and the car lurched to a halt. His chest bounced against the steering wheel. He'd forgotten to put on his seatbelt. "Twenty-something is too old for you." He tried to guess what Saint Signore would advise him, other than fasten his seatbelt, which he did. In his mind, he begged the Saint to return.

"There's a cop!" Panda rose in her seat.

"You're for in it now," Gloria said.

Joey spotted a patrol car zooming in on them from the other direction.

"Start the car," Panda said, "or they'll think we broke down."

With shaky limbs, Joey got them moving again. A blue light on the top of the police car started flashing. Joey was sure he was about to be arrested. But the patrol car sped past them, not taking any notice.

"That was close." Panda looked over her shoulder out the back window.

"You dodged that bullet," Gloria said, "but the next police-man is going to put you behind bars and throw away the key."

Joey concentrated with all his might. He should probably heed Gloria's warnings, turn around, and take Panda home, but the image of Panda hitchhiking prodded him along. She struck him as a girl who'd suffered many disappointments.

As they motored east on NE Forty-Fifth Street few cars were on the road. They crossed I-5; no way would he attempt to drive on the freeway.

"You ain't too old for a heart attack," Gloria told him. "Or a stroke. Maybe you're having one now."

Joey refused to acknowledge her. Staying in his lane - not crossing the centerline or sideswiping parked cars - felt like mowing the yard. This thought gave him a smidgen of self-assurance. In the past, he'd mowed Mama's lawn and never ran into the fence - except that one time.

"Who is this fellow we're going to see?" Joey asked.

"Dirk's just a friend - like you." Panda raked her fingers through her bangs. She sounded relaxed, like it was any old day.

"I'm different, Panda. You know my family. I'd never do anything to harm you - you have my word on it." Joey realized he'd shifted gears, the transmission producing only a mild grinding sound. He was getting the hang of it.

"Unless you collide with a truck," Gloria said. "Or you forget where the brake pedal is. Which one is it again?"

He gripped the steering wheel. He must not land Panda in the hospital. He'd never forgive himself. "What do you know about Dirk?" he asked Panda.

"Don't have a panic attack. He's cool. You'll see. He gave me a couple joints for free and told me if I wanted more, to stop by his place anytime, day or night."

Joey rubbed his forehead as he remembered the Saint mentioning seeing Panda in the U District, conducting some sort of transaction that Saint Signore inferred was a drug deal.

"You smoke dope?" It had been years, but Joey still recalled the free-for-all, ravenous hilarity he'd enjoyed while smoking marijuana. But he would never go back to using mind-altering drugs. He often wondered if they'd allowed the voices in his head to worm their way into his gray matter in the first place. These days, he wouldn't even swallow an aspirin. Who knew what it might really be?

"It's not like I'm addicted," Panda said. "You're beginning to sound like my parents." Panda clicked on the radio - the channel Papa must have listened to last. Dean Martin - an Italian, Papa

269

would tell him for the hundredth time, originally Dino Paul Crocetti - was crooning "Everybody Loves Somebody." Joey was surprised Panda didn't switch stations. But grateful. He hated rap music, which sounded too much like the negative voices already infesting his brain.

"I bet your parents want what's best for you."

"Like, they'd know? My mother's a flake. I don't buy her excuse that her plane is stuck in a tropical paradise for one minute. Makes me want to puke."

"But Cliff…"

"He's a loser too. Used to be a boozer. Now he attends AA meetings. That's why Mom left him."

"How do you know Panda isn't in cahoots with Cliff?" Gloria hissed in Joey's ear. "Maybe she's taking you to Cliff's apartment, where they'll tie you up and stuff you in a closet. Let you starve to death. Or worse, feed you poison."

In the old days, just last month, Saint Signore's soothing voice would fill his head with instructions, but the car resounded with Dean Martin's singing and the rumbling of the motor.

They turned onto Roosevelt Way, heading south on the one-way avenue, then several blocks later approached the University Bridge.

"Bridge alert!" screamed Gloria. "Stop the car. Get out and run for your life."

Joey glanced over to Panda, who'd flipped down the visor and was arranging her hair into erratic spikes.

"I hate bridges." He should said have *I'm terrified of bridges.* "How about you?"

She flipped up the visor. "You're not wimping out on me, are you?"

"If you attempt to cross that bridge, you'll topple over the side!" Gloria shrieked.

Joey gulped. It felt like an unpitted olive was lodged in his throat. "Do you think the bridge is about to open?" he asked Panda.

"Nah, the arms would have come down to block us, and we'd hear the warning bell ringing."

"Don't believe her," Gloria said. "She's a pathological liar."

"You're the liar." He wasn't sure if he'd spoken these words aloud, but Panda was back to fixing her hair, using saliva on her fingertips. So maybe he didn't.

It occurred to Joey that Papa would be proud of him right now. And so would Saint Signore, too. If crossing this bridge meant death, then so be it, he decided. He refused to be Gloria's punching bag any longer.

He coaxed his foot on the gas pedal, and moments later the Alfa's tires squiggled over the bridge's metal grating. Joey was tempted to correct the out-of-control swaying movement, but before he could, the car was on the other side on dry land.

The Alfa labored up the hill, parallel to the freeway. Joey delayed downshifting as he traversed the overpass above State Route 520, but when they came to a red light a half block later, he was forced to stop.

The car's engine sputtered, then quit.

"You forgot to use the clutch." For the first time, Panda sounded peeved. "Now we're stuck on a hill."

"Stuck?" Joey looked in the rearview mirror and was pleased to see no cars behind them. A block or so, down the hill, spread Roanoke Park: a blanket of grass, a handful of trees around the perimeter, and a play structure at the far end. "What should I do?"

"This is a little tricky." She paused, as if she were strategizing. She reached over and took hold of the hand brake she had released when they started this journey. "Okay, put your left foot on the clutch and your right on the brake. I'll release the hand brake when you press the gas, then we won't roll backwards."

After he depressed the clutch, she turned the key, and the engine purred to life again.

"Now what?" he asked.

"With the car in first gear, switch your right foot from the brake to the gas, and with your left foot, let out the clutch."

But when Joey attempted this feat, the engine died, leaving them shrouded in silence, except for the swooshing sound of cars below them on 520—commuters headed to work.

"Foot on the brake pedal!" Panda yanked up the hand brake. "I don't think we can count on this hand brake. It needs to be tightened."

"You're going to kill us and wreck your father's car," Gloria said. "You're almost out of gas."

Joey scanned the dashboard and saw a needle that could indicate a low fuel level. Or was it engine temperature or oil pressure? These were terms Papa used. Life was so much easier when Papa was alive.

"Your father never liked you," Gloria said. "You were a giant disappointment."

"Yes, he did. He loved me as much as he loved Moni."

"Joey, you're talking to yourself again," Panda said.

A chorus of voices - with Gloria as their cheerleader - yammered in his head, spewing negative remarks. "You'll never amount to anything! You're stupid! You belong in a loony bin! The world would be a better place without you!"

Attempting to quiet them, Joey clamped his hands over his ears, but he couldn't block out the racket.

"Joey, pay attention. Put your foot on the brake pedal!" Panda's head snapped around. "We're rolling down the hill!"

CHAPTER FORTY-THREE
Cliff

Ascending from the basement, Cliff loped halfway up the stairwell before spotting Figaro in the doorway to the kitchen, blocking his and Mona Lisa's path. The Doberman snarled, saliva dripping from his mouth, his feet planted like a martial artist, ready to take down his opponent.

Cliff halted so quickly that he almost toppled backwards; he grabbed onto the hand railing for support. "What's going on?" he asked Mona Lisa over his shoulder. A metallic taste coated the inside of his mouth. "Doesn't the dog recognize us?"

"I have no idea." She cleared her throat. "Figaro, good boy, fella, everything's all right." She tried to sweet-talk the dog, to no avail. He growled and woofed another warning, making the hairs on Cliff's arms stand on end.

"If only Mama were here..." she said.

"Well, she's not, is she?" He felt dampness gathering under his armpits from sprinting through the house searching for Panda. He wiped his forehead and recalled that, as a kid, the neighbor's boxer had bitten him. Eight stitches at his hairline left a white scar he noticed when he combed his hair after a shower. His mother had said, "You're lucky you didn't lose an eye," as she drove him to the ER, then complained about the cost of the visit. "Why did you have to go and get yourself bitten?"

He thought he was over his fear of large dogs, but apparently not. His gut cramped with panic, and his hands rose, ready to protect himself from a frontal attack. "Is there a house phone down here?" he asked without turning away from the dog.

"No, there never has been, and my cell phone's in my purse in the kitchen. Did you try calling Panda?"

"Not yet. I would have if you hadn't insisted we look in the basement."

"Maybe her phone's upstairs."

"No, I checked all around the bed. It's not there. And my phone's on your father's desk."

Mona Lisa back stepped down the staircase. "We could go out the basement door, but we'll be locked out of the house."

Cliff felt foolish for not thinking of that route himself. Earlier, he saw the door at the far end of the basement, next to the washer and dryer. "Okay, we're getting nowhere here." Taking a chance Figaro would jump him from behind, Cliff spun around. He and Mona Lisa both dashed for the washing area. Cliff listened for Figaro's footsteps; thankfully, the dog wasn't following them.

Mona Lisa lifted a key from a nail next to the back door and jammed it in the lock, then twisted a dead bolt. Cliff shouldered the door open. Judging from the cobwebs on the outside, Cliff doubted it had been opened for months. He swatted the spidery debris aside and barged up cement stairs over dried leaves and bits of lint from the dryer. The sun was rising, lurking behind a gray mattress of clouds that promised to lift later in the morning. But Cliff couldn't bring himself to feel thankful for a new day.

"We just wasted ten precious minutes," he muttered, not trying to mask his anger. "I could kill that dog."

"You can't dislike Figaro any more than I do," Mona Lisa said, but Cliff didn't buy into her attempt at camaraderie. Panda's safety was all he could think about - and what that scumbag Joey might be doing to her. Cliff's mind was gnarled with hatred, as if all the demons of his past were gathering into a tangled knot of electric eels. He would love to unleash his thoughts and verbally bash Mona Lisa with his bitterness, but he knew he would regret it later. And he needed her help locating Joey.

"What were we thinking? Mona's voice broke into his thoughts. We should have looked out here first." Instead of running to the back porch, she headed for the garage, its side door cracked open. "Oh, no! Someone stole Papa's car."

Sure enough, as Cliff entered the garage, he saw the large door up and the Alfa Romeo gone, leaving a gaping space next to Barbara's Cadillac. He rebuked himself for repairing the garage's door. "I'd bet anything Joey took it," he said.

"Impossible, he doesn't know how to drive."

"How do you know?"

"I know my brother."

"You know nothing!"

"I tell you, Joey cannot drive a car. And a stick shift? Impossible. If they're together, and we still don't know they are, they're on foot. Unless Panda can drive a car."

"Don't be ridiculous. She's only fourteen." He inspected the circles of dried motor oil on the garage's cement floor and hoped the Alfa had run out. Out of coolant and gas would be helpful too.

"Why did you fix this garage door?" she said, as if there were a way to turn back time. "I bet the Alfa's key is on the key rack where it always is. Mama leaves it there for old time's sake."

"Yeah, well, how are we going to get in the house to find out?" Filled with disgust, partly toward himself for not hearing Panda's movements during the night, Cliff turned on his heel and jetted up onto the back porch. Figaro glared at him through the door's glass windowpanes. Cliff tried the handle and found it locked. "Do you keep a key hidden somewhere outside?"

"No, not anymore."

"How stupid is that?" Cliff knew he was acting like a jerk and could see by Mona Lisa's solemn expression that he was hurting her feelings; she was on the verge of tears.

He glanced up at Mrs. Warwick's window and waved,

hoping she was watching and would come down to fill them in on who took the Alfa.

With Mona Lisa standing by, he dashed down the porch steps, grabbed one of the bricks edging Barbara's rose garden, marched back up, and punched it through the windowpane nearest the handle. The glass shattered across the kitchen floor, but the dog remained a few feet inside the door.

He yelled out, "Panda? Are you in there?"

No answer.

Cliff reached through the broken hole and felt a sting as a chard of glass pierced his finger. Would Figaro smell blood like a shark and rip him apart?

"You're bleeding," Mona Lisa said. "Are you okay?"

Cliff ignored her question; he didn't have time to be injured. He twisted the handle, and the door opened. He bumped it further with his hip and said to Figaro, "Go ahead and try to kill me, you stupid mutt." Then he brushed past the dog on his way to the phone on the counter. Out of his peripheral vision, he saw Figaro backing away, his head and tail lowered. The dog seemed submissive now, but no way did Cliff trust him.

Cliff dialed Panda's number, but after one ring, her cell phone switched to her message. His mouth went dry.

"Maybe the battery's low." Mona Lisa moved to his side, holding a paper towel.

He punched in 911. His hand shook. A stream of blood was winding its way down his little finger. Mona Lisa tried to dab the blood from his hand, but he snatched the paper towel, tore off a strip, and wrapped his finger.

"My daughter disappeared," he told the 911 operator, a woman who sounded in her fifties.

The operator asked how long she'd been out of the house, then explained she hadn't been gone long enough to be considered missing. He heard rage exploding out of his voice box, but the operator remained calm.

"Have you checked with her friends?" she asked. Cliff was too embarrassed to admit he didn't know who Panda's friends were, let alone their telephone numbers. "Could she be a runaway?" the operator asked.

"An adult male abducted her," he said.

The operator's tenor changed to one of concern. "Was she taken against her will?"

"I think so."

"We don't know that," Mona Lisa cut in, loud enough for the operator to hear.

He said to Mona Lisa, "Would you shut up?" Then he turned away from her and described Panda, Joey, and the car. "There can't be many red Alfa Romeo Spiders out on the road. Can you have your patrolmen stop the car and bring my daughter home?"

The operator told Cliff that, officially, they couldn't pick Panda up.

"What do you mean? She's a minor. I'm her father." As the operator explained the legalities that gave girls Panda's age the freedom to be in a stranger's car without her parents' permission, Cliff turned back to Mona Lisa and saw her hollow cheeks and her pinched mouth. "Do you have the car's license plate number?" he whispered to her.

"It's written down somewhere." Her voice was lifeless. "In a file, in a box."

"A lot of good that does." He begged the operator to pass his cell and the house's telephone number on to the police.

A minute later, he slammed down the receiver. "According to that operator, Panda hasn't been missing long enough to be worth their trouble." He felt frustrated enough to throw the phone against the wall. "She could be dead by now." Mona Lisa dropped onto one of the kitchen chairs. "Does Joey have a cell phone?" he asked her.

Her mouth bent into a crooked smile, like he'd said something funny. "No, he believes they cause brain—never mind, he doesn't own one."

"That figures."

"Listen, we still don't know they're together. Joey could have walked to Booty's. He could be prepping for lunch at this very moment."

"Then let's go check." Cliff hustled upstairs for his keys and phone. He scanned Panda's bedroom again, looking for clues, but found only the empty bed, her bag—collapsed flat—her skirt from last night draping a chair, and clothing laying willy-nilly on the rug. She certainly hadn't packed and left in an orderly manner. He couldn't remember his pulse ever racing with a river's force - not during a high school football game or even when he and Janette vocally duked it out. It felt like his heart might burst.

When he returned to the kitchen, he found Mona Lisa sweeping up the glass. Figaro was resting in his basket, his breathing steady and his eyes shut.

"No time for sweeping," Cliff said.

"If Figaro cuts his paw, I'm the one stuck carting him to the vet." She mounded the chards into a corner.

He jiggled his keys like a rattlesnake's warning. "Come on, we'll take my car."

"No, we should use two cars." Every word she said barbed into him. But he didn't want to be alone. Because he'd stop off at the nearest liquor store? No, he didn't crave that crutch. He figured Mona Lisa had the best advantage in finding Joey.

"What if someone calls the house? Who will answer the phone?" she asked.

"You can check for messages from your cell phone. The police have my number."

"If Panda's not at Booty's with Joey, are you planning to drive up and down every street in Seattle?"

"If I have to. Please, can you just do this one thing I ask?"

"One thing?" She thrust her chin up at him. "Look, I'm worried about Panda too, and I feel sorry for you - I really do. But I didn't want you two spending the night here in the first place. You brought this trouble upon yourself."

CHAPTER FORTY-THREE
Mona Lisa

The moment I stepped into Cliff's Porsche—before I completely sat down and closed the door—he zoomed away from the curb. I was thrown back into the passenger seat at an angle, wrenching my shoulder and neck.

I was about to have a meltdown. After Figaro's vicious confrontation, Uncle Vito's revelation that I have a sister, and the fact that Papa lied to me my whole life, then Mama's getting married, not to mention Panda's disappearance, my emotional battleground was waging one war too many. I felt like screaming.

I couldn't bring myself to contemplate where the Alfa Romeo was. This last twenty-four-hour roller coaster ride must come to an end. And I was desperate for my morning coffee.

As I strapped on my safety belt, I glanced over and studied Cliff's stern profile, his jaw jutting forward. Until this morning, I was beginning to trust him, but what did I really know about the man? I'd never seen him angry, and his intensity frightened me. Sure, Papa used to get mad and curse in Italian, his arms and hands speaking volumes. But I was never afraid of him. Right now, Cliff scared me. Why did I agree to get in the car?

While he swerved to miss a pothole, I recalled how I'd checked Mama's key rack when Cliff was upstairs and discovered the Alfa's key missing. Joey could have taken it, unless Mama did. I didn't dare mention my thoughts to Cliff.

"I still think I should have brought my own car." My hand rested on the door's handle as he slowed for a stop sign. Should I leap out and walk home?

"If you don't mind, I'd like your company."

"What for?" As far as I could tell, I was his least favorite person - except for Joey. "You insinuated I'm stupid and careless."

"Can we put aside our differences until we find Panda?"

I knew I was being uncharitable, but I was not in the mood to accept his half-baked peace treaty. I thought about Bernie and Chick, his high school buddies, not to mention Cindy, whom I'd bet anything he'd prefer to have by his side.

"By the way, I'm retiring from the reunion committee." I voiced my random thoughts. I saw him frown. I was tempted to add that I didn't want him or his high school chums eating in Booty's anymore either, now that I was turning petty.

We neared the restaurant, only two blocks away. I figured anything that could go wrong today would. My mind was filled with ill omens. I imagined us turning the final corner to find the building ablaze. Or flooding - an old pipe bursting, spewing water across the kitchen and into the seating area.

We pulled up in front of Booty's to find the street deserted. Not that I really expected to see the Alfa lazing out front. I wondered if the person skulking around Mama's house the other night broke in and stole the key.

I could see through the restaurant's wide front window the kitchen lights were still dimmed - our usual procedure at night - and the newspaper hadn't been brought in. But to be safe, I entered the building and called Joey's name.

Finding the restaurant empty, I returned to Cliff's car and spoke through the Porsche's open door. "I should stay here and start the soup. It's almost six o'clock. Time to get to work."

"Please, no. Come with me until we find Panda - and your brother."

I was tempted to ignore him but reminded myself his daughter was missing. Behind his brusque exterior, he must be petrified.

Standing on the sidewalk, I said, "I'll need to call Ramon." I fished through my purse and brought out my cell phone. His phone rang several times before his groggy voice answered, "At this time of day, this had better be good."

"Hi, it's Mona Lisa. I'm sorry to wake you." I wondered if he was alone.

"It's okay. I told you to call anytime you need me." He emphasized the word *need* in a way that brought warmth to my face. I could use a sympathetic shoulder to lean on.

"I have a huge favor." I hated to be a bother. "Can you come in early today to open up?"

"Sure, anything for you, my beautiful boss lady. I'm at your disposal." He sighed into the receiver. "How about you swing by my place and pick me up? I'll serve you breakfast or whatever your heart might desire."

So he was alone. "Ramon, I'm grateful you're a friend I can rely on, but I can't come get you. It's too complicated to explain. I'll fill you in later."

Once I was back in the car, Cliff veered away from the curb. "Do you and Ramon have something going on?" he asked.

"No, not that it's any of your business." I dropped my phone in my purse.

"It's obvious he's got the hots for you."

"Why would you care? Can we stick to the problem at hand?" My jaw hurt from clenching my teeth. "What's the strategy, Cliff? Where are we headed?"

"I have a hunch. I'll check the avenue first."

The avenue was the north-to-south street near the University of Washington campus. But we found the ten-block strip of buildings deserted, except for one down-and-outer cradling a brown paper bag and sleeping on a bench in front of the optometry shop where I used to work - what seemed like a lifetime ago. I longed for my former humdrum, boring life again.

As the car crawled down the avenue, I asked, "Have you called Panda's mother?"

"They're three hours earlier with the time difference, so they're still asleep. I hope we find Panda before Janette wakes up. If anything happens to Panda, I'll be held responsible. I'll never see my daughter again."

"Of course you will."

"You don't know Janette. She's the judge and jury rolled into one."

I kept my vision fixed on the passing buildings, searching the doorways. My thoughts were igniting sporadically, like overturned bottle rockets.

"I have an idea," I said. "Maybe Panda went to your apartment. She might have forgotten something she needs for school today."

"It's a long shot but better than anything I can come up with." He motored toward the University Bridge. "At least we'll be moving. I can't sit around doing nothing." His tires gripped the concrete, then we fishtailed across the bridge's metal grating.

"Aren't you afraid of getting a speeding ticket?" I hoped he'd slow down.

He gunned the engine. "Every cop in town had better be looking for Panda."

We sped south, gaining altitude on Capitol Hill. At a stoplight, he made a short left through an amber light. Less than a half block further, as we were about to take a right to span 520, I noticed blue and red lights flashing in the middle of small Roanoke Park, a flat city block of mowed grass and a sprinkling of trees. I craned my head and saw two squad cars and an aid vehicle.

Cliff punched the brake pedal. "What the—" He roared the engine, made a U-turn, and pulled into a residential side street next to the park.

My jaw dropped open as I spotted Papa's Alfa Romeo. The Alfa's crumpled rear bumper rested against a small hawthorn tree. The Alpha sat amidst the emergency response vehicles and a tow truck.

I hopped out of Cliff's Porsche and jogged across the grass to Panda, who sat near an aid vehicle. Joey stood nearby, speaking to a police officer. The tow truck operator was about to hook the Alfa's front bumper.

"Hey, stop! You're going to ruin the car. That bumper isn't strong enough." All heads turned my way.

The man said, "Lady, I've been towing cars for forty years. I know what I'm doing."

"Who cares about that stupid car?" Cliff sprinted past me to Panda. "Are you all right, honey?" Panda wrapped her arms around herself for warmth.

"She seems okay," a paramedic said.

"Did Joey kidnap you, honey?" Cliff asked Panda.

She pushed her fingers through her bangs so one eye glared out. "I'm fine."

"You can tell me the truth," Cliff said. "You're safe now."

"You're putting words in her mouth," I said to Cliff.

I turned to Joey. "What happened? How on earth did Papa's car end up in the middle of this park?" I scanned the level surface, then glanced up the inclined road that stretched across 520. The highway below was already streaming with commuters.

"Joey?" I said when he didn't answer. After gawking at me like he didn't recognize his own sister, he turned his attention to the ground.

"Officer, arrest this man," Cliff said. "He abducted my daughter. She's only fourteen years old."

We all waited for Joey to speak up, but he remained silent. Was he unwilling to defend himself? A long hollowness filled the park—just the flashing lights and the aid vehicle preparing to leave the scene. It was like an old black-and-white movie with the sound turned down.

"I woke him up and asked for a ride," Panda finally said in a meek voice.

"According to his sister, Mona Lisa Buttaro, here, Joey Buttaro doesn't know how to drive," Cliff said. "Did you get his name, officer?"

"Yes, we did," the officer said. "He doesn't appear to have a license. Not on him, anyway."

"He doesn't have a license, period," Cliff said. "Unless his sister is lying."

I gave him my rendition of Mama's evil eye but let his accusation pass. I couldn't help it. Joey had summoned up the nerve to drive. In a crazy way, I was proud of him.

"How did you manage to drive Papa's car?" I asked, but Joey didn't respond.

"I taught him." Panda sounded elated.

"I don't believe it," Cliff said. "How would you know?"

"I know a lot more than you think I do." Her voice was turning sassy and confrontational.

"If you needed a ride, why didn't you ask me?" Cliff asked.

"Like, at four in the morning?"

"First things first." The officer cut in, aiming his question at Panda. "Did Mr. Buttaro take you against your will?"

"Nah, it was my idea. He didn't even want to go."

"Then what are you doing here?" Cliff glanced around the park.

"I guess I was sleepwalking, but Figaro woke me. I couldn't get back to sleep. Then I thought about how much fun it would be to freak Mona Lisa out if I wandered into her room like a ghost. Have a laugh, you know. But then I got a better idea to go visit a friend, someone you don't know, Daddy, so don't even ask. I wanted to get away. Run away, maybe. To scare Mom. Nothing else gets her attention. So I got dressed and woke Joey up."

I waited for Joey to defend himself, but instead he started mumbling, catching the officer's attention.

"Is your brother all right?" he asked me. "Maybe he sustained a head injury or he's high on something?"

"He's a nutcase," Cliff said. "If you won't arrest him for abduction, he should at least spend a few days in Harborview being evaluated for mental illness."

"How dare you?" Yet, if honest with myself, I had to admit

Cliff was right. Joey needed to be evaluated. He had always refused psychiatric care, and now might be the perfect time to accomplish that goal. But they might lock him up - his worst fear. His fears could get worse.

Panda stepped closer to the police officer. "I wasn't kidnapped. I hatched this whole plan. It's my fault, not Joey's."

"You, young lady, are a minor," Cliff said. "Joey is - what? Thirty-five years old, never married, and lives at home with his sister at their mother's house."

I felt protectiveness covering me - a suit of armor building itself across my chest. I must protect Joey, for Mama's sake. "It's not against the law to live with one's mother," I said. "I do. You know how high rent is these days."

Another policeman - a burly guy who looked familiar - moved forward and gave Joey a look. "Hey, aren't you the guy I talked to outside the Dawn to Dusk Bakery the morning it burned down?"

Joey continued staring at the grass like he was searching for a four-leaf clover.

"That was a coincidence," I said. "He had nothing to do with it. I was there too. We were on our way to work." I wouldn't mention I was driving, and Joey was walking with matches in his pocket.

"Hey," Cliff said, "we have all the proof we need right now. Joey stole this vehicle."

Did Cliff have a personal vendetta against my brother or what?

"He did not." My hands grasped my hips. "It belongs to me. My mother, that is. She wouldn't mind any family member using it."

"On top of that," Cliff said, "he's driving without a license and the car's tabs have expired. They're over ten years old. I'm not letting Joey wriggle out of this."

I shook my head. I thought I had a crush on Cliff in high school, and only days ago I thought I still did.

285

CHAPTER FORTY-FOUR
Joey

Stranded in Roanoke Park waiting for Moni and Cliff to quit arguing with two uniformed officers, Joey gave Joey the willies. He couldn't believe his ears when Saint Signore said, "You've gotten yourself into a fine vat of minestrone soup this time."

Joey was ecstatic but also startled at the sound of Saint Signore's voice. "You're back?" He pursed his lips so they wouldn't move. "Where have you been?"

"Nowhere."

"But Gloria said you had an audience with the Pope in Rome."

"Jo-Jo, I've warned you not to believe her."

Was someone impersonating the Saint? How could Joey tell? "Is this a trick?"

"Don't you recognize me by now?"

"You were gone so long." Joey felt an expanse of sadness in his chest. He'd been lonely without the Saint. And afraid. He could still hear Gloria's voice blathering in the background, but her volume was turned down and waning. Joey could cry with happiness, but he mustn't give the police any further reason to detain him.

The mini-drama continued to play out. The tow truck driver was hauling away Papa's Alfa, which looked harmless now, not like a lethal weapon anymore. Panda was tugging on Cliff's sleeve, insisting she wanted to take the day off from school. Cliff ignored her and aimed more accusations about Joey at the officer.

Saint Signore said, "Jo-Jo, time to gather your courage and speak up, or you'll land in jail."

The officer drew within a couple feet of Joey's face, sniffed the air, and peered into his eyes. "Are you high on something?"

"No, sir. I never take drugs of any kind or drink alcoholic beverages. Honest." Joey straightened his collared shirt. He was tempted to divulge Cliff's previous drinking problem—he'd heard Cliff refer to it.

"This is no time to turn spiteful," Saint Signore said. "Defend yourself. You're the one in the hot seat."

Joey tried to look normal, whatever that meant. He thought of Ramon, his friendly demeanor, and how easily he spoke to strangers.

"Officer," Moni said, "I promise my brother will be evaluated by a mental health professional."

What? She wanted him to see a shrink?

She laid her hand on Joey's forearm. "Will you agree to go if I set up an appointment?"

He forced himself to look his sister in the face and saw what seemed to be an expression of genuine concern. But could he trust her?

Saint Signore told him, "Go along with her. I haven't accomplished much to help you. You don't want to live with Gloria's prattle in your head for the rest of your life, do you?"

Joey heard the thrum of traffic picking up on 520 as the morning commute increased. He mashed his lips together to keep them from moving. "You mean, see a real psychiatrist?" he asks Saint Signore.

"If that's what it takes. I'm beginning to think I've mismanaged you."

Looking over at the sorry hawthorn, Moni said to a cop, "I'll pay to have the tree replaced."

Joey was grateful the tree had stopped Papa's car from rolling any farther. He and Panda might have hit one of the less forgiving evergreens. Panda could have been hurt or killed. It occurred to Joey that it would have been easier if he'd died in the accident. What he had to face now seemed too hard. He was a failure and wanted to give up, to collapse on the grass and die, to be buried in this park.

"Life is never easy," Saint Signore said, which Joey already knew too well.

The other officer approached the policeman. "Hey, Mac, can we wrap this up? We have another call. A burglary is in progress."

The officer tucked a notepad in his pocket and turned to Joey. "Seeing as we're so busy I'll let you off with a warning."

"Hey, where did you say you live?" the other officer asked Moni, and his sister repeated Mama's address.

"That's where we're headed. A woman called to report a break-in three minutes ago."

"I'll bet that was our nosy next-door neighbor, Mrs. Warwick," Moni said.

"Did you leave your doors unlocked?"

"Maybe. We were in such a hurry—and the glass in the kitchen window is broken. But my mother has a Doberman pinscher."

"That dog won't let anyone in," Cliff said.

The officer shook his head. "There's no dog there now."

"His owner nabbed him," Saint Signore informed Joey. "I told you it was going to happen sooner or later."

"Can my brother and I hitch a ride with you?" Moni asked the cop. "There's no way we can all cram in Cliff's Porsche."

"Ride in a police car?" Joey recoiled. The doors would automatically lock. He knew it was a ploy to cart him off to Harborview. "If you don't mind, I'd rather take the bus or walk."

"Suit yourself," Moni said. "I'm going home with them."

"Go with your sister," Saint Signore urged. "*Andiamo*."

Holding his breath, Joey tried to take a step toward the patrol car, but his feet wouldn't move.

CHAPTER FORTY-FIVE
Mona Lisa

I cajoled Joey into the squad car. He agreed to climb in only if I sat in the molded plastic back seat with him. Yuck, even I hesitated.

What were you thinking? - words of chastisement wanted to stampede out of my mouth, but I felt numb, like I was coming out of the dentist's office with my lips injected with Novocain. It was just as well, Joey and I should converse in private without the patrolman listening through the heavy gage wire and Plexiglas window. Not that Joey and I talked much anyway.

I saw Cliff and Panda proceeding across the park toward his Porsche. Cliff was right. Joey had borrowed Papa's car and had Panda with him, exactly as Cliff predicted. I couldn't blame him for being distraught. If she were my daughter, I would have been engulfed with fear.

Much as I wanted to hug Cliff with all my might and thank him, I didn't have the time. I imagined his strong arms around me, supporting me, and realized I'd grown to rely on him. I'd fall for him if I were honest with myself. But his daughter came first. As she should.

I reckoned he would swing by Mama's house later to pick up Panda's things, but I'd be at work. Like a gust of wind swirling past me, our time for intimacy had vanished.

With the patrolman behind the wheel, the squad car exited

the park. Its tires spun on the dewy grass. As Joey and I rode along like caged animals, the patrolman spoke to his dispatcher. I wondered how he'd describe the incident when he was back at the station later. I bet everyone would get a belly laugh as he portrayed the Alfa rolling backward into the park and hitting a tree. Would the day ever come when I could smile about it? Unlikely. My brother could have been seriously injured or killed. I was struck by how much I cared for him, idiosyncrasies and all.

I wanted to blame Joey's outing on Panda, the little green-haired stinker. But she was only fourteen, acting out of impulse. Why would Joey take her out of the house without Cliff's permission? And driving Papa's Alfa? In my mind, I listed all Joey's transgressions, hearing them through a judge's ears, and I was grateful we were not in court at this moment.

The fact is, I didn't know what made Joey tick or what went on in his brain when he talked to himself. I assumed that when his face wore its usual expression and he was clad in a clean and pressed outfit, he thought like other folks. But I had no idea what he'd do next. I felt the sting of guilt for not insisting he be examined by a mental health professional years ago. Instead, I'd followed Mama's routine and pretty much ignored Joey's plight. Like a drowning man, was he crying for help, but I couldn't hear him? Or did I choose not to?

Okay, I inadvertently assisted him by forcing him to work at Booty's out of spite rather than equipping him with restaurant skills so he could support himself. It had all been about me.

Using the siren twice to pass through intersections - Joey plugged his ears - the policeman whizzed us home. We found Frank DiAngelo's white Lincoln and another squad car parked out front of Mama's house. It is very strange because my mother loves to sleep late. I assumed she and Frank would lounge around eating breakfast in bed at his house. Ugh, there I was envisioning the two of them together in Frank's decadent mansion, not here. I shuddered to think about their wedding night. No, I wouldn't let myself envision Mama with Frank.

The house's front door gaped wide open. Mama and Frank stood on the porch talking to an officer and Mrs. Warwick, who must have called Mama and summoned the police. But why?

The patrolman brought his squad car to an abrupt stop. He opened Joey's door, and my brother leaped out. I must say I was glad to leave its confines when the cop opened my side. Who knew what grubby criminals had sat on that bench seat?

The patrolman made a beeline for the officer standing on the porch. The two greeted each other, then strode into the house.

"Be careful, officers." I mounted the steps, leaving Joey at the bottom. "There's a big dog in there."

"No, not anymore," Mrs. Warwick said. She wore her bathrobe and her red satin slippers.

"Where's Figaro?" Mama sounded frantic. Frank stood next to her sporting a jogging suit and mouthing an unlit cigar.

"I have no idea," I said.

Joey shook his head, then shuffled around the side of the house to the kitchen door.

"Mama, aren't you curious about the Alfa?" I tilted my head toward the garage.

"I already told everyone I saw Joey drive it away," Mrs. Warwick chirped, recapturing our attention. "I assumed there was nothing wrong. After all, the car belongs to Barbara. But then that big goon in the van returned, let himself in through the kitchen door, and took the dog.

The fact that a stranger broke into the house sent a chill up my spine. But he stole the thing I most wanted to be rid of. How's that for irony? Yet I had to wonder who would dare take a snarling Doberman pinscher.

I filled Mama in on Mrs. Warwick's late-night visit several days ago, the footprints in the grass, then Figaro's frightening actions earlier this morning while Cliff and I searched the basement for Panda and Joey.

"He wouldn't let us up the basement steps," I said. "No, he wasn't smiling," I assured Mama before she could defend the dog. "He was downright ferocious."

291

The house telephone rang. Now what? It must be Ramon reporting a problem at Booty's. I took the call in the kitchen so Mrs. Warwick couldn't overhear the conversation and spread more gossip. She'd have the neighborhood buzzing over the fact that two police cars were here and Figaro was stolen right out of our kitchen.

I lifted the receiver and brought it to my ear. Before I could speak, a woman sounding about my age said, "*Pronto.*" Her tone was belligerent. "Who is this?" She had an Italian accent but spoke perfect English.

"Who is this?" I shot back. "I'm in no mood for guessing games."

"Anna Maria Moretti."

"Really? I'm glad you called." Even after this horrendous morning, I couldn't believe my good fortune. The drama of Joey and Panda's escapade subsided. "Hi, this is Mona Lisa Buttaro." My voice cracked with a mixture of emotions. I was elated but torn inside because the proof of Papa's philandering and deceit was presenting herself in 3D. I understood Italian well enough to speak to her in her native tongue, but I was a bit rusty and realized this could be one of the most important conversations of my life. I stifled a yawn because I still hadn't had my morning coffee. "Uncle Vito must have given you our number."

"Does it matter how I tracked you down? I know where you live now. That you and your brother own a big house and a *ristorante* that should, by all rights, be one-third mine." Her words blared out with what sounded like a lifetime of pent-up rage and resentment.

"That's why you called?" If only Papa were alive to speak to her. "Legally, the house and restaurant belong to my mother, not my brother and me."

"Not for long." She sounded like a bully who wanted to make a quick buck at our expense. Could we lose everything?

Anger kicked in, and heat rose up my neck. "Neither Joey nor I have much money. You'll have to speak to my mother."

"No, I've called Barbara several times in the past year, and she always hangs up."

"This is the first I've heard of it."

"Your papa tried to hide from me by moving as far away as he could. And now you will pretend you don't know me. But I can prove through DNA testing that I'm your half sister."

"I'm not trying to hide anything. I've always wanted a sister." But in my musings, she was sweet and wanted to be my best friend.

"I don't believe you." Anna Maria hung up with a click that resounded in my eardrum.

My legs weakened. My lower lip trembled, and tears pressed against the backs of my eyes. I wanted to let myself cry for an hour. But now was not the time. I needed to speak to the police, then drive to Booty's and help Ramon.

* * *

The next evening at dinner, Mama, Frank, Cliff, and I were seated at Frank's lace-covered table, set with sterling silver flatware and hand-painted Italian dinner plates. Sitting across from Cliff, my face grew weary from keeping up a cheery facade after a long day at work. When I glanced across the table at him, our eyes locked for a moment. But then he looked away. I couldn't read what was on his mind, and I was too tired to play games.

I replayed my busy day at Booty's. I'll give my brother this. He worked harder than ever at Booty's today. Annie's replacement came in for the first time this morning, and Joey helped train her. He must have found her attractive or something, because when she arrived, he removed his shower cap.

While we toiled at the restaurant, Mama had the Alfa towed to a body shop, and then she fluttered around Frank's grand stucco villa, planning a whirlwind remodel with Cliff at the helm. Everything from enlarging the kitchen and replacing appliances to rebuilding the pool house, not to mention changing wall colors, drapery, and carpets.

I straightened my napkin across my lap. Minutes earlier, I'd learned Mama and Frank insisted Cliff move into their daylight basement, formerly the retired gardener and all-around maintenance man's apartment, with two bedrooms and a kitchenette, opening out onto the Olympic-size swimming pool, luxuriating alongside Lake Washington. Frank's mansion was spacious enough to sleep ten guests, but it irked me they'd ask Cliff to live with them without consulting me first.

"Cliff will be here working for at least six months," Frank said as the topic resurfaced. "He may stay as long as he wishes." Frank was sporting a dark three-piece suit and a bow tie. "We've made Cliff an honorary Italian."

I looked around and thought the dining room, with its crimson velvet curtains covering floor-to-ceiling windows and coral-colored walls and white crown molding, was a bit gaudy. But the child in me didn't want Mama investing her talents in Frank's house. I thought she should remain faithful to Papa. That was silly and selfish. Why should Mama die a lonely widow because I was perpetually single?

As Frank's matronly cook of thirty-five years placed a sumptuous antipasto platter on the table, Figaro limped into the room. Quite remarkably, he'd turned up at our doorstep late last night. "An answer to prayer," Mama had said when she'd picked him up this morning. Joey told me he's convinced Figaro was abducted by his original owner, a thug who mistreated him and used the dog to guard his van at night. Joey claimed Figaro was trying to warn Cliff and me; the man was lurking around outside Mama's house attempting to break in, that Figaro's intentions were virtuous - he was trying to protect Cliff and me.

Frank crossed himself and said the blessing. "Thank you, gracious Father, for this meal and for my gorgeous wife, who makes an old man feel young again.

I glanced up to see Mama grinning. "And thank you, *mio Dio*, for protecting Joey and Panda," she said. "And for returning Figaro."

"Amen," I echoed with the others. I told myself I had much to be thankful for. I needed to focus on my blessings, not rehash the past.

"Oh, I almost forgot." Mama placed four twenty-dollar bills on the table. "I borrowed these from the cash register the other day and intended to return them."

"Mama, I was worried sick over that money."

"Sorry. I meant to leave you an IOU note." She drizzled olive oil and a splash of balsamic vinegar onto a small plate and dipped a slice of bread into it. "Maybe I forgot. I've had so much on my mind." She glanced at Frank, who winked at her.

The money lay on the table between us.

"Did you think your mother stole from her own restaurant?" Frank asked.

"No, but I thought maybe Joey..."

Mama swallowed her mouthful. "He never would. What's gotten into you?"

"Well, are you going to take the money or not?" Frank asked me, his voice gruff.

"Yes. Okay." I folded the bills in half and stuffed them in my slacks pocket.

"Stop worrying about everything," Frank said to me. "Life's too short."

Mama patted my shoulder. "*Mi dispiace, cara mia.* After working at Booty's so many years, I didn't give it a second thought. The last thing I want to do is make your life more difficult."

"My life isn't difficult, so no worries, Mama." Whom was I trying to kid?

As we savored the antipasto, Figaro circled the table, looking for scraps. Mama handed him a slice of salami, and the dog swallowed it whole, then begged for more.

Joey and Panda's escapade was never brought up. Not that I wanted Frank's opinion. I hoped to forget the whole ordeal. Maybe Mama asked him not to mention the calamity for Cliff's sake. Panda was back at her mother's house tonight, probably eating dinner with her new stepfather. No wonder Cliff looked so glum. I couldn't help feeling sorry for him. He'd hardly said a word other than, "What's in this seafood salad?"

"Marinated scallops, shrimp, mussels, and calamari," Mama said.

"Calamari? Is that octopus?"

"No, squid. Isn't it delicious?"

Cliff nodded, then swallowed hard and sipped his water.

I still hadn't mentioned my conversation with Anna Maria to Mama. Had my mother really refused to speak to my stepsister when she called? Would Mama be so cruel? The blame should go to Papa, not an innocent lovechild. Or was there more to this story? Was Anna Maria bent on revenge and trying to extort money from Mama?

I plunked an olive in my mouth. My telephone conversation with Anna Maria had been a walloping disappointment. But during the lunch rush earlier today, greeting customers, ringing up orders, and serving coffee—when I was too busy to be irritated and feel sorry for myself—a sprout of a plan took root in the back of my mind. In spite of Anna Maria's threats, I was going to hop aboard a plane in a couple weeks and visit Uncle Vito, who would set up a meeting with her and act as our arbitrator. Who knows where it might lead?

I envisioned myself stepping off a jetliner at Fiumicino Airport near Rome, spending a week there, then renting a car and driving south to my parents' neck of the woods and meeting distant relatives. It's about time I came to terms with the fact that I was an Italian American, what I'd tried to conceal most of my life because I wanted to blend in.

Minutes later, Frank's cook brought out a dish of penne pasta. Tantalizing aromas wafted from the kitchen. My thoughts shot back to elementary school. I loved my first name until show-and-tell in second grade, when I brought a print of Leonardo da Vinci's painting *The Mona Lisa* and explained her unreadable

Giaconda smile, which, I told my classmates, had fascinated viewers since the fifteenth century. By recess, loudmouth Bob Gilligan nicknamed me Lizzy, which morphed into Lizard. All the boys laughed and dubbed me the Lizard Lady, a nickname that stuck until middle school. I was humiliated, but I needed to get over it, as they say. To forgive those boys, who probably didn't even remember teasing me. And it was time to get over the garage fire too. It was an accident; I must come clean with Mama and accept forgiveness.

I set my fork aside so I'd have room for the chicken *parmigiana* - the fragrance of melted cheese, garlic, and basil grew stronger. I imagined myself in Rome and then Naples, touring churches and museums. I was an art history major in college and would finally see the masterpieces I'd studied. I planned to bring my new camera to capture pictures, then frame a dozen or so to adorn the restaurant's walls. My own personal photo show. Not to sell them and make money but to stretch my boundaries. If Joey could learn to drive a car, wasn't it time for me to rekindle my buried passions?

Later, after a dessert of melt-in-your-mouth tiramisu, Frank reached into his breast pocket and brought out a plump cigar. Mama caught sight of it and said, "Remember, no smoking in the house."

He shrugged and put the cigar away, which I found extraordinary. He was putty in her hands. Papa was never like that. Why, if she told my father not to smoke a cigar, he'd light up three just to prove he was the head of the household.

"What can I do?" Frank winked at me. "I married a woman more beautiful than Sophia Loren. When I stood at the alter and said, 'I do,' I also promised she would be the mistress of a smoke-free house."

CHAPTER FORTY-SIX
Mona Lisa

One week later, so much has changed, as if the world has flipped on its head and I'm living upside down and backward in another hemisphere.

I'm in the waiting room of Dr. Anthony Pasquale, Joey's psychiatrist. If that's not astonishing enough, Cliff is seated next to me. I know he's buried in what he calls the Frank and Barbara DiAngelo Project. I'm not sure what motivated him to accompany my brother and me today. When I told Cliff I was capable of getting us here, Cliff wouldn't take no for an answer. Possibly to ensure my brother actually sees a shrink, meaning Cliff doesn't trust me to handle the office visit. But I like to think Cliff's chauffeur service is an act of kindness and an attempt at reconciliation—that he wants to make up for his harshness last week toward Joey and me. Cliff was verbally brutal, but he was right. I was living in denial as bad as Mama. Why didn't I step in to help Joey years ago? I was consumed by my own disappointments and regrets, not to mention learning about Papa's deceit.

When we three arrived today, Joey opted to scale the staircase to the third floor instead of riding the elevator. "Great, I'll join you," Cliff said. "I can use the exercise."

After checking in with the receptionist, Dr. Pasquale, a mild-mannered balding fellow wearing a tweed jacket, invited me to sit in with Joey for the first ten minutes, if Joey agreed. I was surprised my brother didn't mind my being there. Maybe he figured he could count on me to rescue him if the doctor attempted to drop a butterfly net over his head.

Dr. Pasquale was pleased to hear Joey works at Booty's. "We get the best results when patients have a sense of community and family support," he told me, making Joey's recovery sound easy. When I know it won't be.

Minutes later, I was dismissed to the waiting room. A receptionist sits at her desk across the room, speaking on a phone in hushed tones and scanning her computer. No background music.

I should have thought to bring a book to read. Not that I can even concentrate on the lightweight magazines sprawled on the coffee table. I wonder what Dr. Pasquale and Joey are talking about. I can't imagine my brother unmasking his inner thoughts and idiosyncrasies to a stranger.

Seeing movement out of the corner of my eye, I notice Cliff responding to a text message.

"You don't have to wait around," I say. "We can take the bus home. I'm sure Joey knows the route."

He rotates in his chair to face me. "I don't mind." He slips his iPhone in his pocket. "While we're waiting, would it be too nosy if I asked about your half sister?"

"I guess not." I'd mentioned her to Joey on the ride over. My brother didn't seem surprised, as if he already knew about Anna Maria.

"I'm curious about her," he persists.

"You and me both. Yesterday, she emailed me a photo of herself. She looks like me. The same brown eyes and unruly hair—but on her, it looks good."

"It looks good on you too." He cranes his neck to catch my expression. "Everything looks good on you."

It does? I blink and glance away. "She didn't get Papa's nose, which makes me wonder about her mother, not that I dare ask until we meet face-to-face. With the help of my uncle in Rome, I'm going to do just that in a couple of weeks."

"Sounds marvelous."

"It would be if she didn't despise me," I say.

"She won't once she gets to know you." He takes my hand.

My brows raise. "You mean, you don't hate me?"

"I never did." His gaze penetrates mine. "I took my frustration out on you last week when I should have been looking in the mirror. You were right when you said I shouldn't spend the night at your mother's house with an unpredictable teenager who walks in her sleep. And I owe you an apology for the reunion committee's plot to use Booty's. I had no idea what they had in mind, but I should have guessed. I don't blame you for holding me responsible."

"I don't care about that anymore. I might even attend the reunion. As for Booty's, I'll hold on to it. Joey needs a place to work. And so do I."

Cliff and I are still holding hands; our fingers intertwine.

"I'm not the only one who's had a roller-coaster week." I glance up into his face and find myself wondering if I've fallen in love with him. But I say, "How did it go with Janette's coming home as a married woman?"

"Better than I thought. For one thing, I'm not brokenhearted in the least—not since I met you." He moves closer. "I told Janette about Panda's disappearing act, and she took it extremely well. I thought she'd come unglued and threaten to cut off visitations, but I guess she enjoyed her free time without her daughter as much as I enjoyed fatherhood—for the most part."

"How's Panda transitioning to having a stepdad?" My anger toward her has dissipated because I remember what it was like being a self-willed teenager. She charged my new camera, as promised, and even wrote out detailed instructions on how to download photos onto my laptop.

"Panda wants to come live with me at your mother and

Frank's," he says. "Janette claims she's being lured by the swimming pool and the baby grand. Panda asked for voice lessons, and Barbara said absolutely yes. She'd hire a vocal coach who can come to the house after school two days a weekif Panda finishes her homework. And Panda wants to see more of Figaro."

"I can't believe the dog found his way home." I recall how delighted I was to see him. Who would have guessed? "Mama says he's been a perfect gentleman since staying with them."

"Even I'm beginning to like him." Cliff gives me a wry smile. "But are you sure you don't want Figaro to remain with you for protection?"

"I wouldn't want to deny Mama, Frank, and you the pleasure of his company." "I've decided to get a dog." I envision myself cradling a furry little pooch. "A smaller breed. If you wouldn't mind, I'll ask Panda to help me choose it."

"No doubt about it, she'd love that."

"And I've made another decision. I'm holding on to Mama's house as long as she'll let me."

"That means, when I pick you up for a date, I won't have to get past a Doberman pinscher?"

"A date?" I lowered my volume when I noticed the receptionist is glancing our way. "Are you talking about the high school reunion?"

"Actually, I was thinking tomorrow evening we'd go out for dinner—just the two of us—then see a movie."

I try the notion on for size—our sitting in a restaurant at a cozy table, then side by side in a darkened theater—and decide an evening with Cliff would be delightful. I have definitely fallen hard for him. But to keep the subject light, I say, "You don't want to take Joey and my extended family along?"

"Not this time." He brings the back of my hand to his mouth and gives it a kiss. I feel warmth radiating up my arm, planting itself in my heart.

"We both come with baggage," he says.

"That's for sure."

"You don't know half of my story." His face moves closer, and his lips brush mine, then soften into a luxurious kiss I wish would last forever.

When we finally part, he says, "You may not want anything to do with me when you do." He pauses as if retreating back into his shell, then surprises me by saying, "But the burden would be lighter with another set of shoulders. Don't you think?"

"Yes, I do." My half-smile expands into a wide grin I can't contain. And why should I?

TIRAMISU Recipe

1 1/2 cups heavy whipping cream
8 ounce container mascarpone cheese, room temperature
1/3 cup granulated sugar
1 teaspoon vanilla extract
½ teaspoon almond extract
1 1/2 cups cold espresso
3 Tablespoons coffee flavored liqueur, optional
1 package Lady Fingers (16 – 20 lady fingers)
Cocoa powder for dusting the top

1. Beat whipping cream on medium speed. Slowly add the sugar, vanilla, and rum flavors, and continue to beat until stiff peaks form. Add mascarpone cheese and gently fold in until combined.
2. In a separate bowl, add coffee and liqueur. Dip the lady fingers into the coffee, first on one side and then on the other. Dip them just enough to get them wet, not soggy. Place the lady fingers in a single layer on the bottom of an 8x8" pan.
3. Smooth half the mascarpone mixture over the top. Add a second layer of lady fingers and spread the remaining mascarpone cream over the top.
4. Dust with cocoa powder. Refrigerate for at least 3-4 hours before serving.

Acknowledgments

Thank you from the bottom of my heart for reading my books! My readers and their opinions mean everything to me. Much appreciation to Mary Jackson for her never-wavering encouragement. Thanks to my sister, Margaret Coppock, who was willing to share her wealth of knowledge of the English language and a multitude of other things, such as our memories of living in Rome. Thanks to Marta Aldrighetti for helping me with my Italian. (Any mistakes are mine alone.) Thank you to author Peg Kehle for answering my many questions. Much gratitude to Crime Prevention specialist Mary Amberg, who has helped me on numerous occasions. Thank you to Harold at AA for answering my questions about alcoholism. Mega-thanks to my webmaster, Lisa-Ann Oliver of Web Designs by LAO. Many thanks to Kim D for designing my book's cover! Thanks to copyeditor Kathy Burge, and double thanks to proofreader Lori Wilen.

I love hearing from readers!
Reach me at info@katelloyd.com
My Website: https://www.katelloyd.com
Follow me on Instagram: @katelloydauthor
Facebook: https://www.facebook.com/katelloydbooks

If you enjoyed reading Mona Lisa Smiles, please leave a short online review. I learn so much from them.

About The Author

Kate Lloyd is a novelist and a passionate observer of human relationships. A native of Baltimore, she and her husband live in the Pacific Northwest, the setting of several of her novels. She lived in Rome and studied Italian in college. Kate has worked a variety of jobs, including car salesman and restaurateur.

Learn more about Kate on her website:
https://www.katelloyd.com
Her blog: http://katelloydauthor.blogspot.com
Face Book: www.facebook.com/katelloydbooks
Instagram: @katelloydauthor
Pinterest: KateLloydAuthor

Made in United States
North Haven, CT
05 April 2024

50868625R20189